CONTACT WITH STARFIRE

I was watching the couple, smiling at their open joy, when I felt the touch of the starfire on my wrist. I looked quickly at the white tendril that had come to draw me out onto the floor. It burned like a real flame, but it was cool against my skin. In a flash I stole a glance at Jemeret, who was looking at me and the starfire expressionlessly. Then I rose, and since I had already gathered to narrow my irises against the glare, I pulled in a little more strength and tried to pathfind the flame on my wrist.

By the time I tried it, I was already out on the arena floor. For a split second the tendril seemed to freeze, and then it stood away and flowed around me at a distance of about half a meter. I didn't move, afraid I'd broken some sort of major taboo. The white tendril rose in front of me, swaying back and forth, and leaned forward to touch my forehead.

From behind me in the rows of spectators, I heard a few gasps and a low murmur, which stilled instantly as single tendrils rose from the gold, the blue, and the red bowls of starfire and came to join the white one. They all twined together like a snakelike creature and then spiraled upward around my body until I, too, was encased in fire. I became aware, at the very core of my being, that the starfire was a living thing, and living things have no paths . . .

Look for these Del Rey Discoveries . . .
Because something new is always worth the risk!

COMMENCEMENT

Roby James

A Del Rey® Book
BALLANTINE BOOKS • NEW YORK

A Del Rey® Book
Published by Ballantine Books

Copyright © 1996 by Roby James

All rights reserved under International and Pan-American Copyright Conventions. Published in the United States by Ballantine Books, a division of Random House, Inc., New York, and simultaneously in Canada by Random House of Canada Limited, Toronto.

Library of Congress Catalog Card Number: 95-92518

ISBN 0-345-40038-0

Printed in Canada

First Edition: February 1996

10 9 8 7 6 5 4 3

To Keith
Despite his denials, he really is my own Lord Jemeret

To Barbara, for speaking like the starfire

And to control freaks everywhere

Acknowledgments

I express my heartfelt love and deepest appreciation:

For comments on the evolving copies of the manuscript: to Bonnie Fink, Gigi Gilmartin, David Vorspan, Rod and Judy Ditzler, Jim Peterson, David Epstein, Pat Thompson, Linda McKelvey, Georgia Zweber, Lindy Mendelsohn, and Candy Weigand. And, for catching more typos than anyone else, to the dear friend in Phoenix who specifically told me not to mention her name.

For reading the finished manuscript with enthusiasm and encouragement: to Jan Kirshbaum, Bob Woolley, Eli Schochet, Lou Loomis, Neil Hattem, Connie Greaser, Sandy Lewis, Nell Bruegel, Gladys Sturman, Mal Cohen, Virginia Parkum, Frances Nye-Peterson, James Nolte, Les Cole, and Bob Miller.

For an assessment of the accuracy of the psychology (the "science" in my science fiction), to Dr. Stephan D. Schuster. And to Sima, Sarah, and Maita Schuster, his family, who couldn't be kept from fighting over who got to read it next.

To my precious Cousin Ron, who, reading it, told me to my everlasting joy that I had grown up to be the writer my late mother always wanted *him* to be.

To M. Miriam, and to my "family," the Community at Our Lady of the Rock.

For ongoing encouragement without having to read the manuscript, and thus, for blind faith in me: to Valerie Saenz, Ed

Shaheen, Linda Hancock, Cathy Swarts, Dwight Morgan, Bob Melville, Barbara Straus Reed, and Michael Kesler; Mickey and Susie Rappaport, Dick Kirshbaum, Barbara Hattem, Paula Loomis, and Bonnie Vorspan; Doris Isolini Nelson, Janet Sternfeld Davis, Kathy Rousseau, and the other women of the Steering Committee for the Los Angeles Catholic-Jewish Women's Dialogue; Father William Treacy; Lura Dymond; Lillian and Don Smith; Gail and George MacDonald; and Mary Ann Mobley and Paula Butterini, who kept telling me to keep at it when I was getting discouraged.

My gratitude goes without reservation to Shawna McCarthy, my agent. And I am also grateful to Gabriel Cohen, who introduced me to Michele Slung, who introduced me to David Hartwell, who introduced me to Shawna.

And, of course, to my editor at Del Rey Books, Ellen Key Harris.

Any errors or shortcomings are completely my own, but my strength comes from all of the people above, and I wanted them to know that I couldn't have done it without them.

                                               —R.J.

The technical form of almost everything can be studied from books, but the essence of things can only be known through contact, or from life itself.

—MORRIS LICHTENSTEIN

I. A Place Like the Past

I want to write it as it happened—the processes and the progresses that brought me to where I am, the ways I changed and the ways I stayed the same. I want to tell it as if it were a story, even though of all the things I thought my life would be, "story" is not a word I would have chosen. And yet, Jasin Lebec once told me we all write stories with our lives. It's just that we're not aware that's what we're doing, so we never read them as a whole creation. I promise to read this when I've done writing it. It will help build the foundation I can go on from.

I didn't even begin the journal until after we arrived at Stronghome, and life keeps moving forward, even as I write about the things that have happened—are happening—happened before I got to this world. So I may never catch up with where I am. Somehow that's almost fitting.

The first thing I remember is hearing the fire. The crackle seemed to penetrate the darkness in my mind, and then on my closed eyelids I saw the pattern of moving light. I felt the pain simultaneously. It had been years since I'd felt anything more than a minor cramp, and for a moment or two the shock of the pain's intensity made it impossible for me to think clearly.

I fought to master the gather and take a deep breath, and as I felt I could, the reflexes snapped into place and the pain began to lessen. The capacity for logical thought returned slowly. When I had gathered enough to hold the pain back into a dull, aching throb, I concentrated my awareness behind my breastbone and spread it outward, gathering more as I did so. My assessment showed that I had one cracked and two broken ribs, a dislocated shoulder, a broken arm, assorted abrasions, contusions, and scrapes, and a badly gashed ankle. I was bleeding

1

from numerous cuts in addition to the ankle, but those didn't worry me. Without trying to open my eyes yet, I began instantly to seal off the bleeders in the ankle. The protective edge of my gathering had now shut down all the pain receptors from the injured areas, allowing me the luxury of comfort as I slowly knit the cells on both sides of the ankle cut—first deep inside, then closer and closer to the surface.

As soon as that was nearly healed, I went to work on the ribs, carefully joining cell to cell, almost unconsciously blessing my luck that there were no bone spurs at any of the breaks. I got the shoulder and the arm repaired next, and was tiring fast when I heard the voices approaching.

"There's the fireball!"

"Over here, look over here!"

Footsteps came closer, and then, "It's a woman, and she's alive!" It was very near and filled with amazement, but for the moment I didn't want to pay attention to it. I was marshaling my strength to prepare to open my eyes. I couldn't remember having been in anything that could have crashed, not floater, nor groundcar, nor lander. The last thing I could remember was running up the long flight of steps to the entrance of Government House on my way to Mortel John, Kray, and Coney, who stood at the top of the steps, waiting for me. And now the surface under my heels, hips, and shoulders was rough, uneven, softly padded with what felt like vegetation. Clearly, I was no longer in the paved environs of Government House.

"Don't try to move her. Get Dogul, and hurry!"

The crackling sounds of the fire almost drowned out the words. I risked opening my eyes. It was dark out, and the light I had seen through my eyelids came from a huge fireball, several meters away to my left. Whatever I had crashed in would soon be only cinders, ash, and twisted, blackened metal. Several people ran through my line of sight, between me and the flames, dark shadows on the face of the inferno. I hadn't yet tried to move my head, because it would take more energy, and I was stretched too thin between repairing the injuries and holding back the pain.

The fireball flared up suddenly, and then seemed to subside, leaving a softer, darker night. I realized that, incomprehensibly, some of the people were carrying torches, and then, gathering a little more and turning my head slightly, I saw that there were trees in my field of vision, too—huge, old, thick-boled trees that towered up into the darkness.

This wasn't a world I knew. This had to be a natural area, but one that was unbelievably ancient, and the cities had to be some distance away. I ran quickly through a catalog of the worlds on which I had been, and I didn't know any with natural areas as old as this one.

"Here, Dogul, she's over here."

I pulled in my senses to face this person called Dogul—and again I was surprised as the torchlight revealed a woman of great age, but not age as it came in the Com, with dignity, ease, and grace. This was an aging of wrinkles on leatherlike skin, eyes meshed in a net of deep lines between a headbanded cowl and veil and a chin band.

"Are you aware?" she asked. Her voice was raspy, brisk, not unkind, but not deeply concerned. I nodded, just perceptibly, unwilling to risk speaking just yet. "I'm surprised—" she started to say, then broke off in mid-speech. "The torch," she said instead.

Bright light suddenly intruded on me, and I had to close my eyes. So much of my energy was gone now that I did not even want to try irising my pupils down faster than normal.

I heard Dogul say, "Get a litter. Bring it here as soon as you can. You, Vulin, get up to the stonehouse and tell the Meltress—not the Melster, mind you—the Meltress, that I beg an audience. Go!"

She bent over me again, and I felt her hands gently exploring my body and my limbs. The torchlight dimmed a little, and I opened my eyes again, blinking a few times. Dogul's exploration had reached my ankle. I heard a sudden intake of breath, and she straightened for a moment, then leaned close to my face.

"Listen to me," she said in a low voice. "It is dangerous to practice Samish arts here. You may not know, but this is Honish land. If you value your life, do no more, and be thankful one such as I found you."

She straightened and turned away before I could react, but that was probably just as well, because I had absolutely no idea what she was talking about. I understood most of the words she'd spoken, but the sense of her warning eluded me. Because I was exhausted in addition to valuing my life, I stopped any further attempt to gather, ceased repairing my cuts and bruises, and used my remaining strength to keep the pain receptors closed. In my mind I cataloged the planets I'd been to in my slightly more than twenty standard years. I needed a logical train of thought to believe I was still in control, and I fastened onto needing to know where I was. There was Steressor, where I had been born and certified as a talent; Werd, where I had been trained, tested, and graded as the first Class A of my generation; Koldor, where the higher-level Com training was undertaken and completed; and Orokell, seat of the Com. Those were civilized worlds, not one of which had a natural area with trees in it that looked to be hundreds of years old, and not one of which supported wrinkled women in archaic headgear. Then there was the nameless test-world where I had done my Tenday, but I knew it to be all desert, not forested, and not peopled with anachronisms.

Where *was* I? How had I gotten here? How could the Com have misplaced a just-graduated Class A talent? I was too valuable for this.

Trying to think logically—and the growing stress of not reaching a conclusion—drained me even further. Some of the control over my pain slipped, and I began to ache. A soft groan escaped me involuntarily, and Dogul leaned back over me. "Better to be silent," she said.

If I had not been in pain and exhausted, I would probably have laughed. There was something so ludicrous about the strangeness of all this, something bizarre, out of mesh with all objective reality. I even irrationally supposed that I could be dreaming some kind of Arthurian legend.

"Here comes the litter, Dogul."

"Slide it down here beside her. I want to move her as little as possible."

I felt a genuine stab of fear at the idea of being moved. Somehow in my bewilderment, reality had crystallized around the firmness and solidity of the ground beneath me, as once in classes it had centered on my prowess in training. I was too tired to fight both pain and fear.

Several pairs of hands moved me quickly, a little roughly, onto the litter. All my control, exerted hard, didn't keep enough of the pain at bay, and I cried out against my will for the first time since childhood. I felt abruptly shamed by it. A Class A talent should never have been taken unaware by a simple thing like physical pain.

As the litter lifted and Dogul threw a rough cloth over me, exhaustion took over, all the rest of my control slipped, and the world grayed out. I was not really unconscious, just withdrawn and subdued, protected, away from the confusion. Nothing from the outside disturbed me for an indeterminate time, and then the light brightened and a soft, low-pitched woman's voice intruded. "What is all this about, Dogul?"

I brought myself back to some measure of awareness. The litter had halted, but had not been set down. A torch was closer. As I heard Dogul say, "Meltress, please come and see," I opened my eyes. Dogul was bowing to a thin woman of unknown age, wearing a fine but shapeless robe and a much more delicate version of the cowl and veil. She looked at me for a long moment, then looked at Dogul, and seemed to be calculating something.

At last she asked, "She came with the great fireburn we saw from the walls?"

"She was with it when we found her, Lady Meltress," Dogul answered. "I thought you would want to see. The stars have truly blessed you."

The thin woman looked back at me again, and the corners of her lips lifted in what I was hard put to call a smile. "You have done well, Dogul," she said. "You will be rewarded. See that her hurts are attended." Then she was gone from my field of vision.

When Dogul bent over me again, she was smiling. "Now we'll take you to rest, pretty one," she said with satisfaction. I let myself drift back into the grayness. Until I rested, I would be good for nothing. My reserves were low, and I had to deep. I fell asleep and had deeped before the litter stopped moving.

I awoke suddenly, as always emerging from deeping into sleeping first, then becoming fully aware in an instant. The remembered pain kept me from moving quickly, but as I turned my head, I saw a young woman in a clean but worn robe rise from a stool and go to the door. The door was made of wood, banded with some sort of hammered metal. The walls around the low bed on which I lay were of mortared stone.

The young woman slipped out the door, leaving behind some sort of rough cloth she'd been sewing. I knew what hand sewing was, in a historical sense, but I'd never before seen anyone *do* it. Suddenly, there was a logic to the trees, the wrinkles, the clothes, the room, and the sewing. "This is a wilderworld!" I said aloud. What in the name of sentience was I doing on a wilderworld? They were proscribed. And if I had crashed here, would anyone know I was here? Could anyone come and get me from a wilderworld even if they knew it?

The latter thought I quelled quickly as I sat up, damping away the remaining aches and pains. I was the Class A. The Com would move whole worlds to get me back.

I wanted to get up, but first I had to test out my injuries. I had been able to heal nothing fully before I ran out of time and energy. Under the coarse, loose shift I'd been dressed in, my ribs had been tightly bandaged—the cracked one I had not been able to repair at all had obviously been diagnosed. So my breathing was a little restricted. My bad arm was discolored from elbow to shoulder, but I had gotten the break knitted and the shoulder back in place well enough so that most of the surrounding muscles were not badly damaged. The various cuts, scrapes, and abrasions had some sort of salve on them. Nothing was serious—I had taken care of the worst ones myself.

The door opened and Dogul came in, followed by the young woman, who was carrying a tray with a bowl and a mug on it.

"How do you feel?" Dogul asked.

"All right," I said cautiously. "Where am I?"

The young woman put the tray down on my knees. The bowl contained what looked like a thick vegetable broth; the mug, a thick, yellowish, milky liquid. Dogul answered, "You are in the stonehouse of the Melster Lewannee and his Meltress. They have kindly agreed to see to your healing."

"I can see to my own healing," I said. "Where is this stonehouse?"

Dogul gestured sharply to the young woman to leave the room, and she did so, closing the heavy door behind her. When it had closed, the old woman demanded, her face twisted with anger, "Are you mad to speak that way in front of a serving-maid? If it becomes known that you are Samish, you will be put to the ax, and then where will our plans be? We need only two more days, the Meltress and me!"

Common sense told me that I would learn more if I didn't alienate her, and logic said that I needed to learn. What she had said had little meaning for me. "Samish" was a word I had heard her say before, but still didn't understand. "Our plans" meant nothing. "The ax" also meant little, but it sounded ominous in context. One of the things Mortel John had labored long and hard to teach me was diplomacy. I decided to see if I could practice it.

"I'm sorry if I spoke without thinking," I said, trying to sound sincere, "but I'm very confused about how I got here and what's going to happen to me."

Dogul seemed to accept the apology and gestured to me to eat. I needed strength, so I did, even though the soup was unappetizingly coarse and the ivory liquid was warm and overrich. While I ate, Dogul told me that she was keeper of the servingmaids for the Lady Meltress Lewannee. "Now what is your name, and where do you come from?" she asked.

I thought quickly about status and advantages, and then I said, "I am the Lady Ronica McBride, and I come from a big house very far away. It's called Government House."

Dogul's eyes grew wide enough to add to her wrinkles, then narrowed down, and she stared at me for a time. I finished eating and waited her out. Then she made a sound I could only interpret as disgust, and twisted the side of her mouth down. "It'll do you no good to put on airs now," she said. "You're not with the stars, and you're only a filthy Sammat. We'll call you Ronca—that's a good enough name for a servingmaid."

Anger and pride rose up in me at once. How dare she! "I am no one's servingmaid!" I said hotly.

She as good as sneered. "You'll be that, or you'll be dead," she said. "My Lady Meltress owes a debt that she's going to use you to pay. That's what you're worth to us, and what happens to you after we've sold you is no concern of mine."

She was smug, and standing above me, and I was angry. In a second I had gathered and tried to sting her, to hurt her and make her regret her words.

Nothing happened.

The gathering occurred normally, instantaneously, but the sting was not there. I could not project. It was as if I had not even made the attempt. I was shocked into complete silence, my mouth open, my skin suddenly cold. It was horrible.

Dogul stared at me.

I took a shuddering breath, fought for calm, and reached inside me to look for the sting where it had always been, no longer concerned with anger or hurting. The reflexes were there, the paths along which I gathered were there, and my reserves were full, but the sting was totally absent. It was as if that part of me had been amputated. Something seemed to break inside me, and I hurled the tray away from me and swung my legs over the side of the bed, crying, "Bring me a mirror! Bring me a mirror now!" When she didn't move for a moment, I shouted, "What are you waiting for? Hurry! A mirror!"

Dogul debated only for a second. Perhaps, it occurred to me

much later, I had no value to her if I was raving. She went to the door and gave an order to have a mirror brought.

I gathered to exert control on my diaphragm muscles and my pounding heart, for in a few minutes I would have been overoxygenated. But I couldn't stop the trembling.

The ability to project is the sign of Class A talent. Mortel John—one of the overwhelming majority of people who did not have that ability, but perhaps the only one who could train it—called it "stinging." Gathering is the Class C sign. We generally believe that everyone has it to some degree, in muscular strength, in the immune system, in physical ability, in what was once called biofeedback. But those with higher-level, more complexly controllable gathering abilities are very rare—perhaps one or two to a world. Pathfinding is the sign of a Class B, and it is rarer still—perhaps one true talent to a hundred worlds. Pathfinding takes the ability to gather and applies it to inanimate things, to get them to open themselves, to show how they operate, to allow their usage in other than "normal" ways. One true Class B can operate a star cruiser entirely alone, using the cruiser itself as crew.

As the Class A, I possessed all of the signs—gathering, pathfinding, and stinging. I had been told that at the age of two I was in control of a pack of children, some as old as ten, and that that was the way the government of Steressor had identified me for Com testing. My kind of talent was so rare that more than one Class A in a generation was considered unheard of—I was, Jasin Lebec told me, the only Class A to be identified as stable in fifty years. Therefore, I was of the highest possible value to the Com, the confederation of MIs, and all civilized, Com-member worlds.

The Drenalion, the Com's army, came and took me away from what I can only assume were relieved parents—a young Class A is a tyrant by nature. My parents, I had been told, were colonists in the Steressor city of North Gate, and I had had a normal brother and sister of whom I had no memory. The Drenalion brought me to the school for extraordinary talents on Werd.

There, Mortel John was my teacher for the next eighteen years—mine, Coney's, and Kray's. We were the three talents, all of an age, given into his keeping. Coney was several months younger than I, thin and blond and overly wise, as early as age four—and especially after age fourteen, when he was my friend. Kray was several months older, wiry and taller

even before we hit puberty. We were together all through my
memories—the three of us and Mortel John, my only family.

I mistreated them all at first, according to Mortel John. I
was wild with the power of uncontrolled ability, a despot at
four, an unrulable, selfish baby. I have been told about the first
time I didn't get my own way, not what I demanded—it certainly doesn't matter now, and it was probably insignificant
then. Only a rare child, like Coney was, takes a stand on anything of significance. Mortel John said no to me, and I tried to
compel him by projecting to make him give me what I wanted.
Then he set his full strength against me and resisted. I could
not have been more than a baby, and he refused to bend, holding out against the potent force of my stinging. His reserves
were much greater than mine then, and he told me long afterward that he had also taken a very rare drug to make him even
less vulnerable. He stood against me, stolid and unyielding, until I was exhausted from battering on the rock of his will. I
threw a tantrum, and when it was done, he carried me to my
room. The next day, he began training me in earnest. After that
humiliating loss, I never stung him again. But from that day
until the one when I awoke in the strange bed in the tiny room
on this wilderworld, I had never been without my Class A
sign, my weapon, my sting. When I reached for the sting to
touch Dogul and it was gone, I couldn't be sure that I was myself any longer.

The door opened and hands thrust a polished metal circle at
Dogul. In a moment I was holding it. The face that looked
back at me in desperate confusion was indeed my own. My
wide blue-green eyes looked as they had when I last remembered seeing them, under the gold helmet of a graduating Class
A talent. My face was unscarred by the crash, its shape the
same; my long, light brown hair was tangled, but framed my
face as it always had. I studied myself minutely. My face was
a little different, but not in any way I could identify. Perhaps
the absence of the sting was a result of the crash. Perhaps it
would come back to me when my full strength returned. I decided that it would; of course it would. It had to.

I hadn't realized how hard I was gripping the mirror until I
became aware of the ache in my hands. I sent a wave of artificial relaxation down my arms and dropped the mirror on the
blanket beside the spilled tray. Dogul had been watching me
closely, and I suppose she didn't want to risk another outburst,

so when I asked her, "Dogul, do you know how I got here?" she answered at once.

"The stars brought you. I accepted you to fill my Lady Meltress's need."

I tried again. "The fireball that was burning beside me. Do you know what caused it?"

"The stars," she repeated. "It was a piece of the stars, and it brought you to earth." Still watching me to make certain that I did not explode again, she called in the young servingwoman to clean up the tray and the mirror, and then both of them left me alone.

I sat still on the bed for several minutes, not really thinking about anything in particular. Then I got slowly to my feet. The shapeless shift I was wearing was much too big for me, and I was barefoot. There was no hint of anything I had been wearing when I'd crashed on this world, and I had no memory of what it might have been. I moved strength down to my still injured ankle, even though I really hadn't had time to process the food I'd eaten. Then I limped the few paces across the room to the window.

I was about twenty meters off the ground, in a tower behind stone battlements, and the prospect from the window was of a yard within the guarded wall, some fields outside, a stretch of open land, and then the forest, stretching for miles. Truly, a wilderworld.

I hobbled to the door of the chamber and pulled on it. It was locked from the outside. Balancing myself carefully on my good foot, I hesitated briefly in apprehension, then rested my fingertips against the lock mechanism. I gathered and sought to pathfind the lock. The reflex behaved exactly as it always had, and the lock told me, through my fingertips, how it worked. I gathered again, turned the mechanism, and unlocked the door.

The gathering tired me more than I was used to, and I didn't feel strong enough to go wandering yet. So I relocked the door without opening it and went back to the lumpy, straw-filled bed. If you let your jailers know that you can get out, they will only make it more difficult for you.

Kray was actually better at pathfinding than I was—at least at first—but that wasn't uncommon, since it was his highest-level ability. Coney was stronger and more consistent at gathering than either of us—although, of course, he couldn't pathfind at all. Nevertheless, I didn't let them forget that I had the sting.

Once when we were about twelve, we chose a day when we had finished our literature and mathematics and systems sciences, ran down to the groundcar lines, and rode out to Werd's small natural area to scramble on the rocks and race each other around.

But before we reached the natural area, we saw a downed freighter, abandoned and left at the fringes of a busy docking port. Scrambling around on it appealed to us more than scrambling around on rocks, so at the dock stop we debarked the groundcar and doubled back toward the freighter. At twelve we were old enough to know how wearing acceleration was, but not wise enough to avoid it. The three of us gathered, accelerated, and raced to the rusting ship. We had some foodbars with us and consumed them as Kray asked the freighter to open its hatch.

Once we were inside, dilating our pupils fully in the dimness, the hulk seemed somehow ominous, dusty, musty, slowly edging toward decay and disintegration.

"Junk," Coney said softly. "Not worth the scrap."

We moved quickly through the silent corridors to the bridge, where there was outside light filtering in through dirty windows.

Coney found a half-broken, half-missing comset on the floor, and Kray slid into the gunner's seat to pathfind the unloaded energy gun. I lay my fingertips against the compnavigator and pathfound to the ship's log. We played it back. At first we barely listened, being engaged in the novelty of messing around a once-functional starship without any adult supervision.

Fairly soon, however, all three of us sat close together on the bridge benches, listening to the tape tell of voyages to places we didn't know existed—wilderworlds. We had studied a great deal about the Com. All its member worlds were civilized, tame, and, we thought then, every inhabited world was a member.

The ship was telling us it had gone to a place that wasn't in the Com, and therefore was theoretically completely unimportant, but nevertheless still inhabited. The ship had not landed, just jettisoned cargo from orbit and left. When the tape stopped playing, Coney said slowly, "I've heard of something like that.

It's called a wilderworld." He read a lot more than Kray and I did.

"What's a wilderworld?" I asked.

"A place like the past," Coney said. "A world that the government lets stay primitive."

"That's ridiculous," I said with some amount of scorn. "Why would the government want to do something like that?"

"I thought you were smarter," Kray said, and I stung him a little with anger to warn him. "It stands to reason that there are some places more trouble than they're worth."

Coney nodded some agreement with that. "Kray's right, Ronnie. Some worlds are too much trouble to conquer and subdue and modernize. They don't have minerals or resources. The Com doesn't have to pay any attention to them if they don't even have engines yet, let alone be getting anywhere near space."

"Let them be and stay away from them," Kray said, adding, "huh?"

"There's something wrong with that," I said to them. "If we're supposed to stay away from those worlds, what was this freighter doing going there?"

We guessed smuggling, but that didn't work, because the ship didn't land. We guessed scuttling, but that didn't work because it would be far less costly to scuttle in space than to journey such great distances just to dump something. We guessed interfering, power plays, and a few other improbables, but none of them worked, and it all boiled down to we didn't know.

"Let's ask Mortel John," I suggested, and though we debated it for a time, I won, and in our next class, on the history of the Com, I raised the question.

Mortel John was a deliberate man, and he seemed to deliberate a very long time before he spoke to us about wilderworlds. No, they were not part of the Com. Yes, the government did allow them to exist in a state of pretechnological barbarism because they were—as Kray had guessed—not worth cultivating. There were perhaps three dozen wilderworlds, some inhabited, some no longer inhabited, scattered through the quarter-thousand civilized worlds of the Com, their coordinates concealed, their shipping lanes forbidden.

"Then why did the freighter go there?" Coney asked.

Mortel John rubbed his graying brown beard with his hand

and thought about his answer. Finally he said, "Sometimes a person cannot fit into civilization. We do our best to obtain even a minimum of conformity, but if that fails, if someone continues to be antisocial—"

"The government uses the wilderworlds as prisons," Kray said quickly, with a sense of discovery.

"Not prisons," Coney said. "You can get out of a prison. The government uses the wilderworlds as graves."

"Only in very rare instances," Mortel John said. "Now if your curiosity about wilderworlds is satisfied, may I suggest we move on to the analysis of the Surrecipe Rebellion of 722?"

My curiosity hadn't really been satisfied, but I forgot about that and went on with the class discussion. As a matter of fact, I completely forgot about wilderworlds until my Tenday, and then afterward again until I found myself here on one.

I healed quickly, for most of my injuries had gotten a good start on recovery when I knitted bones and cells at the site of the crash. Once I had awakened and eaten again, I worked a little on the subsurface scar cells, but I was afraid to do anything that would show. In addition, I wanted to keep my reserves high so that I would have all my strength when I needed it, when the opportunity to escape presented itself. I was afraid to try reaching for the sting; I couldn't confront the fact that it still might not be there. I preferred to go on believing that it would return when I was really healthy again.

While I was alone in the high tower room, I did some exercise geared at keeping my muscles in tone, even those constrained by bandages. Dogul and the servingmaid provided more information about the world each time they came in—the maid generally to bring me food, Dogul to check on my various injuries and treat them in ways that, while amazingly primitive, were still effective. I learned that it was presently late summer and would soon be harvest time; that the roaring that rose up to the tower window in the late night and early morning was a pack of klawits, the great hunting cats of the plain and forest; that they fed off the herds of wild and tame animals called dralgs—or, when they could bring one down, off another species called tivongs; that dralg meat was for men first and for women only when the men were done. I had classed the society as stiflingly patriarchal and regarded it with some contempt.

More, too—that the Honish were settled in stonehouses and on farms, while the tribes of the Samoth lived in less-settled areas of the world and were hunter-warriors, miners, seafarers, and the like, rather than only farmers. The truce between the two peoples was uneasy at best, but at the moment it had held for two summers and might hold for a time more, since the Samothen seemed to be experiencing some kind of internal power struggle that made them pay less attention to the Honish.

I asked a few times for the name of the world, but it was futile, as neither woman knew it probably had one. It was simply "the world" to them. Coney had called this kind of world a grave, and I kept trying to find hints that I did not have to accept it as such.

Certain facts, however, were indisputable. If there had been any others in the crash with me, they had not fallen clear and had died in the fire. Whatever had taken my sting—the crash, my injuries, or some unknown something in the days between graduation and now, which time was gone from my mind—had also sealed away a portion of my brain that I simply could not reach. I knew where to look for that missing part of my past and my missing Class A talent, but I found there only a blank wall the likes of which all my training had not prepared me for.

I had been raised to rule the Com, but marooned here on this desolation of a world, I could not even rule my own memory. It hurt. The day after I first tried to explore the stonehouse, I stayed in the tower, thinking things through in as logical a way as I could manage. I felt well enough to try to escape by that evening, but a storm moved in and stayed all night.

The storm fascinated me. Only once before in my life, during my Tenday, had I been on a world without controlled weather, and that other had been a desert world, without rain. The rain, thunder, and lightning drew me to the window, where I watched them raptly once I had gotten past flinching at their wildness. Had it not been for the storm, I might indeed have escaped. I do not know if my life would have been any different if I had—though I think it might not have varied, because Jemeret would not have allowed it to be different. I don't regret that—and I did enjoy the violence of the storm.

Toward morning the storm began at last to abate, enough so that I determined I would leave the next night, without fail.

But I had to find out what lay beyond the door of my room, what obstacles were between me and the outside. As soon as I thought of that, I let myself out the tower room door and slid as silently as possible down the steps that curved around the tower, keenly aware that I was moving into hostile territory with no more power to confuse or dissemble than Kray or Coney had. Kray had found very normal ways to prevaricate, but I had based all of my abilities to deceive on the sting, so now I was feeling defenseless. I did, however, know how to sneak.

At the bottom of the stairway a corridor branched away in both directions. It was high, cold, blank stone. I irised my eyes as wide as I could in order to take full advantage of every bit of light. My body was already pressed against the wall, so I pathfound the structure through it, not through my fingertips. One side of the corridor ended in a T without downward access. The other side turned a corner and joined a major downward stair. Walls couldn't reveal anything about the people who might be around, so I went stealthily along the corridor, alert for any sound.

The corridor remained deserted. I wished for a jumpsuit instead of the coarse shift, and kept straining my senses to catch the earliest possible warning of anyone approaching. There was a quality of irrationality to my apprehension, and I was aware even then that they would probably just return me to the tower and lock me in again, but I was unused to taking risks without the sting. In addition, I was unused to *being* afraid. The fear fed on itself, as fear does, and I didn't try to alter my physiology, for too much of my gathering was going to the silence and the alertness. I descended the main staircase about two-thirds of the way before a sound—and, strangely enough, a smell—brought me up short. Below me and a little distance away in the large hall were a guard and a servingmaid, half clothed, standing and groping at each other in a hasty but no less real coupling. There was no chance of slipping past them, and I didn't want to linger. I paused long enough to identify what I thought were the exits from the hall, then turned and climbed back up to the familiarity of the tower room.

I didn't think I was a prude, but then I suppose prudes never do. I wasn't disgusted by their actions, nor envious, nor embarrassed, and I was most assuredly not excited, but I was intolerant. I had at that time little use for the concept of steamy sexuality, let alone of love. Had I had the sting, I could probably have confused them easily and would have moved on past, even though it was starting to get light out. Without the sting, I would not even try.

More than anything else, this made me feel useless—more useless even than a talentless person, for such a person would never have had the expectation of talent. In the tower room, barely aware of the growing dawn outside, I sat still on the bed and fought back the first tears I had shed in my adult life.

Later that morning, as Dogul cut away the bandages from my ribs to confirm that they were healing—unaware that though some bruising remained, the ribs were fully repaired—I asked her what was to become of me.

"I told you once," she said. "You're to be payment for a debt of my Lady Meltress's. Does it hurt when I press here?"

I had turned off all my surface pain receptors before she had begun working on the bandage. "Not at all," I said almost absently, more interested in other things. "But what does that mean? What *happens* to me?"

The old woman hesitated, her feelings clearly in conflict. Her loyalties were to her employer—or owner, I never did find out which—but we'd talked enough and I'd flattered her enough in the past two days that I hoped she would take a chance. I made my voice as appealing as I could. "Please tell me."

She leaned very close and spoke in a voice so low that I had to raise my hearing levels a little to catch the words. "My Lady Meltress gambles," she said, "but the Melster Lewannee doesn't know she does. Someone who held a debt of hers sold it to Jemeret of the Boru, and we have to get it back. The stars gave you to us because you look like the legendary High Lady of the Boru and the Samothen, and we hope that he will accept you for the debt."

Catching the words didn't mean that I understood them. The names, of course, meant little. I had only time to ask, "What are the Boru?" when the servingmaid came in with a pile of clothes which Dogul took from her and laid on the foot of the bed.

Then two guardsmen, struggling under the load, brought in a steaming, sloshing tubful of water, set it down between the bed and the window, and went out again. Dogul took a cloth-wrapped bar of soap out of her robes and laid it on the edge of the tub. "Wash yourself and your hair," she said. "I will bring towels back while you are bathing. We will dry and oil you, and dress your hair." She left the servingmaid in the room and went out. I lifted the top piece of clothing. It was pale gray, and almost transparent. I looked from it to the tub and back again. For the first time I had an inkling of what kind of future was planned for me here, what kind of future women had on patriarchal worlds, and I didn't think I liked it.

"Please get into the tub," the servingmaid said anxiously. "She'll be angry if you don't."

"Does this mean what I think it means?" I asked her, holding up the flimsy garment.

"I don't know what you think it means," she said. Her voice took on a desperate tone. "Please, lady, get in. It'll be easier on us both if you do."

I dropped the gauze, stripped out of the robe, and got into the hot water, more because I didn't want to hear her whining than because I thought she was right. And I needed the bath. Though the soap was harsh, it was effective, and the motions of washing helped me not to think. The servingmaid hovered around, watching, but I refused to let her help.

I had just about finished when Dogul returned with three large, fluffy towels whose softness astounded me, first because I didn't think this world would waste resources on luxuries, and second because I wasn't certain that my status was intended to be anything above the level of the servingmaid. The towels convinced me that, whatever was in store for me, it was going to be better than sex-service worker. After all, in a patriarchal society women were their bodyworth and little more, but history told us there were levels of bodyworth.

Despite my protests, Dogul and the servingmaid dried my body and hair, and Dogul rubbed some kind of fragrant oil into my muscles and limbs. I enjoyed the massage, but it took some real effort to keep from conjecturing. Conjecture would lead to fear, and fear to hasty decisions, usually mistakes.

The servingmaid went out of the tower room and returned with a tray of small jars and a polished mirror. "Makeup?" I asked with some real curiosity. Dogul wrapped one of the towels around me and told me to sit on the bed. I complied, but when she reached for one of the jars, I said, "No, I can do my own face."

"All right," the old woman said unexpectedly. "Let me see it."

So I sat with the primitive cosmetics, some of which were surprisingly sophisticated, and carefully made up my eyes, which were the only part of me I ever amplified. I added just enough dark to the lashes to make them match my hair, instead of vanishing in golden highlights, and enough gold to the lids to darken the aqua of my irises to the clear green I'd always wanted.

"Kadah!" the servingmaid said in astonishment when I looked up. "She *is* very much like the High Lady."

"Now the hair," said Dogul, who clearly approved of what I'd done. She piled the newly dry and shiny brown hair into her hands and began to brush it until it crackled, then divided it into five sections and braided each, wrapping the braids into a smooth, piled crown. She may have seen it as making me more beautiful, but I saw it as a good way to get my hair out of the way in case I had to defend myself physically.

It was getting on toward afternoon, and I was beginning to feel a little hungry, but the sensation vanished as Dogul carefully lifted the transparent gauze so that I could see its construction. It was a shift very much like the coarse robe I had been wearing, but its diaphanous nature was perfectly plain. "Put this on," Dogul said.

I decided that I should take as much courage as I could and ask the question directly. "Am I supposed to be a whore?"

Both Dogul and the servingmaid looked so completely nonplussed that I was comforted. Dogul recovered first, which was, I suppose, predictable. "There have not been whores on this world for two hundred years!" she said briskly. "Put this on."

It turned out to be an undergarment. The overgarment she held up next was strange and lovely. It was composed of two panels of finely woven green fabric edged in intricate gold-thread embroidery. The panels were tacked together once at what would be each shoulder, and several times at what would be, when it was on, the waist and hips. I learned later that it was called a talma, and it was the basic dress among women in the Samothen who had not yet borne children. When I put it on, it felt uncomfortably revealing, but I imagined it was probably flattering.

"The boots are on the bed, and your cloak beneath them," Dogul said. "We will not have it said that we did not equip you for your journey across to the Samish lands. Finish dressing. I will come back for you."

She went out, leaving the servingmaid. I hadn't moved toward the bed or the boots. A journey—I would be going away from here, away from the crash site, away from the place the rescuers would come looking for me. I started wondering if it would be possible to leave a signal, a trail, *something* for anyone who was searching. I had no doubt that they would come and search. I just wanted to make—somehow—certain they knew that I was still alive, that I had survived that awful crash. They would be tearing apart the worlds of the system to find me. They would have to. I was the only Class A of my generation, and that made me infinitely valuable. I was—

Suddenly I gasped, making the servingmaid jump and look at me fearfully. I was barely aware of her. My instinct for self-protection, which had blinded me, fell away and I confronted the true situation. The talent that made me a Class A, that made me infinitely valuable, that thing was gone, sealed away inside me or perhaps excised somehow. If the crash had been responsible, then that talent could return, and more important, the government would not know that it was gone. But what if the Class A reflex had deserted me *before* the crash? What if it was part of the time that I could not remember? What if they *knew* I was no longer a Class A? Then—

I shut off the thoughts and pulled on the soft, tan animal-hide boots. They were knee-high, with thick soles, but no heels, and they fitted themselves to my feet as if they had been cobbled for me. I refused to let the thoughts back in. I knew that I could not continue to exist sane if I let myself think that they would not come for me. And sanity was the basis of talent.

We were six years old when eight-year-old Sarai Gregson was brought to join us. We were seven when she was taken away. Mortel John told us it was very rare for talent to be discovered as late as eight, but sometimes the "normal" parts of the human nervous system suppress it far longer than is usual, and it has to fight its way out. Sarai was thin and quiet and battered from the inside. Mortel John did not tell us much about her origins, and when the three of us got her alone to pump her, she cringed and wept. Because she was to share my room, I saw her naked, her pelvis, shoulder blades, and ribs standing out like peaks. Her back was hideously scarred. Yet we were children who could heal ourselves. I asked her, stunned, what had happened. Why hadn't she closed the cuts before the scarring could occur?

"I did at first," she said, her eyes brimming, as they often did in her tiny, pinched face. "But they wouldn't love me if the beatings didn't leave marks. I wanted them to love me very much."

After she had fallen asleep, I went into the adjoining eliminatory and vomited up my dinner, for exerting control over my sickness made me feel even sicker. I wanted to ask about her world, her family, but after that I couldn't. I told Coney and Kray what I had seen, what she'd said, and the freakishness of it drew us closer together, but away from Sarai.

Her past made her talent a terrible curse to her. Try as he might, Mortel John could not bring her to accept it. Try as he might, he could not give her a substitute for the love she had never found and needed so completely, so openly. She tried to kill herself when the pain grew greater than Coney, Kray, or I could understand. I remember a vivid image of her as a little blond elf bleeding from a slashed wrist that she fought to keep open even as her instincts gathered to fight it closed. Sometime during the battle, her stretched, exhausted system broke in two, reserves gone, and her mind snapped.

At the time, Kray and I had talked about how sorry we felt for her, but what we really felt was superior to her in her naked weakness. Now I think that perhaps she was stronger than any of us could have known.

We asked Mortel John to tell us what had become of her, but he refused, and we had soon put her out of our minds. We were already practiced at shutting out what couldn't be faced, what couldn't be dealt with comfortably. I brought that ability—to close out the inconsistent, the unpleasant, the harshly true—with me as I grew older, and I used it automatically now in the tower room.

Dogul opened the door and said, "The Lady Meltress will have you come to her now. Bring the cloak." I hesitated, then picked up the dark green, heavy cloth and followed her down the steps, across the wide front hall I'd been unable to cross the night before, and to the door of a side room. Dogul said softly, almost with reverence, "The Lady tower," and knocked on the door.

"Yes?" said the low voice I remembered from my first night on this planet.

Dogul opened the door and gestured for me to enter before her. When I didn't immediately move, she gave me a shove on the shoulder. "Here is Ronca, Lady Meltress," she said, closing the door behind us.

The room was quite large, with several windows overlooking a greensward within the stonehouse walls. There was a tapestry hung on either side of a small fireplace, and in front of the fire were three people. The Lady Meltress Lewannee sat in a chair between the windows, looking at those three people with narrowed eyes, rather than at me.

One of the three I recognized as a guard of this house. He was a great, brutish man with an occipital ridge and the smell of blood always about him. I had seen him from my window shouting orders to some other guards during the storm. I considered him a subhuman and dangerous.

The second man seemed to be another guard, but I knew at once that he was not of this house. He was big and well-muscled, but clearly intelligent. His paired swords—longsword and short—were unlike the spears and daggers of the house guard. I saw their handles in his belt under the heavy brown cloak he wore over a dark tunic. This guardsman showed surprise when he saw me. He quickly masked it, but I had seen it, and I knew the Lady Meltress had seen it, too.

The third man was so small as to be almost a dwarf, and so old as to make Dogul look like a girl, but his black eyes were bright and alert as he studied me.

Dogul shoved me sharply, unexpectedly, in the back. "Look only at the Lady Meltress," she said angrily.

I had to beat down the impulse to spin around and knock her flat, for now that my strength was back, I could have. But I thought that Dogul was trying to help me, rather than humiliate me, and if that was so, what she told me to do was based in reason. I looked at the stern face of the woman in the chair.

"Have your hurts healed, Ronca?" she asked. I tried to analyze her voice using the skills I'd learned to bring to the sting. I heard neither kindness nor caring, but instead a suppressed excitement, a budding triumph.

"Yes, they have," I said. Dogul, at my shoulder, hissed at me, and I added, "Lady." It did not, I admit, sound sincere or grateful.

Out of the corner of my eye I saw the small man's lips twitch, but no one moved.

The Lady Meltress Lewannee looked at the old man. "This is the woman the stars provided to me," she said, stressing the last word. "You know we at Lewannee have always been favored by the stars, and have received many gifts by the fireball." She gestured almost languidly with one wrist, and I automatically glanced in that direction. One of the tapestries had been woven to show a starry night sky over a section of field and forest. In the foreground, animals and men were kneeling to a fireball burning brightly in the center of the image. I hadn't time to study it at length, for I heard her say, "You may examine her face to see that I have in no way had it altered."

That statement was bewildering enough, but the small man's response dumbfounded me. He said, "I have no doubts she is unaltered, lady. Her coming was foretold. Ask her to turn to me, please. Gundever, take the cloak from her." The tall young guardsman reached out and took the cloak out of my hands. He was a full head taller than I, but I had time to notice little else, as the Lady Meltress Lewannee ordered me to look at "Ser Venacrona." I turned to the old man. His head came to about the level of my breast, and above his deeply lined face was a huge shock of white hair, partially hidden under the gray hood of his cloak. His hands did not tremble, despite what seemed to be a highly advanced age.

"I believe it is possible that she is the one for whom we have waited," he said.

I could neither deal with that nor block it out. I was perfectly prepared to be the only Class A of my generation, honored and valued, but I was totally unprepared to be a messiah. I gathered and let the reflexes take over. I spun, pushed Dogul aside, opened the door and ran.

I had been trained as an athlete as well as a scholar and a talent. I had healed my "hurts," and during my short confinement in the tower, I had kept my muscles functional. Now this might be my only opportunity. I fled across the hall, in which a pair of lounging guards looked up, startled, as I passed, and into the first doorway I found. It led to a huge kitchen, through which I ran without even pausing, leaping a churn to get out the back door into the kitchenyard. I pumped more energy into my lungs and legs, accelerating. One of the real advantages of being able to gather is the ability to heighten strength and speed. Thus, while I knew they were chasing me by the time I left the building, I had no fear of their catching me unless they could somehow signal people in front of me to cut me off.

The mud in the kitchenyard slowed me down a little, and I let it, because I knew it would hamper my pursuers, too. I anticipated that the gate would be bolted and perhaps locked, so I didn't waste any time trying to open it. I climbed the pile of wood for the kitchen fire, leaped from it to the roof of a shed against the outer wall, and from there to the top of the wall. I had just reached it when people burst from the kitchen door after me.

From the wall to the ground was a five-meter drop, but the grass was soft, and I cushioned the landing as best I could. For a moment I was stunned by the jolt; then the gathering took over, and I ran for the forest, about three hundred meters away across open land. The boots were soft, and I could run very well in them, so while I had no idea where I was going, I gauged that I could run a long way. The talma lent itself to running, and the undergarment, being flimsy, tore easily when the length of my strides exceeded its ability to stretch.

I could hear that they had gotten through the gate before I quite reached the forest, but soon I was in the trees and their view of me was cut off. I could have tried covering my trail, but I opted instead to put distance between me and them. Once I had outdistanced them by several kilometers, I would take the time to cover the signs of my passage.

It was dimmer under the trees than in the open, but soon the gathering began drawing on my reserves, which increased my sensitivity to light to the point where I could see as clearly as if it were an open field at sunhigh. Branches slashed at my arms and legs, but I didn't care about the pain enough to steal strength from my running and seal off the pain receptors.

Once, I passed a startled group of some kind of grazing animals, which I later learned were the dralgs I had heard about, but I was barely conscious of them, for it was clear they constituted no danger. Several times I frightened coveys of some kind of bird, huddled in the bushes, and the sounds of their wings and startled cries unnerved me.

I don't know how long I ran. Although it grew darker, my sensitivity to light kept increasing and counterbalanced the darkness. Finally, the sounds of pursuit had been gone for so long that I felt I would be safe in slowing. Gradually I reduced my speed to a normal run, then to a walk. The ground had grown rocky, with some large outcroppings nearby. I walked to the base of one and stood against it, listening very hard, gasping in great lungfuls of the cold, sweet air. There were no human sounds behind me.

There was, however, a double heartbeat, about ten meters away to my left. I spun in that direction and saw, crouching, eyes burning with inner fires, what was clearly a predator. I later learned that this was a klawit, one of the hunting cats I had heard about in the stonehouse, but at that moment I registered it only as big, furred, sharp-toothed, and looking at me as if I were its next meal.

Had I had the sting, I wouldn't have been afraid of it, but as it was, there was a real fearsomeness about it that completely unnerved me. Yet the gathering reflex was still strong enough so that when it sprang, I leaped backward. The newly returned dimness of the late evening or night fled as my light sensitivity came back in a rush.

At closer range the animal was feline, an overmuscled, long-fanged, horned cat. It seemed surprised that I wasn't beneath it, and tensed to spring again. I kicked up my acceleration to the highest level I could muster, turned, and bolted again, racing at the limit of my ability to get away from the beast. It was very fast, but after a few minutes it seemed to realize that I was faster and it dropped off and abandoned the chase.

I went a bit farther, and exhaustion claimed me. I dropped to normal speed, and into darkness at once. It had become night. The only sound I recognized was alien to me for the first few seconds, and then I realized it was running water. Covered with sweat and gasping for breath, suddenly chilled from the wind, I stumbled to the stream and knelt next to it, scooping up handfuls of the icy water.

There was no sound other than the water moving over the rocks and against the banks, and the sighing of wind through the trees around me. There was no warning at all just before something struck me at the base of the skull with sufficient force to knock me forward into the water, unconscious.

On Werd—and probably earlier, though I never thought about it before—no one at all wanted me to have nightmares. It stands to reason, I suppose, that a Class A with a bad dream can disrupt the lives of the people in adjoining rooms or even adjoining buildings. The part of the sting that projects the nightmares is a relatively weak one, however, so that people are made uneasy and apprehensive rather than fearful or demented. When nightmares came to me at the School for Talent, Mortel John would hurry into my room, wake me gently, and cuddle and soothe me until I was comforted and at ease again. Then he let me drift back to sleep. When I was deeping, I never dreamed at all, and I certainly never had nightmares.

I knew as I regained consciousness now that I was very near real exhaustion, that much of my reserves were gone and only the artificially induced unconsciousness that had allowed me to deep for a time had kept me from draining myself to a really dangerous level. But when I damped down the dull pain in my head and opened my eyes to find myself on a rug in the Meltress Lewannee's Lady tower, I decided it had to be a nightmare, cried out a little, and waited for Mortel John to come and wake me up. Only he didn't, and it wasn't.

The occupants of the chamber hadn't changed. If it had not been full night outside the windows, and if I had not been muddy and exhausted, I might have thought my whole escape attempt was a hallucination.

"Stand up, Ronca," the Meltress said. I was still too tired to damp down very many pain receptors, so the branch welts on my arms and legs throbbed as I climbed to my feet, forcing me to stand unsteadily.

The stonehouse guard and the guard named Gundever both stood between me and the door, also muddy and disheveled. The brute guard was still somewhat out of breath.

"Oh, no," I said to them. "*You* couldn't have caught me and brought me back here! You were making enough noise to drown out a sonic boom! I'd have heard you."

The stonehouse guard took a step toward me and began to raise his arm in anger, but the small man called Ser Venacrona said very quickly, "In the name of my Lord Jemeret, I accept this woman in exchange for the debt. I will not have her touched." Gundever moved instantly between the stonehouse guard and me, his back to me. Almost offhandedly, I calculated his speed, and there was nothing unusual about it in a man trained to fight.

The stonehouse guard stepped back at once.

The Lady Meltress Lewannee smiled. "You will please then give me the debt paper," she said.

The small man pulled a parchment from his sleeve and handed it to Dogul without even glancing in her direction. She took it and carried it to the Meltress. I turned to watch her and realized that my hair had come loose from at least two of the braids and that the others hung askew. I tried to pull all the hair backward away from my face, but my hands caught in its tangles.

Between the weariness and the aches, all caution fled from me and I yelled, "Just who the hell do all you people think you are?"

Either the old man signaled him or there was something in

my voice that made Gundever whirl around and grab my wrists in his hands, holding them out from my body in a grip that I knew I hadn't the strength left to break.

The Meltress Lewannee crumpled the paper in her hands and tossed it into the flames of the fireplace with a sigh of what could only be relief.

Ser Venacrona took from a pouch at his belt something that looked like a small hoop of beaten metal and stepped toward me with it. I had no idea what he intended, but I wrenched against Gundever's grip on my wrists.

Gundever looked down at me, jerked my arms once gently, then said under his breath in a mixture of exasperation and amusement, "Will you relax already?" The utter practicality of his tone and the incongruousness of the words so astonished me that I stopped struggling and stared at him, open-mouthed. He seemed so sensible that I might have laughed, had I not been so tired. He nodded encouragingly at me when I held still, and I really looked at his face for the first time. He was about twenty-five, deeply tanned, and his dark eyes twinkled under light brown brows that probably matched the hair hidden beneath a dark brown helmet. Somehow he made me feel more at ease, and I thought it was because he seemed to have sense, to be somehow more familiar. It seems to me when I think about it that I must have been feeling—and unaware of it— that being more "familiar" made something or someone more "controllable," since I was used to controlling what was familiar to me. But control is an issue I don't want to write about yet—mine, the Com's, Jemeret's. Not yet.

Ser Venacrona took advantage of my stillness to reach up and fasten the ring around my neck, like a collar. It caught in my hair, which he pulled free. I heard it click almost before I felt it, and, like Gundever's attitude, the click was tremendously reassuring. Anything that locked could be unlocked. Anything with a mechanism had an easy path.

The little old man made a sweet farewell to the Meltress Lewannee, and when he finished, he said to Gundever, "Bring her along. We've got a long way to go before we reach the encampment." Gundever bent and scooped me up.

"I can walk," I said.

"Yes," Ser Venacrona said dryly. "You can also run. For that reason, I think we'll keep hold of you for the time being. My name is Venacrona."

I realized that "Ser" was a title as, across the shoulder of the man who carried me, I saw Dogul looking pleased at the way things had gone. The stonehouse guard made no move to open the door, and Gundever had his arms full of me. Venacrona was obviously not willing to do it himself, so for a moment no one moved at all. At last, probably on a signal from the lady behind us, Dogul went to it and opened it. As we went through, I heard her hiss "Farewell" to me, but I didn't have the energy or the grace to reply.

The three of us marched through a crowd of guards in the front hall and out the wicket in the front gate. In the courtyard was a wagon, curtained in gaily colored embroidered hangings and drawn by two pair of large quadrupeds. I learned later that these were tivongs, the best herd animal on this world, strong, fast, and saddle-broken, as well as wagon-trained.

"Get into the wagon with her," Venacrona said to Gundever. "I don't want her jumping out somewhere along the track."

Gundever set me on my feet in the wagon. The inside was piled with rugs and cushions, which made my footing uncertain, and he had leaped in beside me before I had a chance to scramble across the shifting surface.

"Can you drive them all right?" he called out.

Venacrona had climbed up onto the driver's box and gathered in the reins. "I was driving before your na-sires were sucking tit," he said. "Keep the curtains closed."

The wagon began to move, picking up speed as it got out into the open on the other side of the stonehouse walls. I sat down quickly and looked at Gundever, who pulled off his helmet and dropped it on a rug.

"How did you catch me?" I asked him.

He grinned, suddenly looking very boyish and harmless. "My name is Gundever," he said. "You're an awful mess."

"Are you just a guard, like the ones from the stonehouse?"

His grin turned a little sheepish. "Jemeret wouldn't have trusted Venacrona to a plain guard," he said. "Or you, I guess." He studied me frankly, making me abruptly aware that I was nearly naked, then leaned over by the curtains to the driver's box. "We out of their view yet?" he asked.

"Still in open ground," Venacrona said, "but our tail's to them, so you can come out and take over."

I contemplated jumping out the back while they fastened back the curtain and changed places, but until I found out how they'd caught me, there didn't seem to be much sense in running. Besides, my strength was still too low, my reserves too close to the danger level.

Venacrona plumped himself down on some of the cushions with a sigh of relief as Gundever urged the team to go faster. "You're a great deal of trouble," he said to me, "but I fancy Lord Jemeret will think you're worth it."

"Who is he? Why will he think I'm worth it? What did you mean, I was foretold?" I asked him.

His lined eyes narrowed, and he chose to answer the middle question, though it took me a moment to realize that was what he was doing. "You look very much like a woman we—all the tribes of the Samoth, as a matter of fact—value highly, some-one who is dead now, or maybe someone who never lived at all." He dug his hand into the pile of pillows and brought up a flask, which he handed to me. "Here, drink some of this. It's clogny. You're tired, and it will help a little."

I took the flask, but didn't open it. "Look," I said, "you probably won't believe me or understand me, but I'm from the Com, which is outside this world. All I want is to get back."

"People the stars send us often say strange things at first," Venacrona said, unperturbed, "but after a while they get used to it here. If you don't want to drink any of that, hand it back."

I pulled the stopper and sniffed at the mouth of the flask. It smelled like a grain beverage, so I took a swallow and ana-lyzed it quickly as it burnt its way down—fermented, some sort of grain, aged very little, containing no drugs, potent. I handed it back to him.

"Who is *he*?" I asked again.

"Lord Jemeret is Chief of the Boru, one of the tribes of the Samoth," he said. "And he is my friend. He sits on the ruling Council, and many believe that he will be Chief of all the Samothen before he dies." He took a huge swallow from the flask and wiped his mouth on his sleeve. "You want some of this?" he asked Gundever.

"Is a Boru a man?" Gundever asked, reaching behind him for the flask.

"What does he want me for?" I asked, more quietly than I had asked anything else. The relationship I had with these peo-ple was very different from the one I had had with Dogul and the Lady Meltress, and I knew it.

Venacrona retrieved the flask from Gundever and restoppered it. "He needs a lady and an heir," he said, "and he must have a lady who will help him become Chief of the

Samothen. He has chosen you because you are a stargift. You will bear his child."

My breath went out of me as if I'd been punched, and it sounded ragged in my own ears as I filled my lungs again. Without even thinking, I flung myself at the back of the wagon, but I didn't get there before Venacrona had his hands on the collar around my neck and was snapping something onto it.

"Damn, she's fast," Gundever said, with something like admiration in his voice.

It took me a moment to realize I was now chained to the side of the wagon. The second I did realize it, I spun around, stumbling on the cushions, and made a grab for Gundever's shortsword. The move seemed to take both men by surprise, but my stumble gave Gundever time to intercept me and stop my hand on the way to the sword. He let the reins drop to hold me until Venacrona, surprisingly strong, jerked at one of my ankles and pulled me off balance. "By the stars, woman," he said, "you can't mean to tell me you're virgin."

"Would it make a difference?" I asked, shaking off Gundever's hands.

"It would explain this unreasoning terror," the old man said slowly.

As it happened, I was not virgin, but the unreasoning terror was very real, and he had identified it correctly. I probed my own feelings, and said, my voice catching and breaking as I did, "My name is Ronica McBride. I am a talent. People don't—treat me this way!" To my surprise, there were tears in my eyes.

Gundever snorted. "They must've been telling her horror stories in the stonehouse. Us barbarian tribes raping our way across the face of the land."

I fought back the tears for a few moments, but then I turned my face and hair into the cushions, too threatened, too fearful, too helpless to reason. I closed my eyes and sank into my weariness, trying to feel nothing but the jolting of the wagon that sped me toward a man I knew I could never accept.

Kray's full name was Amahd Kriegar, and he had been born on Abranel and brought to Werd from there. He styled himself a prince of some kind in a joking way as we played games as children. He would say he was too handsome and refined to be an ordinary, everyday citizen, and Coney and I would chorus, "But you've got talent!"

It was from Kray that I first heard the word "rape." We were all somewhere in those early throes of puberty, trying to continue the training of physical systems already rebellious and now adolescent as well. We had half an hour for midday meal between classes, and we had sat by the fountain in the school-yard to eat. Kray had been doing some reading, and he said he had "discovered that there was this thing called rape. You two ever heard of it?"

We both said, no, we hadn't. Kray leaned in close and lowered his voice. "A man can make a woman lay with him," he said. "You know, force her to have sex against her will."

"You're lying," I said angrily, but even as I said it, I knew Kray wouldn't lie about a thing like that.

"Why would a man want to?" Coney asked, putting his meal aside.

"To show he's stronger, I think," Kray said. "I heard that soldiers used to do it to the women of an enemy they conquered."

"Men used to own women, too," I said, "but that doesn't mean they do it anymore, and they don't do that rape thing, either."

"I'll bet they do," Kray said.

As always, when an argument seemed insoluble based on what we knew, we took it to Mortel John. I asked him belligerently if there were still such a thing as rape. Mortel John deliberated for a time, and then said, "Yes, I'm afraid there is."

"Hah!" Kray said, delighted to be right, but Mortel John cautioned him against laughter. Now that the subject had been introduced, he wanted to deal with it solemnly. He described some of the history of the act, its political and psychological bases, its painful consequences. He talked about the Drenalion, the government's cloned shock troops, who regarded rape as a way of letting off excess energy and accompanied one another on forays when they went to quell disorder or break up local battles. The fearsomeness of the Drenalion was in itself a great force for law and order—the threat of their deployment had on any number of occasions been enough to bring adversaries to reluctant negotiation.

"No one could ever do any of that to me!" I scoffed angrily, defiantly. "Could they?"

Mortel John reached out and gently stroked my hair. "I pray that you'll never meet anyone who tries," he said.

"We all do," Coney said fiercely.

"We'd protect you," Kray said, and I rounded on him cruelly and said, "I don't need your protection! I don't need any man's. I can take care of myself."

Mortel John lectured me at some length on ingratitude, but I barely listened to him. My own rage at being part of a group that could be considered weak, into which another group thought it could force entrance, had outraged me so that I was blinded to anything else. That day I might have been blinded to more than I knew, cut off from a womanhood I had not yet attained. Perhaps I am beginning to understand it now.

II. Among the Boru

I was vaguely, distantly aware when the wagon finally stopped, but I had retreated deep into myself and neither moved nor opened my eyes. Distantly, too, I was conscious of hearing an unfamiliar voice ask, "How is she?"

Venacrona's voice, somewhat nearer to me, answered, "Like a laba in a snare. She's passed through the shuddering stage now and into the numbness."

Even through closed eyelids I could tell that more light had come into the wagon. The curtains must have been pulled back, or a torch brought closer. "She's really something," Gundever's voice said. "I don't think you made a mistake."

The new voice was deep and level. It had drawn nearer, and now it said evenly, "Ronica, I want you to open your eyes." The speaker waited for a time, and I neither moved nor responded. Then he repeated, "Open your eyes."

There was no anger or force in the words, but I felt a strange compulsion to comply. I did not then think of it as obedience, and I did not attribute it to any cause beyond the strength in the controlled voice. I opened my eyes and saw his face in the flickering light of a lantern that had been hung on a wagon rib. His hair and beard were black, his eyes gray, and his mouth firm. At first I saw him only in those individual bits, and then his face came to me as a whole, and I saw a fine, strong-looking man about twice my age, contained, and somewhat weary. He also looked somehow familiar, even though I couldn't have said how or why, and once again familiarity made me more comfortable.

And he had called me Ronica, my correct name. It brought me back a little, and he saw me return.

"Sit up," he said.

While I didn't feel compelled to obey any longer, I sat up. Gundever and Venacrona were standing about a meter away, both of them holding still and seeming alert. Lord Jemeret— for I assumed it was he—and the two of them were the only people in sight. I gauged it to be false dawn, and we were in an open space among a group of tents. It was very quiet, except for the restless snorting of the tivongs and a far-off staccato sound like barking.

The tent before which the wagon had stopped revealed part of its interior through a tied-back flap. I could see the edge of a table and some hangings. My head was now level with Lord Jemeret's as he leaned on the back edge of the wagon's side; he took a step backward, away from the wagon. "Unhook her," he said to Gundever.

I could have reached up, pathfound the lock, and freed myself, but I hadn't the energy and I didn't want to give my abilities away quite so soon—not until I had rested. Gundever reached over the side of the wagon and unclasped the collar from my neck. I didn't move.

Jemeret said quietly, "I want you to go into my tent of your own free will."

I was relatively calm, still almost detached, and I don't think I shook my head, but instead made no move at all—just stared at him.

He said, not unkindly, but with a peculiar kind of tension that I couldn't identify, "I want you to think that this world is all there is for you now."

My eyes stung, and I hid my face in the tangles of my hair. My breathing accelerated suddenly. I felt the reflexes begin to gather so that I could explode outward in flight, despite any leavening of reason I might have applied. Before I could move, Jemeret spoke. "Yes, you can run, Ronica. But this is a savage world outside the safety of guarded walls or tents, and you haven't seen very much of it yet. I want you to think that this particular part of this strange world might not be so very bad."

The very reasonableness of his tone seemed to blunt the edge of the reflexes, and the gathering melted away. My weariness and confusion were threatening to overwhelm me, but I still could not move, and this time I think I did shake my head.

With a wave of his hand, Jemeret sent the other two men away. Venacrona vanished quickly among the tents, and Gundever went to stand at the head of the first pair of tivongs, well out of earshot. Then Jemeret said very softly, "If you go into my tent now, I give you my word I will not touch you."

I looked at him sharply, uncertain whether to believe he'd really do that, but it occurred to me that he had no reason to lie. As far as he was concerned, he owned me. I slowly got to my feet and climbed heavily down out of the wagon unaided. He did not reach out to help me, even though I was unsteady, and I realized he meant his promise not to touch me quite literally. It made me a little dizzy with relief and hope that when I was stronger, I could regain control. I looked up at him, and he waited, unmoving. He was as tall as Gundever, though not as broad or as heavily muscled. There was a containment about him that I had never seen before. I couldn't call it serenity, but it was a confidence, a self-sufficiency that made him seem somehow remote. This, too, made me feel more at ease, more hopeful.

Most pressing of all, I had to rest, and rest was what he could offer me. When I awoke, I could deal with everything else. So I walked past the Chief of the Boru and into his tent.

It was a reasonably sized enclosure, larger in fact than the tower room in which I'd spent most of my time on this world. Part of the back of it was curtained off from the front, and the curtain was opened to reveal a low platform heaped with rugs and cushions. In front of the curtain was the table I'd seen from outside, containing a dish of some kind of meat and bread and a pair of goblets. There were several wooden chairs around it. Against the side walls were some closed chests, one of them piled with furs. The tent floor was another large rug, and light came from a couple of four-pronged metal stanchions set near the table. After such a long time of plain stone, it seemed a strangely luxurious place.

The tent flap hissed down behind me. I turned, but not in alarm. It was as if his reassurance about not touching me had soothed the fear and lulled the reflexes. Jemeret had come into the tent, too, and was tying the flap shut. I stood still in front of the table.

"Do you want something to eat or drink?" he asked.

I shook my head again. "I need to deep." I didn't notice when the word slipped out, and even more astonishing, I didn't notice that he took it in stride.

"I know you do," he said, "and very soon I'll let you. Just now, sit down." He indicated one of the chairs, and I sank into it. He leaned against one of the chests and crossed his arms, staying fully three-quarters of the width of the tent away from me. I noticed detachedly that he wore a dark blue tunic and leggings, and high black boots, and that there was a dagger at his waist.

"Don't be afraid of me," he said. His hands lay easily on his upper arms, but I found myself thinking that I had never seen anyone who looked so ready to act while keeping so still. "There's no pleasure in a frightened woman."

"Pleasure," I repeated. Something in the tone of my voice made his eyes darken suddenly, but he didn't move. "Is *that* what you expect to get from me?"

"It's what I will get," he said in the same quiet voice, "and so will you."

Something harsh seemed to swell up in my throat, and the words came out without my placing any impetus in them. "They'll come looking for me, and when they find me, I'll tell them the things that were done to me here, and they'll break and burn and tear this place until there's nothing left at all."

Jemeret listened without seeming to react, and when it was clear that I had finished, he said slowly, "It may be well for you to think one more thing. People are not sent to this world by chance. And those who are sent here never go back." Behind his words, I heard Coney saying that these worlds were graves. And for the first time since I'd regained consciousness beside the fireball, I entertained the notion that I might have been sent here deliberately.

The tears came stinging at me again, and I had the pride to beat them back. All the while I struggled for control he watched me, his gaze neither brooding nor compassionate, just level. When I conquered the tear ducts and the damp glaze on my eyes, I looked directly at him again.

He gestured to the platform in back of the curtain. "Go to sleep," he said. "You can wash when you wake."

I went to the bed, pulled off my muddy boots, and crawled gratefully into the heap of cushions, pulling a rug over myself. The pallet was soft and closed around my body as I relaxed. I fell into sleep almost at once, and into deep soon after. I cannot say for certain—I have never asked him—but I fancy he sat awake and watched me for what remained of the night.

A clatter awoke me, and I snapped instantly alert from deep. It was full day, perhaps even afternoon, and a slender, lovely, bright-haired girl in a soft gold talma was pouring hot liquid into a pottery tankard. "Good day," she said, smiling at me. "You were so asleep I hated to wake you, but my lord said I should."

I remembered much of the night before in a rush, sat up and ran my hands backward through my hopelessly filthy and matted hair. Deeping had renewed my strength, and with it my optimism. If I was strong, there was always something I could do. The girl handed me the tankard, and I drank. The liquid was rich and sweet.

"My name is Variel," she said, somewhat shyly, "which means 'child of smiles,' and I am the claim of the warrior Gundever. You met him last night." Her smile went wider with pride, and almost without meaning to, I smiled back. Her face was impish and her gaiety was infectious.

"My name is Ronica, and I don't have any idea if it means anything," I said, a little amused. "Thank you for this. It's very good. What is it?"

"It's shilfnin," she answered, and hurried on, "I know what your name is. We've been talking about you all morning. Do you know how much you look like the High Lady? It's amazing."

"Who is she?"

"She was the one who brought the starsong, scores of seasons ago. She was the only person who ever ruled the entire Samoth. There's a portrait of her at Stronghome, but Lord Jemeret may have a drawing here someplace. I'm sure he'd show it to you if you asked."

I had no intention of asking him for anything. "Was your High Lady this dirty?" I looked at the caked dirt on my arms and hands and realized that my legs and feet were worse. "Is there someplace where I can wash?" And then something else registered. "*Who's* been talking about me?"

"We all have," Variel replied. "All of the Boru. Gundever told us he and Venacrona brought you into the encampment last night, and that you became Lord Jemeret's claim."

I eyed her with sudden suspicion. "What does that mean?"
"What?"

"You said you were Gundever's claim, and now you've said that I am—someone's." I didn't want to say his name. "What does it mean?"

Variel took back the empty tankard. "It means we have gone voluntarily into a man's tent, and we can leave it or be braceleted at Convalee if we and the man and the stars choose." She said it as if it were obvious. Once again I didn't understand some of the words, but the general concept of the speech seemed relatively innocuous, so for the moment I put aside other questions and got to my feet. My shift and talma were in a deplorable condition, and if I'd been in any mood to be amused, I might have laughed. The household of the Lewannees had tried to make me as beautiful as possible, and I had arrived here looking like a creature from some swamp or other.

"There is a streampool above the camp you can wash in," Variel said. "But I have to call Venacrona before I can take you there."

"Why?" I asked quickly. "Is he the one designated to be my keeper?"

"I don't know," Variel answered honestly and easily. "It's what I was told to do." She seemed utterly without guile.

"Do you always do what you're told?"

She paused on the way to the tent flap and thought seriously about the question. Then, with that impish smile, she said, "Well, not always. But this time I will."

I saw some fresh bread on a tray on the table, and I wolfed down a piece dry before Venacrona came into the tent. "How do you feel?" he asked.

"I'm fine," I said lightly. "I'm just very dirty."

He smiled a little. "Before you leave the tent with Variel, I must ask for your word that you will not try to run away to-day."

"Today?" I repeated, fastening on the incongruity.

"My Lord Jemeret has said that we will undertake to ask you only for a day at a time," he explained. "He does not want to put you into a position to break your word, and he believes you will be more capable of honesty if you do not have to an-swer for more than a single day."

Even fully prepared to hate and reject the man who had traded me for a piece of paper, I admired and grudgingly re-spected the strategy. "Very well," I said, "I give you my word that I will not try to run away today."

He studied me more minutely than I would have expected. At last he said, "I take you at your word," and I sensed it was a formula. "Variel!"

The bright-haired girl came back carrying a basket. As Venacrona slipped out of the tent, she said, "You'd better put your boots on. We'll be walking over rocks to get there."

I pulled on the boots. "Couldn't you just show me the way and let me go by myself?"

"I'm not allowed to," she said, "and besides, everyone would be so curious about you that you'd never get there at all. And I would really like to talk with you."

I hadn't actually expected to be able to go by myself, even after my promise. "Talk to me about what?"

"Would you tell me your lineage?" she asked. We walked out of the tent into a circle of tents around a fair-sized fire. Of all the questions I might have expected, that was the very last.

The encampment was alive with activity, and we were noticed, but deliberately not stared at. Women in talmas or heavier robes wove cloth, banked smaller fires over which pots hung, talked with one another, watched or talked to children—all of whom seemed to be older than about ten—brushed each other's hair, and did other such domestic tasks. But I was encouraged to see one or two sharpening shortswords or polishing harness. Men seemed to be doing wagon or weapons repairs, except for the considerable number I glimpsed beyond the tents practicing combat. Once, out of the corner of my eye, I saw a child point at us, but another pushed his arm down. I felt comfortable. I was used to being pointed out and admired, used to being singular.

To Variel I said, "I don't know anything about my lineage."

She seemed astounded. "But most of us can recite backward for generations!"

I couldn't imagine why anyone would want to do that, and said so.

"But how do you know who you are and where you came from?"

"I am what I have made myself to be," I said, more truly than I had any idea of. "Where I came from can't possibly matter." I have only recently discovered how wrong I was. Before she could ask me anything else, I asked her to tell me about the Boru: how numerous they were, whether this was where they lived—at which she laughed—and what their life was like.

The tribe was one of the ten tribes of the Samoth, and its people numbered 612. "Thirteen," Variel corrected herself abruptly, "if you join us." They were not the largest tribe, but their warriors were the strongest and their lord invariably defeated the lords of other tribes in single combat if he were challenged.

We had reached a rock outcrop around one side of which the whole encampment had been established. A path led back into some tumbled boulders at its side, and we took it, climbing onto the shoulder of the rock. We passed a guard stationed where he could look out over the camp and into some of the country beyond. When we had climbed a bit beyond him, I stopped to look around. The ground sloped away from the rocks and the cliffs behind them, a great bowl of plain stretching in grasslands to the horizon, though to my right, beyond the edges of the rocks, I could see the first stray trees of the mighty forest through which we had traveled the night before.

Variel was telling me that the Boru lived in Stronghome, a valley far to the north. They had come to this plain to camp for Convalee. The other tribes would begin arriving in the next tenday. "We came early to Convalee," she added, "because we were to get you from the stonehouses of the Honish."

"What is Convalee?" I asked. "You keep talking about it. And do all six hundred of you come up this little path to bathe?"

Variel laughed as we rounded the crest of the rock's shoulder and started downward toward a sheltered pool fed by a very pretty waterfall. "There are only two hundred of us here, and we mostly bathe from tubs in the encampment, but my Lord Jemeret thought you would prefer the privacy."

It seemed that the rest of the Boru were still at Stronghome, having not made the journey to Convalee this time. Variel set the basket down at the edge of the pool and took from it two large towels, a cake of flaky, coarse white soapstone, a hairbrush, and some new clothes, including boots and a long ribbon for my hair.

"I'll tell you about Convalee while we walk back," Variel said. "I'll wait for you out on the path."

"Thanks," I said. I knew academically that many women bathed together, just as men did, as Coney and Kray always had. But except for the few months I'd shared my life with the maimed Sarai, and my enforced bath in front of the serving-maid, I'd always been alone at very personal times like bathing, sleeping, and using the eliminatory, and I would have felt awkward if Variel had stayed. I stripped off the boots and the two pieces of ragged clothing, found a place among the rocks where I could take care of my waste elimination, then took the soapstone and waded out into the water. Some of its chill had been dispelled by the sunlight, and I closed down my heat/cold receptors to get rid of the chill that remained. There was some pretty birdsong from higher on the cliffs, and I enjoyed it as I washed off the crust of dirt and unbraided, patiently untangled, and soaped my hair. The sensation of being clean again, in addition to being rested, was so welcome and so invigorating that soon I had completely forgotten I was naked out in the open on an alien world. I scrubbed until I shone, and then I gathered and took the time to find the remnants of my injuries, including the branch welts, and healed them cell by cell.

When I was unmarked again, I walked back out of the pool, toweled myself dry, and began to dry my hair. I was a little thinner, but my muscles were in tone and firm under the skin. Suddenly I realized I was still naked, dropped the towel and dressed.

The shift I had been given was pale blue, very soft and gauzy, and fell to mid-calf. The talma was dark blue, embroidered in silver at its neck and hem, and the boots were black. Everything was comfortable, and once again, surprisingly, the boots fit perfectly. I brushed my hair until it crackled, then gathered it up and made a long, thick braid out of it, tying the braid at top and bottom with the silver ribbon that I also worked through one strand of the braid.

I put the old clothes, dirty towels, soap, and hairbrush into the basket and went out of the rocks to find Variel. She was sitting on a boulder by the path, her arms around her knees, singing softly to herself in a high, sweet voice. She turned to me as I came up, smiling at the transformation from mud-caked drudge to woman. Then she seemed to look a little more closely at my arms and her expression changed. "You healed yourself," she said. "That was very fast. It takes me a couple of days."

"You have talent?" First it was a question. Then, "You have talent!" as I remembered Dogul saying something about "Samish arts." It went some distance toward explaining how Gundever might have caught me when I ran from the stonehouse, though I still didn't believe that he had.

"We call it power," Variel said. She slid down off the rock, and we started back on the path. "All of the Samothen have it to some degree or other. The Boru have a good strain of it, but not many of us are that fast."

"Is Lord Jemeret?" I asked.

She smiled. "He's so strong and fast that when he fights I don't think I've ever seen him have to heal."

"A whole population of Class C's," I said softly. When she asked, "What?" I shook my head and said, "Never mind."

She turned shy again. "Gundever and I were hoping you would permit us to serve you an evening meal in our tent," she said quickly, as if she was afraid I would say no.

I almost did, but thought better of it. I liked Variel, and I had no real reason to dislike her warrior. To be utterly practical, I needed allies here—and as far as I knew, I had no other pressing engagements. "I would be pleased to come," I said.

Her smile grew wider and brighter, and she reached out and took the basket from me, overriding my objection that I could certainly carry it. "Convalee is a gathering of the tribes," she said, as if she had been preparing her explanation while I was bathing. "We come to this plain once every four years from our separate places. The Boru come far, but the Marl come farther, as they live on the seacoast, in Salthome. The Nedi and the Paj come almost as far as we do, from Glen Nedi. They live together, because the Paj do not keep warriors. We have five days together on the Plain of Convalee, although we sometimes visit back and forth—well, mostly the leaders do. The other tribes are the Dibel, the Elden, and the Genda, who all live in the area of the Forge." Her voice hardened as she said the rest. "And then there are the Resni, the Vylk, and the Ilto, and the last two are much less to be trusted." She thought about it for a moment or two and added, "They're not nice people." She dismissed the subject and brightened at once. "The five days of Convalee are so we can trade with one another, socialize, play some games, and refresh ourselves by paying homage to the stars. And some of us will ask for the bracelet." She blushed.

I decided, not too incorrectly, that it had something to do with mating and little to do with me, and we had reached the bottom of the path and were back among the tents, so I didn't ask for clarification. There were no children visible any longer, and a lot of the women seemed to be busy cooking. Besides the guards, I saw no men. Variel explained that most of the men had ridden into the forest in separate hunting parties and would be bringing in food for the next tenday, and the children were at lessons, as they were every afternoon.

"What do the women do?" I asked. "Just cook and mend and breed?"

Variel blinked, taken aback either by the question or by my tone when I asked it. "We have some woman warriors in the

Boru," she said, "but this trip to Convalee they were left to guard the people who remained at Stronghome. Also—" Her mouth twisted as if she were debating whether she should say any more, and then she took a breath and went on. "My Lord Jemeret's last claim was a warrior named Shantiah. He never braceleted her, and he asked her to leave his house more than two years ago, but I don't think he wanted the woman warriors coming to Convalee this year. Here is our tent."

She gestured to a tent fronting on the circle that contained Jemeret's tent. "You can honor us by entering," she said. "I must take the basket to the washing pile, but I'll be back very soon."

I opened the tent flaps and tied them back, letting in light from the day. The tent was smaller and simpler than Jemeret's. It contained only a trunk and a pile of rugs and cushions. But on the trunks were some scrolls. I went to one and unrolled it, and it seemed to be a book of short historical sketches and biographies. It didn't appear to be the first scroll in the series, and when I searched for that, I found one called "Lives and Times of the Wintada Period." The first notation under the heading began, "326–328. The Wintada rulers of the Lowlands took control upon the failure of the Lestigan line to produce an heir."

I rolled it back up and set it aside as I heard Variel returning. She was carrying a slingful of wood to build a small fire outside the mouth of the tent. "There's a pot stand behind the trunk," she said to me. "I'd appreciate it if you could bring it here."

I glanced around and found the pot stand. I didn't want her to think I was simply obeying her orders, for I didn't much like obeying orders, even those couched as such polite requests. But it occurred to me that I was more likely to get information and, ultimately, freedom, if I appeared to be cooperative. So I cooperated. As I carried the tripod with its hanging pot out of the tent, I asked, "Is Convalee the name of this place?"

"It's the name of the festival," she said as she laid out the logs. "We are under truce for the five days, and they're called the Day of the Sheaf, the Day of the Laba, the Day of the Clouds, the Day of the Bell, and the Day of the Fire." It sounded like a complex set of rituals, and I had not a lot of academic interest in it, so I moved on to a subject closer to my heart.

"Being a man's claim. Does it have rules?"

"Rules? You mean like a contest, or a market trade?"

"Something like that."

She thought for a moment, frowning. "It means that Gundever and I will be together and concerned about each other as long as we can," she said at last. "But that hasn't to do with rules. That's just the way it is."

"Sort of like marriage," I suggested, and was surprised when she grimaced and spat into the dust at her feet.

"Marriage is what the Honish do. Someone ties them to one another and leaves them to each other no matter what. They don't have tribes for support, just houses. Claiming is a tribal thing, and it doesn't have rules because the *tribes* have rules. Sometimes the rules are the same for most of the tribes, but sometimes they're different. For instance, among the Boru, no man can claim a woman against her will, but some of the other tribes don't have that rule."

"Both you and Venacrona have called me Lord Jemeret's claim," I said slowly, almost afraid that if I spoke it it would become somehow inevitable. "But I didn't want it or have anything to say about it."

Variel's frown deepened. "That's not true, Ronica. Gundever says he witnessed your going into my lord's tent after Lord Jemeret asked you to enter of your own free will."

Trapped! If I hadn't been angry, I might have laughed. "You don't understand," I said carefully, and I think I did it to try to keep the anger from coming out at the girl. "I didn't have any choice."

"I'm very young, I know," Variel said calmly, but just as cautiously. "And I haven't an extraordinary amount of power. But even I know there are always choices. It just seems to me that sometimes people don't like any of them."

I was not used to being lectured by anyone except Mortel John, and I was not used to arguing, either. I had been accustomed to winning by using the sting, and while I could not then admit she was right—and perhaps disconcertingly overwise—I didn't know how to fight back. I fastened my lips together and swore to myself that I would learn.

Variel barely seemed to notice that she'd won an argument. She made sure the tripod was steady, then took the pot off it. "I'm going to the supply wagons for dinner now," she said. "Want to come?"

It was not as if I had a lot else to do.

Across the camp in a direction away from the cliffs were four large wagons, wooden-sided and open at the tailgates. They were just within the path of a guard riding picket on a tivong.

"Are the Boru at war with someone?" I asked.

"Not really," Variel said, "though there's always the chance of a raid. We just maintain alert in case one of the other tribes decides they're at war with *us*."

At the first wagon, she collected a fair-sized chunk of dralg meat; at the second, a good quantity of vegetables; at the third, a loaf of fresh bread, which I carried; and at the fourth, a container of some sort of foaming ale.

"How do you pay for it?" I asked.

"We don't," she answered. "The tribe eats what the tribe has to eat. I told them we'd be four at meal, and we have food for four. If there was a shortage, we'd have less."

"Four," I repeated, but I already knew.

"Lord Jemeret honors our tent, too," she said. "He and Gundever are friends since Gund was a child."

"How old are you?" I asked her.

"I will be twenty at Midwinter. Gundever will be twenty-five at Convalee." She was my age, and I had thought her such a girl.

We started back toward the tent. "I'm twenty standard, too," I volunteered.

"My Lord Jemeret is forty-two at Midwinter," she said. "It is very rare for a chief to reach that age without braceleting someone. So we hope—" She stopped, biting her lip as if she had said too much.

The notion of braceleting was suddenly no longer of limited academic interest. "All right," I said, "if braceleting doesn't mean marriage, what does it mean?"

"It means that a claim is made more," she said. "Two people joined by the bracelet are joined by the fire, and are one in the sight of the stars."

"Joined by the fire?" I repeated. "That sounds a little grim."

"It's really beautiful," Variel said wistfully. "It's the closest the Samothen ever come to being only one tribe. You see, if there's a claim between tribes, one of the people has to change allegiance, and that's hard. But if there's a braceleting between tribes, the couple can belong to both."

I didn't understand, and said so.

"You can't try to learn a tribe or a people all at once, by

asking," Variel said. "You have to live with us and come with us through Convalee."

"I came from a very—very—different place," I said.

She nodded. "It's always that way when someone comes from the stars. Sometimes they talk about it, and sometimes they don't. We're told that mostly they end up with the Honish, because mostly they don't have power."

That made sense, except—"*Mostly?* You mean some come who *do* have tal—power?"

"Well, you have," Variel said, "and the High Lady did."

"The High Lady came from the stars?"

"Of course she did. She brought us the starsong, the gifts, and they say she brought us the power in the first place. She made us the Samothen. We were just scattered and isolated before."

We had reached her tent, and while she hung the pot back on the tripod, I put the bread and ale on the trunk. "There's a waterskin hanging on the tent pole," she called to me. "Will you bring it out here?"

I went and got it, then carried it to the front of the tent. "Who else?" I asked with what I hoped was only casual interest. "Who else has come from the stars with power?"

Variel took the waterskin and poured a little into the pot, then drew a small knife out of her boot top and began cutting up the vegetables. She thought very hard about the question, her brow wrinkled and her tongue caught between the edges of her teeth. Finally she said, "I don't think I know any, Ronica. I think you'd better ask Lord Jemeret."

"Ask him what?" The voice was deep and even, and I recognized it from last night. Jemeret and Gundever, both of them grimy and looking healthily weary, had come up on the side of the tent. They were wearing heavy leather breastplates and carrying helmets. Variel leaped to her feet, threw her arms around Gundever's neck and kissed his sweaty cheek.

"Who else came from the stars with power besides your High Lady and me?" I asked him. "Variel couldn't remember any more." He regarded me steadily with those startling gray eyes, and for some reason my heart beat a little faster and I automatically gathered to slow it. His gaze dropped to my clear arms, the welt marks completely gone, and then he looked back up at me, his face unreadable.

"Sandalari," he said at last, "priestess to the Genda. You will probably meet her at Convalee."

"Did *she* come from the stars?" Variel asked, surprised.

"Are we all women?" I didn't realize I'd asked the question until it was out.

"Sometimes men come," Jemeret said. He nudged Gundever. "Let's wash and change."

As they started away, Gundever said, "We ought to come early to Convalee every time. These long spaces are wonderful for training."

I had put together the only two four-syllable names I'd heard. "Is Venacrona a priest?" I asked Variel.

"He's key priest," she said, "but he is also the priest of the Boru."

It all seemed suddenly overwhelming. I wished I'd spent several tendays asleep after I crashed here and awakened knowing all there was to know about this world, these people. Until I learned it, I could not manipulate it, not control it. And learning about it was so tiring, for nothing was ever quite what I expected it to be. I sank down on the ground inside the tent and rested my chin on my fists.

"What's the matter?" Variel asked, startled and a little apprehensive.

"I'm praying!" I snapped, without thinking. "All this talk of priests has made me reverent."

She left me alone. It must have been my tone, for I did nothing to correct the impression that I was angry at her. She went on preparing the meal in silence, and I sat still and stared at the ground.

I had given up believing in anything or anyone more important than myself when I was about fifteen—if, indeed, I had ever believed in it at all. For several years when we were around the age of ten, the three of us had been systematically exposed to the major religions of the Com: Purism, with its oversoul and the doctrine of self-sacrifice; Responsion, which posited a supreme being's existence in the reactions of the environment and other people to each individual adherent; Epicyclism and its doctrine of the magnificence of a creator through the workings of a balanced, interdependent universe; the Macerates, who demanded worship of a preserver through atonement and proselytization; and Essencism, a pantheon of aspects of a deity said to watch over the great currents passing through civilization.

Coney seemed to take a little to Epicyclism, but Kray and I

didn't find anything to appeal to us in all the superstition we were listening to. Perhaps our scorn at the idea of finding truth in religion kept Coney from being more positive about his own inclinations, but he never made much of it. We teased him a little at first, then let it go without Mortel John even asking us to or lecturing us about it. We felt a kinship with Coney that, even as children, made us wary of undervaluing anything that he valued highly.

Perhaps I might have been more inclined toward worship of some sort if I had not, at about age eight, begun interacting with the MIs, the machine intelligences on which so much of the government's power rested. The MIs—sociological, political, economic, technological, and astrophysical—held the bank of knowledge about the far-flung worlds of the Com. The machines helped the government rule. Each world had governors, and the government was centered on Orokell, but the ruling council was largely composed of the MIs, coordinating among all the other worlds. Other than Jasin Lebec, the only name from the central government known to most citizens of the Com was Pel Nostro, Com Counselor, the nominal liaison between humanity and the machines. Jasin Lebec, of course, was the only other Class A alive, and he was known because it was he who mediated disputes, made judgments, and negotiated from world to world. Someday, I always believed, it would be my role.

The MIs provided information for many judgments, for decisions that needed to be made to keep the processes of life running smoothly, and kept records—the great demographic machine, with which I never interacted, was said to have data on every living being. And the MIs had been created by human beings, none of whom had been as talented as I was. Everything I set out to do—and I was careful what I chose to try—I managed to do. There seemed no reason to believe in any kind of plan grander than the ones I saw the MIs hatching in their strategic forecasting models. There was certainly no reason to conjecture about a being greater than myself. I always thought somehow that people needed to believe because they didn't have talent. Mortel John never disabused me of it, but, then, I never spoke to him about it.

Once and only once—much, much later, just before graduation, in fact—I asked Coney, "Do you still play around with Epicyclism?"

He hesitated for a long while. "I am an Epicyclist. I've been one for years."

"What do you get out of it?" I asked him then. To me, that was a key question, because I couldn't think there was anything religion could provide that couldn't also be attained in another way.

He thought about that even longer. "Two things, mostly, Ronnie. I get a sense of proportion, and I get something to hold on to—a direct line into someplace else."

"Why do you need it?"

"Because I'm human."

It was a strange catechism. I loved him, and so I didn't question any further. It's possible I never accepted my own humanity. I did not have a people. I didn't know I needed one.

The four of us ate the dinner Variel had prepared and drank the ale, which was nutty and flavorful. Gundever was an expansive host, happy to have us there, as proud of Variel as she obviously was of him. The conversation among the three of them was of the elevation to cadre of a warrior named Palenti and the approaching womanhood of a girl named Shefta. Every so often either Variel or Gundever would turn and give me a little background so I could make more sense of the conversation.

I tried to listen as a distraction, but I grew more and more nervous as the evening wore on. The final tankard of ale shook in my hands, and I had to gather and steady it.

"Ronica, are you all right?" Jemeret asked.

We were still sitting across the remains of our meal, crosslegged on the tent floor. Gundever and Variel fell silent, looking at me. I looked back at each of them for a few moments. "You've been nicer to me than I ever expected," I said. "But—" There was no way I could go on in front of their steady gazes, and I looked down into the remainder of the ale in my tankard.

"But what do we expect from you in return?" Jemeret asked. "Is that a fair guess?"

Without looking up, I nodded and corrected, "You. What do you expect?"

He answered at once. "You've entered my tent, and for the time being I expect you to live there. It is my hope—" he stressed that word—"that before Convalee begins you will join the Boru, become part of this tribe."

I looked up at him. "Venacrona said you wanted me to bear your child," I said flatly.

He didn't smile, but there was a sense of amusement in him. "Priests think in destinations because they feel they already know all the paths," he said. "The rest of us think in terms of process. I'd prefer to talk about this in our own tent, not in a tent where we are guests." He got to his feet in a single, graceful movement and held out his right hand to me, gesturing with his left that Variel and Gundever should remain seated.

I hesitated a long time, for I recognized this as a test. At last, nodding a little, with the understanding that it would be to my advantage to be seen as cooperative as long as possible—my eventual escape would be easier—I put the tankard down, put my hand in his, and stood up. His touch was firm, warm, and almost deliberately impersonal. I was far too aware of it as he thanked Gundever and Variel for their hospitality and led me out of their tent into the circle of firelight from the central fire that all of these tents fronted on.

My interior trembling increased and I gathered and pushed it back. "I have to see the guards about their duties tonight," Jemeret said. "You can come with me, if you like, or you can wait in the tent." It was now quite dark, and the stars were out. I wanted a chance to study them, for this was the first time I'd been outside of roofs, trees, or canvas at night.

But there was an issue here that I wanted to confront directly. "If I say I'll wait in the tent, how do you know I won't run away? It's after sundown."

"You can try it," he said easily. "You tried it once before. I'd hate to see you get that tired again." The smile broke through at last. "I'd hate to get that tired again myself."

The truth about my flight from the stonehouse suddenly became clear. "*You* were the one who caught me! But you weren't there."

"Not in the stonehouse. I'd never go into a stonehouse!" His sudden vehemence surprised me. It was the first strong emotion I'd seen come through his iron control. "I was in the trees, watching the stonehouse. I saw you run across the clearing between the wall and the forest."

"So I ran straight toward you," I said.

He shook his head. "I was at the side of the stonehouse, not at the back. I wanted to be able to see both front and back gates. You ran ninety degrees from me."

He was very fast—fast and silent. I pressed my lips together briefly and looked up at his once again impassive face. "I'll wait in the tent."

Jemeret almost smiled. I saw it at the corners of his mouth, and then he let go of my hand and walked toward the edges of the encampment. He didn't look back to see if I was indeed going to his tent, and I guessed that he would not. When he was out of sight, I looked up. What a dearth of stars. I was used to a night sky thick with the suns of the galactic center. This was a fringe world, somewhere far from the center, far from the life I'd known, far from everyone I had ever met. The greatness of the distance, of the gap, was depressing.

Because this was a world with no way to bridge that distance—no ships, and certainly none capable of the super-speed rolls; no eftel, the indispensable real-time comlink between the worlds; and no concept of either. Perhaps that was the greatest distance, greater than the spaces between suns: the inconceivable chasm that created an unbridgeable dissonance between the remote past and the present. Had I been closer in, had the stars more comfortably surrounded this world—

I cut off that line of reasoning and went back into the tent of the Lord of the Boru, where I paced restlessly, clenching and unclenching my fists, until he came in. Then I fell quite still as he sealed the tent flap.

"Should I lie down now?" My voice came out harsh and ragged. I half expected him to be surprised by it, but he was not.

He went to the table and poured two goblets of a liquid I suspected was clogny. "Ronica, it would help if you believed you were beautiful."

"Help which of us?" I asked.

He laughed, which was one of the last reactions I expected. "Here, take this," he said, holding out a goblet. "Lie down if you're tired. If you're not, come over here and learn something." He pointed at one of the scrolls on the table. Out of curiosity, and calming, I took the goblet and looked down at the scroll.

It was a map, drawn in a very old style, so that trees looked like trees and houses like houses. There was a segment of forest, a large plain below it, and two rivers, the small one running along the left-hand edge of the map from the forest, down past the plain, and the larger one running partly across the bottom of the map.

Jemeret tapped the house in the forest closest to the smaller river. "This is the stonehouse of the Lewannees," he said, "and we are presently camped here." He made a small arc with his finger where the forest met the plain, against a rough rendering of the cliffs I'd seen that morning. "This is the Plain of Convalee, from the Palier Cliffs to the Modria River."

"Where's Stronghome?" I asked. "Variel told me your permanent place was called Stronghome."

"A long way northeast of here, in the mountains. Some other time I'll show you that map."

I sipped the clogny, and it was like fire going down. "It looks like you have a good strategic position here," I said. "Do you think you'll need it?"

"It's possible. The fact that we came so early to Convalee won't escape some of the neighboring tribes. I expect the Genda and the Ilto to be the most likely to come first. Sabaran of the Genda is an old friend of mine. Evesti of the Ilto is an old enemy."

"Have they talent? I mean, power?" The clogny had stopped burning, and I drained the goblet.

"Some," Jemeret said. "Not enough. Sabaran tries to make up for it with wit, but I forgive him for it. Evesti tries to make it up with brute force." He tapped a place on the map to the left of the Boru encampment. "If Sabaran comes next, he'll camp here and ask for conference. I'd like you to come with me when I meet him." He refilled my goblet.

"Why?" I asked.

"Because it does me no harm," he said frankly, "to have a woman of power with me. It elevates me, and that which elevates me, elevates the Boru."

I set the goblet down and moved away down the table to say what I wanted to say. "Why should I have an interest in elevating you?"

"You could do far worse without finding a way to do better," he said evenly. "I want you to think about that."

The clogny had made me a little dizzy and a little sleepy, but I gathered it away. "You need my help?"

"I'd like your help," he corrected. "I will not be ungrateful for it. We can probably strike some mutually beneficial bargains."

I decided to take a chance. "My price would be that you leave me alone," I said in a rush. I sat down in the chair at the far end of the table.

"You share my tent and exist as my claim," he said. "It

should be very clear that I cannot leave you entirely alone. State your terms more specifically." He waited, tapping the base of his goblet lightly against the edge of the map, his gray eyes disconcertingly fixed on my face, challenging me not to look away from him.

Each word was a burden and seemed to take an entire breath as I spoke it. "I—don't—want—to—be—raped." I panted a little when it was all out and hanging in the air between us.

His expression did not change at all, but he set his goblet aside and stood up. I must have jumped a little, and he saw it and didn't move toward me. "Ronica," he said deliberately, "I want you to listen to me and believe what I say. I am not lying to you, because I have no reason to lie to you. We both know that I'm stronger than you are. We proved that when I brought you back to the stonehouse." He spaced his next words carefully, utterly serious. "Rape is a game for the weak. I am not an unkind man. Do not make the mistake of thinking that makes me a weak one. Is that clear?"

Slowly, I nodded. It was rational. Had he wanted to take me by force, he could have done so several times over. "I will help you," I said. "As long as I believe you will not physically force me, I will help you."

"Accepted," he said. "I will not physically force you. Now undress, and let's go to bed."

Before I could control it, my entire body jerked as if I'd been lashed. He didn't move, nor did his expression change. I realized it was either a test or a trap, and in any case, I really did have very little choice.

When he saw me infinitesimally relax, he stripped off his tunic and tossed it onto one of the trunks. His upper body was clear of scars or marks, and the hair on his chest was not heavy or matted, but he suddenly seemed bigger as he bent to fold down his boots. He glanced over at me as I sat, still frozen, in my chair.

"Undressing is a simple act," he said. "I can help you with it if you like."

I got rid of my boots and the talma and shift faster than I would have thought possible without acceleration, breathing in quick gasps and fighting to slow my lungs and diaphragm. He looked over at me, seeming not to notice my naked body, then took two steps around the table, reached up, and untied the silver cord in my hair, gently unbraiding it, his fingers never touching my skin. "Now go to bed," he said.

I bolted for the rugs and drew them quickly up around me, almost afraid to look in his direction. There was a thud. He'd dropped the pile of furs on the other side of the curtain and now he was blowing out the stanchion lamps. I saw the fine lines of the muscles in his thighs and back before the tent was totally dark. I heard him roll himself into one of the furs. After a moment I widened the irises of my eyes to gather in every stray bit of light, and found him, a meter away, watching me.

"We have to learn to trust each other," he said. "I want you to think that I'm on your side."

"Thank you," I said, half sarcastically, half seriously.

"I want you to think that I would rather you didn't thank me for *not* touching you," he said. "Quite the opposite. Are you virgin?"

Something in his eyes in the darkness compelled me to truth. "No."

"I've said I won't force you, and you're not virgin," he said thoughtfully. "Why are you still so terrified at the thought of my having you?" The question had been spoken so reasonably, seemed so natural, that I had no idea of its incredible importance.

I looked for an answer and ran directly into the wall that cut off part of my memory from me. "Something happened," I said slowly, sitting up as if to better cope with the discovery. "Something happened that I can't remember."

"You can't remember?" He sat up to keep his face level with mine, but he did not move any nearer.

"Before I came to this world," I said, feeling the truth of it as I spoke, "*something* happened, and it's not in my mind at all. But my body remembers it."

"Perhaps it will come back to you," he said. He held his voice noncommittally detached, and his control was formidable. It always is.

Slowly I lay back down. "Perhaps," I repeated.

We didn't speak again that night, and eventually I tired of trying to find a way past the barrier to the part of my mind that was shut off from me, and willed myself to sleep. When I awoke in the morning, he was already gone, and I had somehow absorbed the idea that whatever had happened was the reason I had been sent here. The government had somehow taken away—destroyed, burnt out, eliminated—my Class A reflex and cast me out. There would be no going back to Mortel John, or Coney, or Kray, or Jasin Lebec. I would have to make a life here. And, as he wanted me to, I found myself thinking that there might be worse ways to make that life than as a Boru. Being me, however, it was also part of my nature to wonder if there might be better ways as well.

Kray was eighteen and Coney and I were still seventeen when we left Werd for Koldor to continue our studies. It was then that I met Jasin Lebec for the second time. The first time I had been just barely thirteen. Mortel John had taken the three of us to Orokell, to the seat of the government, home of the great Com councils, the bureaus that headed the huge bureaucracy, the central offices of the merchant fleet, the schools of standardization—linguistic, monetary, technological—and the Court of Planetary Justice.

Jasin Lebec was also visiting Orokell, and Mortel John immediately set up interviews for us. Jasin Lebec was the other Class A. He was probably in his nineties when I first met him, and dealing with the tricky negotiations for a trade alliance that would bring two more worlds into the Com. We sat in the spectators' gallery and watched several hours of the negotiations. Coney and Kray asked Mortel John several questions based on the politics of the negotiation, but I only stared at Jasin Lebec. He was my kind. I was to be taught to do everything he could do, and the two of us were the only ones in the Com who could do it, the only ones who were alike. He fascinated me to the point where I stopped hearing anything being said and just watched him. He was an old man, but he did not seem to have begun shrinking back on himself the way some old men did. He seemed as big as Mortel John, and his shock of brown hair was just beginning to whiten, though his eyebrows had grizzled to gray-white. His eyes were dark and glistening, and the lines around them could not truly be regarded as wrinkles yet. He never spoke while I was watching, only listened and *leaned* on the actual negotiators.

Because I was wide open to receive with my Class A talent, I knew every time he used his. It was so subtle that I couldn't call it stinging—my own use of the reflex was still very raw—but I could recognize and admire the delicacy with which he was working. He was exerting influence without appearing to do anything. I wanted to reach out along with him and feel the input from the minds and emotions he was touching, but I had sense enough to know that they would sense my presence, even if they were unaware of his. I knew that my own use of the sting could still create chaos; I wasn't practiced enough for his level of control, though I vowed that I would be. I wanted to be the best ever, including him, and if that meant perfect control, then I would settle for no less.

Mortel John had to shake me to get between my gathering to the sting and Jasin Lebec's projecting. When I realized he'd been trying to get my attention, I drew back to the gallery and fought my eyes into focus as I turned to him. He seemed a little surprised—I think it must have been at the unusual depth of my concentration—as he said, "Come on, Ronica. We have an appointment with him down on the ground floor." I realized that Coney and Kray were already at the door of the gallery, looking back at me with puzzled expressions.

I got up and went after them, and Mortel John followed me, glancing back over his shoulder, down at Jasin Lebec. I saw it as I reached the doorway.

We rode down on the slideway and went into a conference room. It was small, paneled in some sort of dark, fragrant wood, and heavily carpeted. The four of us sat in thickly padded chairs on one side of the table that took up most of the room. It was on one side out of habit. Conference rooms like this existed on all the worlds of the Com, and could be linked with each other by eftel vid—at enormous expense—so that conferences could take place with half of the participants on each world. But a Class A couldn't use the talent by way of an eftel, so a Class A had to be met in person.

We all knew the facts of Jasin Lebec's biography, but Coney asked Mortel John about him anyway, and he responded. I didn't really listen. I had suddenly suspected that the meeting had been arranged so that we three could be tested. All three of us had recently undergone the throes of puberty, and puberty could alter talent.

I was taking a breath to ask Mortel John if I was right when the door opened and Jasin Lebec came in. The question died in my throat. He was not as big as our teacher—indeed, he was smaller than he'd looked from the gallery—but he was still substantially taller than we were. We all rose as he entered and shut the door again, slipping the privacy guard on as he did so. I felt all at once a recognition that someday people would stand for me in this way, and what I thought then was pride, but recognize now more as simple arrogance, came over me.

"How good to see you again," Jasin Lebec said to Mortel

John, holding out his arms. The two men embraced, and I felt rather than saw Kray choke back a snicker. Coney was wide open with admiration and awe.

"Let me present my class," Mortel John said. Both men turned surprisingly affectionate gazes on us. "Amahd Kriegar, Shems Conewall, and Ronica McBride. This is Jasin Lebec."

Jasin Lebec acknowledged the boys with their nicknames, then nodded to me and called me by my full name, just as everyone always addressed him. "I'm delighted we had a chance to meet," he said, and I went wide open again, reading his pure delight, but nothing more, even though I knew there had to be more there. He was very, very good.

We all sat down, and he asked us what we were studying, beginning with Coney. "We all take politics and athletics," Coney said, "and history and technology studies, and this year we're beginning weapons training."

"But that's all of you," Jasin Lebec said. "What about you as an individual?"

Coney gathered and controlled a furious blush. "I'm interested in writing and drawing," he said. "I do some if I have a chance."

Jasin Lebec nodded in approval. "I'm one of those who believes that talent should have an artistic side, too," he said. "I wanted to study voice, if you can believe it. Alas, it was one of the things I had to put aside."

And I *knew* with the kind of certainty that comes only viscerally that he had probed Coney in some way I could neither identify nor understand. Coney was completely unaware of it.

Jasin Lebec turned to Kray and, smiling, asked the same question. "Girls," Kray said, almost belligerently, but then, he had been an adolescent a year longer than Coney or I had. "And I'm interested in breeding and racing Pelhamhorses."

"I approve of both interests," Jasin Lebec said dryly. "It's never failed to intrigue me how Class B talents, who deal mostly with the mechanics of things, find such a preoccupation with living beings. Got any winners yet?"

Kray grinned from ear to ear and launched into a catalog of his two best breeding lines. Jasin Lebec probed him when he was deeply involved in the description, not before. I knew that Kray, like Coney, was unaware of the probe, but that his greater strength had made the distraction necessary.

I felt the hairs at the base of my skull rise a little as I realized that I was next, and that I would know he was doing it to me. When he looked at me, I blurted, "I play the nomidar, and I ride Kray's horses," and stared at him, daring him silently to make any try at me, my shields ready to snap up.

Mortel John stirred, but I didn't turn.

Jasin Lebec smiled. "You're turning into a beauty," he said. It was a completely unexpected statement, and I blushed and gasped simultaneously, for all my still barely trained control was being directed to the readiness of my shields, and I hadn't any left to handle my face. I honestly believe it was the first time anyone had ever complimented me on something that had nothing to do with my talent. I was aware suddenly of my newly budding breasts, of the pubic hair that had made me too embarrassed to swim naked with the boys any longer, of the onset of my camenia, which Mortel John had had to teach me *not* to block, as bleeding was something I thought of only in terms of stanching.

In my confusion, I felt Jasin Lebec try to slip his probe in, and my reflexes slammed the shields up before he had a chance. I saw him hastily mask his surprise. He spoke to us for a time on the costs and responsibilities of talent, that like all privileges it had to be earned and paid for.

Kray asked him what he'd paid. Jasin Lebec's voice was warm and steady, pitched for us alone, and not even to reach as far as the walls beyond the conference table. "A home and a family," he said, "that most of all. But more—I can have no real weaknesses. I have too much talent to be flawed. And flaws are such wonderfully comfortable things."

He smiled at them and at Mortel John, and then looked directly and steadily at me. "I want to speak with Ronica McBride alone," he said. When Mortel John hesitated, he said more firmly, "It is my right. It is necessary."

Mortel John nodded slowly, rose, gestured to the boys, and took them out of the room. I watched my two friends go and could read that Coney was concerned for me and Kray was jealous. Jasin Lebec followed them to the door and reslid the privacy guard. I shot the shields back into place and held quite still, gripping the arms of the chair.

Jasin Lebec came around the table, turned my chair to face him and leaned on the arms, so that his face was very close to mine. I gathered to slow the abruptly faster beat of my heart, startled. "Lower your shields, Ronica," he said. "I won't hurt you."

I knew that. I just was having a lot of trouble laying myself open to him. "No one's ever gone into my mind before."

"Not that you're aware of," he said, "although you were probed when you were selected for training. But because no one has since you've grown so much, I sent the others away. They don't know I probed them, and you won't ever have to tell them I read you. As strong as you are, my guess is that no one ever will probe you unless you let them in."

"Why do you have to do this?" I asked.

He drew back a little and seemed to debate whether to answer. Then he nodded. "All right. Your strength gives you the right to ask."

I wasn't, somehow, surprised. I felt that the explanation was neither more nor less than my due. He and I were the only Class A's in the Com—that is to say, in the universe. There should be an equality about us. I did not find it incongruous that he was eighty years older than I was. I did not find it strange that I was stronger—after all, I was used to being the strongest.

"All along the way, there are tests," he said. "You must meet them. You don't necessarily have to pass them all. In fact, some you would probably do better to fail. But meet them you must. The government needs talents. It cannot afford talents who are not worthy of their talent."

"Do I pass or fail this test?" I asked.

"I hope you pass it," he said.

"What's a passing grade?"

"I'll let you know. Lower your shields." He leaned forward on the arms of my chair again.

I wrenched the shields down, fighting against the defensive reflex, and closed my eyes so as not to see the face above mine. I felt the probe, which was gentle enough, but which set my teeth on edge and made me shudder. Fast as it was, I could not escape the knowledge that someone else was inside my mind.

When he withdrew and did not speak, I opened my eyes. He straightened. "You passed," he said. "You will continue in training."

I let out a sigh and relaxed my grip on the arms of the chair. He sat down in the chair beside me and watched me, waiting for something. Finally I asked, "Are you going to tell me things just between us, for Class A's?"

"What things?"

"I don't know," I said. "Things. Secret things, maybe."

He smiled, gently and a little sadly. "You're clever," he said, "and that's good. There is nothing more disappointing than talent coupled with stupidity. Some talents have been depressingly slow. All three of you are bright, and that's rewarding. Do you want to ask me some questions?"

"Do you want to give me some advice?" I countered.

"My advice is that you ask me some questions," he said. "I don't know when we will meet again."

I thought a little about questions, then asked, "What's it like?"

"Define 'it,' " he said. "Be specific."

"What's it like being a full-fledged world-saver? Having all that power?"

He seemed to ponder that question for far longer than I would have thought necessary. Then he said, "Not fun."

"Really? Not? I'd have thought it'd be great."

"Is that what you're looking forward to? Saving worlds?"

I got up and walked across the thick carpet to the wood panel next to the door, as if to take up some time before I had to answer. "Isn't that what I'm supposed to do? Isn't that what the government's training me for?"

He steepled his fingers on the table in front of him. "What you're supposed to do, what the government is training you for, is to learn to become an adult human being, a complete person. That's all anyone expects you to be."

"That can't be right," I said with all the conviction of youth. "Everybody does *that*."

He shook his head and suddenly looked very tired. "Even if they did," he said, "and I assure you they do not, you would have to be more."

"I am more," I said confidently. "I have talent."

His eyes were all at once, bewilderingly, pitying. "My dear child," he said gently, "it's not the talent that makes you more. It's because you have the talent that you must *be* more."

I didn't understand the difference. Not for years. I believe that I am finally beginning to understand it now. And, to whatever degree I do, I owe that to a different teacher from Mortel John.

Four years later, on Koldor, I met Jasin Lebec for the second time, on this occasion in the quiet courtyard garden of a villa where the four of us were staying. He had not changed at all, while I had grown from just blooming adolescence to young womanhood. The four years had been rich ones for the training of my talent, and I was stronger, more confident, and probably more arrogant.

I remember that I was wearing a long gown of apricot-colored satin instead of the standard white jumpsuit of training. I remember that I had been admired enough to be tangentially aware that I had some beauty, but I valued my talent so much more that I never gave much thought to looks. Millions of women were beautiful, after all, and I was the only Class A.

Actually, there were two Class B women—one fifteen years older than I, and one twenty-eight years older—who were far more beautiful than I could ever have hoped to be. We had met them recently at a talent seminar on Werd, and it pleased me to see them step aside for me, and pay me the respect due to a Class A. Coney seemed barely to notice them, but Kray hadn't come back to his room any single night that they were there.

It was some time before the evening meal, and I had decided to walk through the garden courtyard, the likes of which Koldor was famous for. This was a world of perpetual summer, some of its surface jungle, but in this area moderately temperate. Night-blooming varieties of flowers made the air heavy with perfume, and fountains and statues of ghostly white stone glowed softly from reflected moonlight in the darkness.

He came out of a door I hadn't noticed. I stopped walking, surprised to see him, for I had not known he was on Koldor. "How are you, Ronica McBride?" he asked.

I smiled. "Taller and stronger, Jasin Lebec. And you?"

"Older and wiser," he said, returning the smile. "Let's walk a little way."

We turned side by side and walked along the winding path through bowers, artificially built thickets, and riotous flower beds. Once, we passed the entrance to a hedge maze.

"What have you learned?" he asked. "You, individually, not all three of you."

I thought of my Tenday. I had never told anyone about it, or the amazing thing it had taught me. "I learned that everything has a path," I said. "Not living things, of course, but it doesn't have to be mechanical."

"That's quite a thing to learn," he said. "How did you find it out?"

I thought about it and decided that I might get into some real trouble by telling the truth, so I said, "I pathfound a knot in my horse's reins one day. It takes longer, and probably more strength than it's worth. Mechanical things are quicker—other things are very primitive, and you sort of have to pry it out of them."

He was quiet for a few moments, and then asked, "Did you tell Mortel John?"

"No. It didn't seem very important."

"You aren't that naive," he said mildly.

I had to gather to stop myself from flushing. "I thought I might get into trouble."

He accepted the truth in that. "And what other reason?"

It can be very useful to suddenly think of a lie that could be true. "I thought Kray would be hurt," I said. "He's supposed to be better at pathfinding than I am, and he's very proud of it. What are you doing on Koldor?"

We turned a corner in the dark and found ourselves in a sheltered bower with a white lovers' bench. He gestured for me to sit down, and sat with me. "I was on my way from Aubernese to Orokell," he said, "and I requested an hour's stopover here so we could see each other."

"Really?" I wasn't certain I should be flattered. "Is this another test?"

"I'm not going to probe you, if that's what you're worried about. I was just wondering if you had any questions to ask me now."

As it happened, I did. There was something I'd been wondering about for several months and had almost been afraid to mention, but it occurred to me now that Jasin Lebec was the correct person to ask. "Yes," I said slowly, "there is one question." He waited. "There are three or four Class C's born every fifteen to twenty years, and two or three Class B's. And only *one* of us, according to what the statistics say." He neither confirmed nor denied it. "But the only Class A's we know about right now are you and me. What happened to the rest of us?"

I realized instantly that that was the question he wanted me to ask, the one he had wanted me to ask the last time we met. The pleasure he felt was so intense that it leaked around his shields. I became aware that, vital as he seemed, he was nearly a hundred years old, and though he probably had another eighty years to live, when he was tired, he would lose some of his control.

"Things happen," he said. "Six out of ten of us don't survive to our first birthday. We believe—though after-death examination is not much to go on—that the receiving part of the sting is sometimes far better developed than the projection. For a baby, barely formed, unreachable, that kind of agony without insulation would cause insanity and physical overload. Two out of ten enter training, but do not complete it. They—break, you might say, and are sent away. You have not yet graduated. The number might be three out of ten."

"I'll make it," I said confidently. "I'm very strong."

"There is a paradox about strength," Jasin Lebec said. "Limbs fall from the weakest trees when the wind is heavy. But the strongest trees are uprooted."

"Not all of them. There are mighty forests."

"In a forest, no tree stands alone."

I straightened the overrobe of my gown. "I have Coney and Kray," I said, "and Mortel John."

"Just be careful," he said. "Watch where you make your stands. Watch where your emotions come from, and where they go."

I had thought of something. "There is another question," I said. "When do I learn the kind of probing you did on us?"

"Not yet," he answered instantly, and then before I could ask why not, he patted my hand lightly in the darkness. "Do you still play the nomidar?"

"Yes," I said, and my voice went softer than I expected it to. "I'm surprised you remember."

"You shouldn't be," he said. "I'm interested in most things about talent, and everything about you. Do you have your nomidar here on Koldor?"

"I never go anywhere without it."

"Will you play something for me?"

I was utterly flattered. Coney and Kray sometimes listened to me play, but rarely for very long, and Mortel John fussed that my playing took time away from the long hours of study, physical training, and concentration exercises I was supposed to be doing. "I would like to," I said, suddenly almost shy. "I would like someone to tell me how well I'm doing."

We rose and walked back along the garden path in the freshly cool breeze until we came to the door of my room. I didn't turn on the light, for the second of the moons had risen and the brightness came in the open door. He sat in one of the low posture chairs and I sat on the couch, cradling the instrument against me. At first I had played almost as a joke and to irritate Mortel John. Then, after my Tenday, when I learned that everything had a path, I pathfound the nomidar, and it told me eventually how it wanted to be played. Now it and I played in a kind of teamwork. I'd heard a real nomidartist play in person once, and I had stung him gently and absorbed something of his passion for the playing, even if none of his skill could pass between us.

The nomidar had two sets of strings, eight on the straight playing neck and eight on the hollow, curving, sympathetic neck that vibrated with the chords or the melody. The bowl fit into the hollow between my breasts and my lap when I was seated. The flower I'd twined on its head, where the necks met, stroked my cheek. I chose a song I loved. "I will interpret the second stanza of the poem 'Evening,' by Dreyghal Naraz," I said. " 'Twilight comes in shades of red against the clearest blues of day, and brightness grows before the eye as darkness caps the fading sky.' "

The song was gentle and a little sad and bright and wistful all in turn, and sometimes at the same time. It wasn't the most difficult piece I knew, nor the best piece of poetry. It was only a piece I cared about. I forgot who I was when I played the nomidar. I projected against the sympathetic strings and simply became the music.

When the song ended, Jasin Lebec sat very still, allowing the echoes to fade. Then he rose out of the chair, crossed the room, took my face in his hands and kissed my forehead. "Thank you for playing for me."

"Did you like it?" I asked, needing him to answer.

"You might have been a master," he said. "Don't ever give it up. Ever. Promise me."

"I promise," I said, a little bewildered. He bade me farewell, for his time on Koldor had run out, and he left. I played for a while longer in the darkness, so as not to feel alone.

When I awoke from that first night of sleeping untouched at Jemeret's side, it was with tears in my eyes, and instead of gathering to control them, I let myself weep. First, because I had no nomidar. And second, because something *had* happened to me, and I didn't know what it was.

III. Among the Ilto

Though Jemeret was gone when I awoke, I heard him reenter the tent before I had finished crying, so I quickly closed off the tear ducts and wiped my lashes dry. A woman in a long robe brought in a tray behind him, and he thanked her as she set it on the table. He was dressed in a brown tunic, leggings, and scuffed brown boots, and once again he wore a dagger at his belt.

When the woman had gone out again, he asked, "Feel like eating something with me?"

I was hungry, and the smell of whatever had come in on the tray was instantly attractive. I sat up, holding the top rug across my breasts. "May I have my clothes?"

"They're right over here on this chair," he said, gesturing. He was preoccupied with something on the table near the tray and did not glance in my direction.

I took a very deep breath. This was the way it was going to be; and there was, after all, the question of trust. I could have tried to wrap myself in the rug, but it was huge, unwieldy, and heavy. I tried to keep my face expressionless as I got up, walked to the chair, and dressed in the shift and talma. I did not look at him, and I don't know if he looked at me. My nerves were on edge, waiting to see if he would spring at me or say anything, but nothing happened. When I did look up, he'd rolled up the chart he'd been reading and taken a bowl, a spoon, and a mug from the tray. I took the others. The bowl contained a steaming grain porridge thick with what I suspected to be butter and honey, and the mug contained a rich, fresh milk.

The first mouthful of porridge was so good I wanted not to swallow it too quickly, and from that point on I might have

64

gobbled. Jemeret seemed a bit amused by it. "Do you want some bread, too?" he asked.

I shook my head, but I didn't stop eating. When I finally drank the milk, it was also good beyond my expectations. I hadn't realized how completely hungry I was.

"We need to find a prafax for you," he said. When I looked a bit confused, he explained. "A task—a preoccupation—something for you to do all day that will contribute to the tribe. We call it a prafax if you're just trying it, and a fax when and if you become proficient at it and want to do it as a full contribution."

I wiped the milk away from the corners of my mouth with my fingertips. "Variel told me there were woman warriors," I said. "I've had some—" I didn't know quite how to put it best. "—training in that area."

He looked down at the chart he'd just rolled up and tapped it lightly on the edge of the table, leaning back in his chair. His eyes didn't narrow, but I felt as if they had, as if he were somehow measuring me. When he spoke, it was as if he had never paused. "I'm sorry," he said. "If we were at Stronghome, where the other woman warriors are, we could set some tests for you. Men and women both have to prove themselves by deeds to become warriors of the Boru."

"Aren't there some deeds I could do here?" I asked.

The corners of his mouth twitched. "There may be," he conceded, "but you will have to make them for yourself. In the meantime, you still need a prafax. I've been checking what's available." He made a small gesture with the chart.

I pushed the mug away from me. "Well, then, tell me what my choices are."

"I've eliminated certain of the choices myself," he said. "The food wagons need a substitute tender, and we are short one seamstress. I guessed generally that you wouldn't be interested in those." I didn't bother to tell him that he was right, and he wasn't asking for confirmation. "As a matter of record," he added dryly, "I fancied you would probably not be interested in any of the women's prafaci, so I narrowed the list of men's openings to two—wagon repair and tivong training."

I knew which one I wanted the moment he said them, but I wanted to delay the choice a little. "Do I get to wear something other than this?" I indicated the talma.

"If I give you a man's prafax, I will give you men's

clothes," Jemeret said. "Come on, and I'll take you to meet the wagonmaster and the tivong keeper."

We left the tent, and two guardsmen fell into step several paces behind us. "Who are they?" I asked him.

"That's Urichen and Wendagash," he said, half turning toward the men as he spoke. "Friends, this is Ronica."

I nodded and smiled toward them, and they greeted me amicably. Urichen was easily in his sixties, grizzled and hard as the rock of the cliffs. Wendagash was younger than Jemeret, but not as young as Gundever.

"They're my personal guard," Jemeret said. "I rarely leave them behind for long when I'm not in Stronghome."

"Were they with you when you ran me down in the forest?" I asked him.

"For the first five or six steps," he said with a laugh. "After that, you and I were on our own."

The wagon maintenance area was at the far end of the tents, up against the cliffs. Three wagons were up on chocks, the wheels being rerimmed and the axles repacked.

The wagonmaster appeared to be older than Urichen, and he was bowed, white-bearded, and gnarled, but his smile when he saw us seemed to split his face in half. He had no front teeth on top, and talked with a strange whistling lisp. "My lord, I am very honored you chooshe to shend ush sho many good wishesh—and now a vishit." He bowed his bent back even farther. Jemeret caught his shoulders to stop his downward progress, but held him gently, as if he were afraid to try to straighten him.

"Gannelel, my old friend," Jemeret said softly, "I would like you to meet Ronica, my claim."

The old man looked over at me, made a nod of respect with his head, and looked back at Jemeret. "She'sh a beauty, my lord," he said in a whisper which reached all of us anyway. "Hash she Shantiah's temper?"

"Worse, I think," Jemeret said.

Gannelel shook his head, his lips pursing back into the gap left by his teeth. "My lord, you should sheek shem wish shweeter natuuresh. My Lishanie—"

Jemeret overrode him smoothly. "We cannot all be as lucky in our claims as you and Lishanie. Listen, old teacher, my claim seeks a prafax, and you need a wagonhand. Do me the kindness to show us a little of what the tasks are."

The old man was almost overwhelmed at the thought of my

working for him, highly sensible of his honor. He described at shome lengsh the refurbishing operashions, and it was soon clear that the wagons were his pride, his obsession. He knew every one—the ones in for repair and the others the Boru had come to Convalee in—who owned each, what its history was, and how long before it would need what kind of maintenance. He had five assistants working with him, and as he showed us what jobs they were doing, he corrected them gently or gave them hints about shortcuts. He seemed infinitely capable and completely kind, so in many ways it saddened me a little to know I didn't want to work with him. I wanted to work with the tivongs.

We said farewell to Gannelel when the tour was done, with a promise to let him know what I decided, and the old man drew me aside with a little gesture that would have qualified as a hand on my arm, except that he didn't touch me. Jemeret looked at us curiously, but made no attempt to interfere.

Gannelel's whisper was appreciably lower as he said to me, "If you pleash, Ronica, he ish a very good leader. He needs a neshting tent, not a shparring one."

"Did Shantiah spar?" I asked. It was the first time I'd been at all curious about the claim who preceded me. He whistled and hissed and blushed, shook his head, nodded, and shifted from foot to foot as though afraid any answer would be painfully indiscreet. I wanted to laugh at his embarrassment, but gathered and controlled it back. He was the sort of person, good-natured and utterly harmless, to inspire affection in anyone.

Jemeret called me and we set off toward the tivong pens, with the guards several paces behind. "Did you like Gannelel?" he asked.

"He's wonderful," I said honestly, "and I'd wager he'd be a joy to work for."

"He's Gundever's na-sire," Jemeret said, and when I didn't seem to comprehend, added, "His father's father. That family had a lot to do with raising me. I hold them in high esteem."

"So I can see," I said. "What happened to your own family?"

He was silent for a time as we walked. "They were—lost to me. In my na-sire's time, we were at war, before the peace of Jaglith was signed by the Ilto and the Vylk. Many people were lost, and my family suffered along with the rest."

"But you are no longer at war," I said, for Variel had told me that they were not.

"Not officially." I seemed to sense a kind of sadness in him, which he did not control fast enough to shut away. "The Ilto and the Vylk follow tribal laws that are vastly different from those of the rest of us, and they are not to be trusted, except of course during Convalee. The rest of the time we avoid them when we can and deal with them when we must. But at least it's not full-out warfare."

The tivong herd stretched out before us, more tivongs than there were Boru at this encampment. The tivongs were large, impressive quadrupeds, with long, shaggy hair that wouldn't burn because of its high content of alkalines. Its matting was so thick that it acted almost like a shell. The feet were cloven into five toes, each with a giant claw and two lesser ones, and it was maned behind its face and again across its shoulders. Its long, thick tail was doubled back on itself to form a club. Tivongs came in all shades of brown and green, and displayed a natural camouflage; many of the herd had begun yellowing slightly to match the fading grasses of the plains. For such ugly creatures, their faces were deeply, soulfully beautiful, the eyes huge, dark, and fringed with long lashes, the muzzles noble. Their heads resembled those of the Pelhamhorses Kray had raised; the rest of them resembled nothing I had seen before.

One of them, huge and darkly brown, detached itself from the herd and came to the fence as we reached it, making a low snuffling sound. Jemeret reached across the fence and stroked the nose it held down to him, murmuring softly to it.

"Is this one yours?" I asked him, knowing it was a ridiculous question, but he didn't point that out to me.

"I fancy Vrand and I belong to each other," he said. "Tivongs get extremely possessive if you ride one for a while."

A tall, thin, and wiry man walked up from a creek bed where he'd been sitting under the trees. He wore a kind of leggings I hadn't seen before, smooth and leathery on the inside, soft on the outer part of the leg. His face gave away nothing beneath a red-brown beard. It was deeply tanned, and deeply lined, but he was almost startlingly handsome, his eyes intense and pale blue, seeming to weigh me up without looking at me for more than a sliver of a second.

"You honor me with your presence," he said to Jemeret. His

voice was rough and grating, as if his vocal cords had been damaged somehow and never healed.

"Sejineth," Jemeret said, "this is Ronica. Ronica, Sejineth, the tivong keeper."

I nodded to him and he nodded back. His every movement was sharply, visibly controlled, and the impression it left was disturbing. I wondered if he were a great deal happier with tivongs than with people.

"Does the lady need a tivong?" Sejineth asked.

Jemeret's voice went so hard and cold that it chilled me with its menace. "Ronica was not introduced to you as the lady, Sejineth. She is not a Boru, nor has she been gifted with a bracelet. I'll have your apology." His hand had moved to the hilt of his dagger, but I hadn't seen the motion that took it there.

For a moment Sejineth neither moved nor reacted. Then his body bent smoothly forward into a low bow to the Lord of the Boru. "I beg your pardon, my lord. It was that she bears the face of the High Lady. I became—confused."

Jemeret seemed to debate the intent behind the harsh tone, and while I had no idea what might happen, I was aware that both Urichen and Wendagash had reached for their short-swords. Wendagash actually had his halfway out of its scabbard.

"I hear and accept your apology," Jemeret said quietly at last. His hand dropped away from the dagger, and I heard the click of hilt against scabbard lip as Wendagash slid the shortsword back.

Sejineth straightened. His face was unreadable under his control as he turned to me. "Do you need a tivong, Ronica?" he asked.

"I need a job," I said flatly. "I understand you have one open."

He shifted his gaze in a split second to Jemeret and back again to me. "You're here about the tivong-training prafax?" The grating voice showed some real, if reluctant, surprise.

"I'd like to know what it involves," I said.

The tivong next to Jemeret gave a sudden hissing call, and we all looked in the direction it had turned. A red-brown tivong had detached itself from the herd and was moving toward the fence, slowly, but with deliberation, its head raised high in what I would learn was a gesture of submission, exposing the throat.

Jemeret's tivong slowly raised its own head, though not as high as the new beast, and took a step sideways, away from the fence. The new tivong came directly up to the fence then, made a snuffling sound, and lowered its head so that its muzzle reached out toward my shoulder. I put my hand up and scratched between its nostrils, where the skin was soft and velvety.

"I've never seen that before," Urichen said wonderingly. "A stranger to them, and one *chose* her."

"There seems no doubt about the prafax," Jemeret said wryly. "When the herd expresses a preference—"

I turned toward him to ask a question, in spite of the fact that he'd abruptly broken off speaking, then realized that he and his guards were staring out across the pen. I gathered and looked in the same direction, forcing my focus farther out until I, too, spotted the scout riding a pale brown-green tivong at an astonishingly swift speed across the field toward the edge of the pen.

Sejineth clapped his hands twice and held them at shoulder height, palms outward. The two tivongs backed away from the fence, not with haste or reluctance, one step at a time. After they were about five meters from the fence, Sejineth clapped once and turned his hands palm downward. The tivongs stopped and stood side by side, waiting.

The scout rounded the corner of the pen, urging his tivong forward until he was within a few meters of where the five of us stood. Then he hauled the beast to a halt, bolted off its back, and fell to one knee as he hit the ground, rising quickly.

"My lord, the Ilto," he said breathlessly.

"How far, and how fast?" Jemeret asked.

"Less than a day to the southeast, moving well."

Urichen leaned toward Jemeret, his face grim. "They mean to camp against the cliffs."

"It will be all right if they arrive next," Jemeret said evenly. "But they'll camp on the south side of the Modria if they want trouble. If they cross the plain, it's peace."

"I wouldn't trust them anywhere near what you would." Urichen's voice was less than a growl. "By the murks, I wouldn't trust their women to bleed."

"Perhaps you are wiser than I, old friend," Jemeret said, "but I say I won't expect them to strike unless they fail to cross the Modria." He turned back to the scout. "Get some rest, but make sure a replacement goes out before you do."

The scout bowed shortly, tossed the reins of his tivong to Sejineth and sprinted for camp.

Wendagash stepped around in front of Jemeret, waiting for an order he obviously expected.

Jemeret nodded. "Double the patrol. Send Palenti's unit. But tell them I want everyone back to the first ridge if Evesti crosses the Modria."

Wendagash moved quickly away.

Sejineth had busied himself unbridling and unharnessing the tivong. Two young men and a tall girl came out of a nearby tent to take the gear and lead the beast away, but I barely noticed them. Now the tivong trainer turned to me. "Will you begin your prafax in the morning?"

I started to answer, then glanced at Jemeret, who nodded, barely perceptibly. "Yes," I said to Sejineth.

"Then starting in the morning, you will call me Melster," the grating voice said, "as do my other apprentices." His eyes slid defiantly toward Jemeret, who neither moved nor responded.

My deference to Jemeret was one thing, a hesitant recognition of the greater strength he'd been certain to point out to me. I was totally unprepared to defer to anyone else. "All right," I said to Sejineth, perhaps less mildly than I intended. "I agree to do that as long as you know more about what we're doing than I do."

Urichen couldn't quite choke back his chortle.

Sejineth's lined face paled, then flushed, and I knew I'd made an enemy, but I didn't mind. It didn't then occur to me that I didn't mind because I knew he was Jemeret's enemy, too. I wasn't aware that I'd already taken a stand.

Sometimes the MIs and the human forces of government missed the threat of a madman. We called such a man a "hitch" for reasons lost in the antiquity of the government, and such a hitch made it onto Werd at a time when Coney and Kray and I were not really trained yet. I think we were about nine, but I can't be certain. It's one of the few incidents in my childhood about which I am relatively unsure.

I don't know what kind of malcontent the hitch was, and I don't know why his hatred fastened on us. Perhaps because we were privileged and obviously honored. Perhaps because we were healthy and being educated. Perhaps just because we were young and fair. We were playing in the government-accessed wild, that place of so-called natural land on every civilized world. It's meant to seem something of a wilderness, but now I know that it isn't any such thing.

We had had a picnic lunch with Mortel John, who had decided to take a nap on the bright groundcloth and sent us running out into the woods and meadow. If there were MI sensors anywhere near the wild, they couldn't see us. Occasional trips to the wild were thought to be good for growing talents, and we enjoyed the few we got, playing games of the imagination.

Coney was best at inventing them. Once, I remember, he and I were a binary star system, and Kray was a black hole, and we spun dizzyingly around and around each other obeying a law of physics we barely understood until we could no longer gather fast enough to escape waves of nausea. We laughed helplessly, I remember, feeling content and utterly secure in each other's company.

That day, we were lying on a small grassy field beneath the overhang of some nearby limbs, and from out of the trunk shadows stepped the hitch, with a charger in his hand. The last absolutely clear memory I have of it is seeing the point of its discharge tube aimed at the three of us, and Kray's head coming up suddenly as he, too, saw it.

From that moment until the second my clear memory returns to normal, everything is a jumble of noise and twisted emotions, tangled movement, pain, and redness.

My memory clears at the image of the hitch, ragged and unshaven, lying backward against a tree, the charger at least five meters from his hand. Coney was writhing on the ground, fighting to heal a raw wound on his right knee. Kray was burned raw across his shoulder from armpit to elbow of the arm he had thrown up over his face, and I was scored on the left side. For a little while we just cried and worked to gather and heal ourselves, the way we'd been trained. After the first minutes, the sobbing was mostly from fear, because the worst of the pain got blocked off. The healing took a very long time, however. I was first done, Kray next, Coney last. We lay very still, exhausted, when we were through, and by that time we had been gone too long, and Mortel John came looking for us.

Only Kray wanted to go with him to look at the hitch, but Kray also wanted a close look at the charger. Mortel John forbade him to and went alone before sending for the guards. He told us later that the hitch had been very ill, as well as crazy, and that his body had given out after he fired at us. We were to be his last gesture. I don't know if we believed him, but we never spoke of it among ourselves after it was over.

The hitch was my first enemy. The Drenalion are everyone's enemy, not just mine. Sejineth was my second, but his enmity was far less of a problem. Evesti of the Ilto was my third, and entirely the least successful.

Our evening meal that night was shared in our tent—I already thought of it as "our" tent—with Venacrona, Gundever, Variel, another warrior named Tuvellen, and his claim, Morien. Tuvellen and Morien were in their thirties, and the woman was breathtakingly beautiful. She was black-haired and golden-eyed, and completely at ease in life. When she smiled, she seemed to glow. Tuvellen was not bad-looking, his features regular but unremarkable, and his sandy beard was a little longer than any I'd seen before. Most warriors were either closely bearded or clean-shaven.

I'd been spared the chore of cooking, which spared all of them the chore of eating what I would have cooked. Jemeret had instead introduced me to Numima, the old woman who had brought food to me once before, and whose fax was to be caretaker of his house. She was, incidentally, a wonderful cook, and I assured her I had no desire to take the kitchen fire from her.

Tuvellen told a story about an incident among the training warriors in which a very young fighter named Nutin had distinguished himself with the agerin, a projectile weapon something like a crossbow.

"I don't remember power-testing him," Jemeret said, frowning.

"Nutin was not tested this past spring," Venacrona put in. "He had the fevers when we did the testing."

"When was his last test, then?"

Venacrona was momentarily silent, thinking back. "At his naming," he said at last.

"Not even at boyhood?" Tuvellen asked, astonished. "How could a Boru become a true boy without testing?"

"His father died," Jemeret said as if just remembering it himself. "He went to spend his grief, and when he returned, the testing was over. Veen, make sure you get to him to set something up in the next day or so. We've let him slide painfully long."

The small man nodded, looking a little abashed. "We need

a better system for recording the testing and the results," he said. "We're still using the one we had when we were two hundred strong instead of as large as we are now."

"It *is* possible that the boy is just good with the agerin," Morien said dryly. "One of us has to speak up for ability without a solid base of power under it."

Gundever laughed. "But not you, Morien. Not the woman with the power of bewitching people."

I was instantly very interested. The definition I knew of bewitching made it a Class A talent, and I wanted to know desperately if there were any Class A's arising on a planet with Class C's in great numbers.

Morien's expression was mischievous. "I'm sure Variel won't be pleased that you're admitting I bewitch you," she said.

Gundever flushed. "That wasn't what I meant."

Variel had already said, "Oh, but it's not upsetting."

They stopped speaking simultaneously, and then Variel went on, "Morien, everyone knows your beauty is haunting."

"Have I gone from witch to ghost now?" Morien asked. She looked at me as the men laughed. "They tease me because when I was still Moren, still a very young woman, I decided I was not pretty enough. So I left Stronghome a few weeks before Convalee and went to the Willowmere, below Kerlith, and tried to use my power to change my face." Her mouth twisted a little, and Variel blushed as if to protest, but Gundever laid his hand on her arm and she fell silent.

"I stared and stared at myself in the Willowmere," Morien said, "working on changing my face to be more beautiful."

I was about to tell her she'd succeeded admirably when Tuvellen said with a snort, "When they found her, she was lucky they could tell who she was. She looked like a dennipin!"

Morien laughed with him. "My power was greater than my judgment," she admitted. "Chief Brenadel made me go to my classes and tentings even though my face was still changing back."

"Weren't you angry at that?" I asked her.

Morien looked surprised. "Angry? At whom?"

"At the chief."

"But it wasn't his fault I tried to change my face," Morien pointed out.

"Didn't the others laugh at you?" I'm not certain why I had

to pursue it; perhaps it was because of my disappointment over the fact that the story showed her not to be a Class A. Perhaps it was relief.

Morien's exquisite lips formed a very small smile. "We don't laugh at enough power to change a face," she said quietly. "Not in the Boru. Even if I am slow at changing."

"She has a dennipin's determination, too," Tuvellen said with no small pride.

"A dennipin," Venacrona said to me, "is also called a rock-eater. It will tunnel through the world if it takes a notion to. It is, blessedly, quite slow."

"If it bred any faster than it does, we'd be overrun," Gundever said.

Numima came in carrying a platter of roasted laba in greens, and as she set it down, she remarked to herself, "Saw dennipin not half an arc from here, near the armorer just this morning. Told myself if a hunter got one, I could make soup," and went out before anyone else had a chance to speak.

"I'm sorry," Variel said to Morien. "I hadn't meant—"

Morien stroked the younger woman's arm with long, graceful fingers. "It's nothing," she said. "I learned a lesson, that was all."

Jemeret started to his feet as we began reaching for pieces of the roast, and the two warriors instantly dropped their meat or wine and did likewise, but no one drew weapons. The tent flap was flung aside and a young scout bowed without entering.

"Speak," Jemeret said.

"My lord, I am sent from Palenti," the young man said. "He has told me to say: the Ilto have crossed the Modria to camp, but they are missing men. They have enough to provide and guard and keep their women in tow, but Evesti is among the unaccounted." He waited.

Jemeret gestured to Gundever and Tuvellen, and they reseated themselves. He drew his fingers thoughtfully along the edge of his beard. "Tell Palenti to bring his men back to the near ridge, not just the first one. If Evesti plans something, I want them nearer to us. They are to be watchful, but not to engage unless provocation is obvious."

The scout bowed and tossed the tent flap closed.

"I don't trust Evesti," Gundever said harshly.

"None of us does." Jemeret sat down again and took some meat. "The Ilto are a filthy bunch, no mistaking it."

"But if they've crossed the Modria, they must come in peace," Venacrona said.

Tuvellen shook his head. "They haven't all crossed the Modria," he said, looking to Jemeret for the confirmation he knew would follow. "It's the ones camping on the south side that we have to worry about."

Variel suddenly shivered, and Gundever reached out and put his arm across her shoulders briefly. "Don't think of it," he said softly.

I started to ask, but Jemeret caught my eye and shook his head almost imperceptibly, and I decided to acquiesce. Morien leaned close to me, as if reaching for the wine, and murmured, "We'll walk after the meal, and I'll tell you then."

The conversation among the men turned to battle tactics and strategy, and I watched Variel trying to smile and pay attention, but it was as if some of the brightness had gone out of her.

Later, Morien and I walked near the cliff face and she told me that Variel's older sister had been taken in a raid by the Ilto, along with four other women of the Boru, all of whom had been on a trading mission to the Genda. The raid had been swiftly avenged, but three of the women had already been dead.

"What do they do to women?" I asked, horrified.

"Tuvellen said they beat two of those who died until they didn't want to heal themselves any longer." I had a sudden flash of memory—Sarai's lacerated, scarred back. "The third they—" She paused, choosing her words carefully. "—tore inside. She couldn't heal herself fast enough."

"Variel's sister?"

"Was one of the three. Tuvellen said it would be better if we just never asked which one."

For a few moments I thought about the enormity of the crime, and fought with my own rage. Then I asked, "What about the other two?"

"One of them is now the bracelet of one of our finest archers," she said. "The other was Lord Jemeret's claim, before he claimed you."

"Shantiah?"

Morien nodded. "The brave and the strong of us live longer among the Ilto than the weak and the frail," she said. "They keep their women tied up and make slaves of them."

"How are they allowed to do that?"

"They are a tribe," Morien said. "No one may interfere with the laws of a tribe unless their laws impinge on another tribe."

The wind seemed chill, for she shivered and wrapped her arms around herself. I had damped down my cold receptors and was not feeling it. We found a cleft in the rocks that cut off the wind and paused there.

"Are the Vylk as bad as the Ilto?" I asked her.

"The Vylk are almost as bad as the Ilto, but they are a little more honorable." She grinned. "They steal women from the Ilto and the stonehouses, not from us. Thus, we call them more honorable. The best tribes—outside the Boru, of course—are the Dibel, the Paj, and the Elden. They don't believe in warring, and don't keep warriors. Theirs is a different kind of life."

"If they don't keep warriors, why don't the Ilto prey on their women?"

Morien stroked my hair lightly, as if I were a child. "My dear Ronica," she said, "you don't understand tribal ways. It brings warriors no glory to raid those who are weaker than they are, only those who are stronger. That's why the Boru and the Genda raid no one, but are only raided. That's why no one laughs at a child who can make liquid the bones of her face." Her fingertips brushed my forehead. "That's why no one will question a woman with the High Lady's face if she's shown her power." She leaned very close to me, and I realized that if I had just held still, she would have kissed me on the mouth.

I drew back from her a little, disturbed. "I've shown very little power," I said.

"It shows on you," Morien said gently, and did not try to touch me again. "My Lord Jemeret sees it, too."

"I'm going back now," I said.

"Sleep well," Morien said. "You will make a wonderful Boru."

I went quickly back to the tent and found it empty. There was still some wine on the table, and I poured a quick goblet and drank it down. Morien's touch had shaken me, for it was alien to me to find myself suddenly aware of being desired by a woman. It was not a threat, but it was disorienting. I was unaccustomed to women's sexuality, including my own.

Thinking about sexuality made me realize I did not want to undress in front of Jemeret again. I stripped out of my clothes, blew out the lamps on the stanchions, and got under the rugs, but I didn't try to sleep.

If he was surprised to find the tent dark when he came in, Jemeret said nothing. He set something down on one of the chairs, then laid his belt aside and began to undress. I found that I wanted to tell him about Morien, but I could not, so I swallowed it back. I remember thinking that I would have been able to tell Kray or Coney—well, no, not Kray. But Coney. Perhaps I would speak to Variel about it.

Jemeret dumped the furs down on his side of the partially drawn curtain and lay down, his hands linked behind his head, his eyes open in the darkness.

"What does it mean, to be a Boru?" I asked him.

I could tell by his voice that he was not surprised I was awake. "It means to accept the tribe as home and family," he said, "to accept its laws as the rules by which you live. It means you share the triumphs and sadnesses of the others in your tribe, and let them share yours."

I rolled onto my side and irised my eyes out to see the planes of his face faintly in the darkness. "But wouldn't it mean that to belong to *any* tribe in the Samoth? What does it mean to be a Boru?"

He looked at me. "You must accept my authority and follow my leadership."

"Ah." I hadn't realized it was out loud until I heard it. "So it comes down to you."

He reached out very slowly and stroked my hair, as Morien had, but even more lightly. "It always will," he said tonelessly.

I had begun to tremble as soon as he touched me, and as fiercely as I gathered to try to stem it, the fear in my body fought back against the gathering. I fell backward away from his barely felt touch, saying, "I can't. I just can't."

Jemeret drew his hand back to his side. "I know that," he said. "I want you to try to imagine a time when you can."

Removed from his touch, my body began to calm under the force of my gathering. I didn't comprehend the overwhelming fear, the strength of the impulse to run. It was even possible that, because of Morien, I *wanted* him to touch me. But my body did not, with an emphasis that caused me to shake as I conjectured.

"No," I said quickly, "I can't even do that!"

"You will," he said.

And I burst out, "How can you know that?"

"It's just something I know. It's just something I want you to believe."

Even then I had to admit that his confidence was impressive. I had never tamed a tivong, or a Pelhamhorse.

"You're asking me to trust you," I said to him after a while, and at that he smiled.

"To be precise, I have never asked. I have given you orders, and I'm willing to be patient until you begin to obey them." The humor in his voice touched me, even as I didn't doubt the truth I heard in his words.

"What happens if you run out of patience?" I asked, keeping my own voice very small, in the intimacy of the dark.

He was silent for a very long time. "I don't know. I hadn't thought about that."

"Has it never been known to happen?"

He laughed softly, and lay back in the furs again, his hands behind his head. "Ronica," he said, "if I were you, I'd go to sleep now."

I burrowed into the rugs near the back of the tent and closed my eyes, but it was a long while before I slept.

Kray was the one who discovered that some men slept with other men and some women with other women. We were about fifteen, in a class on the philosophy of empire versus that of bureaucratic government, and we were bored by it. Mortel John had been called out, and left us to study.

"Hey, come look at this," Kray said, and called up some very erotic images on his comsole. "Look what I found."

We went, and stared, fascinated, at the display. "How'd you plug into that?" Coney asked, but we knew he'd pathfound to it through some code or other.

"I read some poetry once," I began, and then looked away, suddenly caught by a wholly unexpected wave of arousal.

"What?" Kray asked.

I had gathered and pushed it back before I turned around again. "Are there lots of people who do those acts?"

Kray seemed to debate whether to keep pushing me, but as I saw him consider it, I reached out and stung him a little so he'd change his mind. He went back to his comsole and put in the question. "About seventeen percent of everybody does it once or twice," he said, "and about eleven percent keep on doing it. It's called monosexuality."

"It doesn't sound particularly appealing to me," Coney said thoughtfully. "Two left halves."

"But kind of stimulating," Kray said, without insistence, watching me.

"Is that a proposition?" Coney asked, and I laughed. For a second Kray's face went thunderously dark, and then he flipped the comsole off and made a false kiss through the air at Coney. Coney took a swing at him.

Mortel John was somewhat distressed on his return to find a full-scale battle instead of a well-behaved class. I had retreated to a corner to think over what had just happened. I didn't know many women; there weren't any my own age at the school at Werd. Women were, to me, somehow mysterious, alien creatures. I began to study their writings, and once or twice I slipped away from the three men who made up the major portion of my life to speak with some of the visitors to the school—Liliane Grainger, the government's population officer, and Verlaine Hong, wife to the First Secretary, are the most memorable. But they were fleeting influences on me, their responses always colored by their respect for who I was, and I could never decide whether the MIs had any feminine aspects to them. Now I think that I was raised like a questa queen, the sole female in the hive, catered to, pampered, isolated, and trapped.

My nomidar was female to me, but it was nothing I could speak with or learn from. I was formed entirely by men. If I failed, it must be their failure, too.

Jemeret woke me gently in the morning, and my body did not immediately tense and try to flee, because for a moment I had no sense of time or place beyond the warmth of the rugs and the touch on my shoulder. Then I came aware, and the reflexes snapped into place with a speed and strength that threw me halfway down the rugs away from his hand. He watched me, expressionless, as I fought the reflexes back and down to bring my flight response under control.

"It's time to get up," he said. "You'll have to be at your prafax just after dawn," He started to straighten up.

I said, "I'm sorry, Jemeret. I really have no control over that."

Something swelled up behind his clear gray eyes for a fraction of a second and was gone so fast that I wondered if I'd imagined it and the faint softness in his voice as he said, "The clothes you'll wear to the tivong pen are on that chair."

He dressed swiftly and left the tent. I couldn't shake the

feeling that something important had just happened, and it annoyed me greatly not to have known what it was. I swore to try to remember it for later. Actually, I have been particularly fortunate in life with my memory, which is usually excellent. This made it all the more devastating to me to have parts of it inaccessible. If not for memory, I would have missed completely almost every important thing that happened to me, for I recognized none of them for what they were at the time. In retrospect, what I thought were titanic struggles while they were occurring turned out to be quite minor. Things I did easily, thoughtlessly, have proven to be huge decision points on whose paths I should never have set out without long premeditation and carefully drawn maps.

Thus, memory can bring me back to decision points since I came to this world, places where I looked backward because I could not imagine a future, and I can see that there was always value in me other than my talent, but I never noticed it.

I remember writing when I started this journal that I'd try to tell my story as if I didn't know how it was turning out, to get the transitions correct. And in my story, the next thing that happened was that I went to the tivong pens. The horizon was just beginning to streak with light across the plain and above the cliffs, and there were scattered clouds in the lightening sky. It was still chilly, but I was now well-protected against it in high boots, leggings, and a tunic, an outfit much like Jemeret's own and one in which I was far more comfortable than I had been in the talma.

Though I knew I was on time, I was the last to arrive. Sejineth and his three apprentices were all gathered around a small fire, drinking something. An empty mug stood on a flat stone nearby, waiting. I took a deep breath, said good morning, and joined them at the fire.

"This is Ronica," Sejineth said. "Introduce yourselves." He handed me the mug, and I dipped it into a pot of the thick, hot liquid which their bodies had hidden from me before.

"I'm Pepli," said the younger boy, a towheaded, freckle-faced youth of eleven or twelve. "Glad to see you."

The older boy, lankier, fourteen or so, was sandy-haired, with bright blue eyes. "I'm Lumo," he said. "We can use the help." He'd rehearsed that speech, and I knew he was relieved it was out, but when I grinned at him, he grinned back.

The girl was about Lumo's age, with dark brown braids and eyes and regular features, thin and tall. "I'm Shefta," she said, her voice surprisingly deep and reedy, "and I think it's time we had another woman around here." There was something almost familiar about her, but I could think of no possible explanation for that, because she was nothing like Coney or Kray, the only other adolescents I had ever really known. I shrugged it off.

"Thank you," I said. "I'll try to be a help to you all." It was a little on the humble side, but I think I meant it.

"Drink up," Sejineth said. "We have to get started early with the pad cleaning."

The boys groaned, and we all finished the porridge, which was filling and tasty, though nothing like what I'd had in Jemeret's tent. When we were done, Sejineth said, "Ronica, you team with Shefta. Take the tivongs in the cutting pen. Lumo, Pepli, you work with the tivongs in the eastern pen. I'll mix more of the petcale so you'll have plenty."

"Yes, Melster," they chorused, and I added, "Yes, Melster," quietly after them.

Sejineth looked directly at me for the first time. "Try not to get hurt," he said. "You're my responsibility as long as you're in my prafax."

"Yes, Melster," I repeated, careful to keep my voice even and not to in any way imply the insolence I was feeling.

"Come on." Shefta put her mug down on the flat stone. "Let's get the petcale and get started."

I followed her to the tent where the tivong supplies were kept, and we picked up a large wooden pail full of a yellowish brown liquid and an applicator that consisted of a tube with a plunger. "We cut the tivongs into separate groups after you and my Lord Jemeret left yesterday." Shefta talked as she handed me the applicator and a large pile of cloths. "This can really be messy work, pad cleaning."

"What is it we're doing, and why?" I asked.

She attached a long leather strap to hooks on the side of the pail and slid it over her shoulder. "Tivongs are used to rockier ground than this grassland. This is really dralg land," she explained. "Tivongs are from the highlands under the mountains, and the rocks keep the dirt from balling up between their claws. When we spend any time on the plains, we have to keep the pads hard or they rot. Come on."

She walked with a strange, knee-bent, rolling gait to keep the liquid from sloshing out of the pail, and I followed her, not volunteering to help, because I knew I would probably spill it. "What's Sejineth like to work for?"

"He's all right," Shefta said easily. "There's better, and there's worse, I fancy. He's fair to me."

"Can't ask for more than that," I said, ignoring the fact that I always had.

We reached what I assumed was the cutting pen, a fair-sized fenced enclosure off the main corral, containing about a hundred tivongs. The enclosure was just out of sight of the tents, but in the long run I don't suppose that mattered, because when they came, they knew who they were looking for, and where we were.

"It really is a two-person job," Shefta said, setting the pail down inside the enclosure. "One of us lifts a foot and the other shoots on a dose of the petcale. How are you at foot-lifting?"

"How are the tivongs?" That question seemed to me much more to the point.

Shefta laughed. "I like you," she said, and I recognized something I was not used to hearing: a genuine assumption of equality. All my life I'd been treated with awe and respect, except by Coney and Kray, and even then I'd demanded more than equality. This notion of being equal to people—Jasin Lebec was the only person in my life who could have dealt with me that way, and he had always been better than me—was brand-new. To be honest, this experience of a happy fourteen-year-old girl making a real judgment of friendship and equality and smiling warmly at me because of it was very touching.

I did not name it as such, but I was finding I enjoyed the new sensation of belonging. I had been only a few days among the Boru, and their open acceptance of me, talentless, their willingness to include me as if I were not maimed, as if I still had a use, had disarmed some of my wariness and was increasing my suspicion that I would have to make the best of my life here.

For half the morning I enjoyed the sensation of belonging more and more, as we treated the feet of some of the tivongs in the pen. Shefta chattered on about Pepli and Lumo, about some of the history of the tribe, about how the Boru and the tivongs depended on each other, and about how much she wanted to be inducted into womanhood here at Convalee, because she certainly didn't want to wait until she was eighteen for the next festival.

"I can't decide if I should be Shenefta or Shefrata," she said, refilling the applicator as I picked out a dark green tivong and gave it the signal to stand. After treatment, a tivong's feet would get very pale, and that helped us tell which ones had been treated and which still needed it.

The tivongs were very docile, but not notably cooperative. They stood when told, and they allowed their feet to be lifted and bent back, sole upward, but they didn't shift any of their weight to their other legs. I developed the technique of supporting a lower leg on my thigh, and it seemed to work pretty well. I had toyed with the idea of gathering and using Class C power to support the weight, but I didn't feel it was necessary to waste reserves. The choice probably saved my life.

"Which name do you like better?" she asked me.

"I think Shenefta is a little softer, at least in sound," I answered. "What do they mean?"

"Shenefta means 'breeze in the evening.' Did I get all of that foot?"

"And part of my boot."

"Shefrata means 'crisp twilight.'" She rubbed her arm across her nose to scratch it. "I'm pretty sharp, with bones that stick out all over the place," she said thoughtfully. "Maybe I better hope for better times and be Shenefta. Want to take the applicator for a while, and I'll lift feet?"

I never had a chance to answer her. I was enveloped in a thick, foul-smelling rug and lifted off my feet, and I heard a startled, muffled cry that told me Shefta had had the same experience. For a moment I struggled, but without exerting gathering energy at a high level, I couldn't have ripped free, so I went limp and expanded my hearing.

"I think she's fainted," someone said in a hoarse, strangely accented whisper.

"This one hasn't," said another voice, a little stressed, probably because Shefta was fighting like a fury.

"Knock her on the head," said a third, and there was a rather sickening thud. I had a moment to hope vaguely that Shefta had some talent, for she was going to have a terrible headache.

"Get down," said a new voice, a little farther away. I had increased my hearing enough to try to pick up heartbeats and count the number of men who had taken us, but the powerful hearts of the tivongs interfered and made a count impossible.

I had no doubt from the beginning that they were raiders, and the most likely raiders were, of course, the Ilto. As long as I was muffled in the heavy folds of the rug, with no clear line of sight and no way of gauging the enemy, I had no intention of wasting strength in a struggle. My reserves were close to complete, and I wanted to keep them that way, for a well-trained Class C—which I was—is a powerful weapon with full reserves. From what I knew of the Ilto, I would need all the talent I could command.

Whatever the incident prompting the men to take cover among the tivongs, it passed. They moved swiftly once they were free to, and then I could tell there were eight of them. As far as I could judge, their speed was not so great as to indicate they had talent, or that anyone was pursuing. While I was apprehensive, I was not afraid. I did not analyze this then; after all, there was a great deal going on. But it became clear to me later that this open abduction with baldly threatening violence was less fearsome to my body and reflexes than a gentle touch from Jemeret.

I landed on my stomach, still bundled in the rug, on what I came to believe was the haunch of a tivong. Someone mounted the beast behind my body and we sped up to flee. The ride was a rough one. I was tempted to damp down my pain responses, but decided against it, not only because it would take even a tiny amount of my reserves, but because I didn't want to do anything that would also damp down my awareness.

The ride was longer and bumpier than I would have liked it to be, and once convinced they were safe from pursuit, the men laughed and made lewd comments about us. I heard clearly that I was to provide Evesti's revenge on "that ashadophed, Jemeret." I guessed, rightly, that that comment meant I was safe from the men who had abducted me. I felt certain that Shefta would have no such safety.

Even under the muffling folds of the rug, I knew when we were approaching the river: the relatively flat land of the plain changed into a descending series of rolls. I assumed this would be the Modria. The feet of the tivongs made unexpected hollow sounds.

"Push off," one of the men said. "Let's get there."

We must have rafted across the river, and then we were climbing the banks on the other side. At last we descended a long rise and stopped. I was lifted down off the tivong and carried a short distance. "Get the chains ready," one of the men said, and I felt the rug being pulled upward toward my head. Rough hands hauled my boots off, and some sort of metal bands were snapped on my ankles. I almost smiled as I heard the clicks. The rest of the rug was snatched away, and separate men took hold of my wrists as I adjusted my eyes quickly to the light.

My instant impression was that they were big, filthy, and hairy. And if they truly devalued women the way I had been told by Morien, they would expect little in the way of resistance. In a society where women have no value, a woman can be the greatest weapon of all.

"Put her in the tent before Evesti gets here," said the one who seemed to give most of the orders. "You—woman of the stars," he continued from behind my back. "When our chief is finished with you, you'll not want to go back to the puny men of the Boru."

The two men holding my wrists yanked me along toward the largest of the four or five tents that had been set up here. I didn't see Shefta.

The tent contained a pile of furs and a large wooden stake, from which hung a chain with other bands on it. The men turned my back to the stake, pulled my wrists behind me, and banded them. They hooked chains from the bottom of the stake to my ankle bands, and then they cut off my tunic and leggings. I beat back some rage at the comments they made about my body as it was revealed. I would need to be able to reason, and anger would limit that ability. When they failed to get a response from me, one said to the other, "Perhaps she's feebleminded." They roared with laughter and left the tent, proving to my satisfaction where the feeblemindedness lay.

I pathfound the locking mechanisms in the four bands directly through the flesh they pressed against, and less than a minute later my body was free of the chains. I did not, however, move. The fact that my ankles were free would be concealed by the furs, and I held my hands behind my back as if I were still chained. Had they tied me with thongs, I might not have been able to get free in time. Because they used chains, Evesti had no chance at all.

A man threw open the tent flap and came in, and I had no doubt who he was. He was bigger, broader than any man I'd yet seen, wearing only a fur loincloth and a wide belt. "You are Jemeret's claim?" he asked.

It was not really a question, and I didn't answer it. A sharp, unexpected scream from outside made me jump. Evesti grinned. "You, too, will scream," he said, "but it will be from pleasure."

He stripped out of the belt and loincloth, and I had only

time to notice that he was monstrously erect as he started across the tent toward me. One thing was instantly plain: he had no talent worth mentioning, because men with talent did not need overcompensating muscle development. That made him no better than a Drenalion, and I had dealt with Drenalion before. Then, too, I heard Jemeret saying, "Rape is a game for the weak." I had never feared weak men, and I did not fear this one.

I tensed, letting him get his hands on my breasts, and then I pulled my reserves into a focused gather aimed at my flattened right hand and my pointed right foot. I had not wanted to underestimate his speed, and as a result I overestimated it.

A Class C at focused gather moves faster than a normal human eye can see, and because of the intensity of the instantaneous expenditure of reserves, the Class C is blinded by the light at the exact instant of the strike. It was as if lightning had struck in the tent as I lashed out with an augmented hand and foot movement, knew I'd struck something with each, pumped the unused portion of the reserves back and looked at what I'd done.

My foot had missed his genitals, but had entered his belly several centimeters above them. My hand had struck true to his nose, driving bone back into his brain. He was dead before he hit the tent floor. I let him lie there bleeding as I dried my foot and wiped off the blood that had spattered on me. I felt no remorse over the death of a Drenalion. Now I needed to find a way to get out of here, for me and for Shefta. My leggings and tunic were shredded and my boots were outside. I took one of the furs and tied it around me with Evesti's belt. Then I searched the tent for a weapon.

Before I was done, there were sounds of battle and shouting outside, but I didn't dare look out. There seemed to be many more Ilto than I had seen, and there must have been women among them, for I heard women's voices. I waited, apprehensive, but unwilling to reveal the fact that I wasn't presently being raped; I didn't have enough strength left to face very many of them. My reserves had been seriously depleted by the death stroke.

With abruptness the sounds outside ceased and I heard a shout. "Evesti! This is Jemeret of the Boru! Come out and face me, you meggo-spawn!"

I honestly didn't know what to do. Perhaps I'd committed some awful intertribal act, and would be punished for it. Perhaps I'd robbed Jemeret of his revenge, and he would be humiliated. I was far more confused than I had been before I had killed Evesti, so I did nothing.

There was a low murmur outside. They were all surprised at the lack of response.

"Evesti!" Jemeret shouted again. "Are you a laba as well as a meggo? Come here!"

It was clear that I couldn't just sit and do nothing, so I went close to the tent flap and called out, "Uh—he can't come out right now."

There was an absolute, utter silence for the space of a breath. Then Jemeret tore the tent flap aside and came in, longsword drawn. Over his shoulder I could see Gundever and Urichen standing outside with drawn swords, and then the tent flap fell closed.

Jemeret bent down over the hulk of Evesti. "What happened?" he asked.

"I killed him," I said unnecessarily.

He sheathed his longsword with one fluid motion and came to stand very close to me. "Ronica, are you all right?"

I almost laughed. "He didn't have a chance," I said wearily. "He was very big, but very stupid. Did I do something wrong?"

"That depends on how ambitious you are," he said. "If I'm not mistaken about their laws, you are now Chief of the Ilto. I assume the combat was equal?"

"We were both naked, if that's what you mean." I was annoyed when he started to laugh softly. "Jemeret, I don't think this is funny at all."

He kept laughing, and after a few moments I began to be infected by it, but I fought it back. "Listen, is Shefta all right?"

Again there was that sudden swelling in his eyes, instantly gone. As if he knew he could, he put his arm across my shoulders, and, amazingly, my body did not jerk away from him. "She's fine," he said. "Shaken, a little closer to being hurt than any of us would like, but we got here in time for her."

"I don't want to be Chief of the Ilto," I said. "I'm much more ambitious than that. How do I get out of it?"

"Take the belt off."

I looked down at the belt, realizing it was more than just a belt, then back up at him. "My fur will fall off if I do."

He stripped off his tunic and handed it to me. "You don't need anything of his anyway," he said lightly.

"Least of all, his tribe." I undid the belt, let the fur drop, and

pulled the tunic on. It came nearly to my knees. I didn't notice
that it was the first time I'd been naked in front of him without
feeling any awkwardness about it.

He bent and picked up the belt, opened the flap of the tent
and cast it out.

A cry went up, joyous from the Boru, enraged from the Ilto.
Jemeret gestured to me, and I stepped out of the tent beside
him. Until I drew a lungful of the relatively fresh air outside,
I hadn't realized how foul the air had been in the tent.

Someone among the Ilto shouted, "Vengeance! It is my
right!"

Jemeret, grim-faced, waved him forward, and a broad-
chested, ragged-bearded man pushed between a Boru warrior I
didn't know and Urichen and planted his feet in front of
Jemeret. I gauged my reserves to be about two-thirds gone
from the focused attack, and I gathered a little to feel less
weary. A focused kill-strike is the most devastating weapon in
the arsenal of the Class C, but you can't do it more than once
without dying yourself.

"I am Ustivet, brother of Evesti. Give me a sword," the
challenger said.

Jemeret nodded at Wendagash, who tossed his longsword
onto the ground at the man's feet. Ustivet grasped it and fell
into a fighting crouch. Jemeret reached for his own sword.

"No," I said more sharply than I'd intended. I had never let
anyone fight my battles, and I wasn't about to start among the
repulsive Ilto. "The kill was mine. The challenge should be
mine."

Jemeret glanced briefly away from Ustivet to my face, then
back at the barbarian. Ustivet was staring at me in open anger.
Jemeret relaxed and let his longsword slide back into the scabbard.

Ustivet sneered. "The Ilto don't challenge women," he said
with venom. "We master them!"

I sighed and said clearly, "You idiots wear me out." I gathered, accelerated forward, bent in under his sword guard, broke
his arm below the elbow, pushed the upper arm back enough
to dislocate the shoulder, and was back in the place I'd been
standing before his sword thudded to the ground. It was both
a showy and a dangerous move, because it came perilously
close to draining my reserves, but I guessed I would only have
to do it once, and I was right.

Only Jemeret noticed that I was panting. Everyone else

stared down at Ustivet, who had hit the ground with his knees just after the sword and was grunting in pain. Gundever let out a whoop, and from behind him a thin girl wrapped in a cloak propelled herself forward and threw her arms around my waist. It was Shefta. Her hair was a little matted with dried blood, but the cut looked better than I expected, and she had only a fading bruise on her temple. I stroked her a little as she straightened up and hoped that no one had noticed that her onslaught had staggered me.

"Ustivet," the Lord of the Boru said, "take your life and bring it to Convalee or not. The belt of the Ilto lies in the mud for the taking, and the Boru will recognize its wearer. But be warned. My claim and I will not be satisfied a second time to let meggos get away with their lives."

He gestured with his head and the Boru moved toward their tivongs, Wendagash bending contemptuously past Ustivet to pick up the fallen sword. Gundever lifted Shefta off her feet and away from me, and Jemeret slid his arm around my waist and said under his breath, "You'll have to make it as far as the tivongs on your own."

He was telling me that I couldn't show weakness in front of the Ilto now, and that meant he knew how drained I was. "I can do it," I said.

He stepped back. It was the longest walk I'd ever taken, longer even than the one Kray had taken with me on Koldor after I'd killed the Drenalion. Jemeret mounted the tivong first and pulled me up behind him. I sat sideways because riding astride would have hiked his tunic up above my hips, and I clung to his body with my arms around his waist. As we rode, in weariness, I rested my cheek against the smooth muscles of his shoulders. I wanted to doze, but I didn't, despite the fact that I was, astonishingly, at ease. It was long after dark by the time we reached the tents, but I still saw light as intense as an afternoon under the sun.

IV. Growing

Because Kray was stronger, and because he habitually challenged me, about a year after we arrived on Koldor I seduced Coney. I think we three had always known that someday I would sleep with one of them—maybe ultimately with both— and that it would be at my choice. It was Kray who first used the metaphor of the questa queen for me, and when he did it, I yawned elaborately and made faces at him.

I had known for months before I took Coney that they both desired me—Kray's a strong and open want, Coney's a quieter, deeper need. I wanted a man. Self-stimulation had become boring and ultimately dissatisfying. Sex with someone else was a phenomenon I knew objectively, like I knew what a penis was and how it operated.

Neither of the two men remained virgin as long as I, but then neither of them had as much to lose. I had let no one but Jasin Lebec into what I considered my personal space, and that brief invasion of my mind had set me against easily letting someone into my body.

I'm not at all certain why I picked the day I did to tell Coney to come and see me that night. Once again, the reasons for a decision I made elude me. Perhaps it was because Koldor was our last place together. After we completed training, the government would send us on assignments to separate worlds, and it might be years before we saw each other again. I guess I just didn't want to sleep with a stranger. Like many of my ostensibly intelligent decisions, it was incredibly stupid. But never mind.

Coney came to the courtyard door of my suite about midnight and let himself in. I was playing the nomidar, but I broke off the song and set the instrument aside. Coney had not grown quite as tall as his early promise, and he had a deep tan which seemed to make him all of a color, hair and skin and only slightly darker eyes. He bent and kissed me on the cheek. "What's so important?"

"Don't you know?" I asked him in return.

He did. His face changed suddenly, and he was so openly readable that I didn't even have to scan for his feelings. He was radiating something like joy and something like pain and something like very real disbelief. He was silent for a longer time than I'd expected, and then he asked, "What caused this?"

"What do you want me to say?"

He slowly shook his head. "If you don't know, I can't tell you." Some of the light seemed to go out of his face, and he instantly gathered and controlled it. "Why don't we just forget it?"

He turned back toward the door into the courtyard, but stopped when I spoke. "You can't tell me you don't want to have me."

Before he could control it, his face paled under the tan. "Yes," he said, "I want you. I've loved you since we were children. But you don't really want me—you want a body. Use somebody else's."

"I do want you," I said firmly.

"I'm handy," he shot back.

"That, too." I hadn't meant the honesty to hurt him, but it did. I tried to explain it. "Coney, I do want somebody, but I want it to be somebody who cares about me. Not me, the Class A—me. I trust you. I want it to be you. It's the same thing as loving, really."

"You fool," Coney said. It was the harshest thing I'd ever heard him say. "It's not the same thing at all."

"Then it'll be enough," I said. "I don't want you to walk out of here."

"Call Kray!" he said, really forcing control on his voice.

"No, it has to be you." I reached out and stung him a little bit so that he couldn't leave. It was easy to bring him back, because he really did want to come back to me. He also really wanted to make love to me, so it took very little sting to take him into my bedroom and persuade him to do what he wanted to do anyway. Naturally, it was a failure, but I'm not sure I noticed it at the time. We both had Class C reflexes, and so orgasm was a given. I thought it was all there needed to be. Unfortunately, he really loved me.

Coney and Kray and I shared a sense of humor; I think that the ability to laugh at the same things means not only some values in common, but a common education. The three of us had laughed together for years, and often. After I started sleeping with Coney, however, the three of us stopped finding things funny. The tension that grew among us reached the point where Mortel John could no longer ignore it, and he stopped in mid-sentence during a political economy lecture to say, "All right, I think one of you better tell me what's going on."

Kray looked away, Coney looked down at the floor, and I asked, "Whatever do you mean?"

Mortel John was not very often given to sarcasm, but now he repeated, "Whatever do you *mean*? I see before me the remnants of a good class of talent! I see three people who look just like the students I used to have, but those other students were at least marginally intelligent, marginally curious about the interactions of planetary markets, marginally creative, and more than marginally interested in one another. These three people, who look like my students, are dull, preoccupied, and greatly uneasy in each other's company."

As if he had listened to himself speak and recognized the truth in the words he heard, he snapped his fingers. "Of course. Uneasy in each other's company," he said again. "Get out of here and work it out. Don't come back until you're ready to learn something."

We got out—far out into the natural area, each of us alone, to do some thinking. We had discussed going somewhere together, in the polite, civilized voices we had begun to use on each other, but we finally decided to be alone for a while and to meet later.

I chose to practice my free-cliff climbing on a very respectable face in the center of the area. I wanted to be tired, for being tired made thought more difficult, so I gathered and carefully but quickly climbed the face, using some of my reserves but not very much of them. My caution saved me there, as it saved me later among the Ilto.

The wooded plateau at the top of the cliff yielded to a gentle downslope, but I never got as far as the slope's start. Three of the Drenalion were at the top. To this day, I don't know what they were doing there—they could have been resting or training or any number of other variations on activities. It didn't matter, really, for the moment they saw me, they reverted to what they truly were.

The Drenalion were the beasts of the government. They were cloned, sterile, and totally alien to the notion of civilized society. Mothers used the threat of them to keep children in line, just as the government used the threat of them to keep worlds in line. At the time I encountered them on Koldor, they were fifth-generation clones, and the sixth generation would be the last that was controllable. After it, a new strain would have to be begun.

The Drenalion on the plateau began to separate and work on coming at me from different angles, identical grins on their faces. They were big and slow, but they compensated for lack of talent with muscles. They leered and began to close in as soon as they had decided they were in a formation that would keep me from escaping.

I knew from their reputation what they intended, and rage took control of me. The reflexes threw me into an almost uncontrolled acceleration, the like of which I have never experienced again. I stung one as I just about ran up the face of a second, crushing his larynx across his windpipe. I spun to face the third and realized he had drawn an energy whip, but was waiting for me to slow down to use it. I restung the Drenalion who was trying to rise, closed off my hearing, and gathered to pump volume into my voice by stretching my diaphragm and lungs. My scream full at the third Drenalion punctured his eardrums and threw him backward. I decelerated, picked up the whip, and sat down on a rock to wait for the scream to bring other people.

Only one of the three Drenalion was dead, though I would have killed them all if they had attacked me again before help reached me, for my reserves were very low and I would not have been able to hold them off. I turned the whip all the way up to full, so I know I would not have hesitated, but neither the one I had hit nor the one I had screamed at got to his feet. It never occurred to me that there might be more of them.

Kray and five more clones reached me simultaneously. "Can you take those two?" he shouted, pointing. Then he accelerated and flung himself among the other three. I went only partially into acceleration to preserve what I could of my remaining reserves, but the whip served me well.

When I slowed again, staggering, Kray was standing among the three huge corpses of the Drenalion he'd fought. I was breathing so hard I thought my lungs would burst, and my heart was pounding in a sea of loose adrenaline. I dropped the whip, trying to gather enough to shut down my adrenals completely. The light around me was blindingly bright.

Kray still had a good portion of his strength left, and he scooped me off the ground without hesitation. "We've got to get out of here," he said. "I'm sure there are more of them."

"I'm at my limit." I was dismayed at how much my voice trembled. My eyes shut as if I were seeking darkness I would not find.

"Just hang on." He accelerated into a gathered run, carrying me. At some point Coney joined us, but I don't remember where it was, and he was there to fight off another pair of Drenalion who happened across our path. We had to go the long way down the slope and around the plateau to the face of the cliff to get to my floater, but by that time some of the armed guard from Government House had reached it, and we were in no more danger from the Drenalion.

Kray dumped me in the floater's riderseat and got behind the controls. "Come *on*!" I heard him yell, and Coney piled onto the floater's luggage rack, locking his hands on it and shouting, "Go!"

I heard it all as if through a gentle haze, needing to deep so much that I wasn't certain if I could keep myself from sliding downward into the shimmering brightness. Both of the men spoke to me from time to time, asking me to look at them or say something in response, and I suppose I did, but I was barely aware of it.

Kray must have radioed ahead, for when the floater jerked to a stop and Coney leaped off, Mortel John was waiting with a pressure ampule, which he broke against the artery in my neck even before he lifted me out of the floater.

I slept for two days after that, most of the time deeping, and I know they gave me massive doses of restorers, because Mortel John told me later how fortunate I'd been. If there was any kind of scandal concerning the deaths of the Drenalion, the government hushed it up.

Coney and Kray came to visit when I was just about ready to get up. They came together, and I hugged them both, but by tacit agreement, we didn't talk about it. I told them I'd be back in class soon, and we talked about the upcoming election on a world wavering in its commitment to remain in the Com.

When they got up to leave, Coney kissed me lightly and

went out first. Kray lingered long enough to say, "Ronnie, there are times when I wish you were less of a talent and more of a normal, ordinary woman."

I was feeling quite well again, and I smiled. "I'm sure there are." We stared at each other for a moment longer, and then he turned and left the room.

We were all friends again, and I didn't sleep with Coney anymore. I never talked about it, and neither did he. Kray wouldn't mention it, either, and for a while we tentatively joked about everything but ourselves. Then slowly the old relationship came back. The wedge I had driven between us had been withdrawn.

I was not nearly as bad after the Ilto as I had been after the Drenalion. Clinging to Jemeret's waist as we rode into camp, I had more reserves left than I had had in the floater, but I needed to deep and I knew it. I even knew that this world was a much more dangerous place to drain my reserves than Koldor had been, for this place had no restorers that I knew of. A planet of Class C's would go lightly on healing potions, for they would be so very rarely needed.

So I was well aware, if a little lethargic, when Jemeret and the other riders pulled up by the circle of tents that held the chief's tent. Unlike during my first arrival among the Boru, there were many people standing around, and I recognized joy on Variel's face as she rushed to greet Gundever.

Venacrona hovered at Jemeret's stirrup, his face open and anxious. Jemeret made him a sign of some kind that I couldn't quite see, and the priest disappeared from my view. I unclasped my arms from around Jemeret's waist as he swung a leg over the tivong and dropped lightly to the ground. He turned and held his hands up to me, and I slid down into them.

"Urichen, take Vrand to Sejineth," I heard him say. "Tell him I'll speak with him at the court tomorrow afternoon."

He supported me with one arm around my waist, but didn't lift me off my feet. Gundever, leading his own tivong, stopped and asked a question so softly I didn't hear it at all, nor Jemeret's answer. Then the Lord of the Boru turned to the waiting crowd. "We are all safe," he said. "Shefta and Ronica have been brought home, and the Ilto have a new chief. Return to your tents. Tomorrow evening we will meet at the sacred spring and give thanks to the stars for our strength."

He stood, still supporting me, until the crowd had dispersed, and then he helped me walk to his tent. It was the darkest hour of the night, the one I later learned was called the Hour of the Eclipse, but he didn't light the stanchion lamps, which were out. I didn't need them, for I saw the interior of the tent as bright as day, and Jemeret knew that I did.

"I'll deep now," I said, and relaxed my control enough to sway in his arm.

"Not yet," he said quietly. He leaned down toward me, and I felt his lips lightly brush my forehead. With the hand that was not holding me, he stripped out of his boots and leggings, but the motions were so swift that I barely noticed them. "I have asked you for nothing until now," he said, his voice soothingly steady above me. "Now I ask you to remember, when this is over, that I want you to forgive me."

In my lethargy, I was bewildered. "I don't understand," I said, looking up at his expressionless face. "What have you done?"

"It's what I'm about to do," he said. "I may never find you this tired again." Moving faster than I could have followed, accelerating, his free hand ripped the tunic that I wore from neck to hem, stripped it off me, and flung me, naked, backward onto the rugs.

Lethargy fled as the reflexes slammed me into awareness. Frantically I groped to gather for a sting that wasn't there, fighting physically now as he knelt beside me, still accelerated, and caught my wrists, pinning my legs down with one of his. Despite everything he'd said, everything he promised, rape was what I expected. I had never before seriously battled anyone with as much Class C power as my own, and it soon became clear to me that I could not hope to win.

I had one defense reflex left, and I used it almost without being aware I was doing it, tamping down my sense receptors bit by bit until I had closed off my body from my mind, until I could not have felt him thrust into me. His face was still strangely expressionless, but intense as he studied me, one hand imprisoning my wrists, the other supporting his weight above me. I stopped struggling and received a shock so great that my whole understanding of reality twisted out of shape around me and left me gasping with fear and amazement.

It was not my body he penetrated, but my mind, sliding in past nonexistent shields as if he'd always known the way. He'd tricked me, most of my reserves gone, into using a good deal of the rest in trying to guard my body, and when I was totally preoccupied, he'd thrust a mental probe into my brain. Jemeret of the Boru was a Class A, and he was using the sting.

It is impossible to describe to anyone who has never felt it the sensation of someone else inside your mind. Jemeret was strong, firm, and determined, taking possession of my consciousness with almost no disruption, but I hated this kind of invasion as much as I would have hated the other kind. My diverting of reserves to my shields was too late to keep him out, but I fought his possession as strongly as I could, feeling sensation returning to my body as I threw my fading strength into the immobile battle inside my head.

He was trying to soothe me, to relax me, moving in places inside my brain that Jasin Lebec had never touched. In rage, I committed myself utterly to the fight, throwing more and more of my failing energy into the defense of an already breached wall. The room grew brighter and brighter, and though I knew shutting my eyes would do nothing to reduce the light, I closed them. The glare was almost overwhelming.

I knew in an instant that I'd gone too far, that I'd used up all my reserves, that I was drained, and that I was dying. My resistance failed as my reserves did, and Jemeret was firmly implanted in every part of my mind that was not locked away from me. I had not surrendered, but I had lost.

From what seemed to be an immense distance, I heard Jemeret say, "Ronica, you have to want to live. I can help you, but you have to want me to."

And suddenly I realized that I'd been taught all my life to be a survivor. I very much wanted to live, even if living meant yielding, past regret and past hope. As soon as I wished it, with a surge of power, Jemeret began to pour strength into me. The glare in the room, which had become unbearable, dropped to bright, then to what I'd think of as early morning, then to dim. His reserves were unimaginably greater than mine, and I believe now that he must have given me at least half of them, if not more. He brought me back from a nearly certain death by willing me part of his own survival.

When he knew I was truly going to live, reading that *I* knew it, he dropped down onto the rugs beside me and slowly, gently, withdrew his presence from my battered mind. The two of us lay naked, covered with sweat from the exertion, panting, and nearly exhausted.

I turned my face away from him and began to cry, but he turned me back with his near hand and let my tears mingle with the glaze of sweat on his shoulder. "I was afraid I'd lost you," he said, his voice thick and edged with emotion. "That time you almost got away."

I wanted to ask why he had done it, but the sobs were sweeping up from inside me in long, uncontrollable waves until my whole body trembled under them. With his free hand he stroked my face and hair, my breast and hips, calming me as he'd calm a frightened animal.

Once again I felt his lips lightly brush my forehead. "Deep now," he said, and pulled a rug up over our bodies. It was a long while before the sobs subsided and I finally slept in his arms.

I awoke past midday the next day, coming alert at once, feeling strong and shaken simultaneously. Jemeret was still deeping, his breathing too slow and even for simple sleep. I realized then, if I hadn't fully the night before, how much of his own strength he had poured into me. But I would not let myself be grateful. Now that I was recovered from my touch of death, I was angry at the man in whose arms I still lay, for he had turned me into a person he had had to save.

He had drawn me back, not from the edge of the pit, but from the pit itself, and what I felt as I lay looking at his profile was an absolute rage that he had put me in it in the first place. I need to be clear about this: I did not hate him. In fact, I may already have been half in love with him. He had shown himself to be completely my own kind, even more than Jasin Lebec—for I had already spent more time in his company than my total acquaintance with the older Class A—more than Coney and Kray, who had never known the power of using a sting. But he had been stronger than I, and he had probed me against my will, and those two sins seemed unforgivable.

I deliberately blocked out the voice that rose instantly to memory, saying, "I ask you to remember, when this is over, that I want you to forgive me." I was not in a forgiving mood. As I slipped out from the circle of his arm, being careful not to awaken him, I wondered at the absence of an open impulse for revenge, but I knew that I probably could not hurt him. For one thing, that morning I *was* too much of him. For another, my own sting was gone. I still felt nothing of people's minds, and thus I could not influence his.

Had I been, at that time, a fair person—as I have since then been shown many times what "fair" really means—I might

have understood that he had not hurt me by his penetration of
my mind. He had done nothing to influence me, except to ask
me to choose life; he had only probed me, more completely
than Jasin Lebec had done, in an act that was a Class A's right
to perform on those around him or her. I had always taken for
granted my own right to do it; in that light alone, I might have
granted the same right to him. But I was not fair. I truly believe that no one ever sees both sides of a question in which
they have a stake.

Someone, probably Numima, had brought in fresh clothes
and left them on the table. Mine was a deep gray talma,
trimmed in pure white. I assumed that I was not to go to the
tivongs today.

After I'd washed and dressed in the talma and braided my
hair with the white cord I found under the gown, I sat in a
chair and watched him sleep, winding the end of the cord
around my finger, then unwinding it again. Even my boots
were white today. It occurred to me to check his clothes, and
I found his tunic to match mine, though his leggings and boots
were black. Under his tunic was a thin silver band of beaten
metal, and after I studied it for a moment, I realized it was a
brow-crown.

I looked up and found him awake, watching me. I let his tunic fall back on the crown and stood up. "Should I undress
again?" I asked.

"You're free to do as you like."

"In that case, I'd like to leave," I said.

His eyes clouded. "There are ceremonies today, and I'll
need you with me."

I sat down again and held my hands tightly clasped in my
lap. "I don't see why I should feel obligated to help you any
longer," I said, trying to sound reasonable. "You've freed me
from that, too."

He sat upright, his body somehow negligent and tightly
coiled at the same time. "I don't remember doing that. Perhaps
you can refresh my memory." His self-possession made me
nervous.

"How can you pretend?" I cried out. "You—violated me,
and after you said you wouldn't! You told me to learn to trust
you!"

A quizzical, bemused expression passed swiftly across his
face and was instantly gone. "I said I wouldn't physically force

you," he said, "and I haven't. And I won't. You'd hate rape, and I want you to enjoy me as much as I intend to enjoy you."

"I won't forgive you for last night." My voice rasped more than I'd intended, but there seemed little sense in controlling emotion he would know I was feeling.

He threw the rug aside and got to his feet, but I neither jumped nor drew back from him. His self had become too much a part of me for my body to recoil from him any longer. "What I did to you last night is neither more nor less than I've done—without their knowledge—to the members of the Boru at manhood or womanhood ceremonials. You were aware that I was doing it. That's the only difference. That, and the fact that I had to wait until you were worn-out. You are stronger than even I guessed." He came to the table, splashed water from the basin on his face, and dressed with spare, economical motions. "I paid a tribute to your strength, but that's all."

"I am not a Boru yet," I said steadily. "It is possible that I will choose not to become one."

That hurt him, and I knew it instantly, even though I couldn't have said how I knew. I turned away, not wanting to confront his hurt—my having been responsible for it. But I wouldn't take it back.

He set the crown on his brow and faced me directly. "The next tribe in strength to the Boru is the Genda. If you stay with me today through the ceremonies, I'll take you to the Genda, and you can decide if they suit you better."

I felt a pang I barely understood, a certainty inside me that here was where I belonged. But I said, "All right, I agree to that."

He held out his hand, and I put mine into it, feeling as I did so a slight, inexplicable tingle run up my arm. "How ever could I have your child if I were not a Boru?" I flung it at him in confusion at my own reaction to him.

Jemeret smiled. "You are a highly intelligent woman, Ronica, and like many highly intelligent women, you tend to overlook simple things. With your power, even if I impregnated you against your will, you wouldn't have to carry the child an hour." His words were not patronizing, just informative, and I was astonished, because that had never occurred to me before.

With genuine surprise at my previous failure to have thought of something as elementary as that, I said wonderingly, "You have to have my consent."

"Consent is a momentary thing, while a pregnancy tends to drag on a bit," Jemeret said. "I have to have more than just your consent. I want—I *will have*—your enthusiastic cooperation."

"I can't imagine why you would ever possibly have that." My reply was out of my mouth instantly, an instinctive declaration. I don't know how I expected him to respond, for I saw it as a challenge.

His expression softened, blending the lines of his face to smoothness, and his free hand moved up and gently pushed a curl of hair off my forehead. "I know you can't," he said, and despite his trying to mask his compassion, I sensed it clearly. "But I think you will someday. You have the strength to."

"Strength!" The word exploded outward from my lungs as if he'd punched me.

And as if that had been a signal, Venacrona flung open the tent flap. I barely had time to notice that the priest wore a long black robe, heavily embroidered in coils of red, gold, white, and blue. On his head he wore a pyramid hat, each side one of the colors from the robe's embroidery. Then Jemeret led me outside to a low platform in front of one of the other tents in the circle, and we mounted it.

Two things were instantly apparent as we turned around at the top of the steps. First, every Boru who could fit into the circle and the area of surrounding tents was there. Second, there was something wrong with the fire in the center. Instead of blazing from the logs, as I'd been used to seeing it, it grew from a wide metal bowl. Instead of the usual way a fire moved, it danced and writhed with a rhythm that seemed to have nothing to do with wind or crowd movement, and its interior shone with separate strands of the same four colors that Venacrona wore on his robe and hat.

The colors were, I realized abruptly, star colors—the red of red giants, the white of white dwarves, the blue of the hot young blue stars, and the gold of the middle-aged, yellow suns. While I wasn't then aware of it as such, I was looking at starfire. A tingle like the one I had felt when Jemeret took my hand ran up the back of my spine.

The crowd of massed Boru shouted Jemeret's name once, and their leader held out his hands to ask them for quiet. "This is the Boru Court of Justice," he said. "Let all with claim before this court come forward."

The men who had ridden with Jemeret to retrieve Shefta and

me from the Ilto found their way through the crowd and knelt in rows between the platform and the fire. I picked out Gundever in the second rank, but watched Jemeret more than I watched the kneeling men.

"These warriors have gone into danger and have returned," Jemeret said, his voice full and carefully pitched so the crowd could hear. "For a successful foray, each man here is granted half a tenday of rest this winter."

The men cheered. I noticed out of the corner of my eye that Venacrona held a golden bowl full of metal tokens, and he took his place with another man and a woman, both in plain white robes, to the left of the platform. The warriors rose and walked past the platform, each bowing to Jemeret and taking a metal token out of the bowl.

I was not accustomed to a court that dispensed rewards. Most of the courts I had known had been constituted to punish, and if a reward was judged to one claimant, it was at the cost of another.

Jemeret waited, not moving, until all the men were back in the crowd. Then he said, "Let the girl Shefta come forward."

Shefta, wearing a green and brown talma and looking very adult, came to kneel in the open space between the fire and the platform. She smiled broadly at me, then blushed furiously and looked at Jemeret.

"This girl," Jemeret said, and he smiled down at her, "was carried into danger and has returned. From this time forward she will be a woman of the Boru, with the name Shenefta. Her womanhood ceremony at Convalee will only confirm what each of us knows. Shenefta knelt as a girl, but rises a woman. Fortunate the man who chooses to share her courage."

Shenefta reddened, but stiffened her back and raised her chin. Venacrona gestured, and the two assistant priests helped her to rise. The three of them bowed to Jemeret, and Shenefta threw me another wide smile as she returned to her place.

Jemeret put his hand out to me and drew me forward, but kept me facing the crowd of people. "I present to the Boru the woman Ronica, my claim," he said, "who was carried into danger and has returned. She was carried away as a prafaci tivong trainer, but she has returned a warrior of the first rank, having proven herself by deeds. Greet her as befits a new warrior."

I felt tears sting at me, and I controlled them. The shout of

"Boru!" went up from almost two hundred throats, male and female alike.

Jemeret squeezed my hand lightly and I stepped back to the place I'd had before. The tears had been born of confusion that he would honor me when I had just hurt him, but then something inside me told me that this was a fair man, and we were in a Court of Justice.

My attention was immediately diverted by Jemeret's next words. "Let the man Sejineth come forward."

The crowd parted a little on the far side, and Sejineth walked forward between the platform and the fire. He bent forward onto one knee and waited, his eyes on Jemeret's face. For the first time, Jemeret did not speak to the crowd.

"A woman and a girl of the Boru were in your care, and were carried into danger. Sejineth, you have failed in your responsibility to your prafaci. Do you doubt this?"

Sejineth slowly shook his head. "The facts are as you have spoken them, my lord."

"Both the woman and the girl have returned to us, however, and their harm has been minimal," Jemeret said. "Thus I do not believe the Boru should exact a great price, but only a small one for your failure. Do you agree with this?"

The tivong keeper's voice was clipped as well as harsh. "You are generous, my lord."

"There is no justice without balance," Jemeret said mildly. He nodded to Venacrona.

The small priest had gotten rid of the golden bowl. Now he said, "The tivong trainer's share of the sale of tivongs at Convalee is a five-percent share. This year it will be halved, with the unawarded half going equally to Shenefta and Ronica. Is this a fair judgment on you?"

Sejineth's eyes glittered angrily, and I wished I could read him, but of course he was closed to me. "This is a fair judgment," he said. He rose, bowed, and turned back into the crowd.

Jemeret spoke again, his tone much colder. "Let the man Kowati come forward."

Again there was a parting of the crowd, and a young guardsman was brought forward by two warriors. His hands were bound, and his eyes darted from one side to the other. When they reached the area between the platform and the fire, the warriors pushed him to his knees.

Jemeret spoke to him. "Kowati, you were on guard at the

time when the Ilto raided us, and it was past your position they came. This in itself is not a life-taking error. But examination shows that yours was not a failure of vigilance, but a failure of loyalty. You let the Ilto in, and you showed them their targets. Do you agree with this?"

The young man looked up with a face all at once alive with hatred. "Why should *you* have her?" he shouted.

The warriors on either side of him started to bend closer, but Jemeret said, "No, let him be on his own."

Kowati wrenched briefly at his bindings. "My sire was once chief of this tribe, and my brother or I should have come after him! Not you!"

Venacrona stepped forward, but was very careful not to get between Jemeret and Kowati. "Do you agree with the reporting of this matter?" he shouted to the Boru at large.

Most replied, "The facts are as spoken."

"This is a fair judgment," Jemeret said.

And Kowati slumped, lifeless, to the ground.

I heard myself gasp and slammed the reflexes into place, which caused me a sudden stab of pain. It was much too soon after the draining of my reserves for me to use them; I should have waited at least a tenday before risking them again.

"Does anyone else question my right to be chief?" Jemeret asked calmly.

The crowd was completely silent, and in the stillness the starfire's sinuous writhing seemed to create a kind of hum. Without moving, I fought the reflexes down. Jemeret put his hand on my waist, as if casually, and the pain ebbed. I glanced at him, then glanced away in time to see the two warriors lift Kowati's body and carry it out of the circle.

"Does anyone question the judgments of this court in any way?" Venacrona asked. Again there was silence.

"Those who can will assemble in an hour at the sacred spring," Jemeret said. "Those with duties are free to stay away." The hand on my waist went to my hand, and he led me off the platform and back into our tent.

Venacrona closed the tent flap behind us.

Jemeret let go of my hand and took the silver crown from his brow. "Are you all right?"

I stared at him, unable to find the words I wanted.

"There wasn't time to warn you," he said. "It's not something I do very often, but there are times when it does no harm to remind the Boru that I can." He sat down at the table, where there was a decanter with two goblets. "We shouldn't eat until the ceremonies are over, but a little wine would be bracing." He poured some into each of the goblets, pushed one in my direction, fingered the stem of his own without lifting it, watched me and waited.

I had never known anyone with such power. I couldn't even call it talent any longer, not under these circumstances. Its very existence made him totally remarkable, totally unexpected, and so impressive that I did not think I could deal with the fact that he had slept beside me for four nights and had just recently saved my life. In a way, such a use of Class A power both horrified and fascinated me. I found my heart pounding and my palms damp.

Jemeret just waited.

At last I took the other chair and sat down in it, for my knees had gotten weak. I didn't reach for the wine, only laid my hands flat on the table and stared at them.

"Just say it," he said.

My head came up quickly. "How did you do that? Can any of the rest of you do that? Did you know I could feel it go by me? Did Venacrona feel it, too?" I had run out of breath.

Jemeret chose a question to answer. "Not many can do it," he said. "It is said the High Lady could. And I can. That's not very many."

My mind had leaped forward, ignoring the rest of the questions I'd asked. "Why did you agree to take me to the Genda?"

"Because to live on this world, if you are not a Honish, you must have a tribe. If you choose not to become a Boru, then becoming a Gendal is the next best thing." He finally took a swallow of his wine. "Unless you're sorry you didn't stay Chief of the Ilto."

I started to reply angrily, then realized that he was teasing me. His confidence was breathtaking, but now that I knew what his power really was, I could understand it. He wanted me to be a Boru very much, but he could joke about it.

"You frighten me," I said.

"No, I don't. I unsettle you, and *that* frightens you." He rose slowly and moved the second goblet closer to me. "You know I don't want to hurt you."

"There's hurt and hurt," I said, and suddenly gasped, plunged into a memory of pain. It wasn't my pain; it was Coney's. As if a closed door had opened on a truth I had locked away inside and ignored, I understood the pain I had caused

Coney by sleeping with him without loving him, when he loved me more than he loved fresh air. I understood how much I'd violated his self by bringing him back to me with the sting when he wanted to leave while he could. I understood that I had made him do badly things he would have given his life to do well. And I had done all that to a man I considered one of my only real friends.

I couldn't stop the tears that came. Jemeret stood above me, holding his own goblet, but he did not move or touch me, and he held his face carefully expressionless. I was realizing that I had been flawed in the mold, that the absence of my sting was not what flawed me. I knocked my goblet over and covered my face with my hands. I tried to hold on, but there was a slippage, and for a moment I truly hated myself.

It passed. I believe the fact that I was so much made up of Jemeret gave the hatred the impetus to flow through me and leave me, sadder, alone with myself.

Only then did Jemeret ask, "What's wrong?"

I looked up at him, blurry behind the wash of my tears. "I harmed someone I cared about, and never knew it until now. And I'm crying because I'll never have the chance to tell him I'm sorry."

I thought I might have felt an instantaneous probe, but it was gone before I could be certain. "We all hurt people we care about," he said steadily. "It's part of being alive. Drink some of this."

He made me take his goblet, and I obediently swallowed twice. The wine warmed me. "I thought it was something only normal people did," I said.

"We're all normal people."

"No." It was a tribute to his power, but somehow it caused him to wince. The reaction was minuscule, and I was surprised that I recognized it.

"All of us," he said. "Finish that, and we'll start for the spring."

I drank the rest of the wine and ran my fingers under my eyes. It would be good to have something to do other than think. Jemeret lifted the brow-crown and put it back on.

"Do you need to warn me about anything here?" I asked him.

"No, this one will be very simple," he told me. "You'll only have to sit, and drink a little fresh water."

"I can do that," I said. "Even today, I can do that."

"Ronica, I don't know what just happened to you. If you want to tell me, I'll listen, but if you don't, I won't ask. I only tell you that I want you to think you are the same person today that you were yesterday."

I found I could smile. "No, Jemeret," I said with real conviction. "Today I am partly you. Yesterday, I was only me."

V. Among the Genda

The sacred spring began just at the edge of the trees about a kilometer out of the Boru camp. It was edged with silvery rocks and long-fronded ferns, and it gave out a silver thread of water that sprang downward into the Plain of Convalee for some distance before it curved westward to join the smaller of the two rivers, the Tran. It did not sink into the surface of the plain, which was remarkable, but hardly inspirational.

Venacrona and his two assistants had set a golden tripod near the mouth of the spring; on it was a bowl in which danced the four-colored flame. Under the tripod hung a golden scoop, its handle decorated with multicolored ribbons. The three priests sat around the head of the spring, on the grassy face of the plain. Jemeret and I sat on the grass just where the tiny pool spilled into the ribbon of stream. Many of the Boru had come to the stream, and sat in long lines on either side of the water. I had seen Tuvellen and Morien, but I was still preoccupied with myself and not in a mood to be sociable. We sat more or less in silence as the late afternoon wore on toward twilight, and I began to sense the reverence, the prayers that were rising around me. The very serene atmosphere became charged with a tension composed of the workings of all these people's minds. It was not a threatening tension, but rather one filled with energy, exhilarating.

My tears were no longer wrenching, but they still flowed. I had always known myself to be selfish, had even prided myself on the fact that in my case the value of my talent made selfishness no more than simple wisdom. But I had not known how thoughtless the selfishness had made me, how unaware of the feelings of someone I thought well of.

There was a stir beside me, and I looked up. Shenefta had

come up the rows of people sitting by the stream until she had almost reached us. I smiled at her, for something in the hesitancy and defiance of her manner told me that this was an audacious act for her. She smiled back at me, though it was plain she noticed my red, wet eyes, and sat down in the small space between me and the next Boru along the stream, who happened to be Gundever, though I hadn't noticed him before.

The sun set completely, and in the growing dimness a woman began to sing. Others along the stream took it up, for it was obviously a familiar song, and its slow beauty climbed around us. I was touched and enchanted and saddened simultaneously, first because it was the only music of any kind I'd heard on this world, and I hadn't been aware of how much I needed music; second, because it was in and of itself of surpassing loveliness. I didn't listen to the words, only to the rise and fall of the melodic line. It soothed and calmed me as it washed over me.

The song ended just at last light, its echoes fading along the walls of the cliffs behind us. Venacrona rose. "People of the Boru, we come again to the Plain of Convalee, where we meet as the Samoth with others of our race. We sit again beside the fire and the water, and we give praise and thanks that we have remained a tribe, that we have grown in strength, that we have prospered. People of the Boru, think on our greatest gift this season—that some among us who have been alone have found others to share their lives, and that some who are now alone may find others waiting on the road just ahead. People of the Boru, so that none may be alone at this moment, join hands."

He bent a little and gave one hand to Jemeret, while the priestess took his other. She linked a hand with the remaining priest, who took the hand of the young girl sitting across the stream from us. Jemeret took my left hand in his, and I gave my right to Shenefta. The link flowed down the stream in time with the sound of the water until one continuous chain had been formed, the last people on each side reaching across the water to clasp hands.

"My lord," Venacrona said, "the Boru are joined." And Jemeret blazed out with an energy that seemed momentarily to link all our minds. I felt the oneness which rose and faded at the same instant, recognized some individuals standing out as motes of light in the sea of brightness that was Jemeret, and then was alone again within myself. But I had known an utter belonging unlike anything I had previously dreamed of or experienced—a warmth and acceptance that left my spirit tingling in its aftermath.

Tearless now, I looked at Jemeret in complete awe. There were more than a hundred people along the stream, and he had touched every one of us. I was barely aware that he and Shenefta had kept hold of my hands when everyone else had separated. I was shaken from my self-pity by the sheer vastness of the power this man bore, the power that lay hidden on this wilderworld, for which the government would have given anything to bring into the Com. At that particular instant, if he had asked me for anything, I would have given it to him without a second thought. Perhaps unfortunately, he did not ask.

Venacrona had begun again. "People of the Boru, we give praise and thanks. Praise to the fires of the heavens and the waters of the world. Thanks to the spirit of light and that of dark, the male and the female, the fire and the water." It seemed a basic prayer, of the kind I'd always been able to disregard before, but now there was something strangely satisfying about it.

The assistant priest and priestess rose to their feet, cupped hands held outward in front of them. Venacrona took the ladle, dipped it into the spring, poured a scoop of water into the priestess's hands, and then repeated the maneuver with the priest. They seemed to hold their hands in such a way that no water dripped out. Then Venacrona dipped the ladle in the pot of fire and transferred the flame to their cupped hands. It continued to burn.

I was past astonishment. The light of the world had gone, and the glow of the three multicolored fires was the only illumination under the forming stars. The song began again, softly, almost as background, and the people leaned forward to scoop a palmful of water from the stream and sip it. I followed Jemeret's lead and did the same. The water was fresh and sweet, but unremarkable. I wanted to analyze it as it entered my system, but that would have meant gathering, which I could not do. I also wanted to pathfind the fire, but I could not. They would have to remain mysteries for now, and I grew frustrated when I had to accept mysteries. The song, slower and softer this time, ended again, and the priest and priestess opened their hands, letting the water and fire sink into the ground. Venacrona moved his hands over the last fire, and it fell back into the metal bowl. The stars overhead seemed very close, touching the grass and our heads with silver.

"People of the Boru, go in peace," Venacrona said.

Jemeret got to his feet and drew me up beside him. I squeezed Shenefta's hand once before she moved away.

Still holding hands, we walked slowly back to the tents, with many of the Boru walking near us. I was calm, almost contented. Just as we reached his tent, Jemeret let go of my hand. "I've got to speak to the guard," he said. "I'll be back in a little while."

He turned without waiting for a response and disappeared into the darkness. I went to the campfire, which was normal again, took a sliver of wood, and carried the flame with me into the tent to light the stanchion lamps. When I blew out the splinter, the lamps seemed too bright, so I extinguished all but one of the lights I had just kindled.

I undressed slowly, almost absentmindedly, and got in among the rugs. Something in what had happened had touched me very deeply—not just the music, but the unity, the closeness. The faith. Jemeret's power.

I lay watching him as he came into the tent and dropped his brow-crown on the table. "The Genda were seen across the Tran, just above the Modria," he said. "We'll go there in the morning."

Stubbornness rose in me and refused to let me say no, that I would stay here. Despite how much I was drawn to this tribe, speaking now smacked too much of capitulation. He needed, after all, to be punished for showing me that he was what I could no longer be. "All right," I said, and turned my face to the tent as he started to undress. I heard him drop the furs beside the rugs, and I drew a little more back into myself. I was lonely, and I honestly don't think I'd ever in my life let myself feel lonely before.

Jemeret, Urichen, Wendagash, Venacrona, and I set off on tivongs just after the morning meal, all of us dressed alike. Jemeret had given me a shortsword to wear, but had refused to give me a longsword to match it until after I'd had some training with the larger weapon. I wore the shortsword tucked into the belt over my tunic, and ached as I rode.

Somehow my personal calendar had snuck up on me, and I was beginning my camenia without benefit of gathering to soothe the ache away. I discovered I did not know how to relax from within, that all my relaxation had been as a result of my self-induced physiological changes. And now my body clenched under the cramping and I didn't seem to be able to do anything about it. What I wanted to do was stand up under the unfamiliar pain and not show anyone that I was feeling it. A part of proving—even to myself—how strong I was made me choose not to ask for help. I was always the one who fulfilled requests, not someone who had to make them. I could surely pretend I was not in any pain.

All the same, I had an idea that Jemeret knew. I had begun to feel that he knew everything I felt, and while I told myself it was a bit paranoid of me to react that way, I also knew very well that it was possible. If he wanted to look at my emotions, he could do so. What he could not do was to influence me without my being aware of it, and so far he had not tried. I failed to see then that everything that had happened to me since I left the stonehouse was influencing me. I thought that influence was a direct, deliberate process, a function only of the Class A mind.

We rode in silence across the Plain of Convalee, south and east, avoiding the tiny silver stream by skirting it instead of crossing it. I wondered briefly if we had not ridden across it for religious reasons, but didn't ask and soon forgot about it.

Venacrona spoke briefly to Jemeret and then urged his tivong ahead. He looked like a child on the back of the immense beast, but he handled it well. The two guards rode some small distance behind us, and Jemeret and I seemed more or less alone on the broad face of the plain. He was silent and preoccupied for a long time, then looked over at me and smiled a little. "Sorry," he said. "I didn't realize you were alone."

I almost said, "Neither did I," but that could have led down paths I did not want to travel. Instead, I changed the subject. "I was just wondering what the Genda are like."

"They're like us—the Boru—in many ways," he said. "We have a lot of the same customs, the same beliefs, and the same sense of the history of the Samoth. The Boru generally have more power, and we're in a different business."

"Business?" I realized I knew nothing at all about the economics of the tribal cultures.

"The Boru breed and raise tivongs," he explained. "We sell the males to the other tribes at Convalee. The Genda are metal-smiths. They forge our weapons, our lamps, our wagon parts, and our jewelry. A Gendal made the brow-crown I wore yesterday. Each tribe has its own speciality."

"What do the Ilto trade in?" I asked.

"Slaves," Jemeret said. "The Vylk and the Resni buy them, and I've heard tell that the Marl have been known to purchase a few, though they generally deny it."

"Wait," I said. "I thought they enslaved their *own* women. They deal in slaves as a commodity?" It was a horrifying thought.

He looked at me wryly. "Ronica, I don't know why you're so surprised. The Lady Meltress Lewannee sold you to me, you know."

"So the Boru buy slaves, too," I said.

"You know better than that. You're no more a slave than any of us."

"But slavery—" I found myself somehow stunned by the whole concept. Free citizenry had been an ideal for so very long.

Jemeret smiled, a little curiously. "There has to be a system in any group for punishing people other than killing them or slapping their hands," he said. "Sometimes people find it impossible to follow rules."

I heard echoes of Coney and Kray and me talking about people who couldn't fit into the Com.

"Exile," I said softly, the word cutting down inside me, hurting, as an admission of my own situation.

His smile faded. He might have understood quite well what I was feeling. "I told you this is a savage world," he said. "Exile here is a death sentence, so we don't force it on anyone. Slaves get taken care of, fed, sheltered, and usually not worked too hard. Slave owners aren't out to destroy them."

"The Ilto killed those Boru women—" I began.

He shook his head sharply. "The women the Ilto take from us are not taken as slaves, but as symbols." He glanced down at the ground as if concerned about where the animals were putting their feet. "Symbols are almost always treated worse than something as mundane as slaves."

I looked down at the neck ruff of the tivong I was riding. He was the one who had chosen me when I first went to the tivong pens, and I felt secure on his back, despite the ache in my belly.

"You said the leader of the Genda was someone named Sabaran," I said, wanting to change the subject. "What's he like?"

"He's a fine man," Jemeret said. "We have tried our strength against one another for many years. His bracelet is a wise woman named Clematis, whom I once courted when all of us were younger. But the Genda I really want you to meet is the priestess Sandalari. She's the most beautiful woman in the Samothen, or was before you came."

"Better not let Morien hear you say that," I said lightly, because I recognized that he did not mean it as flattery. "Does beauty matter so much here?"

"Beauty always matters," he answered. "What changes is the way people think beauty is formed. In the stonehouses, wealth makes beauty no matter what the physical appearance is."

"Where I come from, talent makes beauty."

He smiled. "To some extent here, too."

A very strong pain stabbed at me, and I winced and bent forward a little. Jemeret pulled his tivong close to mine and took my wrist. "What is it?" he asked.

"Embarrassing," was all I would say.

He studied me for a moment or two, then let go of my wrist, turned and whistled sharply. Urichen urged his tivong faster until he had caught up with us. "Yes, my lord?"

"See if you can find some wardroot," Jemeret told him.

Urichen turned the tivong's head and galloped off toward the Tran. Wendagash moved his own mount a little closer to us, but did not catch up.

"You should have said something," Jemeret told me.

"I'm used to being able to handle it myself. It isn't anyone else's business."

"You cannot always be alone," he said quietly. "You cannot always face things alone. You must have a people around you."

"I don't know how," I said honestly.

"Try to start by relaxing. Try to like people."

That made me so angry I forgot my pain. "I like people," I said hotly. "Shenefta is very likable, and so are Gundever and Variel." I paused, and it sobered me. I decided that I might as well continue to be honest, despite the fact that I had to force it out of myself. "I like you."

His expression gentled. "Well, that's progress," he said. "You like me despite the fact that I betrayed your trust and violated you?" The question was serious, not teasing. I knew I was angry at him for asking it, but I still did not dislike him. I thought about what he had asked, and it sank down inside me and rose up as words I couldn't have explained. "I used to be a greater person than I am now."

"Nonsense," he said. "Your future is greater than your past."

"You didn't know me," I cautioned, and was astonished to feel tears coming from somewhere again.

Jemeret leaned over and took my arm. "I know you now," he said. It was undeniable. What there was to know about me, he knew. What existed in my mind, he had seen, touched—and yet, astonishingly to me, he seemed not to have judged me, or if he *had* judged me, he'd still found me worthy, despite whatever had happened to send me here. "I have never known anyone like you," he added. He looked up then and saw Urichen coming back. He let go of my arm and turned his tivong's head away from me.

"Chew the wardroot slowly," he said, "and don't swallow the pulp, just the juices."

I had blinked back the tears before Urichen reached me.

The Genda sent a delegation to meet us, bearing a brown and gray banner that I assumed was a symbol of their tribe. Venacrona was riding with them. One of the five Gendal riders was a big, blond, bearded man with a thin gold circlet on his brow. He and Jemeret greeted each other with genuine pleasure, and clasped both arms. Jemeret clasped a single arm with one of the other men, almost still a boy, also blond, but cleanshaven. I realized that the big man must be Sabaran, and rode closer in time to hear him ask, "And what prompted the beard?"

Then he saw me. "Kadah!" he said. "I see why you came here early." He held out his hand to me. "I am Sabaran of the Genda, and I greet you in the name of my people."

"I am Ronica," I said, adding after a breath, "Lord Jemeret's claim." Out of the corner of my eye, I saw Jemeret look quickly at me, then away again. I lightly touched Sabaran's big hand.

"This is my son, Sheridar," the Lord of the Genda said. "These others are my guards. Come—we set camp early when we heard you were coming. The ford across the Tran is just to the south of here."

He rode beside me, Sheridar beside Jemeret. The others, including Venacrona, rode behind the four of us. I would catch Sabaran's or Sheridar's gaze on me as we rode, but Jemeret did not look at me again, and I was not surprised. I watched the Tran draw closer, its expanse broken occasionally by low bars of rock or sand around which the water rippled.

The rhythm of our even-paced ride became comfortingly the same, and I sank into it, relieved of the necessity to talk. Slowly, as if a sealed room were opening, I remembered something of the beginning of the time I had forgotten, the time that was shut off from me. I saw my face again, in my dressing room mirror, under the edge of the gold helmet just before the graduation ceremony. I was wearing the gold jumpsuit and black sash of highest government service, and there were several bouquets of flowers on the dressing table—white and yellow from Coney, blue and orange from Kray, pink from Mortel John, bright red from Jasin Lebec, and gold superblooms from Pel Nostro.

I felt again the relief of having training over with at last, of being on the threshold of all life had to offer me, of being almost a free citizen of the Com, without restraint. I remembered how intrigued I'd been about the idea of learning what my first assignment was to be, researching the worlds of the Com it would take me to, and then *acting*, making an impact, becoming the second Class A loose in the universe. The eagerness of that evening in my dressing room swept over me again. I had thought that the galaxy lay at my feet, and I wanted to get out there and walk on it.

There was a knock on the door, and I called, "Come in." Coney and Kray entered, Kray in the silver jumpsuit of second-rank service, Coney in the bronze of third-rank. Their faces looked strangely unfamiliar under their helmets until they smiled, and then we embraced each other. We had another two days together, after the great graduation gala, before we would be separated, and we had been planning to spend the time in a quick trip to Nanseda, an amusement world about which we'd heard a great deal but had never been permitted to visit.

I remembered that Kray had brought a holocube they'd sent to confirm our reservations, for the trip had been his idea, and he set it up on my dressing table. We watched the spokesman lay out a map of the world and point out its attractions—for the literary, there was live theater, performing modern, ancient, secular or religious drama or comedy, some of it revolutionary; for the musical, the best musicians in the Com, singly or in groups, orchestral, dance, and voice; for the athletic, individual and team competition, in everything from ballyball to air skating; for the lascivious, the pleasure rooms; and all of these worlds within a world giving ample opportunity for participation or observation, depending on your desires. Food from all the worlds of the Com could be provided, and an animal park displayed all sorts of life.

"How are we ever going to see it all in two days?" Coney asked with a laugh.

I had said, "You and I can see some of it. I'm sure we won't be able to get Kray out of the pleasure rooms." Kray turned dark, burning eyes on me, really angry, but I laughed it off and took one of the superblooms out of Pel Nostro's bouquet to hand to him as a peace offering. As Kray put the cube away in his jumpsuit, a liquid tone echoed through the room to tell us that it was time to go up to the stage.

The memory ceased. Try as I might, I could not get any farther into the missing area of my recollection. I realized that we'd arrived at the ford and that Jemeret was now staring at me. I smiled at him a little tightly and guided my tivong into the shallow water after Sabaran's mount, which was already halfway across the river. It had begun to rain lightly, and I watched the ripples formed by raindrops distorted and whisked away by the current as we crossed.

Now that some piece of my memory had returned to me, I was impatient beyond words for the rest of it to arrive. If the government's mind block or the trauma of the crash here had begun to lose its hold over me, I could at least find out what had happened—what had brought me, stingless, to this world. For a moment or two I may also have imagined that remembering would make me able to repair whatever had been wrong, and then I could go back again, but rational thought cancelled that out very quickly, and the hope died. We could stave off going to our graves, but we did not rise from them again.

The tivongs were steady-footed through the water, and soon we were on land again. Jemeret drew his mount beside mine and spoke in a barely audible voice. "Are you all right?"

"Of course," I said lightly. I wanted not to share either the memory or the fact that I'd begun to remember. "The wardroot's just wearing off a bit."

His eyes narrowed a little, and I knew at once that he knew I had just lied to him, and that he was far from pleased about it. I looked quickly away from him. Easy lying had always been a good refuge, but I used it rarely, for it would lose its value if it became too common. I was unused to being found

out, because my projective abilities had always assured acceptance. In the pit of my stomach, I disliked the feeling of being
seen through.

We crested the rise on the tivongs and through the light rain
saw the encampment of the Genda. The tents were mostly a
soft, light brown, and I didn't think there were quite as many
of them as at the Boru encampment. They were spread over a
wider area, because a wagon stood between each pair of tents.
Tivongs were picketed in several locations, and there were
warriors in evidence on the rises around the camp. The glows
of many small fires looked welcome through the dampness,
and we hurried our pace.

It was the first time I'd ridden astride on a quick-paced
tivong; I found the gait almost restful. The big animals were
graceful and solid, but different from the Pelhamhorses I had
once ridden with Kray. I thought I could enjoy this as a pas-
time.

There were no circles of tents here, as there were in the
Boru camp, and we rode to the largest tent. We dismounted, all
but Wendagash, who led the riderless tivongs toward the nearest picket area. Sabaran's tent had a canopy that reached out
toward the fire in front of it. Under it stood a woman I immediately identified as Clematis. She was honey-haired, about
half a head shorter than I, and though no longer slender, she
carried herself so well that I barely noticed her size. She was
not beautiful, but she radiated warmth. She wore a russet robe
with ties from throat to hem, which swayed around her like a
bell as she and Jemeret embraced each other.

"So you've grown a beard," she said to him as they parted.
"How fine it looks on you."

"How fine *you* look," he said. "Clematis, this is Ronica, my
claim."

I held out my hand, but was swooped into her embrace.
"The woman who brought us early to Convalee," she said,
holding me out from her by the shoulders. "Another quadra of
peace won't harm any of us, my child. Come in."

The inside of the tent was so comfortable as to be almost
messy. Cushions and rugs were piled everywhere, even on
trunks, and beautifully decorated lamps stood on tripod pedes-
tals all around the interior. Jemeret and Venacrona followed us
in, along with Sabaran and Sheridar. I did not see where
Urichen went.

Clematis sat down on the rugs, and we ranged ourselves in

a rough circle. Sheridar opened a tall metal wine jug and passed it to his father, who poured the red liquid into a series of stemless cups he drew from the chaos of the room.

"Am I late?" a musical voice asked from under the canopy.

"Not late to this tent," Sabaran said. Jemeret got to his feet again and held out his hands, and a thin flame of a woman glided across the rugs and put her hands in his. Her smile at him was a marvel. Then he turned and knelt before Venacrona, who rested his hands on her white-gold hair.

"Thank you for blessing me, my father," she said.

"My daughter, blessing you *is* my thanks," Venacrona replied. She leaned forward and kissed his cheek, then sat down beside him in the circle.

"Ronica, this is Sandalari," Clematis said, and the woman and I nodded to each other. I'd already guessed who she was. Her vitality, her sheer joy at being alive, surrounded her and radiated outward like a beacon. I couldn't take my eyes off her at first, for here was the only other person I'd met who'd come from the worlds outside this one—probably from the Com, since no world without Com technology would have the ability to roll the great distances involved. Clematis held out one of the full cups of wine to Sandalari, who took it with another smile.

Sheridar said abruptly, "Venacrona says you've come looking for a tribe."

I realized he was speaking to me, and looked over at him. Clematis tsked audibly at his blurting, and the young man reddened, but jutted his chin forward, not retreating. I felt Jemeret tense slightly as he sat directly to my left, and I recognized that what I said to Sheridar had some kind of real meaning. I had a flash of wonder that I could read him, asking myself if he were deliberately controlling himself less in front of me, and then I put it aside and smiled at Sheridar.

"Not exactly, no," I said gently. "I have a very important decision to make, and I've been taught that I shouldn't try to make important decisions without collecting information first. So you could call this a research trip." I didn't intend to stress the last word, but it came out that way.

I felt, rather than saw, Jemeret relax. The image was so clear on my nerves that for one breathless moment I thought my Class A talent had come back. I scanned the rest of the group, but there was nothing. Disappointed, but not really surprised, I sipped some of my wine. It proved to me that Jemeret was projecting, letting me know how he felt about what I was doing. I might have resented it; I did not.

"So you'll be seeing all the tribes, then." Sheridar was persistent.

I glanced sideways at his father. "Do you think I'll need to?"

Sandalari laughed, her voice as rippling and liquid as the sound of the Tran. "No one thinks you need to, Ronica," she said. "But some people fight the choice of the stars, instead of giving in to it."

"Did you fight it?" I asked quickly. I think I would have gone to great lengths to get her to talk about her arrival here and her life before.

Venacrona sat up straight and pointed at me. "That's rude," he said, "and I tell you because you cannot be expected to know all our customs yet."

"Let her be, Veen," Jemeret said easily. "If Sandalari wants to answer, then she should."

Sandalari nodded at him and replied to me, "I fell to the Genda, and with the Genda I have stayed."

"Of course," Clematis said smoothly, "since Ronica fell to the Honish, it's clear she already knew she could move around." She was a natural diplomat, and I admired her skill.

"The Honish!" Sheridar's voice rippled with anger.

Jemeret's head came up and he looked directly at the youth for a moment, then turned to Sabaran. "Trouble?" he asked.

The big man shifted his place a little and said reluctantly, "There have been stirrings behind Reglessa Fen."

"And you never sent a Paja messenger?" Venacrona asked. He looked, for some reason, both distressed and angry.

"We had no Paj with us," Sabaran said. "They'd gone back for the tribal meeting before Convalee. And the Honish wouldn't dare make trouble at Convalee."

"But you've left your home behind, man," Venacrona said sharply. "What about the Forge?"

Sabaran half rose, and Clematis laid her hand gently on his arm. His face was flushed with anger. "Do you think I'd leave the Forge unprotected?"

Venacrona made a soothing, conciliatory motion with his hand.

Jemeret broke in calmly. "I fancy the best Gendal warriors will have to miss Convalee this time, Veen. I fancy we'll lend Sabaran a few of our warriors, if he asks."

Sandalari laughed, and such tension as remained in the room dissolved. "I fancy he won't have to ask," she said.

Sabaran had calmed himself, his equanimity as quick as his temper, and now he sat back down. "From what I hear, we have nothing to fear from the Ilto, at any rate."

To my astonishment, I found myself blushing. It was terribly inconvenient to be unable to use any of my talent, but the reserves had to be given time to heal. All of the Genda were watching me, but I hadn't the slightest notion of what I was supposed to say. Jemeret came to my rescue. "You are well informed for a tribe without a Paj."

"The Boru rarely move without knowing what lies in front of them," Sabaran said. "The Genda cannot do less than likewise."

I raised my head, my face still hot. "The Ilto tried to take what was not theirs to take."

Venacrona put in dryly, "Their mistake was not that they tried to take it, but that they were not strong enough to keep it."

"They underestimated their opposition," I said to him. "People who think women are weak are destined to be unhappy with them."

"Some women *are* weak," Sandalari said, surprising me. "You must not fall into the trap of judging all women by yourself, just as you mustn't judge all men by Evesti or by Jemeret."

She was right, and I nodded at her. "They underestimated me."

Sabaran laughed, and its deep boom seemed to shake the sides of the tent. "That's not a mistake any of the Samothen will make again. No one will be foolish enough."

Sheridar gestured with the metal jug to ask who wanted refills, and when I saw that everyone else had held their cups out, I held mine out, too, even though it was still three-quarters full. "The Elden are only a day or two behind us," he said. "The Boru have started a fashion for coming early to Convalee."

"I fancy we'll be back to our normal schedule by the next festival. Coming early this year seemed more sensible than lingering." Jemeret swallowed half his drink.

Everyone in the tent looked directly at Venacrona, who sighed a little and toyed with his cup. Then he looked up. "Yes, this is going to be a bad winter for storms. I'm going to advise the Marl to stay in port and cast their nets only from Salthome. The seas will be too dangerous to risk."

Clematis leaned forward. "Will it come early, or stay long?"

"The signs say both," the old man said almost reluctantly. "All the signs say this will be a year of Severance Storms, the first in living memory."

I wanted to ask all sorts of questions, but decided I shouldn't interrupt. The idea of predicting weather by signs instead of both predicting and controlling it by MI was fascinating to me.

"It doesn't surprise me," Sheridar said. "In the year of the Foretelling, there were storms, so it's fitting there should be storms in the year of the Fulfillment."

That was too much to let pass. "What foretelling?" I asked.

Sandalari looked down into her cup as Clematis rounded on Jemeret. "You didn't tell her? Jemeret, I'm amazed at you!"

He grinned at her with a very little bit of sheepishness. "You may find this hard to believe, Clematis, but she really hasn't been here that long, and there's been a lot going on. I haven't had a chance."

Clematis said something under her breath that sounded rude, and Sandalari looked up swiftly. "May I tell her, Jemeret? I will be talking with her later at any event, and I'd like to. We have other things to talk of here and now."

Jemeret nodded at her, his motion barely detectable. I suppressed my curiosity and leaned back as the men and Clematis talked about the stores needed for a winter of this magnitude. I gathered that it snowed heavily only in the high mountains, but that the rest of the land was vulnerable to water and air disturbances, and there was some discussion of who should be warned earlier than whom else, and under what circumstances. I was distracted from the conversation by the thought of speaking to Sandalari alone.

The discussion ended with a group of serving people bringing in many dishes of hot food. I realized when I smelled it that I was ravenous, and at the same time that the wardroot was starting to wear off. I tried to put that out of my mind and eat heartily, for that seemed to be the style of this tribe, or perhaps just of this tent. The food was generally richer, more sophisticated, and more highly and complexly seasoned than the food of the Boru. I found myself trying to remember when I had last had a meal as elaborate.

When we were done eating, and had consumed enough of

the wine so that, while I still ached, I no longer cared, Sandalari rose gracefully to her feet and held out a hand to me. "If you will come with me now, Ronica, we can talk in my tent. I will return you to your lord's tent before the Hour of the Moon's Descent."

I rose, uncertain if I should thank Sabaran and Clematis for the meal, but sensing that I should not. I nodded to each of them and followed Sandalari out into the rain.

It was only a short walk to her tent, two wagons distant, and inside she gave me a towel to dry my hair. Even before she'd taken the towel back, I burst out, "What world did you come from? Excuse me if it's rude, but I have to know. You're the first other outsider I've met here. What did you get sent here for?"

She held out her hand for the towel, seeming to debate what to say, and then she smiled at me and said the last thing I expected. "I came from your world, Ronica. I came from Werd."

My shock must have been obvious. "How did you know?" I asked in a whisper that sounded harsh even to me. "How did you know Werd was one of my worlds?"

"Because we knew each other," she said, the smile fading as she spoke, dissolving into something sadder and less vital. "When I was a child, my name was Sarai."

"I don't believe you!" It was out before I had a chance to subject it to any reasoning.

Sandalari undid the shoulder ties on her talma and pushed it and the shift down over her shoulders. She turned her back to me. Almost all of the horrible scars I remembered were gone, and the skin was smooth and healthy. But one ridge of scar tissue stood out from her left shoulder to her right kidney, left deliberately, as a symbol. Even before I saw it, I believed her, for my memory had conjured again the picture of the teary-eyed, pinch-faced little blonde, and the lines softened and flowed into the vibrant woman in front of me.

"I do believe you," I said quickly. "I don't even know why I said that. How—"

The overwhelming magnitude of the list of questions came flooding in on me, and I stopped as she pulled up and retied the talma. "They made me whole again," she said, "or perhaps it was really for the first time. They valued my strengths and understood my weaknesses."

"But you were mad," I said. I waved as if to discount having said it, once again nothing of a diplomat, but Sandalari smiled.

"Madness is not a permanent condition. All I needed was love and acceptance. I found that here, and it made the madness unnecessary."

"It was a long time ago," I said, unwilling to admit but unable to hide that this subject made me very uncomfortable. "We couldn't—Coney and Kray and I—couldn't have helped." It felt so good to speak their names again honestly and freely to someone who had known them.

Sandalari's voice went very gentle. "I am a priestess of the stars now, and truth is one of our great values. So is kindness. Sometimes the most difficult task I have is choosing between the two."

The edge to my voice wasn't deliberate, but I recognized it. "Go ahead and say it. I'm strong."

She took her time sitting down on the cushions, gesturing for me to do the same, and I guessed that she was choosing her words with some care. Finally she spoke. "It is your strength which has caused you your greatest harm and your greatest pain, Ronica. You have become its servant, rather than making it yours. No, let me finish."

I hadn't been aware that I had opened my mouth to say something.

"You are so entirely afraid of weakness," she went on, "or have such contempt for it. You have since you were a child. All three of you were afraid of me because I was the thing you couldn't allow yourselves to become. Coney was the best of you—at least he tried."

"And I was the worst," I said harshly.

Her voice was still mild. "Of course. You were the strongest. You felt you had the most to lose. When I most needed love and acceptance, you were busy shutting me out. You were afraid of me because I was needy—I needed something I couldn't get for myself—and to you, that was weakness." Her eyes narrowed. "You still think needing equates to weakness."

"Thinking has nothing to do with it," I said. "It's a body reaction, not a mind one."

"Your body and your mind are both part of you, part of your person, part of your wholeness. You hurt yourself when you separate them."

Her words struck a core of something real inside me, and

before I was aware of it, the reflexes took over and I had gathered to reach for the sting that wasn't there. The pain of the gathering ripped through me on nerves already raw from the camenia ache, and I doubled over until the reflexes relaxed and the pain receded.

Sandalari laid a hand on my arm, but didn't move or speak until it was clear that I was all right. Then she said quietly, "I had not expected my words to cause you such pain. Let's talk of the Foretelling."

It seemed that there was a legend among the Samothen that the High Lady would return to unite the tribes under her rule. She would again descend from the stars, and she would pass a number of tests, only some of which were known to those other than the priests and leaders of the tribes. She would be known by her power, by being honored by the animals, by being honored by the stars; the man who won her love would rule with her, and their children would make everywhere a good place to live.

"Almost the standard stuff of prophecy," I said thoughtfully. "The difference is that this time it's supposed to be me."

"Time will tell," Sandalari said. "What kind of prafax will you have here among the Genda? What was your work among the Boru?"

She waited patiently for my answer, and she had to, because I was trying to escape from the thought of the Foretelling. Then her last questions finally registered. "Among the Boru I am a warrior of the first rank."

She smiled. For the first time since we had sat down, she looked away from me, down at her hands. "The woman warriors of the Boru are well known, and I'm certain that you must be very good, but the Genda have only men warriors. Lord Jemeret will be a Gendal warrior of the first rank while you are here."

My head came up as if I'd been challenged. "Jemeret is going to be a warrior to Sabaran? Why?"

"Everyone in a tribe for any longer than a visit must have tribal status," she said. "The laws of the Samoth make that necessary."

"What about the others who came with us?"

"Venacrona is returning tomorrow to the Boru," she said. "A tribe cannot be long without its priest. Jemeret's guards will become warriors of the second rank. It's you we need to find a place for."

Even before she finished speaking, I had made the decision, as though it had taken almost no conscious effort on my part. "No, I don't think we do," I said. "Sandalari, I'd like to speak with Jemeret, please."

She rose instantly and went to the tent flap. I don't know who she spoke with, but someone dashed away into the now heavier rain. She turned back to face me as I got to my feet. "Is it because of the things I said to you?" she asked me. "I gather you don't want to stay with us, and I would like to know if my being here is part of the cause of that."

Her words astonished me, because my thoughts had been in another place entirely, so I spoke with less discretion and more fervor than I might otherwise have done. "No, not at all, Sandalari. It hasn't anything to do with you. Jemeret must not make himself less than he is, not for me, not for any reason."

Jemeret came in then, cloaked and hooded against the rain, but his hair was still plastered down on his forehead. He seemed as calm as usual, and I was glad to see him. "You wanted to talk to me, Ronica?"

"There is no need for us to stay here for any length of time," I said to him, "or for any more time at all, really. I will become a Boru."

His gray eyes were suddenly filled with a warmth the like of which I hadn't seen before, and I had to look away from him because of the abruptness of my trembling.

"We will welcome you to the tribe," he said. "We ride back in the morning."

Because we had been returned to the status of guests, the Genda put Jemeret and me in a tent near the edge of the encampment. We made plans to assemble with the rest of our party at the ridge above the Tran at dawn, and then Jemeret and I were closed into the unfamiliar dimness, with the sound of the rain beating on the tent roof.

I realized that my trembling had grown worse, and that I was having trouble looking at him, but how much of the arousal was because of my camenia and how much was prompted naturally, from his strong presence, I didn't know. I had come, somehow, to want him, and I was afraid of wanting him, because I couldn't understand it, and I wasn't sure I could control it; because it smacked of need, and Sandalari had been correct about me and need.

He lit the lamp. The tent was smaller than Gundever and

Variel's, no more than a sleeping area, really. There were no furs, just a pile of thin rugs under a blanket of woven material. Jemeret dropped his cloak to the floor and stripped out of his boots, but did not remove his tunic or leggings. Instead he sat down on the bed. "I want you to tell me why you made this decision now."

I couldn't conquer my restlessness, so I paced a little at the bed's edge, then said honestly, "Because you would have had to make yourself less. *Why* would you have become a warrior of the Genda for me?"

"Some things have high prices," he answered, "and I believe you are worth whatever price I have to pay for you."

"But I'm not a Class A any longer!"

His voice was harsh. "Ronica, you persist in thinking that your worth is caused by your power."

"It always has been," I said. "All my life—"

He rose swiftly and put his arms around me, holding me still against the trembling that I was simply ignoring now. Only part of it was the unusable reflexes, reacting in fear, but I couldn't have told him that. "I want you to think that all your life has gotten you *here*," he said. "Here is where you must begin to do things differently."

I shook my head. "My worth to you is because of my talent."

"Partly," he said, stroking my shoulders. "But only partly. The rest is because of who you are inside your power." I didn't want to listen, and he actually shook me a little to make certain I could hear him. "The power in me may seek out the power in you, but the person I am under the power is what seeks out the person you are. I want you to think about that."

I couldn't explain the anger that washed over me, and I didn't try; I just gave in to it. "Why are you doing all this?" I shouted at him, pulling away. "What possible difference can it make to you whether or not I do or think about any number of things?"

And he said quietly, "It makes a difference to me because I love you."

My breath went out of me in a whoosh, the anger dissolving, and I looked at him with what must have been absolute wonder. There is no doubt that I believed him, that I drank in the words so thirstily that I instantly mistrusted myself. And mistrusting myself, I mistrusted everything. I knew instinctively that this love was different from what Coney and Kray had felt for me. Jemeret was more than my equal, and just as I couldn't allow him to be less than his potential, he couldn't allow it in me. And yet I was less.

I wanted to leave, but it was not possible. I wanted him to go away, but that wasn't going to happen, either, and I knew it. Over and around it all, I did desire him. The part of me that was him, poured into me two days before, was being drawn more and more strongly back to him. He waited, watching me.

"Jemeret, I'm not very good at this," I said at last.

"I agree with that."

I almost laughed, but it was all too serious for laughter. "I don't understand how you can love me. I haven't even been here for a tenday."

"Love isn't a time-bound phenomenon. It's a choice," he said. "I have been inside your mind, and I felt at home there. You have agreed to join my tribe, and you are beautiful and strong. Of course I love you."

His calm confidence gusted past my senses and left me once again in awe at his strength. Even knowing as I did that he had held my mind entirely in his, that he had read my spirit and knew it, I marveled at him and could not believe I would ever be capable of such risk-taking.

"I'm very confused."

"Confusion is often a sign of growth," he said. "Why don't you try to sleep now? Things will look clearer in the morning."

Suspicion bloomed inside me, and he saw it and gently shook his head. "I won't try to influence you while you sleep," he said. "I don't do that."

"I used to," I said. "I used to have that talent. We called it the sting, and I used it a lot. The government trained me to use it."

He looked away from me and began to undress, saying only, "I can't answer for your government."

I took off my tunic, but left on the leggings to hold the camenia cloths in place. I curled against the side of the tent under the blanket as he blew out the lamp. Despite the confusion and the uneasiness and the fear, despite my recognition of the need, despite any doubts I might have had, I was glad that we were going home in the morning. I didn't understand love. I'd seen too little of it for it to have become controllable.

A Class A had to have people to practice on. Class C talents practiced on themselves, and Class B talents practiced on things, but a Class A learned on people or not at all. Mortel John, Coney, and Kray were my targets as a child, most readily available. As I developed some scruples—never enough, I fear—I wanted to practice on them less and less. It never got to the point of unwilling subjects—that is, I don't think it did. And I actually got to do some good.

There is a time I remember like a shining jewel out of the grayness of adolescent schoolwork. Mortel John was called out of the classroom in which I was studying the physiology of the human brain. I was the only one of the three of us who had to study neurology, because a living brain has no path, and I was the only one who would have to find my way around the landscape of the mind.

That day, I was memorizing connectors through the corpus callosum when Mortel John came back and said, "Ronica McBride, you're needed at the hospital near Government House. Come with me, please."

I rose and followed him, excited by being needed, and excited, too, because I rarely got to go anywhere without Coney and Kray. "What is it?" I asked him. "What am I going to have to do?"

"The ambassador from Auburnese is visiting here with her husband and daughter," he said as we made for the floater garage. "The little girl has contracted therios fever."

"Wasn't she inoculated?" I was truly horrified. Therios fever was an ancient ailment, causing unbearable burning and frightening delirium. But it was relatively easy to guard against, and it usually cropped up only in someone who had been shamefully, deliberately infected.

"There was an inoculation," Mortel John said shortly, and I guessed that there was some intrigue to it that I didn't know and wasn't about to be told. We got into the floater and lifted off immediately. By that, I knew that we had top clearance, and all other floaters had been grounded to keep them out of our way.

I had been to the hospital on a day tour to see the facilities and observe the workings of physiology in vivo, but I had never come to visit anyone; the people I knew never got sick. Now I felt a thud of excitement that I was going to get to work, not just do childish influence experiments on people who mattered little in the scheme of things.

We got to the hospital faster than I would have believed we

could, but then this was the first time I'd ever been through the city on a priority clearance. Someone was waiting to take the floater as we alighted, and the staff of physicians was waiting just inside the entrance, along with some government personnel. The respect everyone showed me was a little awesome and entirely gratifying. I smiled through the introductions without actually listening to any names, until I got to the Honorable Letitia Ver Lenghy and her husband, Mockin Ebisco. The ambassador was close to tears and clasped my hands as if I were her savior. Her husband was grim-faced, trying to comfort her and regain control of himself simultaneously. Their fear and anguish were so apparent that I didn't have to read them, but I did anyway. To my surprise, I discovered that in spite of the undeniable genuineness of the emotions they were radiating, what they were really feeling, down at their most basic levels, was love.

The people on whom a Class A practices rarely feel any love during the sessions, and the depth and color of this particular emotion as I read it seared me. I stared at them, and with a completeness I cannot even now explain, I envied that little girl with therios fever—I, who had always been the envied, never the envier. At the same time that I recognized the envy, I vowed I would save the child's life for these two strangers who cared so much for her.

"Come this way, Ronica McBride," Mortel John said in a tone that made me believe he had said it once before without getting any response from me.

I followed him down a hall, with the child's parents and the assorted government officials behind me. The room we entered was divided into two by a clear lead-base acrylicine, and the child was in a bed beyond the wall. I guessed her age at almost seven. Her straw-colored hair was plastered to her head with sweat, and she writhed and tore against the restraining shield that held her to the bed.

Letitia Ver Lenghy gave an involuntary cry, quickly stifled. The girl was worse since she had last seen her.

"The inner section is very close to the freezing point," Mortel John said to me. "You'll have to adjust before you go in." He indicated a sphincter door in the side wall in our part of the room.

I looked at the ambassador. "What's her name?" I asked. I believe it was the first thing I'd said since I entered the hospital.

It was her husband who answered, his voice breaking. "Lanya."

I turned, pressed open the sphincter door, and stepped into the tunnel connecting it with the inner part of the room. Each step I took made the cold worse, and I adjusted my body temperature upward to compensate almost automatically. By the time I had crossed over the acrylicine barrier, I began to encounter the terrible power of the delusions—not the delusions themselves, but the brutal results of them on Lanya. The emanations—confusion, horror, rage—were so horrific that I bent my head to push forward through them as though a strong wind were blowing in the room. I could not shut them out and hope to reach the child, for if I did not share her pain, I could not reduce it. With as much of my strength as I could spare, I reached backward along the narrow tunnel and recontacted the outpouring of love from Ver Lenghy and Ebisco, gathering with it to give myself the will to continue.

If the battering was intense for me, I could barely imagine what it would be like for the tiny girl. Once inside the room, I had to control myself to walk steadily to the bed, still holding firmly to the thin line of love leading back through the tunnel to the other side of the clear wall. My pride would not allow me to stumble where the watching people could see it.

I rested my hand on the child's forehead and had to adjust the temperature of my palm rapidly downward to avoid being scorched by my own heat combined with hers. It took all my courage to slip through the curtain of pain and into Lanya's turbulent mind. The fever nearly knocked me off my feet. I gathered with every bit of strength I had or could draw from her parents and began calling her name, searching through the whirling storm of hate and rage for the nugget that was still the little girl.

I don't know how long it took until I found the spark and carefully surrounded it with my own being to protect it from the delusions. Lanya's body relaxed into the restraints with such suddenness that the people watching from the other half of the room must have thought she had died. Fear flooded in along the connection, and I hastily withdrew from the ambassador and her husband, signaling Mortel John to tell them what I had done.

I could barely see in the real world; all my vision was now grayness shot with discordant colors of madness. Slowly I worked my way along the girl's synapses and nerve endings, driving the fever's chemical matrices back out of the brain centimeter by centimeter. It seemed to take forever, but then I became aware, as Lanya did, that the room was very cold, and the haze of roiling delusions began to subside.

The brightness of the room startled me as my sight returned. My reserves were low, but not untenable. And the fever was back down in the child's body, at a level that could be treated. I looked over at Mortel John and saw him say something, at which the ambassador, her husband, and the medical personnel rushed through the sphincter door into the inner section of the room.

Letitia Ver Lenghy threw herself at the now sleeping child. I drew out of the little girl's mind and opened myself wide to drink in the beautiful, intense outpouring of love, even though it wasn't aimed at me.

As I lay beside Jemeret in the darkened tent among the Genda, I remembered what that had felt like. Coney's love for me had been a different thing, always constrained by who we were. Kray's love had been angry, possessive. Jemeret was the first person in my life with the potential to help me produce what I had felt in that hospital, and I so wanted to believe that he would. Sandalari had helped me to admit to myself—if not to her—that I, too, needed something. It was a desire I could not destroy, because just then I had no Class C ability available to me. I was forced to be—until I recovered—not just a person without Class A talent, but a person without any talent at all.

I must have made a sound, because Jemeret looked over at me. "Ronica?"

I honestly had no idea that I was going to say the words until they were out of me. "Make love to me."

"I want to," he said, "but I will wait until you can use your power again."

I wanted to say that I would never get all my power back, but it seemed too likely to shatter a moment I wanted to keep.

He reached out and drew me in against his side, my head on his shoulder, and I rested comfortably there for the first time. He stroked my hair and soothed me gently to sleep.

The delight shown by Gundever and Variel, and Shenefta's open joy at my return, made me conscious that I had made friends here to whom my presence or absence made a difference.

According to the laws of the tribe, once I had agreed to become a Boru, the ceremony could be scheduled for a tenday in the future, and I was to spend that time—in the words Venacrona quoted to me—in rites of purification and in learning the history and the laws of the tribe I was to join.

I learned a great deal about the Boru in that period of time—tribal rules, customs, songs, dances, history. Venacrona's assistant, the priestess, whose name was Mardalita, worked with me. It was the first time I'd ever taken instruction from a woman, and I discovered something that intrigued me. Mardalita took her tasks very seriously, but she did it with an amazing sense of fun. Mortel John had never seemed to think anything he was teaching us could be considered humorous. Mardalita found many things absurd, but liked them anyway.

During the tenday I spent mostly with the priestess, I saw very little of Jemeret, except that we still slept side by side on the rugs. There was no sexual threat from him, however, because I knew he would not touch me until my reflexes were healed. And on the day that I became a Boru, my convalescence ended, and I could gather again without pain. I suspect that Jemeret arranged it that way, though at the time I deceived myself into thinking it was a coincidence.

The Genda had camped next to us, and the Elden and the Dibel had arrived and camped beyond them. The Dibel were musicians, singers, dancers, minstrels, and showfolk, according to what I'd been told. While I hungered to get into their camp to search for a nomidar, or what passed for one here, my time was completely filled with the rituals of preparation. By the time I was to be embraced into the Boru, three more tribes had arrived: the Nedi, the Paj, and the Resni.

The embrace was scheduled, as were many Boru ceremonies, at last light. All day I had been kept with Mardalita, though Variel came in once to bring me my talma for the ceremony. The priestess fed me, bathed me, oiled my body, dressed me, fixed my hair in the series of braids coiled to make a shining crown that I'd first worn at the Lewannee stonehouse, and talked with me about incidents in her childhood, leading up to her own embrace into the tribe. "I was too young to understand," she said with some real regret, "even though I had been bleeding for two years by the Convalee of my embrace. I was originally a Nedi." She was decorating the shoulders of my silvery talma with midnight-blue rosettes. "I envy you, really. You are old enough to understand and young enough to still grow with us."

I didn't respond much. I had been conscious in the morning that my talent was accessible to me again—though of course the sting was still gone—and aware at a lower level of my being that Jemeret was also conscious of it, and that he had said he would make love to me when I had my power back. So, though I didn't try to concentrate on it, I was feeling ripples of excitement most of the day, sometimes seeming to emerge as uneasiness and sometimes as downright hunger.

By twilight I tried gathering to suppress the undercurrents, and it worked as well as it ever had. I felt a swell of gratitude and relief, but promptly put the excitement down and helped Mardalita set the silver-spangled veil over my head. We walked slowly to the sacred spring, and as we made our way through the silent camp, I asked Mardalita, "Why is it that this ceremony didn't wait until Convalee?"

She smiled gently. "I am acting at the command of my Lord Jemeret, as are we all. You had best ask him."

There was a crowd at the spring, as before when Jemeret and I had come here, but this one was smaller, more intimate. I picked out no individual faces in the dusk, and didn't iris my eyes to make it easier. Jemeret and Venacrona were standing by the head of the spring, and despite my gathering, my heart jumped at the way the new starlight highlighted the smooth planes of his face. Then I was swept up in the ritual.

Venacrona raised his hands, palms outward, and began the short series of ritual questions. Mardalita had explained to me that, if I'd been a baby of this tribe, my parents would have answered for me, but as I was grown, I would be able to make my own replies.

"From whence do you come?" the priest asked.

"From the stars," I said, as someone would have said for a newborn, only in my case it was true. Most new Boru of my age would have declared a past tribal affiliation but, of course, I had none.

"What do you seek?"

"The family of the Boru." I'd practiced saying it, but I wasn't prepared for the warm ripple that washed through me when the words were actually out.

"What are you prepared to swear?"

"Loyalty to my people, obedience to the tribal laws"—My voice trembled slightly now, in spite of my attempt to control it—"submission to my Lord Jemeret—" I forced the words to be firm. "—and an existence as part of the people of the stars."

"Who of the Boru will speak for this supplicant?"

Mardalita had told me that no one would be ordered to speak for me, and if no one spoke for me, I would be rejected. But almost before Venacrona had finished the question, Shenefta bounced to her feet, and Variel and Gundever rose almost immediately thereafter. Morien stood next, sinuously graceful, and then Urichen, Wendagash, and Numima, which I learned was astonishing, for she had never before spoken publicly.

Under the glittering veil, I looked quickly sideways at Jemeret, but he was holding his face sternly impassive.

One by one each of the tribe members who had risen spoke, saying things about their interaction with me, some of which I'd never realized they felt. It was touching, moving. Darkness set in as they talked, and when Numima was done, Venacrona spoke as well, and that I knew was unusual from the reactions of everyone else. When he was done, he added, "The speaking of the Boru is acceptable. Now the seeker may speak for herself."

This was the only part of the ceremony that Mardalita had not talked to me about. She had told me that I could not even ask her if what I wanted to say would be acceptable; I would just have to say it. I had thought long and hard about what I might say, almost wishing I *had* been an infant, so someone else could speak for me. I sensed that this would be important to everyone, and I didn't want to disappoint them by saying the wrong thing. Even now, I hesitate—I didn't want to disappoint Jemeret.

But the job of a Class A, really, is to create alternate scenarios and try to see which would work out best. So I'd tried out all kinds of replies on myself, guessing which would be likely to please the Boru most.

I took a deep lungful of air, observing that Jemeret seemed to be holding his own breath, waiting. *I am the Class A,* I said to myself, ignoring the verb tense, *and I can do this.* I said clearly, "A part of me was missing, and I did not know it until the Boru filled the emptiness."

I heard the murmurs of approval traveling through the watching tribe members, and Jemeret expelled his pent-up breath slowly and evenly. I'd guessed right. I was as pleased as if the scenario had saved the peace on a two-million-citizen world.

"I proclaim you a Boru!" Venacrona shouted in a great voice, "and we welcome you."

All of the Boru except Jemeret echoed his last words in a volume calculated to try to shake the cliffs. The Lord of the Boru stepped carefully around the springhead and drew me into his arms in what Mardalita had described as the symbolic embrace of the tribe. Only then did I lift off the veil and cast it aside, showing the face of a Boru to the tribal family.

There was no feast or celebration. Once I was actually a Boru, no further fuss needed to be made. Jemeret carried my veil and held me lightly by the arm as we walked back to his tent. We didn't speak, and I gathered continuously at a low level to keep myself from trembling visibly. At the flap of the tent, he handed me the veil and his brow-crown. "I'm going to see to the guards. Don't get undressed." He was gone before I could ask why.

I entered the tent and dropped the things on the table. There was a small flask of clogny on one of the chests, along with two cups. I eyed it, then looked over at the pile of rugs, on which a fresh blue and silver coverlet had been laid. Under the gathering, something barely recognizable stirred inside me, part known desire, part unknown fear. I ignored it.

Jemeret found me sitting on the edge of the table, beside the veil and crown, waiting for him. He fastened the tent flap and dropped his cloak on a chair. He was not smiling at me, and I became a little apprehensive.

"Do you want some clogny?" he asked.

"I'd rather you just told me what's wrong," I said.

He seemed to consider that. "I think we're about to find out. You have access to your power?"

Slowly, I nodded.

"Then it's time to see if you trust me," he said evenly, and reached out to draw me into his arms.

I want to be utterly frank about this. I wanted him to touch me. He had just embraced me at the spring, and I had not re-acted to that public, impersonal touch. I wanted him to have me. I had spent the day eagerly anticipating this moment. And as his hands slid from my shoulders to my back, to draw me closer, the reflexes I wasn't expecting at all slammed into place and hurled me across the tent away from him. He was not at all surprised; I was completely horror-struck. I think I might have screamed, "No!" but I'm not certain. I accelerated, ripped open the tent flap, and ran out into the night at full speed.

Even in the lightness of hard gathering, I stumbled a bit, but so committed was I to flight from what I didn't want to confront that it made no difference to me. Jemeret must have been cautious about expending his reserves, because it took him a surprisingly long time to catch me. I think I must have been halfway to the Tran before he brought me down, hard enough to have killed someone not under acceleration. We lay still in the grass of the silent plain, and I let go of the energy I was drawing from my reserves. Night returned as the gathering light faded. We lay still, breathing hard.

"I didn't want to do that," I said at last, my voice trembling both with fatigue and with something close to despair. "I didn't think I was going to. But you did."

He said nothing, nor did he relinquish his hold on my hips.

"How did you know?" I demanded.

Again he did not respond. I struggled upright, pulling against him with all my strength, but not gathering. He let me fight until I was exhausted and fell back, and then he released me and sat up beside my prone body in the tall, waving grasses.

"Help me!" The cry came from somewhere I didn't recognize inside me. It was as if I had used up all my resources. Yet it might have been as much rage as despair, as much demand as plea.

"You will have to help yourself, Ronica," Jemeret said expressionlessly. "Even if I were to come into your mind, I couldn't change it until after you begin to reclaim what is locked away."

I didn't want that answer; I wanted a man who, in addition to being strong, could show me what I had to do, just as Mortel John had always shown me. We slowly got to our feet. Hardly knowing I was going to do it, I swung open-handed and without gathering at his face. He was not where I was aiming when the blow passed, and his expression was unreadable in the darkness.

We went back to camp without touching, and in the tent he slept on the furs again, as he had before we began sleeping side by side in the camp of the Genda. He did nothing to try to alleviate my rage, as if I were capable of recognizing that it was directed at myself, not at him.

* * *

Coney and Kray had always been quick to try to deflect my anger. As a spoiled child, I could make life utterly miserable for them; as a spoiled adolescent, I could make it considerably worse than that. Only once that I recall did either of them stand up to me when I was in a rage, and of course it was Kray who did it. I cannot now remember the incident that originally sparked my anger, only the circumstances that resulted. We were probably about thirteen, just into the unpredictability of adolescence and the full flush of what our bodies were experiencing now that we were changing. In addition to not recalling the precipitating event, I don't remember the argument, but there was one. I only remember the fight.

We were in the common room, and I remember that I started the fight by lashing out at Kray with my still unpracticed, unrefined sting, in absolute rage that he had not given in to me. He launched himself forward despite the mental force that I was directing against him, struck me with his shoulder at about the level of my waist, and catapulted me backward onto the floor. I knocked my clenched fists against the side of his head, and he swung an arm out to knock my hands aside. By an unspoken but all-too-fully realized mutual consent, neither of us gathered to enhance the blows, and neither of us made a sound.

He tried to catch my wrists and I struck at him with the sting again, staggering him long enough for me to kick free. He pulled me down when I tried to get to my feet, and I kicked his bicep. He slapped me, open-handed, and at that my control snapped and I shot into acceleration and punched at him. Had the blow landed, I could have broken his jaw, but he accelerated a split second after I did and evaded it. As he yanked me by the arm out of the striking position, I lashed him with the sting a third time, more weakly now, and this third lash seemed to enflame him more.

Fighting while accelerated is very difficult unless you mean to kill, for it becomes harder and harder to keep the blows from reaching murderous levels. Kray lost it first, and I felt my arm snap. I closed off the pain receptors instantly and stopped trying to control my own blows.

By the time Mortel John got to us, Kray had a broken nose, a fractured cheekbone, four broken ribs, and a cracked pelvis. I had, besides the broken arm, a broken collarbone, a cracked kneecap, a dislocated wrist, and multiple contusions. Only our acceleration had saved our lives. The lectures went on for a long time after that, even as we were healing, but for some reason, after the fight was over, we seemed to have no lingering animosity toward one another—only a lasting caution about not getting ourselves into a situation like that again.

Coney, who had been away, was stunned on his return at what had occurred, but both of us just shook our heads, and I might even have said, "Being out of control isn't any fun."

"It's like going mad," Kray said.

"Make sure it doesn't happen again," Coney said, looking first at me, then at Kray, then back at me.

"It never will," I said, and Kray agreed with me.

VI. Music

Two days before Convalee was to finally begin, two very important things happened: I finally got into the camp of the Dibel, and the Marl arrived for the festival. I'm not sure why the important things in life sometimes come in bunches, as if they've been lined up beyond the horizon waiting for a gate to open, and when it does, they rush in; but that day, they did.

When I awoke, Jemeret was already gone, the furs piled away at the side of the tent. We were barely speaking. I was still angry, and both bitter and childish because of it. Jemeret seemed more sad than anything else, but it could have been my own guesswork, for he gave away very little. There were moments when I longed to return to our past easiness, but I didn't have any idea what to do to recapture it. And, to be honest, most of the time I didn't try. I was caught in my anger. It may be that I enjoyed it. And it may be that I saw any attempt at conciliation on my part as capitulation, which was, to me, shameful.

I was dressing as a warrior most of the time now, but since there was no one with enough leisure to begin training or working with me until we turned to Stronghome, I had no real fax. I had taken to returning to the tivong pens and working with Shenefta, but I had not returned to calling Sejineth Melster, nor had he demanded that I do so. He was well aware that my status had changed and that my work with him was voluntary. He didn't seem unduly discomfited by it, and Shenefta welcomed my presence.

This day, however, I was feeling particularly defiant. Even though the tribes were supposed to mingle only on invitation until the start of Convalee, the wind had brought bits of music across the open fields the night before, and I hungered for it too much to worry about obeying rules. Once I was dressed and had eaten, I slipped out of the tent and past the perimeter guards, setting off swiftly across the field toward the Dibeli camp. The day was beautiful, the wind light, and the sun pleasantly warm on my face. I had almost forgotten my anger, my frustration, even the fact that I really shouldn't have been on this world in the first place. There is a rightness to being out walking in the sun and wind that transcends personalities.

I was still several knolls off from the Dibeli camp when I heard the music begin, and I sat down on a small hill to listen for a time. I was, of course, unfamiliar with the tune, but the type of music was what we called a lasten—selections of vastly varying melodies between passages of steady, almost predictable patterns. I could pick out at least four individual instruments, and I found it strange that they were all familiar to me. The beat was being kept by a large, deep-voiced throm, hand-beaten, rather than with sticks. The major melodic instruments were the canita, a larger, nonsympathetic version of the nomidar, and the stigol, a wind instrument whose reedy voice could both sink and soar. The back melody and the undercurrents were carried by the diplick, a keyboard device with metal strips plucked or rubbed by pressure on other pieces of metal.

The musicians were very good. The melodies were fairly complex and relatively independent of one another, and I didn't hear a single missed note. When the song ended, I got up and walked toward the camp again. There were no guards, nor did I expect any. The Dibel were pacifists—there was no honor in attacking them, so they were safe from attack.

I slipped in among the tents as quietly as I could. I did not want to cause any kind of incident, but I wanted to see if there were nomidars here. I had higher hopes now that I had heard other instruments I knew. I extended the range of my hearing outward, and there was music everywhere: singing, playing, the rhythmic clapping and outcries that came with dancing. These were happy people—just the fact of their singing made them seem effervescent and alive.

Some saw me and smiled at me, but seemed to pay little attention to a stranger in their midst. I was about to approach one hurrying woman with a bundle of laundry in her plump arms when my augmented hearing picked up the characteristic sounds of a nomidar off to my right among the tents. I spun and ran in that direction, feeling the hunger to have the instrument in my hands again.

The nomidar music grew more distinct as I approached. It was a sweet country air, wandering, gentle, and comfortably simple. I rounded a corner of a tent and came upon a young man dressed raffishly in an outfit that contrived to look like multicolored rags, strumming a lightwood nomidar whose head was strung with ribbons. The instrument had a thinner, brighter tone than mine had had, but it seemed to have a slower action. The young man looked up and saw me gazing at his fingering and at the nomidar with what must have been the face of a starving woman looking at food. His cascade of notes trailed off, and without a moment's hesitation he spun the instrument out at arm's length and offered it to me.

I reached out as quickly as I could, without acceleration, and the feeling of the smooth, highly polished wood against my palms was so familiar and so welcome that I almost cried. Without being aware of anyone or anything around me, I sat cross-legged on the ground, rested my cheek against the head of the nomidar, and began to play one of my favorite songs, "The Music." It was a fast, searingly bright melody that danced along the scales of the neckboard to resolve gaily in a satisfying major run at the end.

As it always did, the music enveloped me and enriched me, to the point where its ending left me feeling bereft. I sat still in the fading echoes of the notes until a voice said, "Go on, play again," and I opened my eyes to see the colorful young man leaning close to me, also cross-legged on the ground, with an expression on his serious face much like the one on mine must have been before he handed me the instrument. Reluctant to surrender the nomidar, but unaccountably shy, I asked, "What do you want me to play?"

"Something sympathetic," he said.

I knew at once what he meant, but I'd never played a sympathetic piece without my projective abilities, and I found myself hesitant to leave the technical for the emotional. The nomidar had a resonating capacity of its own, but I had always augmented that. Then I took another look at the intense concentration on his face, and I knew I had to try it. I chose a very simple piece, one from my earliest days as a nomidartist.

"I will interpret a line from a rhyme by Odenska," I said. " 'The child who sleeps is a hesitation in the dance.' "

My fingers fell into the quiet chords almost automatically, and I was carried back to the small, tree-shaded courtyard in the home of the teacher Maur, where I'd first picked up a nomidar. I closed my eyes and was again somehow a child, still innocent, still amazingly tyrannical, but also still utterly convinced of the rightness of my actions and my choices. The melody rose up, simple and true, gentle and soft. The song wasn't long, and very soon I let the echoes fade and slowly, almost reluctantly, opened my eyes.

"My name is Dirian," the young man said. "How can you know such music and not be Dibeli?"

"I am a Boru," I said. I realized I was still holding the nomidar. Since I didn't want to give it up, I had to force myself to extend my arm in his direction. When he took the nomidar back, I felt such a wrench that it must have shown.

"They will be for sale on the Day of the Sheaf," Dirian said. "Some of Tendoro's best work, I think."

"For sale? You mean I can get one?" My voice scaled up in hope and disbelief.

"Of course."

Then I became aware that a group of people had gathered, probably while I was playing, and that I had to get away, fast. I got to my feet.

"Wait. What's your name?" Dirian asked quickly, scrambling to his feet as I got up.

But by that time I was nervous. Too many people had heard me declare a tribal affiliation. I spun and ran.

In one of his more pedantic and pompous moments, Mortel John had said that life was only a very small part planning, that most of life was simply a reconciliation of the "ifs." Coney, Kray, and I had laughed about that later, and Kray had done one of his more incisive Mortel John imitations. Kray had begun perfecting his impression of Mortel John one day when we were nine. Long observation had lifted it from parody to true caricature, and affection tempered both his actions and our response to them.

I didn't know what Mortel John meant by the "ifs"—I had remembered what he said as much because of Kray's imitation as because of the words themselves—until that day on the plain, fleeing from the Dibeli camp. I was by myself when I saw the Marl arrive. I've gone over the ifs so many times in my mind since then: If I hadn't run off from the Boru camp to follow the music; if Jemeret had found me later than he did; if I had played only one piece, or three; if the Marl had arrived a little earlier in the day, as they were supposed to; if—in short—I had first seen the Lord of the Marl in the company of Jemeret, then it is possible that my reaction to him might have been unstoppable, and a great many subsequent events might have been pushed off course.

But because I was alone when I first saw my Lord Ashkalin, there was an unrecognized inevitability to my future, as there had been to my past.

I had run headlong from the Dibeli camp into the afternoon without a real destination in mind. Perhaps I was on my way back to the Boru camp. I topped a rise in the long grass and saw the train of the Marl riders and wagons just in front and across from me. I could have accelerated and run in front of the column, but I was uncertain if an accelerated approach might be seen as a threat. Instead, then, I sat down in the tall grass to wait for them to pass.

Ashkalin rode at the head of the second portion of the column, so I didn't know at first that he was the tribe leader. Nor would it have mattered. Because when I saw him, I thought I was looking at Kray—bearded, twenty years older than I remembered him, but Kray as he would become, a familiar, much valued person from a world and a life I still wanted to return to.

I may have cried out; I don't remember. I did leap to my feet, and Ashkalin's eyes found me at once—piercing, brown, so utterly well-known to me. Then, totally unexpectedly, the field of my vision went dark red with a rage as unmotivated and uncontrolled as my fear of Jemeret's body had been. Ashkalin's tivong shifted under him and reared up, and he fought it back down and forced its head toward the hillside.

In the grip of the rage, I started toward the side of the hill myself, and then I was flattened by a flying tackle from behind. The ground struck me with a force that knocked the rage out of me, even through the cushion of the grasses. As I returned to control, I recognized Jemeret's hands on my arms and felt his mouth lightly brush my hair before he jerked me to my feet.

Jemeret and Ashkalin faced each other directly, and I felt like an unimportant bystander in the confrontation. Neither man spoke for a moment as Ashkalin pulled his tivong more firmly around. Then Jemeret nodded, and Ashkalin said, "We got here a little late."

"So I gathered," Jemeret said. "My Lord Ashkalin, Chief of the Marl, this is the Lady Ronica, my claim."

Ashkalin nodded to me. "An eventful acquaintance, my Lady Ronica."

And I said steadily, "I thought you were Kray."

"Crazy?" he repeated. "You're the one who frightened my mount."

I wasn't sure how he had misheard me, but I didn't get a chance to correct him. Jemeret's hand tightened abruptly on my arm. "She didn't say crazy," he said carefully. "She said the name of someone she once knew and deeply cared for."

Ashkalin returned his gaze to me and made a half bow. "In that case, my lady, you do me honor. I hope I may look forward to a touch of yours on the Day of the Clouds."

He even sounded like I thought Kray would have sounded when he reached the age of forty. His face, deeply tanned, deeply lined, was Kray's face made more complete, more fulfilled, with more of life in it and on it, but otherwise the same.

Jemeret realized I was not going to respond. "The lady would be pleased," he said. He and Ashkalin exchanged another glance that seemed charged, nodded to one another, and then the leader of the Marl turned his mount's head back and rejoined his train.

"How did you know who Kray is?" I demanded of Jemeret, pulling my arm free of his grasp.

"You persist in forgetting I've been inside your mind," he said calmly.

I shook my head. "I've been inside minds," I said, "and you don't get names out of them."

"I do," he said. "Come back now."

"And, wait, why did you introduce me to him as the Lady Ronica?"

"You're a Boru now, and as my claim you carry that status. I thought you understood that."

I had missed it somewhere along the line, in the tenday of training. But I had another issue to pursue. "I was in the camp of the Dibel," I said to him as if he'd asked me where I'd been. "I could have been a Dibel."

He smiled and gently shook his head. "Not you," he said. "Not once you killed Evesti. Had you been a Dibel, they would have had to sell you or cast you out, because to harbor you would risk attack on the whole tribe."

I remembered in a rush that in a very real sense I *had* been cast out. The only "tribe" I had ever known had sent me here. In the echo of reawakening to exile, my anger at him died away, following the unreasoning rage that had hurled me at Ashkalin. "Jemeret, would the Boru ever cast me out?" I asked him, suddenly worried, aware of how even this morning I had defied their rules without thinking twice about it.

He took my arm again, and I did not pull away. "I want you to think that *I* will never cast you out," he said deliberately, "and I am the Boru."

I wonder now why I didn't wonder then where the rage had come from. It had washed over me and let me be, and I had simply let it go. Of my own volition, as we walked back toward the camp of the Boru, I gently, slowly, thoughtfully drew my arm out of his and took his hand. It was a concession, but it was not a conciliation, I thought then. It was a recognition that I didn't know what was going on but that I did know, having become part of the Boru, I wanted to remain there.

The Day of the Sheaf

Bright sunlight moved from behind the morning clouds on the first day of Convalee. Jemeret had gone from the tent early to arrange for the transfer of the tivongs to the fields where they would be sold. He still slept on the furs, but we were both aware that I had started to miss his presence beside me. I thought that perhaps he would not reach for me again because he'd reached once and I had flung myself away from him. I thought perhaps he was waiting for the initiative to come from me, but that I couldn't do. I had been able once to ask him to make love to me, and he had chosen not to. I knew I would never bring myself to ask again.

Instead of warrior garb, I had been left a bright blue talma edged in a soft, smoky silver. I put it on over the pale gray shift without hesitation. These were the colors of the tribe, and I was pleased to be wearing them. I was also very excited, for today I might be able to get myself a nomidar. While I was binding my hair the trumpets that heralded Convalee sounded, and I hurried out of the tent to join Variel and Shenefta, who were eager to begin exploring the marketplace. Morien had wanted to join us, but I wasn't distressed not to see her. Shenefta talked on about this first Convalee as an adult, and perhaps I should have listened, for it was my first Convalee ever. But my mind was on the nomidar—getting it, cradling it, uniting with it to lose myself in the making of music.

Now that all the tribes of the Samoth had assembled, there were over two thousand people on the plains, in different costumes and different colors, but most wore their tribal colors somehow in their clothes. Variel looked flushed, bright, and lovely, and I envied her simplicity without realizing that it was actually the healthiest thing about her to envy.

There were guardsmen everywhere, in outfits of their tribes, and all three of us shied wordlessly away from the brown and red of the Ilto. They also seemed interested in staying away from me, but I barely noticed, just as I barely noticed that the three of us made our way very easily through the crowds that seemed to part for us.

Variel touched my arm as we neared the booths of the Elden. "Ronica, I need some cloth for a talma for the Day of the Fire," she said.

Shenefta bounced excitedly. "You will be braceleted by Gundever!" she said. "We all guessed it."

Variel's color heightened and she seemed embarrassed, but she spoke with dignity. "We intend to ask, and we can only hope that the stars will find us worthy."

I didn't want to be drawn away from my quest for a nomidar, but I also did not want to be alone, so I went with them to the Elden booths, bright with heaped fabrics, finely woven rugs, cushions and drapes, from light materials to heavy knits and trappings for the tivongs. Variel and Shenefta headed along the booths chattering about the tribal colors until they reached a booth of blues. Then they stopped and held various shades of blue talma cloth across Variel's creamy, high-colored cheek. I had barely paid attention until I saw Shenefta hold up an exquisite length of sky-blue edged with deep violet flowers. It made Variel look almost as beautiful as Sandalari, and I said, "Yes, that's the one. You ought to get that."

Variel smiled at me, her eyes alight, and then turned to the Elden manning the booth and asked the price. A long negotiation followed, during which I stood amazed. Though I knew they were for sale, it had never occurred to me that I would have to *pay* for the nomidar. I had no money, and had not thought to ask Jemeret for any. Now, as Variel concluded the negotiation, she drew a small bag from under her talma and gave the man a number of bead tokens.

Shenefta prodded me surreptitiously. "What's the matter?" she asked in a hiss that nearly qualified as a whisper. "You look green."

"I don't have any money," I whispered back. "I don't think I can get the nomidar I want."

She wrinkled her nose. "Let's see what they want for it anyway."

Variel had wrapped up the length of blue cloth and now she looked over at me. "Ronica, you should pick out some talma material for the Day of the Fire, too," she said softly. "My Lord Jemeret will certainly seek to bracelet you."

I shook my head automatically, but only said, "Everything he wants me to have he has someone bring to me. If he wants me to have a new talma, he'll give me one."

Shenefta and Variel exchanged a quick glance. Variel was gently insistent. "No, the talma for the Day of the Fire must be of your choosing. It's a Boru custom."

"I don't have any money," I said. "I couldn't buy any talma material anyway."

"I have enough," Variel said. "Let me buy it for you. You can repay me after you get your settlement from the tivong sale."

I thought of refusing, but both women seemed to want me to agree, and I was interested in getting to the booth of the Dibel Tendoro. So I reached for the lengths of talma material, but the Elden boothholder stopped me. "I have a length set aside."

He bent down and picked up a small parcel, which he laid on the counter. I opened it. Inside were two lengths of fabric, a gauzy deep blue for the undergarment, and a metallic silver shot through with threads of five shades of blue, from pale to midnight. It was among the most beautiful pieces of material I had ever seen. I ran my hand lightly over it, almost afraid I'd injure it, but it was sturdier than it looked.

"Did my Lord Jemeret arrange this?" I asked him.

The Elden shook his head. "I have heard of the Lady Ronica," he said. "The Elden, too, hope for the Foretelling."

"How much for this?" Variel asked, reaching for her purse again.

He named a price and said, "There can be no bargaining on this."

Variel paid, and I noticed that she used fewer tokens than her own talma material had cost. Shenefta rewrapped the parcel and handed it to me.

"Thank you," Variel said to the boothholder, and I nodded to him, uncertain what to say. He shrugged a little and smiled as we left the booth and went back into the crowd.

I felt embarrassed and touched, and didn't realize how far I had come from the time in which I felt reverence was expected and kindness no more than my due. "I don't know how to sew. Who makes this up?" I asked.

"You do, despite your lack of ability," Variel said, unperturbed. "We'll make our talmas together. We better start when we get back this evening, because we won't have much free time in the next couple of days."

Shenefta skipped a little as we went past the booths of the Resni, who were selling drink. They were doing a good business, for many of the tribes could not make their own liquors, lacking access to the ingredients. I wondered briefly at some of the more exotic-looking bottles—another product of the Genda—but we didn't stop to sample. Up ahead were the Dibeli booths.

The other women let me lead—and this area was not as populous as many of the others. It was a small tribe, and the most crowded booths were those that booked performing schedules, for all the tribes wanted singers, dancers, or showfolk to stop by and play for them during the year. Farther on, where the individual instruments were for sale, not that many people had gathered. I hesitated for a moment at a fine display of stigols, for I loved the rich, reedy voice of the instrument, but I played only at a base level of competency, and for me that wasn't nearly enough. Then I looked ahead and saw Dirian standing in front of a booth, restless but obviously unwilling to leave.

He saw me just after I noticed him, said something to the man in the booth, and sprinted toward me. "There you are!" he said. "Come on. Tendoro's been waiting to meet you."

He gestured back toward the booth he'd come from. Shenefta pushed up against my side and cleared her throat loudly. I glanced at her, a little bewildered, and realized from the expression in her eyes that she liked the way Dirian looked and wanted to meet him.

I was getting better at reading people in the small ways they read each other, rather than with Class A talent. The process was subtle, and made easier by the caring I felt for Shenefta and Variel. Slowly, I was starting to understand what was possible without talent.

"Hello, Dirian," I said, a little bemused. "This is Shenefta and Variel, both of the Boru." I looked at the other two women and added unnecessarily, "Dirian is Dibeli." They murmured hellos, and Dirian nodded hastily, barely seeing them. He half urged, half herded us toward the booth.

I saw the nomidars before I saw Tendoro. There were five of them, slightly different sizes, in different woods, all highly polished, each with a decoration of ribbons or flowers at its head. Tendoro was almost as old as Venacrona. His skin was pale, and soft with the softness that great age brings, and he seemed so fragile as to be easily broken. His hair was white and thinning, but shoulder-length at the back, and he wore the violet and yellow Dibeli colors with the kind of pride that indicated he felt a sense of ownership.

"So this is the nomidartist," he said, his voice stretched and brittle, like parchment. "The other musician among the Boru."

"I am Ronica McBride," I said to him, but I didn't offer to shake hands, out of fear of hurting him somehow. I wanted to be polite and keep looking at him, but I couldn't take my eyes off the nomidars.

"Try them," Dirian urged. "See which is for you."

"I don't have any money," I said reluctantly.

Variel stepped up to the counter beside me. "The Lady Ronica can speak for the tribe's debt," she said firmly to Tendoro.

He smiled. "I would not be concerned with putting the Boru in debt for a true musician," he said, his voice barely audible. "Here." He handed me the nearest nomidar, and it did not waver in his hand.

It was heavier than I was accustomed to, and the first few notes showed me that it was tone-bound. The instrument would be fine for group work, but it would never stand alone. I shook my head and laid it aside.

Tendoro gave me another. This was far above average in tone, but it lacked the rich undertones so essential to sympathetic melodies. For a moment or two I was tempted, knowing how weak I now was in sympathetic music, but just as I could not have seen Jemeret be lessened, I could not deliberately choose to lessen myself. I shook my head and gave it back.

Tendoro's eyes glistened. He reached behind him for a nomidar made of a kind of richly dark wood I had never seen before. Its ribbons were the Dibeli colors, and its bowl and fingerboards almost sweetly curved to match one another. When I cradled it, it fit me perfectly. I ran a scale on its straight neck, and knew in an instant that this was the best instrument I'd ever touched. Its voice was rich and full, the sympathetic undertones powerfully available. In the higher ranges it had a brilliance that almost awed me, and its depths were sonorous. I looked at Tendoro with astonishment and deep respect. "This is a master nomidar," I said. "You must truly have been inspired."

"I would like to hear you play it before I set a price," the old man said, his voice less wispy than before.

I hesitated, not knowing if it was proper. Variel and Shenefta looked at one another, then smiled and sat down on one of the benches scattered throughout this market. Dirian bounced impatiently at the side of the booth, nodding. I wanted to play; I did not want to perform. I had never been a performer. My music had always been mine, revealed only to those I felt close to, except for Dirian, when I needed to play more than I needed to be private. But I wanted this nomidar, and I saw that I would have to earn it.

There was a nocturne I had taught myself while I was still on Werd, written by someone blind from birth, as my first teacher had been—blind in a way that would not lend itself to repair, for repair can only take place when the structure is there to begin with. I had never really been satisfied with the way I played it, for it spoke deeply of a sorrow I had not previously felt and a hope I had never thought I needed. I cradled the wine-dark instrument, closed my eyes, and began to play. It was not a piece to demonstrate technical virtuosity, but it was hauntingly beautiful. It was not a piece to demand great sympathetic power, because it was masterly in itself. Even as I lost myself in the delicacy of its growth and grandeur, I knew that I had never played it better.

It was not a long piece; I rarely chose to play long works, because I was uneasy about losing myself in them for too long. The nomidar was magnificent. In the silence of its last reverberation, I heard Dirian exhale, releasing such a burst of pent-up breath that I wondered if he'd stopped breathing the whole time I was playing.

Shenefta got to her feet. "Was that as good as I thought it was?"

Variel shushed her and pulled her back down, but Tendoro just nodded gravely at her. "It was superior," he said, and to me, "My dear, I have set the price."

"What is it?" I asked, my fingers tightening on the finger-board in reflex against letting the instrument go.

"Tomorrow is the Day of the Laba," the old man said. "The game of the Dibel will be the nomidar. You must enter, and if you win, the nomidar will be yours."

"That's not fair!" Dirian said hotly. "You know she'll have to compete against—"

Tendoro raised his hand and Dirian fell instantly silent.

"This nomidar," Tendoro said, his voice now surprisingly strong, "will be the prize in tomorrow's game." He held out his hands for it.

I wanted just to take it and run, but that would have dishonored me, and my honor had somehow become the tribe's honor. I looked down at my hand, which had not unclenched, and exerted my Class C skills to make my arms move the nomidar away from me. As he took it back, I asked Dirian, "Who do I have to compete against?"

He glanced at Tendoro, then shook his head. I guessed.

Variel gathered up her package and mine, and said to me, "I can tell you that, Ronica." She and Shenefta rose, and the younger girl took my talma material from Variel, who added, "You will have to compete against my Lord Jemeret."

I should not have been surprised. "Jemeret is a nomidart-ist?"

"He won the game twelve years ago," Tendoro said. "It is not played every Convalee."

"Is it against the rules for me to best the man who claims me?" I asked. All four of the people shook their heads no, but even as they did, I realized that if I beat Jemeret, he would, once again, be lessened. And then, belatedly, it occurred to me that I could not win a contest against someone whose sympathetic skills had to be so superior to my own. I felt many emotions in rapid succession—sadness, anger, self-pity—and then I looked straight at Tendoro.

"You've heard me play," I said. "Do I have a chance?"

And he said, "Yes."

It was enough. I took my package away from Shenefta and asked Variel, "Where else do we need to go?"

In all the worlds of the Com, there was no drink to match shateen. It was made from the flowers of the banade, a shrub that grew only at the highest area of vegetation on Ludurn and bloomed only once in twenty years. If any mechanical devices were brought near the banade before or during its blooming phase, the blooms died immediately, so the flowers had to be harvested by hand, by climbers who took extreme physical risks to bring the blossoms back for distillation.

Coney, Kray, and I had drunk shateen only once, just before graduation, at a dinner in our honor given by the governing council on Orokell. There was one bottle of shateen on the table, and the minister opened it himself and poured it into the long-stemmed gold and crystal cups. My first sip was like distant thunder that rushed closer as I swallowed it. Kray whistled softly under his breath, and Coney made a small gasp, as if he had risen from deep water with aching lungs. The second sip was like being dipped in fragrant feathers—every nerve in my body began to hum and vibrate, and my thoughts drew inward. The third sip put colors on all the people in the room, a kaleidoscope of hues and shades, bright and pastel in turn. I think I may have started to giggle, and I don't remember much of the rest of the evening. We knew, Kray and Coney and I, that we would never again drink anything as fine.

I reflected on the shateen as I sipped clogny at the evening meal on the Day of the Sheaf, alone with Jemeret. I knew as surely as I knew about the shateen that I would never again play a nomidar nearly as fine as the one I'd given back to Tendoro. Jemeret had been quiet during most of the meal, but I'd only noticed it in passing, for I was self-absorbed. Finally I looked over at the Lord of the Boru. "Would it humiliate you if you were to lose one of the games tomorrow?"

He almost smiled, and I sensed that in his quiet he had been waiting for me to start the conversation. "Do you think I'm going to lose a game?"

"The Dibeli game," I said, and watched my hand playing with the stem of the clogny goblet. "They say you play the nomidar."

"And they say I won the game the last time it was played." So he had known about what happened at Tendoro's booth. "I gather you want to play."

"I *have* to play." The words leaped out of me. I looked up at his level gaze. "I have to have the nomidar that's going to be the prize." He said nothing. And I, unaware, said a great truth: "I need it. I've lost too much else."

He didn't nod, but I sensed an understanding. "Are you asking me not to compete?" he asked reasonably.

I couldn't respond to that. It seemed to me that he shouldn't have had to ask the question. I wasn't asking him to do any-thing; I was telling him he had to lose. The silence stretched on between us because I didn't know what to say, and it must have been clear on my face. Finally Jemeret said, "There are very few nomidartists outside the Dibel, and, of course, no member of a tribe can enter its own game. I would hate to see you succeed by default."

"*Will* I succeed?" I asked him.

His face was unreadable, probably by his own design. "I haven't heard you play," he said. I knew then that he would not let himself be beaten. If I were to win, it would have to be because I was better than he was—significantly better, too, for he was a tribe leader, and he was a Class A talent. Something twisted deep inside me at the thought of not having that nomidar, of not being able to play it again, and then I slammed a rigid control around it and lifted my head.

"You'll hear me tomorrow," I said as steadily as I could.

His eyes gleamed suddenly with an emotion I neither recog-nized nor understood, but he only said mildly, "I'm looking forward to it."

Then Variel scratched at the tent flap, her arms full of talma material.

The Day of the Laba

In any given Convalee, four of the ten tribes of the Samoth sponsored games on the Day of the Laba. The tribes to sponsor and provide prizes were chosen by lot by the priests, and the members of a sponsoring tribe could not play in its game. In this Convalee, the sponsoring tribes were the Genda, the Nedi, the Paj, and the Dibel. Most tribes picked games in which they themselves excelled, even though they could not compete; that told me why the Dibel always picked something having to do with music or the performing arts.

The order of the games was chosen by lot, and, according to the rules, anyone who wanted to could enter up to three games, but few did. Many people simply preferred to watch, for the games were revealing of strengths and weaknesses, and pride dictated a good showing. The only exception seemed to be made for the children, who were encouraged to play as often and as far above themselves as they could, even without a chance of winning, and who were never castigated in defeat, but only praised for trying. Besides, entertainment was rare enough in the Samothen that an opportunity to be a spectator was not often passed up. One of the attractions of Convalee itself was the chance to be amused.

The Genda had won the right to put their game on first, and they had chosen a marksmanship contest using the agerin, the pellet-armed weapon used by many of the guardsmen. The pacifist tribes—the Paj, the Dibel, and the Elden—all chose to be spectators, rather than contestants, and the Nedi preferred the longbow to the crossbow and did not have many practitioners. So after Sabaran of the Genda announced the first qualifying round, in which fifty people could shoot, aiming at bales of straw with target cloths draped over them, the field seemed crowded with Ilto, Vylk, Resni, Marl, and Boru, about ten each.

Jemeret, Gundever, Variel, and I were at the front of the great amphitheaterlike bowl in which this game would take place, and it was crowded with Samothen. I listened vaguely to the two men discussing the merits of some of the contestants, then watched as the Genda set the qualifying rules: the top score would move into the second level, no matter how many people attained it. The first batch of contestants yielded two qualifiers, a Resni and a Marl, who had each scored eight center hits out of ten. The other forty-eight people were eliminated.

"I can do eight out of ten," Gundever said. "I'm going in."

"The stars guide your hand," Jemeret said warmly. "I'm not a proponent of the agerin."

And I heard myself ask, "Can women play?"

Variel's eyes grew momentarily larger, but Jemeret said, "If a woman can use an agerin, she can play."

"I want to play," I said.

Variel took my arm and pulled, which was so unlike her that I almost thought Shenefta had snuck up on us. "Excuse us," she said to the men. She drew me aside in front of the crowd as the next first-level qualifying round began.

"What is it?" I asked her, curious.

"A tribe lord—and his lady—have to be very careful what they play," Variel said, with some urgency in her voice. "Ronica, if you are badly beaten, it will mean a loss for my Lord Jemeret."

I recognized her concern, smiled, and patted her hand lightly. "Variel, trust me."

"Have you ever fired an agerin?" she asked, persisting.

"No," I said honestly, "but I know about ballistics, and I've fired lots of other things. I want a chance to try."

Then the second of the first-level rounds was done, and Gundever called to me. "Come on, if you're coming, my lady." By that, I knew Jemeret had told him it was all right for me to go into the game, and so did Variel. I seethed a bit at needing his permission, but I was beginning to understand it.

Gundever and I took targets next to each other, close to the near end of the line. I was the first woman to have entered the game, and I was dressed in a talma, not as a warrior, so there were some murmurs as I picked up the agerin. It was heavier than I had expected, and I adjusted my muscles to compensate for the weight. The Gendal who was distributing pellets gave a handful to Gundever and then paused, my pellets in his hand. I watched his glance stray over my shoulder—to Jemeret, I knew, asking permission. For a moment the anger swept over me, and I stood perfectly motionless, hand outstretched. When the Gendal put the pellets into it, I knew that Jemeret had nodded. I wanted to throw the pellets back into the Gendal's face, but if I had, I would not have been able to participate in the game.

The men slid their pellets into the sleeves of their tunics, but the talma presented me with no such opportunity. I knelt on one knee, rested the agerin on the other, and let all but one of the pellets slide out of my hand onto the ground beside me.

Gundever made a slight noise. When I glanced upward at him, he pulled his bowstring taut past the pocket in which the firing pellet was to lie. I smiled fleetingly at him, nocked the bowstring, loaded the first pellet, aimed from my knee, and fired. The pellet pulled down and to the left. I nocked, loaded, compensated, aimed, and fired again. This time the pellet struck a hair higher than center, and to the right. I'd overcompensated minutely.

But now I had the distance, the angle, and the parabola. The next eight shots were true. The Gendal judges waved me to the group that had qualified for the second round, and Gundever joined me there.

"Very good," he said. "I didn't know you knew the agerin."

"I know shooting," I said. I didn't look over at Variel and Jemeret; I didn't want to know what expression was on Jemeret's face.

Forty-five of us qualified for the second round, and one of

the targets was taken away, target cloths replaced on the other nine. I was, indeed, the only woman. The second round consisted of thirty shots, and the first top score was twenty-seven true. I could get neither the target nor the agerin I'd used in the first round, and the agerin I got had a slightly longer tip-to-pellet ratio. My first shot was directly above center; the other twenty-nine were true.

Sixteen contestants qualified for the third round. Gundever and I were the only Boru, and I realized with a start that one of the five qualifying Marl was Ashkalin, looking more than ever like Kray in a deep gray tunic edged with shiny red-gold. He nodded at me once in mixed recognition and respect as the Genda removed another target and replaced the cloths.

Sabaran announced that the third round would require fifty shots, of which forty-six had to be true, no matter what the first group of contestants did. It was a stiff order. Most of the contestants were tiring slightly. Pulling the bowstring was a strain itself, but aiming was even more debilitating. I had entered the edges of my reserves, gathering to hold the heavy weapon steady.

For this round I was able to keep the agerin from round two, and all fifty of my shots were true. Ashkalin, one of the Ilto, and I survived into the final round. Gundever had missed by only one shot, and had acquitted himself well. I realized that I could also withdraw now with honor, but the presence of Ashkalin made it impossible. Kray and I had fought for dominance for too long.

"When did you learn to shoot an agerin, Lady Ronica?" the Lord Ashkalin asked me as the Genda removed all but the last three targets.

"Just now," I said honestly, hearing Kray's mocking voice under the polite tones of the Marl leader.

His eyes widened a little at the response, and he bowed his head almost imperceptibly as he moved back to his own target. I still could not look at Jemeret.

Sabaran announced a round of a hundred shots, the best score to win. It would be grueling, but that was the point. I turned off my mind, fixed my arm and the trajectory, and simply fired until I had no more pellets. When the pellets were gone, I got to my feet and put down the agerin. The Ilto had missed with his sixtieth shot and stopped to watch. Ashkalin had missed his eighty-ninth shot and stopped. I had not missed a shot.

My arm was trembling with weariness as I rose, and I became aware of the low, appreciative mutter of the crowd. For the first time, I looked at Jemeret, and even though his face was held carefully expressionless, his eyes were glowing with a fierce pride. It might have vanished or lingered—I couldn't say. Without warning, another door opened in my memory.

The graduation program took place in a large hall with a great many government dignitaries on hand. I remembered being seated on the platform with my two classmates, listening to Com Counselor Pel Nostro praise our accomplishments openly to the audience. I remembered fastening on Mortel John, huge and solid in the first row, not looking to me any older than he had when he had begun training me so long before.

"These three people have made choices of sacrifice," the Counselor said, his amplified voice rolling out over the assembled officials. "The Com is proud to number such citizens as part of its own."

The memory shut down, and I found Jemeret at my side, his hand on my still-trembling arm, leading me back to our places in the crowd. "Is everything all right?" he asked, his voice barely audible.

I nodded. Variel squeezed my hand as I sat down beside her. "You were wonderful," she said. "I should never have thought of stopping you."

"My Lady Ronica."

I looked up, startled, to see Ashkalin of the Marl standing in front of me. "My Lord Ashkalin," I said almost automatically. He nodded once, deep enough to constitute a bow, then nodded more briefly to Jemeret and moved away, toward a group of his own people partway around the bowl.

The prize was a fine new agerin, carefully crafted, and I accepted it with pleasure.

The second game was the Paj's, and they had decided on a footrace, as their messengers were the swift carriers who kept the tribes in contact with one another. The qualifying heats were of about six kilometers' length. The race itself would be twenty kilometers. A number of the Boru went to enter, but except for Wendagash, none were people I knew. Variel talked softly to me of her last Convalee, of how proud she'd been of Gundever even then, and I smiled and nodded; I was trying very hard to recapture more of my memory, but it eluded me.

Then I felt Jemeret's fingertips lightly brush my arm, and I turned toward him. "Come with me," he said. We left the great bowl, heading back to the encampment. I realized that there were a number of other small groups making their way back—I identified the form of Venacrona among them, and I thought I also glimpsed Sabaran and his son.

All at once Jemeret stopped and turned. Behind us came Sejineth, looking sober. I think now there must have been great rage under his seemingly placid exterior, but I still could not always read the subtle clues. I was therefore surprised at the harshness of his voice when he said, "I *am* still a Councillor, my lord."

"So you are," Jemeret said easily, "but this is not a full Council. Your presence is not sought."

Sejineth thrust his chin at me, his eyes glittering, and said, "She isn't a Councillor at all."

"You know full well who she is," Jemeret said, his tone a little harder.

"I know what you hope she is!" Sejineth said shortly.

Jemeret drew in a slow breath and slowly released it. "If you are a Boru only by virtue of your fax, and not by your own inclination, you are free to choose your own path."

Sejineth seemed to stumble even though he had not been moving. He spun and ran back toward the crowd gathered on the gaming field. Jemeret took my arm again and led me in the other direction.

"He's angry," I said unnecessarily.

"He's been angry for a long time. Try not to let it worry you."

I almost laughed. It was as if I hadn't enough things to worry about and would therefore worry about Sejineth, whom I thought about as little as possible. I recognized Ashkalin, and beyond him, Ustivet. I guessed that this was to be a meeting of the leaders of the tribes.

"This is the Inner Council," Jemeret said, as if reading my mind. "We bring two people from each tribe and two of the priests into session."

"Was this expected?" I asked.

"Not until the Day of the Bell," he said. "But we've gotten a message that a group of stonehouseholders is meeting at the Lewannee stonehouse. That may mean nothing, or it may mean trouble."

"What kind of trouble?"

He cast me one quick, sidelong glance, then took my hand and led me to the growing circle of people. Venacrona stood at its center. When he seemed satisfied with the attendance, he sat, and so did everyone else. "I am Venacrona," he said, though I was certain that everyone in the circle knew him. "I speak for the stars with my friend Sandalari." The tall blond woman, about a quarter of the way around the circle from me, nodded.

Beside her, Sabaran spoke. "I am Sabaran, and I speak for the Genda with my son, Sheridar." On his other side, Sheridar nodded. There was a lithe, graceful woman beside Sheridar, who said, "I am Lyrafi. I speak for the Dibel, with my brother, Orion." They were both young, relatively handsome, and seemingly quite at their ease. In spite of my minute as Chief of the Ilto, I had not seriously entertained the notion that a woman would be a tribe leader, and I was quite interested in studying her, serene under the thin gold circlet of leadership. I missed the leaders of the Vylk and the Resni introducing themselves and the men they had brought with them.

Then I heard Ashkalin say in Kray's voice, "I am Ashkalin, and I speak for the Marl with my companion at arms, Moonelin." I realized that I was the next person in line, sitting beside the stocky Moonelin. I looked at Jemeret, uncertain. "I am Jemeret and this is Ronica," he said evenly. "We speak for the Boru."

Before I even had a chance to calm my nerves, I went ice cold all over. He had put me in a position of equality with himself. It seemed to me there was a hesitation before the introductions went on with Henion of the Nedi, but I might have imagined it. I had to exert a great deal of force to keep from grabbing at Jemeret's arm to steady myself, and I knew that he knew it.

The world fell away as a bit more of the forgotten past unlocked itself and surrounded me, still unfolding in a kind of episodic revelation. On the dais, Com Counselor Pel Nostro had turned toward Coney. "I want to present to you Shems Conewall, Com Class C of the first rank, free Com citizen of the third rank. He has spent his younger life learning to serve, and he will spend his adult life serving. We are unworthy of his service, but we will accept it in the name of the Com. We salute him."

The audience cheered, ten thousand voices washing over us in waves.

Pel Nostro repeated his speech for Kray—except that Kray was a second-rank citizen—and there was another cheer. Then the Com Counselor looked at me. Touching just at the edges, I felt a surge of his most immense pride, as if I were somehow his personal accomplishment, the triumph of his life's work. "And now," he said, his voice plainly showing what he was feeling, "I take pleasure in presenting to you Ronica McBride, Com Class A of the first rank; free Com citizen of the first rank. She—" Applause and cheers drowned him out, for everyone in the audience had risen to their feet. Kray reached over, took my arm and squeezed it briefly, no jealousy apparent in him at all, and Coney glowed at me with his own pride. The applause tapered off, and Pel Nostro resumed, "She has spent her life learning to fill a void that has existed in the Com for the many years since our highly honored Class A, Jasin Lebec, sat here in gold for a long-past generation of government officials to revere. This, my friends, is the first Class A to complete training successfully since that time." Again applause erupted, and again the audience sprang to its feet. This time Coney and Kray rose, too, also applauding. I remembered thinking that what I had done was neither more nor less than I was supposed to have done, and wondering why the other Class A's had broken under it.

When the applause died at last, the audience sat down, and the three of us remained standing to swear the Oath of Government Service, giving our lives over to the Com. It might have been overwhelmingly troubling to promise so much, except that we'd been carefully prepared for it, had always known we would take it, and I, for one, had always known I had been raised to be the controller, not the controlled. I spoke the words of the oath almost carelessly.

"Ronica." I became aware that I was hearing Jemeret's voice. For a fleeting, disoriented moment I wondered what he was doing in the auditorium, and then the past dropped away as suddenly as it had risen, and I was sitting in the Council circle.

"I'm so sorry," I said, embarrassed. "I didn't hear what was said."

Ashkalin's voice cut in smoothly. "I asked you if this meeting of stonehouseholders could have anything to do with your time there."

I shrugged, but I did know what he was asking. "I can only guess. There was an old woman, a servant named Dogul. She knew I had tal—power. She cautioned me against using it. She and her Meltress tried to keep it from the Melster. I don't think they knew how much I had."

"That's the key, then," Venacrona said firmly. "If Lewannee learned of it, and guessed at the power, then the superficial resemblance to the High Lady is suddenly harmful, is suddenly worth calling a meeting about."

"Can we infiltrate that meeting?" Sheridar asked eagerly.

"It's done," Sabaran said, hushing his son, "just as they have probably got informants at Convalee."

"Will it mean war?" Lyrafi asked regretfully. "We have done so well for so long in the absence of war."

"It need not mean war," Venacrona said, "but we cannot stop our growth because it may."

"How can it be growth if it leads to war?" Lyrafi asked sadly.

"How can we," Jemeret asked, "allow the stonehouseholders to define this situation for us? Venacrona has said it need not lead to war. Will we war because they feel we must?"

"If they war on us, we must reply in kind," said the leader of the Vylk, whose name I had missed. "It is our duty as the Samothen."

"War is never a duty," Lyrafi said sharply. The Vylk leader sneered in response, but generally into the circle, not at her.

Ashkalin spoke. "I believe there is much to be learned from war, if it is a worthy war. But if the stonehouseholders want a war over that lady, the war should be between them and the Boru, not them and the Samothen."

There was a very long moment of silence, and then Sabaran said quietly, "The Genda stand with the Boru."

A man I didn't know, short and stocky, with tousled brown hair and a boyish grin, lazily said, "The Resni stand with the Boru."

Then Henion, old enough to have silvery streaks in his dark hair, said, "The Nedi stand with the Boru."

Ustivet shifted once, uneasily, and said, too loudly, "The Ilto owe a blood price." He moved his bandaged arm and shoulder a little. "The Ilto stand with the Boru."

Another long moment of silence followed, and then Venacrona said softly, "The stars stand with the Boru in this. The lady's coming was foretold."

"Ah, then," Ashkalin said—and I had the feeling the entire game had been played for his benefit—"the Marl stand with the Boru as well."

Jemeret hadn't moved once since Ashkalin had raised the point at issue. Now he shifted slightly and looked around the circle at the tribal leaders who had spoken. Because the Paj, the Elden, and the Dibel did not keep warriors, their loyalty to the Samoth was given over. That meant that all the tribes but the Vylk had indicated they would be with the Boru in any fight. Jemeret seemed to think for a long time. "I would still believe that we have choices other than war, and I would ask those who stand with the Boru to consider that."

Before anyone else could speak, Venacrona raised his hands. "Then until we receive word of the meeting of stonehouse-holders, this Council is suspended."

When we arrived back at the contest ground, the footrace was in its final heat, and it was won by a young warrior of the Marl.

After the break for the midday meal, it was time for the game of the Nedi, and, in announcing it, Henion said some things that it was clear no one expected. "We of the Nedi believe that sometimes a game must be more than a game. We are a forest people, and we believe in living in harmony with the forest. Our game, therefore, is a new one, being played for the first time at this Convalee. The prize will be worth the risk."

At the word "risk," there was a stir, and then a hissing sound like wind through tall grass. A number of the warriors of the Nedi drew up a draped wagon, and Henion pulled aside the drape. There were eight cages on the wagon bed, and in each cage was a young and somewhat subdued klawit.

"I'll be damned," Jemeret said under his breath. "That old meggo went ahead and did it." He wasn't angry, but I didn't hear an edge of amusement in his voice, either.

Ashkalin rose from his place by the tribe flag of the Marl and walked to Sabaran. The two of them came across to Jemeret, who got to his feet. "Do we go along with this?" Sabaran asked.

"I don't know that we have the right to interfere," Jemeret said. "The rules of Convalee are that the tribe chooses the game, and the Nedi have chosen."

"It's likely to be a short game," Ashkalin said, "especially if no one enters it."

"I'm going to enter it." The three men and I turned to see Morien on her feet, her exquisite face alive with an eagerness and excitement I would have been hard put to match under almost any condition.

Tuvellen pulled at the hem of her talma. "Sit down."

Henion was explaining the game. "The drug slows the beast's responses enough to give a prospective tamer a chance. Remember that a klawit can be tamed, and once tamed, can be a formidable ally." His voice indicated that he didn't truly think anyone was likely to succeed. "Any klawit that isn't tamed will be permitted to go free back into the forest."

"When was the last time you saw anyone with a tame klawit?" Sabaran asked.

A warrior from the Vylk, lean and scarred, rose and came forward, eyes narrowed. "I'll play your game, my Lord Henion," he said. "I've crossed the beasts before."

Morien had twisted her talma out of Tuvellen's grasp and walked past the three tribe leaders toward Henion. Two warriors of the Ilto, goading each other in a way that indicated personal rivalry, came out of their tribal group. Then one of the biggest men I'd ever seen, a Gendal with arms like cargo ships and a great blond beard spilling halfway down his chest, came down front and bowed to Sabaran. "My lord." His voice rumbled as if it came from the depths of the earth.

Sabaran smiled. "Go on, Gradiard," he said. "Aim your heart at this one."

Gradiard bowed again and went to join the line at the front.

Jemeret turned and looked back into the ranks of the Boru, and when I followed his gaze, I saw Sejineth rise and come forward to stand beside Morien.

"There remain yet two cages," Henion said, "and we can supply additional klawits if there are even more who wish to enter."

But no one else came forward.

"The rules are simple," Henion went on after a moment. "The winner of the game is the one who comes closest to the ideal—beast out of the cage and under control."

"What does Morien think she's doing?" I asked Jemeret.

He shook his head briefly. Shenefta drew out of the ranks of the tribe and came to sit beside me, her hand on my arm. "It's really some game, isn't it?" she hissed. "Sejineth's in for it."

"I don't know about that," Jemeret said to her. "The bond he has with the tivongs should serve him well."

"Gradiard had a klawit kitten when he was young," Sabaran

said. "He grew to manhood as it grew older. I've heard that the cat bond is unforgettable."

The six people had begun to approach the eight cages, and it was quickly clear that the two Ilto warriors were the only ones who knew nothing at all about what they were supposed to do. Any approach of theirs to any of the cages raised great agitation in the cats, and once one of them was almost caught by a slashing paw.

The Vylk, Gradiard, Sejineth, and Morien approached more slowly, provoked much less reaction. I began to suspect that each of the four of them had a minute amount of Class A talent—not an unknown factor in the worlds of the Com, but not encouraged or taught, for it was dangerous without giving any serious benefits. Class A talent in tiny amounts is highly unstable, almost ephemeral. It is inherently uncontrollable, and undependable.

I fastened on watching Morien, so tiny among the men, for the excitement she was feeling surrounded her like an aura. I remembered thinking when I first met her that she might have had Class A ability, and then dismissing that thought. It returned now.

There were not many fluctuant Class A's in the Com, and for a long time I never knew they existed at all. I think now that perhaps I was sheltered from the knowledge. When I did learn that Class A talent had a low, uncontrollable side, and that some people who had it never knew they had it, I was first astonished, then horrified, and finally angry. Class A was special; it should have been sacrosanct. I found it impossible to deal with the idea that some people had it in useless, harmful ways.

Class B and Class C reflexes were logical, dependable things, present in greater or lesser amounts, and the amount you had didn't vary. Training only sharpened and defined what already existed; it could not add. The innateness of talent—and the government's much-discussed inability to identify the elusive genetic component—was what made someone like me valuable to the Com.

Usually fluctuant Class A's did not know they were Class A at all. Their unusual ability to influence people when the reflex was present was put down to charisma, charm, good nature, uncommon common sense, or beauty. Some of them might grow strong without being aware of the source of that strength. Mortel John, Kray, Coney, and I had once become involved in one of the most notorious scandals in the Com, and it resulted in the revealing of a powerful fluctuant Class A, previously unknown.

Messianic movements only concerned the Com if they disrupted trade or caused attempted renunciation of Com influence. They were usually limited to single planets, and most of them died out quickly. The major religions of the Com did not support messianic movements, and were too well established to admit new ones to their ranks without a fight. Even the Macerates' preserver was not supposed to be manifest in a fleshed being.

When I was thirteen, a man named Ghefir M'Cherys broke away from the planet Jann-Bime with a hundred thousand followers who believed in forced conversion and were willing to be extremely uncivilized to bring it about. The government debated for some time whether or not to send in the Drenalion, but in the end—probably at the insistence of Jasin Lebec—they decided to use us.

A crack contingent of Drenalion did infiltrate different parts of M'Cherys's followers, and they stole him off the ship he was riding in. A skilled Class B went in with them and stopped the engines of the ship, leaving the life support. The troops then jettisoned all the escape pods and landers and brought the man M'Cherys to Werd, where we were studying.

Mortel John met with him first, while he was still drugged, and what went on at that meeting, he would not reveal. The three of us sat outside in the paved courtyard, and I concentrated on *not* sending a sensory scout of any kind, because the whole idea of encountering a fluctuant Class A repelled me utterly. The problem I had was that Kray seemed to know how I felt.

"Listen, Ronnie," he said to me with real condescension, "if you need us, we'll be right out here, and all you have to do is holler." Kray had learned early that he got stung a lot less if he hid his teasing under the guise of concern for my welfare. He reasoned that I then couldn't sting him, out of the sense of fairness that Mortel John was working so hard to encourage in me. Sometimes I stung him anyway.

This time I just twisted my mouth a little and looked away from him, gathering and calming myself. The overlay of serenity was much more cosmetic than therapeutic. I didn't want to go into that room.

Mortel John came out, far too soon from my point of view,

and said to me formally, "All right, Ronica McBride, you may go in and meet the man M'Cherys."

Coney reached out and squeezed my hand in a quick gesture of support. I gathered and forced my body to rise and walk to the door, wishing that Jasin Lebec were not three-quarters of the galaxy away.

Ghefir M'Cherys was a nondescript man. His sand-colored hair was thinning, and his face was puffy with the fat of good living and self-indulgence. At the moment, he looked a little frightened and very subdued. The drugs were almost out of his system now, and I realized that Mortel John had estimated his emergence from the drugs so that I would see him at this moment.

I couldn't think of a single thing to say to him. I just stood there and waited, holding on to my nerves.

"It wasn't my fault, you know," the man finally said to me. "I didn't ask for it. They followed me."

That told me what to say. "They couldn't have followed you if you hadn't been willing to lead."

"You weren't there. You didn't see it."

"No," I agreed, "but I know how careful you have to be with talent."

"I didn't know I *had* any talent," he said. "It just snuck up on me."

I read him and realized that it was true, and I suddenly had to gather to stop an intense shaking. I couldn't see its source. "Do you know when you have it and when you don't?" I asked him.

He allowed himself a small smile. His fear was beginning to fade. Perhaps he was aware of the fact that I was a very young, very small girl. "Other people," he said.

I knew what he meant—he was told he had talent by the reactions of others. It reminded me a little of the Responsionists, whose doctrine I had found silly. "How often?" I asked.

He shrugged. "Sometimes every week. Sometimes for weeks at a time, and sometimes not for months. You can't know what a torment it is." In his eyes I saw the pain, and I knew it was utterly real. I wanted to be anywhere else.

Morien had almost succeeded in reaching the door to the cage, and her klawit sat quietly, its eyes never leaving her, when I was struck by a thought brought to me partly from watching her and partly from that distant past with M'Cherys.

Suppose *I* was a fluctuant Class A on a very, very long cycle. Suppose the powers had cut out on me unexpectedly. And I found myself staggered as something twisted inside me. If they had gone away, they might come back.

For the first time in days and days, I felt hope. If my Class A talent came back, I might somehow be able to find a way to get out of here. Deep inside, a small voice asked, *Is that still what you really want?*, but I stifled it. And if I couldn't find a way out, I could use the talent here, as Jemeret did. That might not be so bad.

The klawit rose to its feet and pressed its shoulder against the bars of the cage. Morien reached out, her eyes shining, and stroked its pelt. It turned its head to her in something like surprise, and I was startled to see that its eyes looked very much like hers.

Then something changed. I saw it instantly, and started to shout to warn her, but she was aware of it and jumped backward at once. The klawit shook itself, with great speed, as if waking up, and lashed out at the spot where she had been standing. If it had not stopped to shake, she would have been cut apart by its claws.

"So much for the drug," Ashkalin said dryly. Tuvellen had stepped forward to help Morien to her feet. I glanced at the other contestants, and found only Gradiard still working up on the cat. Over the next half hour he actually got into the cage with it, but he did not have enough control to bring it out of the cage. None of the others even came as close as Morien.

When Tuvellen brought her back to her seat, Morien was lovelier than before, if that was possible, flushed with pride at having been able to touch a klawit. She clung to Tuvellen, happy and a little tearful. "I never played such a game before," she said to me.

"I have," I said under my breath, thinking of M'Cherys's trial, and the exile of himself and his followers to a world without means of escape. I wondered if it had been this one, but somehow I didn't think so. This was a world that got its exiles one at a time, not in the hundred thousands.

At the time, I had thought that removal from technology was the worst possible punishment. Now I regarded it as nothing very much. It all depended on what you considered important. I glanced in his direction, and found that Jemeret was studying me. "It's time for the game of the Dibel," he said.

VII. Open to the Sky

A stage had been set up at the front of the bowl, and Lyrafi stood on it, waiting for us. As Jemeret and I approached, she raised her hands to call for attention. The crowd seemed to have grown larger since the klawit cages were taken away, but I couldn't guess whether it was because the Samothen were all nomidar lovers or because it was known that the competition would be between Jemeret and me. As the spectators grew silent, I found my heart pounding, and I gathered to calm myself. My nervousness was greater than I wanted. I loved playing the nomidar, and I knew at an almost instinctive level that I could play the wine-wood nomidar better than any other, but I didn't like performing, and this audience was a huge one. For a moment I actually toyed with the idea that Jemeret was influencing me to nervousness, but then I recognized that I was just afraid that he would be far, far better than I. I brought up Tendoro's reassurance and held on to it.

Lyrafi had gotten the silence she sought, and now she smiled. "Once again the Dibel have the distinction of putting on the most exclusive game in the Samoth, though this year the Nedi came close." There was a ripple of laughter, filled with anticipation, and then Lyrafi's clear, trained voice went on. "This year we chose a game of the nomidar, and as we have only two entrants, we have dispensed with the qualifying rounds and devised a set of seven exercises as challenges to the contestants. The winner will be the person the judges hold to score higher in four of the exercises."

Jemeret took my hand. I jumped a little, not expecting his touch, and looked quickly at him. His gaze was warm, supportive, and genuinely affectionate, and he made no attempt to screen it from me. My instant, overwhelming response was a

170

serene calm, and I knew he had not projected it onto me.
Whatever happened, he was on my side at least as much as he
was a competitor.

We got to our feet and went up two steps onto the stage
where Lyrafi stood. She gestured, and Tendoro, Orion, and
Dirian brought up onto the platform a brace of nomidars,
among them the wine-wood nomidar I knew to be the prize of
the contest. My fingers curled when I saw it. The men set the
instruments down gently and waited.

Lyrafi spoke to Jemeret and me in a voice that carried
clearly to the crowd as well. "You will agree to select one instrument, and you will both use the same instrument. In the
game of the nomidar, the instrument itself can be a player."

I looked at Jemeret.

"Go on," he said. "I'll accept your choice."

I'd studied game theory; his tactics were intriguing. It stood
to reason that if I chose, and he matched me on my choice of
instrument, he would win. If I refused to choose, the advantage
in such a tie would be mine. But I wanted to play the wine-
wood nomidar, and if I refused to choose, he might select a
different instrument.

I reached for it, and Tendoro handed it to me.

"You will agree which one of you will play first," Lyrafi
said.

"I will play first," Jemeret said.

Again it was an intriguing choice. Mine would be the performance in each round with the opportunity to surpass. I nodded agreement and held out the nomidar, even though I was
reluctant to let it go. Jemeret dropped my hand, took the instrument, and sat down at the edge of the platform. I sat beside
him, watching the nomidar in his hands as the three Dibeli
men picked up the other instruments and took them off the
platform.

Lyrafi had remained. "The first exercise," she announced,
"will be a children's song. Each of you is to interpret the
rhyme, 'The laba hops, the laba glides, the laba stops, the laba
hides; it knows its way; it scents the air; it spends the day deep
in its lair. The laba stays away from harms, and so do I, in
mother's arms.' "

I was nonplussed. In the first place, I'd never seen a laba, so
I didn't know what the creature looked like, even though I'd
eaten servings of its meat on occasion. In the second place, I
didn't remember a mother, so I would be hard put to effec-

tively capture a sense of absolute safety arising from the trust in another person. My trust had always been in myself and my own power, which was notably shaken right now. Third, I realized with a sinking heart that if the contest started with sympathetic music, every piece would be a sympathetic one.

Jemeret began to play, and I sensed in the music a small, quick, timid, perhaps even slightly comical creature. If I closed my eyes, I could almost see it. The piece was very short, and he did not make it sympathetic. It was a relatively simple rhyme, and he must have made the decision that it was so simple it did not need any augmentation. When I searched at the end for the sense of safety I expected, I couldn't find it. I wondered if the fact that he was a man, a warrior, and a chief made him draw away from it.

And then I wondered if I could capture it.

The audience stirred, and I was aware of some whispers of approval. Jemeret handed me the nomidar. I cradled it gratefully, feeling its already familiar contours, warm from his hands and body.

I chose a higher register than he had and used the sympathetic strings nonsympathetically to create a background wash against which the swift, tinkling notes of the laba could dart. I brought up the background to a heartbeat rhythm, and repeated the rise and fall of the creature at a slower pace until the foreground notes blended into the heartbeat. I gave the heartbeat four bars alone, and then stopped.

Jemeret smiled, and I reluctantly gave him back the nomidar, but there was a challenge in his eyes as well. We both scored the first round to me—but it was only the first round.

Lyrafi nodded at each of us in turn. "The second exercise," she said. "While we Dibel keep no warriors, we lean on the warriors of the others in the Samoth. We value the powers of those who have chosen the way of peril. Therefore we ask for an interpretation of one of the sayings of Romalux, once a fine warrior of the Genda: 'To know whom to strike is competence; to know how to strike is skill; to know where and when to strike is art; to know why to strike is victory.' "

I didn't agree with the saying, and I didn't know if Jemeret agreed with it or not, but he was obviously familiar with it. He played brilliantly, his sympathetic tones a rousing to patriotism that I knew I would not be able to match, his melody more complex than it seemed, inspiring both dedication and admiration.

The nomidar felt like it carried some lingering harmonies of his when I rested my cheek lightly on its head. He had chosen the brigade approach; I chose that of the individual warrior. My melody was jaunty, a little discordant, a little risky, and I kept the sympathetic strings low, overwhelmed by the melodic line at the end. Jemeret's was the better interpretation. I reckoned the score to be one-all.

Lyrafi rose from her seat at the back edge of the platform. "For the third exercise, we chose a saying from the time of the ancients, before the joining of the tribes into the Samoth. 'Life which is here is life from the Fire. Only sleep lies in the spaces between the stars.' "

I jumped when I heard the saying. It had been days since I'd really thought about space, about traveling between worlds, about the strange regions of superspeed rolls where light and sound became intermingled, about the viewport filters that illuminated brilliant points of incandescence and long strings of gases in vibrant, changing colors. Jemeret played of blazing starfires and empty spaces between; I could not. I had seen too much of the spaces between the stars, and I knew they were far from empty.

I tried to shut the knowledge out of my mind when my turn came, but it kept seeping through into my playing, muddling the melody I had chosen. I probably didn't play badly, but I don't think I played well. I determined to make it up in the next round.

"Secrets," Lyrafi announced, "are exercise four. Not a poem, but an idea to interpret. From the small parts of childhood kept from parents and friends, to the major intrigues of tribes and of nations. Secrets are hidden in all the relations between people and between peoples."

She waited, as did we all. Jemeret seemed to retreat back into himself, head bent over the smooth curves of the nomidar. Although he was both motionless and expressionless, I sensed in him a turmoil so strong that it hinted of itself past his formidable shields, even to someone, like me, as deaf to other people's thoughts as an untalented person was. Finally he lifted his hands to the strings, but he did not look up.

The first few notes were so muted I think almost no one heard them, and as the deep, rich tones began to rise in volume and make their way out over the crowd, I became aware that there were no sympathetic tones at all. Jemeret completely suppressed them.

I couldn't call what he chose to play a melody. It was a stately series of tones, progressing until resolution seemed inevitable, but then avoiding it, so that a dissatisfying undertone of anxiety and restlessness set in. It built toward a strange sort of climax, in that the notes were not discordant, but they refused to let the listeners make a whole of them. It was becoming unbearable when suddenly Jemeret stopped playing. The echoes had died completely before I could reach out and take the nomidar.

I cradled it, but I hadn't assembled any thoughts. I realized that the silence was stretching on, fastened my mind on the single word "secrets," tried to tamp down my higher consciousness and just let my fingers play. Jemeret had suppressed all the sympathetic tones; I couldn't amplify them without my Class A talent, but I could let the instrument resonate to them, and I did.

I don't remember the melodic line. I was barely conscious of playing. When the song was done, I looked up and found Jemeret staring at me, white-lipped, his face pinched with an effort I didn't understand. A murmur from the audience drew my attention, and I looked outward.

People seemed to have been deeply affected by my playing, even though I didn't know what I had played. I reckoned the score at two-all.

Lyrafi sighed and rose. "We will observe a short pause now," she said. "Too much nomidar is like too much rich food. Stretch—and reassemble in a handspan."

I wanted to go on playing the nomidar, but it wouldn't have been fair in the context of the contest. I set it down by the cushions Lyrafi had been sitting on and hopped off the platform. I wanted to go off somewhere, but the Plain of Convalee offered little in the way of shelter, and the tents of the Boru were a long way off. I didn't realize that my whole body was trembling until a flurry of hair and talma embraced me to hold me steady. Shenefta said in my ear, "It was wonderful and horrible both, Ronica. How could you do it?"

I stared at her, bewildered. "How could I do what?"

She shook her head, and I saw tears in her eyes. Once again something had happened and I had missed it. I was trying to phrase a question when her gaze moved beyond me and she took a step backward. I glanced back, and it was Jemeret, just come down off the platform.

"Do you know what happened?" I asked him.

He nodded slowly.

"Tell me—*will* you tell me?" I corrected.

Just as slowly, he shook his head. "Not this day," he said. "Perhaps after Convalee ends." He held out his hand, and I put mine into it. I didn't dispute his decision, because there was so much I didn't understand that this was just a bit more.

"You play the nomidar very well," I said to him, meaning it, not knowing I was only moments away from finding out *how* well.

"So do you."

"I'm holding my own," I said with what I thought was a fine sense of objectivity. "Considering I can't do anything with the sympathetic strings except let them resonate."

"That's all most nomidar players can do," he said. "Even those who can do more usually hold back."

"Are you holding back?" I asked him.

He grinned, and the tiredness around him seemed to slip away. "I don't think I dare to," he said. "Not if I want to win."

My hands suddenly itched to get back to the nomidar, but at the same time I felt my face growing hot. I, for so long used to so much adulation, was somehow embarrassed by praise from him. I tried to block it, but of course he sensed it at once and squeezed my hand, then let it drop.

"You're growing up," he said softly.

Lyrafi called the reassembled crowd back to order as Jemeret and I returned to the platform. This time, for some reason, I was aware of the individuals I knew in the audience, many of them Boru—but Ashkalin's brooding presence was somehow prominent, too. I had not realized before that he was there.

"The Dibeli contest continues," Lyrafi said. "There will be three more rounds, and for the first we will ask the contestants to interpret a piece of the Song of the Outcast Tribe: 'Where pride walks, regret fills the footprints. In the stride of arrogance is the stumble of contrition.' "

Jemeret leaned for a moment on the nomidar, his hands resting lightly on the strings, and then he played. He chose to divide note by note, then chord by chord, then phrase by phrase, each alike yet very different, the first harsh, edging on dissonance, the second softened, harmonized, infinitely sad. It was a truly brilliant performance, perhaps the best I had ever heard.

And I realized as he finished that I was afraid to reach for the nomidar. It was as if something had taken hold of my arm and weighted it down so that movement was impossible. I felt a kind of panic rising inside me.

He must have felt it instantly. He looked up, emerging from the spell playing the nomidar can create, realized I hadn't moved, probed me swiftly, and then made some adjustments in my mind that caused the panic to drain away.

There was some restlessness in the crowd, for the delay had been lengthy. I took the nomidar from Jemeret as slowly as I could. If I defaulted on the song, I would lose the contest, and I couldn't allow that to happen. But I didn't want to play this selection. Usually a strong challenge forced me to a greater effort, but something about this particular poem made me want to turn and run away.

I cradled the nomidar and looked directly at Jemeret. It wasn't that I asked him to help, only that he hadn't completely left my mind yet, and he knew I couldn't play. So he did the absolutely impossible. He played for me, through me.

What the piece sounded like, I don't know. I also don't know if anyone suspected what was happening. Certainly Mortel John would have discounted the likelihood. We were both tired, even sweating, when he judged the piece to have gone on long enough to allay suspicion, and I imagine it wasn't very good, but at least I was through it and we could continue. I gave him back the nomidar. It was only fair that he win that round—he was the only person who had played in it.

If there was a moment when it became possible for me to love him without reservation, it was that moment. I felt not the awe at his greatness I'd felt that night at the spring, not deference to his superior strength, not even the natural kinship of two like people. When he had saved my life, it had been against my will until the very end, and he had himself been the cause of my near suicide; but now he had protected me against public humiliation in answer to a very real plea of mine, without hesitating, without exacting any price. He was, I had to admit, unceasingly loving.

Lyrafi had risen and was speaking. I wrenched my thoughts around to pay attention to her. ". . . sometimes difficult to play both sides of an argument with the same skill," she was saying.

"We've set that test for these nomidartists. Having just played the fall of pride, we now play pride's grandeur. The lines are from a verse of Jenothera: 'The fires of the stars burn through time and are not consumed; there is no body great enough to contain the heart of a victorious warrior, or a mother with a newborn, or a lover who dances with Fire.' "

Jemeret, though tired, clearly knew the verse, and perhaps had even played it before. He began at once, with a stirring series of strong melodic chords that blended into a rousing melody, and subsequently into a series of melodies. Each series was grander, finer than the one before, and it was all brought together in an exquisitely rousing theme, uplifting and magnetic, whose resolution at last was immensely satisfying.

The audience was deeply moved, and very pleased, and so was I. I took the nomidar from him and cradled it. I was filled with gratitude to him for saving me in the last round of the contest, and gratitude is inimical to pride. I fastened on some of the specific words in the poem—fires, victorious, dances—and played them, instead of playing the poem as a whole. The fact that by my reckoning he had just won the contest did not seem to distress me, even though before we began competing, I had been certain that defeat would devastate me.

I was surprised when Lyrafi did not say that the game was over. Instead she announced the last round. "Our last exercise will celebrate love, that most elusive of emotions, whose description has challenged our finest poets and our most talented singers. The poem is of unknown origin: 'To the hills and valleys of one world, the valleys and hills of another. The rhythms of two—joining, merging, continuing as one, through and beyond life, lighted in the face of the stars, in the glorious crimson heart of fire.' "

I was stymied. How could I sing of love when I was so convinced that I had never known it, when I had used Coney's honest love for me in a selfish way, when I flung myself away from Jemeret when he tried to touch me?

Jemeret paused briefly. Then he began to play softly, steadily, a poignant and supportive tribute to all the beauty in the world, rising high, sinking low, growing more complex, then combining in an even warmer, richer theme. He built upon it the second time through, making it even more complex, with brilliance and clarity—like the bright flame of a rocket in space, hot and distinct against a background far away. It was over too soon.

He had to hand me the nomidar, because once again I couldn't reach for it, but as soon as I had it in my hands, I knew what I was going to do. I believed that he knew more about the subject of love than anyone else I had ever known or was ever likely to know.

I drew a deep, calming breath, let it out slowly, and then I played his song back to him again. I may have fooled myself into thinking that I did it purely as a way out, because I couldn't have played my own song. Now, trying to be honest, I think it was only partly that. Partly it was my tribute to him.

I didn't think I'd changed it, except perhaps for a slightly greater hesitancy at the poignant beginning, a slightly higher treble in the soaring conclusion. But when I finished, in the pool of silence that invariably follows a skillful nomidar song—whether sympathetically augmented or not—something in Jemeret blazed upward and outward to envelop me and hold the two of us, for a full second, away from the rest of the world.

Then it was gone, and Lyrafi rose and held out her hand to me for the nomidar. I surrendered it, with reluctance, but not as much as I thought I'd feel. "The judges will now deliberate," she said, "and we thank the contestants for their participation."

I wasn't sure what there was to deliberate about, but anything that hinted I might have a chance to win was welcome. I glanced down into the audience through the gathering twilight, and saw:

Variel, wiping tears from her eyes and holding tightly to Gundever; Shenefta, grinning at me so fiercely that I thought her face might split; and Ashkalin, staring at me with a vulpine hunger he instantly masked, but too late.

Shaken, I looked down at my hands in my lap.

I had seen that look before. Not a look like that, but *that* look, on Kray's beardless, years-younger face. It had resided there before I slept with Coney, while there was still a chance I might choose Kray—while he still thought of me as an object of desire, before I hurt him because he was too much like me.

I became aware that Lyrafi was asking the contestants to rise, and I turned my attention gratefully back outward and stood up there on the stage, beside Jemeret.

"The Dibeli judges have rated the contestants on seven rounds of nomidar songs," Lyrafi announced, "and here is the outcome: Lord Jemeret has won four; Lady Ronica has won three. The prize goes to the Chief of the Boru."

I felt a pang at seeing the nomidar pass to another pair of hands, even if they were Jemeret's, but of course I was not surprised. I started to turn to leave the stage, but Jemeret called me back.

"I appreciate the victory," he said to Lyrafi. "What chief would not? But Ronica is my claim and, perhaps, more. We should not take competition seriously, she and I, and thus I have no victory here, but only the honor of your choice. I believe it could have as easily gone to her. Besides, I already have several nomidars. Therefore I would like to pass this one on to a nomidartist certainly worthy of it."

The audience applauded. Shenefta actually cheered. My palms tingled for the nomidar even before I reached out for it. Something in me was prodding me to think that the gift was patronizing and that I shouldn't take it, but it hadn't a chance in the face of my desire for the instrument.

But I couldn't say thank you; I could only nod to him as he handed it to me.

The crowd began to disperse, except for the watching Boru, Lyrafi and her brother Orion, who had joined her on the stage, Dirian and old Tendoro, and Ashkalin of the Marl with some of his men.

Dirian seemed to be having a low argument with Tendoro, something relating to "erratic genius," but I had no time to listen, as I was riveted by Ashkalin's bow to Jemeret and then to myself.

"I would like a moment to speak with you," Ashkalin said to the Lord of the Boru. He didn't look in my direction, and I got the distinct impression he was making a special effort not to.

"I am honored," Jemeret said in a voice that almost, but not quite, matched his words.

Ashkalin glanced at me as if he expected me to step backward, but I felt strongly that Jemeret would want me to stay, so I shifted my grip on my new nomidar and waited. Jemeret waited, too, and Ashkalin understood that he would not be able to speak without me there. His eyes darkened, and he said to Jemeret distinctly, rudely, "I seek to challenge for her."

Jemeret did not immediately react, but I did, almost unaware of what I was doing. "No!" I cried out. Both men started, and Lyrafi and Orion exchanged a quick glance. In the silence that followed, as the Boru moved closer to their lord and the Marl to theirs, I bent, carefully set the nomidar down, straightened up, and almost detachedly watched my hands curl into claws. I felt my body gathering to spring. Jemeret moved so quickly his motions were lost to sight, fastening his hands around my wrists from behind me and lifting me up off my feet and away from Ashkalin. Holding me off the ground, he shook me once, hard, to break into the gathering, and I heard him say, "Ashkalin, the challenge is unwise. Do not put the Marl in jeopardy before a winter of Severance Storms."

I stilled, shocked at my own reaction, and looked back over my shoulder at the leader of the Marl. The expression on Ashkalin's face told me several things. First, that my reaction had shaken him almost as much as it had shaken me. Second, that Jemeret had enforced his words by using the sting.

Ashkalin bowed very slightly. "I withdraw the challenge," he said, his voice toneless, that of a lesser talent who has been stung by a greater. He turned on his heel and strode away, and his men followed.

"I'm all right," I said to Jemeret. He set me down, holding on to my wrists a moment longer.

"Ronica, you can't go around trying to kill all the leaders of the Samothen," he said, half seriously. "People will begin to believe you're a Honish agent."

"I didn't even know I was going to do it," I said, almost afraid to look at him. "Jemeret, I think I must be mad."

He took my chin in his hand and forced me to meet his level gray eyes. Almost offhandedly, I noted that I was not reacting at all badly to his touch. "It isn't madness to do logical things."

"Logical?" I repeated, disbelieving. "How can—what do you mean, logical?"

Now that he knew I was paying attention, he let go of my chin. "Everything you do comes from something else, perhaps something that was done to you, something locked away in that dark section of your mind. Everything has a path."

Even as I was shaking my head in denial, I knew that he had chosen an expression for this which had very real meaning for me in another context. I had learned it on the only other wilderworld I had ever touched—an uninhabited one, where I had done my Tenday when I was sixteen.

The Day of the Clouds

I never learned the name of that world, but I had been told there was no one on it but me. Mortel John had been very clear about that, describing to Coney, Kray, and me what this "ultimate" survival test would be like.

"You will each be dropped on a deserted world," he said, "but one on which air and gravity will permit survival. You will have a pack with essential gear, and three days of food and water. You will need to find food and water to sustain you for the rest of the tenday, until the lander returns to pick you up."

"I don't understand," I said a little petulantly. "The government spent a complete fortune to train us and educate us for service, and now it's going to try to kill us?"

"Yeah," Kray said approvingly, for although we had discussed the issue privately, none of us had had the courage to raise it in class before now. "It doesn't make a lot of sense."

Mortel John didn't have to deliberate about that question. "We all know that there are costs to training talent," he said. "We all know the government is willing to spend a fortune. You must understand that, until graduation, when you actually take the oath and enter government service, we are also willing to spend your lives."

The three of us sat as if struck, for no one had ever said anything so outrageous to us before. Then Coney said carefully, "I don't believe that. I don't believe you're just willing to let us die."

Mortel John nodded. "You're correct. But you see, in this class, we've studied a great deal about the physiology of talent, and only a limited amount about the *psychology* of talent. It is now time to tell you that talent is to a great extent a problem for its holder." He paused as if debating exactly how to say what came next. We hung on every word. "In the last hundred years," he said, "we have lost more talent through madness and suicide than in any other way."

I frowned. Kray gaped, astonished. Only Coney was unmoving, seemingly unsurprised.

Mortel John went on. "Talent is a lonely thing, isolating. The greater the talent—and you are very talented—the more the isolation." I thought suddenly of Jasin Lebec, whom I might never see again, whose time was scheduled minutely, who shared his life with no one, and I felt myself repress a shudder. Mortel John said, "Isolation requires certain inner strengths, because without them, you cannot hope to succeed. The Tenday tests those strengths in ways you cannot hope to imagine and we cannot duplicate in any other way."

"How many trainees fail the Tenday?" Kray asked.

Mortel John shook his head. "That information is not available."

"So we're on our own," Kray said. Coney grinned and added, "I think that's what he's been saying."

Mortel John looked at me as if he expected me to say something, but I had nothing at all to contribute to the discussion. I am almost astonished to admit it now, but I saw nothing wrong with isolation. I knew—knew beyond any fear of contradiction—that I could depend on myself, that I belonged with myself. I believe that conviction came from two sources. First, it was my reaction to the feeling of distaste I had experienced when Mortel John spoke of isolation, and second, it was a defense against the thought that a Class A might need something other than him- or herself. I was a Class A. I didn't need anyone else. Oh, it was all right if they were there; I certainly liked the three men who had made up all of the family I'd ever known. But I could get along fine without them if I had to. I was sure of it.

Unfortunately, the Tenday proved me right.

The planet I was brought down on had one great land mass, and I was dropped right in the middle of it. The recall beacon I carried would not operate for the first nine days and twenty-eight hours, for this planet had a thirty-four-hour day. I suppose I could have pathfound it and reset it, but that would have been a humiliating admission of failure. It would be up to me to stay alive until recall. I calculated that I could stretch my water to four days in a pinch, and about the food I cared little.

For the first hour I sat quietly where I'd been dropped and studied the landforms around me on this desert world. As the sun rose, I put a hat on and watched the shadows of scrubs on the dry soil. The day would be cloudless, and there were no dramatic changes in the land that I could see. That ruled out making a wide spiral.

At last I rose, chose a direction at random, and struck off in a straight line. There were, I had been told, neither insects nor animals on this world. "All flora, no fauna," Mortel John had said. It took until mid-afternoon to reach the horizon point I had set myself for, and from there I could see two very differ-

ent kinds of landforms. Far to my left were what looked like
upthrust mountains, sharp-edged, perhaps fairly young geolog-
ically. To my right, the dry ground seemed to give way to
gracefully curving sweeps of rock and slot canyons. They appeared to be water-formed, and while I knew the formation
could have taken place hundreds of centuries earlier, it was at
least a sign that water had run there once. I set off in that direction.

The day grew warmer and warmer, and I stripped out of my
jacket. I could have equalized my temperature to remain comfortable, but I didn't want to gather unless it was necessary.
Ten days was a long time, and my entire life was reduced to
the need to find water, because if I did, I would survive until
recall.

For almost three days I wandered through a desert world of
incredible beauty without seeing any foliage I would associate
with water. I found roots I analyzed as edible, and some ber-
ries that tested out as wholesome, if bitter. There were some
succulents that held moisture within them, and perhaps they
would have been enough, but I was convinced I needed a good
source of fresh water, and I meant to find one.

I made a choice on the morning of the fourth day that I
would probably not be lucky enough to locate the water on my
own; if I were to find water, the world would have to show me
where it was.

And so I set my pack aside in an open space of land, took
off all my clothes, and stretched out flat on my face, arms
spread wide, cheek pressed against the earth. Then I did a
thing no one had ever done before, because no one had known
it was possible. I pathfound the planet.

In essence, I asked it to tell me where its water was hidden,
much as I asked the nomidar how it wanted to be played. Because a planet is immense, and because things that are not mechanical take a long time to reveal their path anyway, I lay
there unmoving for almost an entire day before the path revealed itself to me. Then I rose, measurelessly weary, drank
the remainder of the water they'd given me, dressed, shoul-
dered my pack, and set off at a mile-eating run. I was dangerously tired and very thirsty when I got to the water, but it was
never a life-threatening experience, and once I reached it, there
were no further problems surviving.

For five days I stayed in the gardenlike area near the waterfall formed by the spring I'd found, recovering from the exer-

tion of pathfinding an entire world. I slept a great deal, never really needing to deep, and when I was awake I explored, perfectly safe and only a little bored. I never dealt at all with being alone. I never needed to.

The night of the Day of the Laba, Jemeret slept beside me again, and I welcomed his presence, because I had so little to hold on to any longer. I lay awake for a long time after he fell asleep, thinking about the fact that I had ceased to know myself at all, even though the idea that I knew myself was one of the only things I had ever really depended on. That night I was visited by a strange phenomenon, though I didn't recognize it for a recurring motif until after Convalee. My dream was somehow edged in a strange wash of golden sparkles, a glittering veil, a patternless pattern of changing light through which shapes seemed to make their presence known without indicating anything of their true form. The first time it happened, it seemed nothing special; momentarily inexplicable, it disturbed the surface of my consciousness and then vanished in the normal activities of the day.

Jemeret woke me at daybreak, and he had not gotten up. I looked at his face, touched with fresh morning light, and, as the dream faded, I found myself smiling. He smiled in response. "Today you will need to be a little less guarded, if you can. This is a social day, when we interact with one another across tribal lines, as chance takes it. Many Sammods and Sammats will want to speak with—or dance with—the woman who looks like the High Lady."

I was well accustomed to being stared at and sought after for a word or two. At a series of receptions before graduation, some people in the crowd had reached out to touch my sleeve as if contact with me could in some way ennoble them. I would be very used to that, and although the idea of dancing was not really welcome, I didn't think it would present any problems. And yet I heard myself ask, "Will you be there?"

Neither his smile nor his expression changed, but there was somehow more warmth in his face, and I wondered how he did that. "I can be, if you want me to be," he said. "I can't dance with you all the time, but I can be nearby."

"Good," I said. "Then you can stop me if I try to kill anyone else."

It was the first time I'd heard him laugh, full, hearty, and utterly carefree. I had no idea where it came from, because I was very serious in what I had just said, but I enjoyed the good humor that seemed to wash over me as he laughed. It gave me a sense of well-being. He stopped laughing and his eyes searched my face.

I felt an odd urge to reach out and touch his cheek. "Are you doing that?" I asked him, but it was not a hostile question. "Are you stinging me?"

He didn't answer.

"It's all right," I said. "I don't think I mind." But I exerted just enough pressure on myself not to obey him, waiting to see if he would increase the power.

He gave one short laugh and withdrew the sting. "This isn't a contest, Ronica," he said. "You have to learn that. This doesn't have a winner or a loser." He tossed the covers aside and got swiftly to his feet to dress. "This time, we can both win."

I lay on the rugs for a time longer, not watching him, thinking about what he'd said. It was not a concept with which I was familiar. When I truly thought about it, it was clear to me that Variel and Gundever were not engaged in any kind of contest, and it was also clear to me that they were wildly, almost embarrassingly, happy. I thought back to other ongoing male-female relationships I had known, and realized that in my entire life there had only been one—no, two—others that I was aware of: Letitia Ver Lenghy and her husband supporting each other in the hospital in mutual love and the avoidance of despair was one. The second was Com Counselor Pel Nostro and his wife, Jara Deland, who worked with the MIs on the highest levels. They had been involved in something which, if it couldn't be characterized as a contest, certainly qualified as open war. How did I know who was normal and who was not?

The only time I had seen the Com Counselor with his wife was at a dinner they gave for Kray, Coney, and me before graduation, but I had been hearing about their battles for years. Even in our company, their verbal sparring was intense, and, I admit, extremely entertaining. It was what I thought relationships were all about.

Jemeret had left the tent, and I arose, washed and dressed, and was ready for breakfast when he and Numima came in, almost simultaneously. He was still smiling, and I smiled back.

Music was literally in the air when we left the tent for the bowl of Convalee. The flattened area was filled with people, laughing together, singing, dancing. Though I had never danced before, by afternoon I had learned how the Samothen danced—great circle dances of a hundred people, dances in which only the women participated, pair dances in which partners changed often, and pair dances in which they did not.

During a partner-changing dance, I spun away from Sheridar, laughing at something he'd said, and found myself partnering Ashkalin. As we made the required opening bows to one another, I said softly, "I apologize, my lord, if I was—unwise."

Without smiling, he said, "You are, my lady, a woman of very strong opinions." And then the elaborate figures of the dance and its very newness made me concentrate on my steps. Once or twice I caught sight of Shenefta, dancing with an earnest young man of the Genda or with Dirian, and another time with a Boru adolescent.

The dancing continued most of the day, its practitioners changing as some people rested and others arrived. In the middle of the afternoon, breathless and laughing, Lyrafi, Clematis, and I sat sipping shilfnin and nibbling on clover cakes. Lyrafi complimented me on my dancing, and I told her, almost shyly, that I was learning it as I went along. "The way I learned to shoot the agerin."

Lyrafi swallowed hastily. "You weren't learning to play the nomidar as you went along! Who was your teacher?"

I thought about that long and hard, and then answered slowly. "It's a complex question. There was a blind man named Maur who made me a nomidar when I was eight years old and taught me the fingering and chords. But from that point on, I listened to nomidartists and took what I believed was good about their work."

The other two women exchanged a glance, and Clematis said softly, "Imagine what she could become with a nomidar teacher!"

"I think," I said, almost with wonder, "that I wouldn't know how to behave with a teacher. I've been on my own for so long now."

"And you're very good," Clematis said seriously. "It would be hard to find a teacher who had greater skill."

"Jemeret could teach her," Lyrafi said to Clematis, with a sidelong glance at me, "but it might be unwise."

"Why unwise?" I asked.

Clematis broke another piece off the clover cake in her lap

as Lyrafi answered. "You and the Lord Jemeret seem to compete in a number of ways, and it seems—important to you that you do well against him. You would have to let go of that competitive spirit."

My first thought was that everyone around here knew everyone else's business, and my second thought was that it would probably do me a lot of good to escape any need to compete with Jemeret. My third thought was that it wouldn't be an easy thing for me to do. "Is Jemeret truly so much better a nomidartist than I am?" I asked Lyrafi. I wanted her opinion, because I respected it greatly. I was also fishing for compliments, because after all, the score had been four to three the day before. Now that I had lost the unshakable foundation of Class A status, it was even more important for me to seek security in other areas.

Clematis started to shake her head, but Lyrafi gestured to her and considered her answer. "It's difficult to describe," she said at last. "As far as technique is concerned, the two of you are different, but about on a level. Neither of you has had the practice time to attain full mastery of the technical details, but we don't have time to miss that when you play because the emotional elements are so rich. What Lord Jemeret has is—a fullness of soul. It may come from his age and experience, or it may come from something in himself."

"What you've just said is that what makes him better is something that can't be taught," Clematis observed before I had a chance to say the same thing.

Lyrafi smiled. "I didn't say that at all," she said serenely. "All I said was that Jemeret could teach her to be a better nomidartist, and that is true."

I became deeply concerned with the composition of the shilfnin, and Clematis diplomatically changed the subject, debating with Lyrafi who might be braceleted on the Day of the Fire, and who might ask and be turned away. Of course they concentrated their analysis on the Genda and Dibeli couples, as well as one cross-tribe Dibeli-Paj match.

"I think Variel and Gundever of the Boru will be in that group," I said when there was a pause in the conversation. "They seem very attached to one another."

And Lyrafi stunned me by asking, as she brushed the crumbs off her lap, "But what has that to do with it?"

"Pardon?" I asked.

"The attraction between people sometimes isn't enough,"

Clematis said, "and the stars have the final choice. Variel and Gundever have been together only since a midsummer ago. Sometimes the stars will approve, and sometimes they will not. We will have to wait and see." Briskly she rose to her feet. "I want to dance again."

Lyrafi and I also got up, but more slowly, and out of the corner of my eye I saw Jemeret disengage himself from a group of men and move to intercept me. He had been careful to remain somewhere near, but he was never intrusive, and I was grateful.

The dancing went on into the night, and under the stars we parted and returned to our separate encampments. While Jemeret was consulting with his guards over night positions, I set two cups on the table and filled them from the flask of clogny. Then I sat down in a chair and waited for him to come in.

It was quiet in the tent, and I was at ease, feeling calm and strangely contented. All at once it came to me that sometime during the day I had recognized that I belonged here. I had ceased to view this world, this place, as transitory or as alien. I believed now that I was here to stay, and I was determined to make a success of it. It could, realistically, have been a lot worse.

I had just reached the dangerous part of the conjecture—the part where I would try to deal with the fact that I didn't think I was fluctuant, and therefore would never be a Class A again—when Jemeret came in and sealed the tent flap. I put the thought aside as he turned and looked curiously at me and the two cups.

"I want to talk," I said.

He came to the table and leaned back against it, near my chair, picking up the closest cup of clogny. Silently, he waited. I was having a hard time choosing the words I wanted. He sipped some clogny, his face impassive, his gray eyes disconcertingly fixed on my face.

After a very long pause, he grinned. "You certainly don't expect me to start, do you?"

I laughed with him, and suddenly it was easier. "I would like to ask you if you would consider teaching me more about the nomidar."

He was taken by surprise, and he didn't try to hide it. "You are an excellent player," he said. "The contest proved that. Why would you want lessons at this point?"

Without thinking about it, I answered, "Well, I've never had a nomidar teacher, because the nomidar wasn't something the government thought was worth my learning, and I'm used to studying. I just never got to choose what I'd learn before."

He considered it at some length. "There's a saying on this world: 'We can learn something from even the smallest blade of grass.' I don't know if I can teach you anything about the nomidar, but when we get to Stronghome, we can begin to play together. Will that do?"

Slowly I nodded. I finished my clogny and carefully set the cup back on the table, aware in the silence as he studied me that there was a sting in the tent and that he wielded it.

Meeting my gaze when I at last looked up, he slowly shook his head. "Not yet," he said. "We are too close to the Day of the Fire now."

I didn't understand what he meant, but I was grateful for the delay. "You probably don't have to worry about me trying to run away any longer," I said, and he laughed.

"I haven't been worried," he said. "Not for days."

He extinguished the stanchion lamps.

The Day of the Bell

It occurs to me now that one of the reasons I like classes and structured learning is that they encourage—and contribute to—the belief that life is orderly, that things happen when they are supposed to happen, that actions have predictable results, and that events are controllable. The Com fostered this belief, and every Class A scenario is built on this foundation. Now I suspect that it is not only illusory, it is destructive. And even knowing that, I cannot escape its seductiveness.

I went to the tivong pen early on the Day of the Bell, because I wanted to ride again. Jemeret had not given orders that I could not ride alone, and I felt fairly safe on the plains between the two rivers. Most of the people in the Samothen knew who I was now, and the story of Evesti had gotten around. In addition, I was a Boru, and no one else was likely to make the mistake of the Ilto. As soon as I neared the pens, the tivong that had presented itself to me on the day I chose a prafax broke away from the herd and trotted up to the fence.

"Working today?" Sejineth had come up behind me, and I had been hardly aware of him because I was concentrating so

hard on the grace and power of the tivong, whom I had named
Rocky. I turned.

"No, I'd like to ride this morning, and my friend here wants
me to ride him," I said. "I'll saddle him myself, and I'll rub
him down when I bring him back, so you won't have extra
work." It came out faster than I would have wanted.

He bowed shortly and walked away. There were only a few
hundred tivongs left now, for most of the huge herd had been
traded or sold on the Day of the Sheaf. Across the compound
I could see Shenefta and the boys mixing feed, and when she
glanced in my direction, I waved, and she smiled back and
shouted a greeting.

In less than a handspan, I had the tivong saddled and was
riding off down the plain, feeling the wind whip my hair
around my face. I had forgotten how much I loved this.

Pelhamhorses were different from tivongs, in that they were
closer to the primitive horse stock. Unlike the tivongs, there
was no predator strain in their breeding. Kray and Coney and
I loved every opportunity we got to break away from training
and ride on the bridle paths of our study complex on Werd.
Kray was proud of his breeding stock, and because he wanted
to race them, he bred them for speed. When we really wanted
to let them run, they had the stamina to oblige us.

With a sense of fairness that governed few of my other actions, I refrained from stinging my mount to urge him to win.
The race had to be fair because it was a test of Kray's horses,
not us. Sometimes I lost, but I didn't mind. A horse was a
wonderful companion, strong, beautiful, happy, and utterly focused on running, which gave it a selfless joy, and I opened
myself to it completely, because it was one of the few times I
ever felt pure, uncomplicated emotion. I fed on it.

A tivong was much more intelligent, and therefore much
more complicated. It, too, loved to run. That seemed to breed
true down all the mutations in horse stock. But the purity of its
joy was tempered, even as it is in human beings, by wariness,
by an apprehension about what might be around the next bend
or over the next rise. A horse lived second to second, but a
tivong, like a person, lived in the moment and in the future at
the same time.

Rocky sped up a hill and paused at the top. From here I
could see most of the separate encampments of the Samothen,
and both rivers. The view was really breathtaking. It was

closer to the forest than I had thought when I let Rocky choose
his own path up here, but I suspected no menace from it, so I
dismounted and let the reins drop. Rocky might wander a little,
but he would never run off and leave me. Tivongs didn't.

I sat cross-legged on the hilltop in the waving grasses, encir-
cled my legs with my arms, and started to concentrate on relaxing, only to discover—to my complete surprise—that I was
already relaxed. Rocky dropped his head to graze idly at the
grass, and I watched the breeze stir the edges of the trees and
listened to the singing of birds as they swooped overhead.

Perception is an amazing thing. It differs for each of us, because each of us is different, and we filter it through that different self. What each of us knows about objective reality, we
know through our subjective senses—an unyielding paradox.
So when I describe what happened next, I describe it through
my own senses, and while I ordinarily trust my senses concerning the external world, the next hour had such a hypnotic
quality to it that I'm not sure I'm reporting it accurately.

On the hilltop, despite the distance I could see, Rocky, the
birds, and I seemed to be the only living beings in the world.
If people stirred in the encampments—and I'm sure they
did—I simply was not aware of it. Strangely enough, I don't
even know what I was thinking about.

Between one moment and the next I realized that there was
movement along the edge of the forest, where the trees met the
grassland. The movement was gentle, and in many places at
the same time. Even Rocky seemed to sense no menace. And
as I watched, idly attracted by the motions, face after face appeared, distinct from the trees and undergrowth.

They were klawits, about twenty or thirty of them, their eyes
aglow with their inner fires, but the normal feeling of predator
that surrounded them like a halo was somehow absent. Slowly,
but not cautiously, four or five of them stepped from the cam-
ouflaging trees into the open field. From this smaller group,
two continued to move forward—one a huge female, and the
other, at her side, a much smaller, younger male. The male almost qualified as a kitten. The curiosity on its face was evident
as it cocked its head and looked at Rocky and me. Beside me,
Rocky lifted his head and looked at the cats, but after a moment he lowered it and pulled at some grass again.

The two klawits came closer; then the female put her head
down and nudged the kitten out in front of her. They pro-
ceeded up the ridge that led from the forest to the hill on

which I sat. There the female stopped. The kitten looked back at her over his shoulder, and she nodded him onward. He turned toward me again.

Moving slowly, partly not to startle him and partly because of the peculiar lethargy that hung over the scene, I got to my feet. The kitten's ears reached almost to my waist as he approached. When he was close enough to touch, he stopped and sat on his haunches, looking at me.

His eyes glowed mutedly, but still entirely without menace, and he showed neither claws nor fangs. Rocky went on grazing as if there were nothing unusual about this. I was fascinated by the kitten.

When I still hadn't moved after a minute or so, the kitten came even closer but without getting up from his sit, lifted his paw, his claws still retracted, and rested the pads against my knee. He was waiting for me to do something, and so was the much larger cat behind him. I thought idly that I could recover quickly from any injuries the kitten might inflict, but the big cat would be a problem.

The kitten pushed firmly at my knee, which had the power to almost stagger me. Clearly, I could not just do nothing. I reached out and laid my hand on his head. His paw dropped from my knee and he made a noise I could characterize as a "purr" the same way I might have characterized the galaxy as a "place."

I scratched the slightly speckled baby fur, which was amazingly soft to the touch, and the kitten wriggled and rolled onto his back. The large female moved closer until she was so close to me that she had to lower her head to put it on a level with mine. She turned her face past me, and her whiskers stroked across my forehead, tingling. I stared at her as she looked back at me, where I stood over the upended kitten, and her eyes were opalescent, as well as lit from within. We confronted each other directly for a moment or two, and then she dropped her head, nuzzled the kitten, turned and walked away, back into the trees. The other klawits retreated, too, and the forest was still, except for the breeze's movement of leaves and branches.

Rocky, the kitten, and I were left alone on the rise. I could not help but feel that the mother cat had just given me her kitten.

Wonderingly, I sat down beside the kitten, who squirmed his huge head into my lap, purring away. Rocky took a step closer and nudged the kitten's side with his nose. It gave him a glance, but did not otherwise pay attention. I rubbed its up-turned belly, where the fur was even softer and paler. The edges of things seemed somehow hazy. I went on playing with the kitten, who responded enthusiastically, rolling and even licking my hand with a raspy tongue big enough to envelop it. I was conscious of the sun on my skin and the breeze ruffling my hair.

The feeling was a kind of calm, relaxation, and satisfaction I almost didn't recognize. Even now I have a difficult time be-lieving that I was, at that moment in my life, fully *happy* for perhaps the first time.

By the time the sharpness returned to the edges of things, it was mid-afternoon. The kitten had curled up against my thigh and was sleeping. Rocky had grazed his fill and rested his nose on my shoulder, almost dozing himself.

It occurred to me that I probably should be getting back. I shook myself as if to doff the lethargy, but when I was sure I was awake and the dream was gone, the kitten was still there beside me.

"Will you come back to camp with me?" I asked him as if he would understand. It might have been the first time I had spoken aloud since I got to the hilltop. The kitten got up, his movement not as graceful as it would grow to be, not as pow-erful. He yawned and stretched, first front, then rear, and then stood still, waiting. I swung up on Rocky and picked up the reins, expecting the kitten to run alongside as we headed down the hill and back across the plain, but with a balanced leap, claws still fully retracted, he leaped up behind me onto Rocky's broad back.

Rocky glanced around, but otherwise did not react to what might have instinctively been seen as an attack. Soft-pawed, the kitten lay down. "All right," I said. "Let's go back."

We were never taught that happiness was something to be desired or sought after. Happiness was the logical result of doing our duty, serving the government and the Com. We got no lessons in being happy.

Once, in a class when we were about fourteen, Mortel John was having us study different forms of poetry. We were read-ing examples of a form called "sendav," in which syllables were rigidly defined and vowel sounds were limited in relation to one another. The poem we were studying was:

"Clear smile / tears so few / Home waits there / These are the signs / We know joy."

"What do you think of this poem?" Mortel John asked.

Kray made a face behind his hand. Coney asked, "What's the difference between joy and happiness?"

"Joy fits the syllable requirements," I said, and Kray gave a snorting laugh.

"Joy is felt," Mortel John said, "and happiness is experienced."

We all three glanced sideways at each other. Mortel John was being obscure again.

"It's something you'll have to learn as you mature," our teacher said now, "so don't ask me to explain it to you." But I could not resist that challenge.

"Are they mutually exclusive, or are they sequential, or what?"

Mortel John sighed. "You will have to learn for yourself how it will be for you," he said, "as this is one area that is different for all of us."

"How is it for you?" Kray asked, jumping in on the challenge before it could get away.

Mortel John hesitated for what seemed like an inordinately long time, especially in light of his answer. "It would do you no good to hear my answer," he said at last, "and it could do you appreciable harm. Let's discuss the form of the poem."

The first tribe I encountered as I returned was the Elden, the tribe of cloth-makers from the plains near the Forge. They lived nearest to the Dibel and shared the protection of the Genda against any incursions by the Honish. As I drew up to the tents and wagons that marked the outer edge of the encampment, an Elden who was gathering wood saw me and looked twice at the picture we made, me and the two animals. He gave a sharp, multitoned whistle, and people began to gather, at a respectful distance.

I knew I needed to get back to the Boru and the tivong pens, but I kept Rocky's pace down because there were soon so many people around that I was afraid he would trample someone.

Before I had even reached the end of the Elden encampment, Sammods and Sammats from the Resni and the Nedi were beginning to line the route as well. The kitten sat up and pressed himself against my back, not out of fear, but almost to reassure me that he was still there. Many of the people I rode past fell into step behind me.

Finally the tivong pens came into sight, and I realized that the four people I had seen that morning—Sejineth, Shenefta, and the newly named adults Pepali and Lutamo, fresh from the manhood ceremonies that had taken place during the day, while I was gone—were literally surrounded by members of the other tribes. To the side, by Sejineth's tent, stood a group of tribal leaders, including Sabaran, Lyrafi, Ginestra of the Paj, who was the other woman leader, Zunigar of the Resni, Ashkalin, and my Lord Jemeret. Uniformly, they looked astounded. I hoped I wasn't in some kind of trouble.

Rocky, still steady in pace and temperament despite the crowd, reached Sejineth and his helpers, and I reined him in. Sejineth took hold of the tivong's bridle, and I waited for the kitten to lean away from me, then swung down. As soon as I was on the ground, the kitten leaped lightly down to my side. The nearest people backed up a little, and though Sejineth didn't move, his eyes were so wide I thought they'd split apart.

"I'm sorry," I said to Sejineth. "I don't think I'll be able to rub him down after all."

I expected sarcasm, but he said only, "I'll take care of him."

Then I turned to the group by Sejineth's tent. Of course, my concern was largely for what Jemeret would think or say. The kitten walked at my side as if I had trained him to. It was humorous, somehow, that all these people were standing around staring.

No one crowded me. I went directly to Jemeret and waited in front of him. He was letting nothing show, and I was apprehensive. He looked at the kitten, who returned his gaze, then looked back at me. I felt strongly that he expected something of me—that everyone did—but I hadn't any notion of what I was supposed to say or do. I looked at Jemeret with an appeal in my eyes.

At once I felt an impulse to lay my hand on the kitten's head. The klawit looked up at me as if it, too, were waiting for something.

I felt a tickle in my throat and heard myself speak. "I name this cat Tynnanna."

Too many things happened at precisely the same moment. First, Jemeret tightened his lips and paled with the enormity of the effort it had taken to speak through my voice. He staggered infinitesimally and had to control himself absolutely to keep from falling. Second, the klawit kitten stood up on its hind feet and roared, but he still did not extend his front claws. Third, two or three of the people in the crowd started to cheer, and others took it up until the noise of it was like a wall of sound, beating at me in waves. And fourth, I gasped and twisted around—toward the cat, as it happened—stunned by what Jemeret had accomplished and by what happened inside me as I realized he had given me the words and made me speak them. Thanks to the antics of Tynnanna, no one was watching either Jemeret or me as we reacted to our separate and shared experience. And as I moved, I was assailed by another memory.

I remembered that the graduation gala had been a huge celebration, beginning several hours after the graduation ceremony itself, in a hall as large and vaulted as a hollow mountain, where the leaders of worlds, of merchant fleets, of the great universities, of the numerous religions, of the Com itself, came to pay homage to us—but especially to me. I could see in my mind's eye, even as I noted and worried about Jemeret's weakness, that I had chosen to wear a gown of midnight blue shot through with silver threads, and that these were the colors of the Boru. I could feel that I was triumphant, but I was also aware, looking back from the perception of a Boru, that I had no grace, in the spiritual sense of that word. I might have been disgusted at this revelation, but my concern for Jemeret overrode both the feeling and the memory.

I didn't wait to see if he wanted me to approach him, or if Tynnanna would follow. And I didn't move too fast, because I knew that Jemeret would not have wanted anyone to know how weak he really was at that moment. As I reached his side I realized that the other tribe leaders had fallen back a step or two, so I guessed that the kitten was right behind me. My Lord Jemeret had not moved, and was looking at me with such love on his face that I wanted to weep. I bit back the impulse to ask him how he could love me when I had behaved so awfully, and probably would again, but I remembered that Coney had not stopped loving me when I destroyed his hopes, and that Jemeret knew me better than anyone else alive.

"Come on," I said to him in a voice audible to no one else. "I'll walk you back to the tent." I threaded my arm through his as if it were a casual motion, but in reality I wanted to support enough of his weight so that he could walk with ease.

We moved through the encampment at a normal pace and

Tynnanna walked just behind me, drawing enough of the attention so that very few people looked closely at Jemeret. It was approaching sunset when I sealed the three of us into the tent, and Jemeret sank gratefully into a chair.

"The day's activities aren't really over yet," he said, "but I fancy we'll live without most of the rest. You created quite a sensation. How did you know?" He wearily started to unlace the neck slot on his tunic.

"How did I know what?" I asked him. "Why was this so important that everyone wanted to see it? Why did you have to exhaust yourself? What is going on? And *how* did you do that?"

He almost laughed. "There are some parts of the Foretelling that are more specific, and they are never to be told to any candidate for the Fulfillment. You are not to know the criteria by which you will be judged, except in general terms. You will be honored by the animals, is one of those general terms. The specific is that the High Lady will have a klawit companion named Tynnanna."

The kitten, who had lain down by the tent flap, raised his head at a name he already, eerily, seemed to know.

Jemeret had finally gotten the lace undone, but it was an effort. I reached out and helped him strip off the tunic. "How did you find him?" he asked me, rubbing his eyes.

"I didn't. He found me." I judged that Jemeret was really too weary to hear the story now. "Here, let me help you." I slid my hands under his armpits to gather and almost lift him out of his chair. He seemed amused, but he let me support him to the bed.

"I haven't time to deep," he said. "There's one more meeting I have to go to."

I sat down beside him. "Jemeret, you need to replenish your reserves. Can you draw strength from me?" It was a perfectly logical question. Since he had given me so much of his own strength the night he probed me and saved my life, it was as if now—gratitude having been lost to me that night—I had found a way to give him some of his own strength back, to meet a need of his in reply to the needs of mine he had met.

"Do you really want me to?" he asked, self-contained and unreadable even in his weariness.

"Yes, I do," I said, and meant it.

"Lean toward me," he said, and I obeyed, swaying in his direction. "Let me do this my way."

I didn't know what he was going to do until he drew my face to his and fastened his mouth on mine. My body did not pull away, and I welcomed the kiss almost with relief. His mouth was incredibly soft, gentle, and sweet, moving on mine in a way that sent waves of feeling coursing along all the nerves in my body. For the longest moment he let the kiss stand alone, and the weak melting that flowed through me was entirely natural. Then his arms came up strongly around me, and he gathered and began to draw strength from my reserves.

I interpreted the growing weakness as arousal, and it nearly overwhelmed me. Without realizing I was doing it, I clung to him, gasping. He was very careful about how much energy he took, but I was beginning to understand the meaning of the word "swoon" when he stopped.

Almost abruptly, he broke off the contact. All the questions I had wanted to ask about how he had been able to speak with my voice were driven clear out of my head. "Soon," he said roughly. "Very soon."

I forced my eyes to focus to see his face, then gathered and fought down the arousal until it abated to manageable levels, although I was still breathing very hard. I did not understand why my body no longer rejected him but I had not understood why it was rejecting him in the first place. I wanted to know what had changed, but at the same time I didn't care, because now we openly wanted each other.

And his desire for me was no longer a threat. It was a promise.

He got to his feet, much stronger now that he had resupplied his reserves, and I felt a languor that was partially the drain on mine and partially the aftermath of the kiss. "I'll be back in a few hours," he said. "Try and get some sleep."

He put his tunic on again and went to the front of the tent. Tynnanna rose and moved away from the tent flap toward me. "Amazing," said Jemeret at the cat as he left.

I must have fallen asleep shortly thereafter, and when I woke up in the morning, he had already left the tent.

The Day of the Fire

There is a difference between being given honor and earning honor. I believed the night of the gala ball after graduation that I deserved the homage bestowed on me, and the entire Com conspired to reinforce that belief. I know now that they honored me not because of what I was, but because of what they hoped I would become. All I had done was finish a very flawed education. I am not one of those people who can pretend to be an MI, and that was all my education prepared me to be—because it was all the government and the MIs needed me to be.

I cannot now say what would have become of me if it were not for Jemeret.

The kitten was pressed up against me when I awoke, and Jemeret was not there. The memory of my helplessness in the face of arousal the previous night made me sit up in surprise. Why hadn't I gathered and kept it down? The answer came almost instantly: Because I felt as if I had been waiting for it all my life.

Numima let herself in, glancing at Tynnanna with a look at once wary and full of "don't-give-me-any-of-your-nonsense." Moving to the table, she set down a tray with bread, a berry spread, and milk. "Your clothes for today are on the chair, my lady," she said. "It is late morning now, and my Lord Jemeret will be back to get you in a little while." She threw another fast look at the klawit, who elaborately yawned in her direction. To show she was not afraid of him, Numima snorted as she left the tent.

I got up, washed, threw a small rug around myself, and ate before I looked at the clothes. This time the gauzy shift was dark blue, the talma the silver material I had cut and imperfectly sewed. But it boasted a trim I had not seen before, embroidered from blended threads of blue, and the work was exquisite. I didn't know who had woven it or sewn it onto the talma, but I was grateful. The boots were dark blue, and the hair cord was a rich, deep sky blue that seemed to glow almost as much as Tynnanna's eyes.

The material was so smooth it made me wish I had some kind of hand lotion, but all I could do was gather and soften my hands. Then I dressed in the finery.

It was strange. In the same colors at the graduation ball, I had been wearing almost a million credits' worth of ice gems as necklace, earpieces, and tiara. The gown had been created by the top designer on Marpeta, and I knew I looked spectacular in it. Yet I believe the talma I wore on the Day of the Fire was the most flattering, ennobling outfit I ever put on.

I had just finished braiding the cord through my hair when Jemeret pulled open the tent flap. He was wearing a midnight blue tunic so dark it was almost black, and its silver trim was very subtle. He wore his brow-crown and smiled broadly when he saw me. "You're lovely," he said, holding out his hand.

Tynnanna moved toward the open flap, paused to look back at me, and darted out. I wondered for a split second if he'd be back, but I guessed that if he had no intention of returning, he had never needed to come in the first place.

"We have an Inner Council meeting now, then the intertribal banquet, and finally the Starfire Ceremony," Jemeret said. "It will be a long day."

"I rested plenty," I said. "I'm sorry I missed all of yesterday."

"Not important," he told me. "Only today matters. The Council should be interesting. We'll hear the first reports from the spies among the Honish."

"Will it be war?" I asked him as we moved among the tents toward the meeting ground.

We were the first there, and in the next half hour the leadership of all the other tribes arrived while the guards from the Boru, Genda, Marl, and Nedi stood in a wide circle around the meeting, out of earshot and facing outward. We sat on round, barrellike stools with backrests but no arms. For the first time I formally met Tatatin of the Elden and Krenigo of the Vylk. Tatatin was almost as old as Tendoro, and I began to wonder if my time here would be spent meeting an endless series of old men. He was round, with a wide smile and finely developed sense of humor, and he seemed genuinely pleased to have met me at last, fingering the edge of my talma and remarking proudly, "That's a nice piece of goods." Krenigo was another story entirely. He was thin as a rail, dark, greasy, and whiplike, but the intelligence behind his eyes was unmistakable. There was malevolence here—not an open, brute malevolence like Evesti's or Ustivet's, but something darker and fouler. I felt glad I would not have to spend much time in his company.

Ashkalin nodded to me as he took his seat, and I looked past him, expecting Moonelin at his side. Instead there was a lad of about fourteen, and my heart wrenched almost unbearably inside me. For if Ashkalin looked as Kray would grow to look, this boy looked as Kray had looked when we were growing up together. I nearly rose, nearly cried out at him, but I felt the restraint Jemeret laid on me with the sting, and I acceded to it, gathering to close my tear ducts before I could begin to cry.

Venacrona and Sandalari arrived last, and the priest announced that everything was in readiness for the service later. We performed the ritual of the introductions. When it was Ashkalin's turn, he said, "I am Ashkalin, and I speak for the Marl with my son, Danaller."

His son. I was aware of how much control I was now exerting to keep myself from running to the boy and embracing him. He reminded me so strongly of Kray when we were at our best with one another. Danaller hadn't Kray's sense of self-confidence, but he did have the bravado. It was almost painfully endearing.

"Here comes the messenger," Sheridar said, pointing.

A Paj, wearing muted reds and blues, sped up to the line of guards, which parted for him. He ran to Ginestra and knelt. "Rise," she said. "Is it known?"

"It is known," the messenger said, his voice clearly carrying around the circle.

"Speak it, then," Ginestra said.

The messenger turned and took one step backward so that he stood between Ginestra and Zunigar, facing the entire circle at the same time. "The meeting of stonehouseholders at the Lewannee stonehouse is ended," he said. "The Honish have resolved to provoke an attack by closing the borders of their lands to the Samothen. Their guards have already been dispatched to accomplish this. They intend to defend their lands, and armies have been assembled and alerted."

Sabaran rose slowly. "This most affects the Marl, the Resni, and the Vylk, as these are the folks who have to cross the Honish lands to get back to their homes. The Genda will stand with them, if they request it."

Henion also rose. "And the Nedi."

Ustivet spoke for the Ilto in the same vein.

As the Paj, the Dibel, and the Elden kept no troops, they could not speak. That left only the Boru undeclared. Everyone in the circle—including me—looked at Jemeret, who sat very still and seemed to be in deep thought.

The silence grew so thick that no one else was willing to break it. At last Jemeret rose slowly. "We have been given a great opportunity here," he said, surprising the entire group, for this was not the formula, "and it has come earlier than we might have expected it. We have been separate for centuries,

since the death of the High Lady. We have seen some of the
omens that the long time between is coming to an end. But the
omens have not been enough, not yet. And now something has
forced us to consider some things we might have chosen to
defer for other seasons.

"We have always argued whether to stand together or individually. We decide it each time, sometimes one way, sometimes another. Yet we stem from the same roots, and we all
worship the stars. I believe we must address the question of
uniting in peace as well as war, at Convalee and away from
Convalee, as once we were, long ago."

Ashkalin also rose. "I am concerned here in two ways," he
said. "First, the Marl need the tribes at this time, because without them, the Marl cannot get back to Salthome. I recognize
that, and I welcome the support that has been offered. But the
question of reunifying is more serious than this incident. It is
a question of 'Who rules?' "

"The Council does." This, unexpectedly, came from Lyrafi.
"No single person—aside from the High Lady—has ever ruled
the Samothen."

Venacrona raised his staff, and all eyes went to him. "We
must recognize the Foretelling."

Ashkalin started to speak again, but Tynnanna chose that
moment to come running over a rise from the direction of the
forest, carrying something in his mouth. The line of guards
separated out of his path, and most of them kept looking over
their shoulders into the circle when they reestablished their
line. The klawit entered the Council circle between Ashkalin
and Henion, dropped his speed to a prancing walk, came directly to me and proudly laid at my feet the carcass of something he had just killed. He then walked around and sat at my
side, between me and Sheridar.

"We must," Venacrona said again, with emphasis, "recognize the Foretelling."

"Rule by the Council implies that we would live together,"
Krenigo said, rising, "and that would mean changing our way
of life. That is a serious consideration."

"But not a necessary one," Ginestra said unexpectedly. "The
messenger system could keep us informed quickly. The ships
of the Marl and the tivongs of the Boru can make communica-
tion regular and certain. These are details to be settled if we
decide, not factors to keep us from deciding."

Now Zunigar rose. "I, too, am concerned as my Lord

Ashkalin is, as the Resni also have to cross the Honish lands to get to the Hive, and to conduct our trade. I believe we must consider unity, but not today, as the Foretelling has further steps to run. My question is, if we delay this choice, how do we get home?"

"More to the point," Ashkalin said dangerously, "do the Boru stand with us or not?"

"Of course the Boru stand with you," Jemeret said almost offhandedly, "but if there are to be losses—and we must face the possibility that there may—I believe those losses should be in a greater cause than the immediate one."

"I agree," Sandalari said firmly. "And I believe that tomorrow we will know more than we do today."

Ashkalin leaped on that like a predator. "What do you mean by that?" he demanded. "What do you know now that makes you believe that?"

Sandalari was unmoved by his vehemence, and I reflected on how strong she had become, from the trembling, battered child I had known on Werd. "Why, only that the stars make their choices tonight," she said gently. "And we will be able to see if they find her worthy, as indeed we can see that the klawits and the tivongs have found her worthy."

As if he understood, Tynnanna chose that moment to lay his head in my lap, and I rested my hand on it almost absently. Part of me had started to bristle at the idea of being judged, but another part clamped down on it. I thought that my Lord Jemeret would not want me to make a scene of any kind now. At the back of my mind, however, I could hear Kray laughing, for Kray had always wanted me to defer to him, but could never make me do it, and now I was choosing to do it —though for someone else. "Sorry, you weren't man enough," I thought at him, as if he could receive that thought on a world light-centuries away, as if the sting could carry words—as if *my* sting could; Jemeret's had that power—as if I had a sting any longer.

And all those "as ifs" notwithstanding, I went on holding a one-sided conversation with Kray, looking at Danaller as I did so.

You wanted me, and maybe you did love me, Kray, but it was in your way, which meant trying to prove that you were better than me or stronger than me, and you weren't, so you were basing yourself on a lie. You needed me to be less, so you could be more, and I couldn't do it.

I realized suddenly that I had missed something in the Council meeting, that the voices had stopped, and that when Danaller looked over at me, it was because everyone else was staring at me, too.

Jemeret said carefully, "My Lord Ashkalin has asked you if you lay claim to the title of High Lady, Ronica. Our laws say that you must answer."

I knew I had to rise to speak, and so I gently pushed Tynnanna's head from my lap to do so. I looked directly at Ashkalin—so very like the younger man with whom I'd just had an inner encounter. Because he was so like Kray, I knew that part of the tension he held himself under now was caused by what he perceived as my ignoring his question. I thought of how Kray reacted to what he thought of as humiliation, and I wanted to soothe and reassure him.

"I beg your pardon, my Lord Ashkalin," I said sincerely. "I was a long way away from here at the moment that you spoke. My name is Ronica McBride, and I am Lord Jemeret's claim. If time and the stars show me a different path, I may have to walk it. But for now, I am content."

Jemeret relaxed instantly, almost imperceptibly, but I saw him do it. The relaxation seemed to flow outward along the circle, until even Ashkalin, appeased by the response, nodded and sat down again, satisfied.

Venacrona raised his staff once more. "Let us agree, then, to defer until the morning any plan of action. We worship together only one day a year. We will dedicate this day to that worship and allow the stars to guide us."

One by one the tribe leaders agreed, and the formal Inner Council began to dissolve. Sabaran nodded in my direction as he told Jemeret he'd see him later, but Sheridar, eyeing Tynnanna a little warily, came over to take my hand. "I hope you will honor me with a touch later."

Not knowing fully what he meant, I remembered that Ashkalin had said a similar thing when I first met him. Sheridar needed a reply, so I said, "I will if I can," which seemed innocuous enough. He squeezed my fingers briefly and was gone after his father.

Jemeret touched my shoulder, and I turned my face up to him and said softly, "Sometimes I wish I knew what the hell was going on around here."

He smiled and kept his own voice low. "You did fine."

Before he could say anything more, Lyrafi and Orion had come up to us.

"We wonder," Lyrafi said, "if we could prevail on the two of you to spend part of the banquet at the table of the Dibel. No matter what happens tomorrow, we will soon be parted, and it is a sadness to leave talent such as yours behind. Music is, after all, what *our* tribe is supposed to be known for."

"We would be honored," Jemeret said with a genuine smile. "I hope you will play for us, as well."

Lyrafi actually colored prettily. "It would be a pleasure."

Jemeret took my hand and we walked back toward the edge of the Boru encampment, Tynnanna following along, tossing his kill in the air and pouncing on it on occasion. "We of the Samoth have been at odds for a long time," Jemeret explained, "because our people have a history of being ruled separately by men and in unity only under a woman. But it's been a long time since a woman was good enough, or strong enough."

"Do you think I'm strong enough?" I asked it almost wistfully. All my life I had been told how important it was for me to be strong enough to shoulder the responsibilities the Com had for me. I had been so certain I was more than a match for whatever the Com could throw at me, and obviously I was not.

"Not now," Jemeret said in reply, "because you still have a great deal to learn about both strength and goodness. But I believe you *could* be strong enough at some point if you wanted to."

That confused me. "What does strength have to do with learning?" I asked. "You either have it or you don't. Learning is a veneer on top."

"You're wrong," Jemeret said, adding with a mischievous grin, "with all due respect. Strength and learning are tied together in very interesting ways. Each makes space for more of the other."

Mortel John had taught us all sorts of things, from the basics of communications and access through advanced astrogation and politics. But he had never taught us anything about learning. The physiology of talent we got aplenty, the ethics of talent we studied to some degree, the political use of talent was a major concern in our final year, and the psychology of talent got only an odd mention now and then, as there had been one before our Tenday.

"What happens," I remember asking him in class one day

when I was about thirteen, but before I encountered the man M'Cherys, "if the person with the talent misuses it?"

"Renegades happen," Mortel John said, "but they are almost always talents who have not been through the rigorous training the Com supplies to you. There is no place in the Com for a rogue talent."

"But where do rogue talents come from?" I insisted, while Coney and Kray sat very still and stared at me as if I were crazy. It wasn't as if we hadn't talked about it by ourselves; the boys just didn't want it brought up to an authority. In my view, they preferred their conjectures to a factual answer.

I smile now as I realize that I have always confused "facts" with the truth. I somehow thought that if Mortel John or the MIs told me that something was a fact, it had to be true. When Mortel John told me no renegade had ever been through training, I believed him.

Mortel John considered my question, and then asked, "Do you remember Sarai?"

Our heads dropped, and we looked down at our comsole tops. Of course we remembered, but it was still an embarrassment to us.

"Sarai was a renegade," Mortel John said. We all looked up again in surprise, for that poor, broken child hardly fit our description of a renegade. "A rogue," said Mortel John, "is someone in whom talent was not encouraged or encountered until it was too late."

We all felt very comfortable, very safe with that explanation. We knew our talent had been identified and encouraged at the earliest possible moment in our lives—after all, we remembered nothing but being here on Werd in training.

What we didn't know, and never thought to ask, was how anyone knew when it was too late.

The banquet was actually about fifty different banquets, from the guards out on the picket line to the priests and priestesses of every tribe. Many of the women had spent the entire day at the cooking fires, and all dishes were equally shared among the people gathered at Convalee.

Jemeret and I actually spent some time at a number of different tables, as some groups dissolved and re-formed in different configurations throughout the sunset and early evening. I learned the true meaning of the term "feast," though I actually ate and drank very little, as we dined with our tribe, with

Sabaran and Clematis and the people at their table, with Henion and his bracelet Andala, Tatatin and his claim Fidasya, and Lyrafi and Orion, and then later with some groups of people I barely knew at all. While we were with the Dibel, Jemeret and I played separate, short, lively songs on the nomidar, and Lyrafi played a haunting tune on her diplick, making the little harp sing with a genius I had barely suspected of her.

If anyone had asked me why I ate and drank so little, I might have said that I just didn't want much, but the truth was I was apprehensive about what the evening would bring. The Council meeting had made me aware that something was to happen, and it would be meaningful. Not only did I hate not knowing what it was, I was afraid that, as during so many other important happenings, I would not notice it and would end up not understanding what was going on again.

Just as full dark fell, the women who had done most of the cooking cleared away the food and drink that was left, while the men took the benches on which everyone had sat and set them out along the sides of the bowl of Convalee, in increasingly large concentric circles, making a large stadium. The flat area inside the seats became a performing floor. By the time the setup was done, with several long aisles leading to the center, the stars were out overhead.

I still found it difficult to look up and see so few stars, but now I saw the beauty of it as well. Where the stars were massively plentiful, in the galactic core, no single star could pretend to beauty or singularity, but here where they were rarer, each individual star could truly be said to shine like a jewel.

The members of the Samothen began to gather on the rows of seats, more or less in tribal groupings. As always, the tribe leaders were to the front, but I noticed in a number of cases that they sat three or four rows back, not in the front row to which Jemeret led me, just at the end of one of the aisles. Tynnanna, who had also feasted when the dish was appropriately meaty, sat up in the aisle against my side.

"What happens now?" I asked Jemeret, but he said only, "Wait and see."

There was a light touch on my shoulder, and I looked at the row behind me to see Variel, exquisite and flushed in her sky-blue talma. Beside her sat Gundever, looking proud and a little nervous. Both of them smiled at me, and I smiled back.

"You look wonderful," Variel said admiringly.

"And so do you," I responded, meaning it. She positively glowed with excitement and hope, and her gentleness magnified her beauty. Everyone looked their best for tonight, but Variel somehow surpassed all the other women. Farther back behind us, about ten rows or so, I saw Shenefta, still all bones and angles in a plain blue-green talma. She saw me glance at her and waved.

Behind me I heard music begin, and when I turned back to the floor, there were six musicians standing in the very center of the area, shoulder-to-shoulder in a circle facing outward. Two played stigols, two throms, and two canitas, making a breathy, reedy melody underlain by a strong beat, just slightly removed from the primitive.

Jemeret rose and held out his hand to me. All around us, in the front several rows, I could see couples rising as well. He started to lead me out onto the floor, but paused because Tynnanna had risen also. "Not this time," Jemeret said softly to me. I looked down at the klawit and said, "Stay here." The kitten sat back down again, and Jemeret and I continued out onto the flat surface at the center of the bowl.

This was not a dance. It was somehow more of a parade, with stately steps and patterned movements. My right hand remained firmly in Jemeret's left. The couples were all in a line, women behind one another on the men's left. The line made one circuit around the arena and then individual couples moved to other places on the floor. At that, many of the people observing came out onto the floor and went to couples they knew, each "touching" the free hand of the man or the woman. Sheridar and Ashkalin, true to their words, were the first to touch me, followed by many of the other Sammods I had acquaintance with, including, much to my surprise, Sejineth. Jemeret was claimed for a touch by Clematis, Lyrafi, Ginestra, Morien, and a number of other women, including—just at the end of the time—Shenefta, who came up quickly, squeezed his hand, and darted away, as if she really didn't have a right to be there. When the music faded out, trailing off the notes of the song, the parade was over. We all left the floor and returned to our seats.

I have always believed in that old saw that a sufficiently advanced technology is indistinguishable from magic. When I first encountered all that was to follow that night, I automatically relegated it to the realm of a technology so advanced that it was inexplicable to me. I had, after all, been raised to believe in the ever-increasing complexity of technology. I was wrong about that. What I was watching—what I continue to watch—is part of the ever-increasing complexity of life itself.

I'm stalling. I have to stop commenting and just tell the story.

Into the arena came Venacrona, followed by Sandalari, two priests, and another priestess, each of the four bearing on his or her upturned palms a large metallic silver bowl. All five people wore robes of a peculiar matte gray. The robes had hoods, but the hoods were folded back off their heads.

"Tribes of the Samoth," Venacrona said in a voice that carried to the last row of people, "we come to pay homage to the stars, of whose stuff we are made, of whose stuff this world is made. We praise them for our very lives."

Sandalari and the other three assisting Venacrona began to sing—at first quietly, and then with more and more power, first on the same notes, then each singing a separate note that blended with the others in a wonderful polyphony. As they sang, each set his or her metal bowl down onto the floor of the bowl of Convalee. The singing was sweet and pure, rising and falling hypnotically. After a moment or two, still singing, the four backed away from the metal bowls, which remained on the floor, equidistant from some center point. When the others were off the floor itself, Venacrona walked to stand between the bowls.

"Let the stars honor us with their presence," he said. "Let them find us worthy enough to praise and thank them. Let them choose from among us those who are especially worthy." Then he left the floor, and every light, which had been illuminating the floor from stanchions at the ends of the aisles, went out.

For a time there was only silence, the faraway cold silver light of the stars overhead, and the glow of the klawit's eyes. Then the bowls began to softly give off light, each in a separate star color—blue, red, white, yellow-gold.

I was interested, but still a little detached. Then, without warning, from each bowl grew a column of live flame, which shot straight up to almost stratospheric height, illuminating the entire area with starfire. The priests and priestesses began to sing again, and in time to the singing, the starfire began to rock and sway, the columns to writhe, snakelike, to twine around and through one another, and to make organic patterns so surpassingly beautiful that I found them difficult to take in.

The dance of the flames was spellbinding. But it was only the beginning.

The song came to an end. The columns of flame fell back into the bowls with a quiet whoosh. I had no idea how much time had passed since the singing began, nor how much time passed now, with the afterimages of the flames slowly fading from my field of vision. Then the bowls began to glow again, and I was once again transfixed.

This time the flames did not shoot upward; they flowed out of the bowls as if they were overflowing, welling up and moving waterlike until the mingled colors covered the entire floor, breaking like waves at the feet of those of us in the front row. I became aware with a shock that they emitted no heat. But it was undeniable that they were flames, that this was fire.

When the blue and red flames mingled, they did not make purple—they were simply mingled red and blue. All the colors behaved similarly. The floor of the arena had become an abstract pointillist work, brilliant and challenging at the same time. Even without music, the rhythms of the flames seemed to generate an accompaniment of sound that surrounded us. I felt a little breathless at the wonder of it.

Shifting, the flames sorted themselves back into the four separate colors. A murmur of expectation rippled through the spectators. The thrumming took on melodic aspects that were clearly inhuman, but nevertheless very pleasing. It seemed a long while then before anything else changed. The four separate star colors pulsed in time to the unearthly music, and the glow created dancing shadows on the faces of the Samothen.

Then, slowly, the surfaces of the roiling fire began to sprout bumps, like nipples, which—still slowly—increased in length into tendrils, and the tendrils continued to lengthen, pulsating in time to the music, or, perhaps, causing it. They grew ten, twelve, fifteen meters tall, still no wider than a finger, until a forest of grasslike stalks covered the entire arena floor, grouped by star colors.

The slow pace of the process became even slower, developing into an almost-stasis in which nothing at all moved. The sound died, and the silence was complete; everything seemed to be holding its breath.

In the stillness, Tynnanna turned and darted up the aisle to the back of the arena, as if he knew he would now somehow be in the way. The night then froze again, everyone watching the motionless tendrils until it was almost unbearable.

And then the tendrils began to reach out into the group of spectators, stretching or shrinking as needed, twining around and across one another without blending. Some of them flowed up the aisles—Tynnanna had been right—while others dropped down above the heads of the Samothen. Each tendril tip touched lightly on the forehead of a man in the crowd. I saw the golden one that touched Gundever, leaving no mark behind. Very few of the Sammods were actually touched. As the tendril retreated from Gundever, I turned to ask Jemeret what the flames were made of and saw a blue tendril touch him lightly. I couldn't move, and the question died on my lips.

All the tendrils retreated back into the bed of flames, and once again everything was still.

After a pause about five breaths long, a single tendril rose from the white area and moved into the crowd, choosing a red-haired woman of the Nedi. It fastened a loop around her wrist and drew her out of her seat and onto the arena floor.

The white fire retreated before her as she walked, so that she was walking on the solid ground, with the flames on either side of her. At a point in the circle, the tendril stiffened and stopped her forward progress. And then the flames rose up and encased her, surrounding her completely. The human music, which had softly begun again with the tendril movement, went steadily on in the background.

She looked untouched, but a little anxious, as the tendril rose again from her feet and hovered in front of her, forming the loop it had put around her wrist to bring her to the floor. This time the looped tendril did not encircle her wrist. Instead the loop remained in front of her, at the level of her breast, offered to her. I realized that this was a bracelet.

The redheaded Nedi reached up with both hands and lifted the bracelet of fire away from the tendril, which sank back into the other white flames. She turned and walked off the floor on the path the fire had left for her. A Nedin man rose as she came closer to him, his smile welcoming and wide. The woman knelt in the aisle and held the bracelet toward him, over her head, saying something I was too far away to hear. The man took the bracelet from her and slipped it on her left wrist, where it glowed unbearably bright for a moment or two and then simply seemed to dissolve away.

I had been so fascinated with the unfolding of the drama involving the Nedi that I hadn't been aware of the other tendrils, but tendrils had risen from the gold, red, and blue areas in sequence, drawing other women from among the spectators. Each was now at a different point in the sequence, but in the furthest along, where the flames had fallen away from encasing the woman, no bracelet was offered, and she had to go back to her seat without one.

Over the next two handspans or so, the process was repeated again and again. Only about a third of the women got bracelets, and the rest were turned away.

When the red tendril came for Variel, I was nervous for her, and it was clear that she, too, was very nervous. She squeezed Gundever's hand quickly, and then let the red flame around her wrist draw her onto the arena floor. The flames engulfed her, and I wondered if it was for a longer or shorter time than anyone else. The fire fell away and lingered at her feet for what seemed a very long time, and then the tendril rose and offered her a bracelet.

Variel's delight was utterly apparent on her face, as was her sense of wonder as she took the bracelet with trembling fingers and a little cry of joy. Dignity almost abandoned, she positively scampered back to Gundever, then remembered the rest of the ritual and dropped to her knees, the bracelet upraised. "My love, the stars have found us worthy," she said. "Will you do me the honor of braceleting me?"

Gundever had risen, and now he took the bracelet and slipped it on her left wrist. I was close enough to study it minutely, and I irised my eyes down so that the hot glare as it brightened didn't make it impossible to see. The bracelet didn't dissolve into the air; rather, it was absorbed into Variel's skin. She leaped up and threw her arms around Gundever, laughing.

I was watching the two of them, smiling at their open joy, when I felt the touch on my wrist. I looked quickly at the white tendril that had come to draw me out onto the floor. It burned like real flame, but it was cool against my skin. In a flash I stole a glance at Jemeret, who was looking at me and the starfire expressionlessly. Then I rose in response to the tug against my arm, and since I had already gathered to narrow my irises, I pulled in a little more strength and tried to pathfind the flame on my wrist.

By the time I tried the pathfinding, I was already out on the arena floor. For a split second the tendril seemed to freeze, and then it broke off contact with my wrist and stood away from me, as if uncertain what to do. I became aware that there was no singing at all anymore, and that there were no other women out on the floor except me.

The tendril flowed around me at a distance of about a half meter, and I didn't move, afraid I'd broken some sort of major taboo. Then it spiraled back from around me, rose in front of me, swaying back and forth, and leaned forward to touch my forehead.

From behind me in the rows of spectators, I heard a few gasps and a low murmur, which stilled instantly as single tendrils rose from the gold, the blue, and the red and came to join the white one in front of me. The four tendrils twined together into a snakelike creature and then spiraled upward around my body until I, too, was encased in fire, but a fire composed equally of all the star colors. My mind and body were permeated with a gentle warmth that seemed to spread along my nerves and into my flesh. I became aware, at the very core of my being, that the flame was a living thing, and living things have no paths.

Suddenly the flames were gone from around me and the sinuous column was standing in front of me again, swaying to the sound of the starfire's own music, which had risen while I wasn't aware of it. It swayed toward me, then away from me, then coiled about my waist, my shoulders, withdrew, returned, withdrew again, and swayed again.

I became aware with absolute amazement that the fire was dancing with me. It was an endearing thought somehow, and without meaning to, I started to laugh. The twisted column of fire shivered as it danced, and small teardrop sparks shimmered free into the air around me. I held out my hands, and the sparks skittered along my palms and lower arms.

The strange dance didn't last nearly long enough, and then the tendrils drew apart. I waited a moment or two to see what the fire might do next, and when it didn't move, I reached out to caress it one last time. But before my hands could touch it, the four tendrils melded their tips into a bracelet, which hung before my eyes, offered by the starfire.

As touched as if this bracelet had nothing to do with Jemeret and me, but only to do with the starfire and me, I smiled and took the bracelet with my fingertips. The starfire clung to the bracelet for a second longer than I expected it to, and then the contact was broken. I thought the tendrils would sink back down, but they did not, and I nodded to them and carried the bracelet back toward Jemeret, who had risen and was almost, but not quite, smiling.

I had never knelt to anyone in my life, but I knew I would need to do it to complete the ritual. His eyes held mine steadily until I reached a spot directly in front of him. I didn't know if he would sting me to help me kneel, but he did not. I understood then that this was something I had to do entirely on my own. I made myself drop down and raise the four-color bracelet above my head, but I could not look down. My gaze meeting his directly, I opened my mouth to say the ritual formula I had heard Variel say, only to discover that I could not—in the utter silence of the arena—call him "my love." So I made a tiny alteration.

"My lord, the stars have found us worthy. Will you do me the honor of braceleting me?"

Jemeret reached out and took the bracelet. My fingers tingled a little as I gave it up. But he did not slip it directly onto my arm—he held it up above his head, the starfire colors reflecting from the silver of his brow-crown, and only then lowered it onto my left wrist. The bracelet seemed to writhe on my skin for a moment, and its sudden brightness exploded through the arena. I felt coolness diffuse into my arm and vanish inside me.

Then Jemeret lifted me to my feet and folded me into his arms, his lips against my forehead. "You were wonderful," he whispered.

When I turned back to the arena floor, the starfire had returned to the separate metal bowls, where a domelike glow of each color lingered over the bowl tops. The priests and priestesses came back onto the arena floor. The four who had carried in the bowls picked them up and began to sing again, their voices full and rich. It seemed as if the ceremony was continuing unbroken, as if what had happened in the middle was just a dream.

Indeed, sitting beside Jemeret with my hand firmly in his, I felt as if it *had* been a dream, except that my fingertips still tingled.

Late into the final night of Convalee, when the Starfire Ceremony was over, Jemeret and I rose, and Variel threw her arms around me and hugged me so tightly I almost couldn't catch my breath.

"What did it feel like?" she asked me, and I heard echoes

of the question in the crowd, for there were a great many people around us.

"It was fun," I said, telling the complete truth. "Carefree. The starfire is alive."

Variel nodded, but I knew she thought I was speaking metaphorically. "I've never seen anything like that."

"No one's ever seen anything like it," Gundever said. "You never do things by halves, do you?"

"I didn't do anything deliberate," I said, almost defensively. "I don't think I've done very much on purpose since I got here."

Jemeret took my arm and pressed gently with his fingers. To the entire assemblage he said, "Tomorrow will not be an easy day. We'd better all get some rest if we're to get the Marl, the Resni, and the Vylk home." To me, he added, "Come, Ronica."

We passed slowly through the crowd, accepting their congratulations with grace. Tynnanna fell into step beside me as the crowd thinned out, and when we reached the edge of the Boru encampment, Jemeret turned me to face him and said softly, "I have to set the guards. Go to bed. I'll be there in a little while."

There was something in his voice that coursed along my nerves the way the starfire had. The starlight on the planes of his face dazzled me, but I was totally unprepared for the rush of arousal that swept over me. He nodded, a smile playing at the corners of his lips. "Go on."

I heard my voice tremble as I spoke, and I made no effort to control it. "How do you know I'll be there?"

The smile widened, and his hand gently brushed across the front of my talma, making me shiver. Then he said words that would once have enraged me but now made my knees nearly buckle. "You're out of control," he said in a quiet voice. "Go to bed."

He turned and was gone in the darkness.

Caught in the desire, I had to fight to walk, fight to keep from touching myself, because while I could have produced my own orgasm instantly, with or without external stimulation, somehow I knew that this time it would not do. He had brought me to this, and its completion was in his hands.

Tynnanna and I reached the tent, but he didn't come in, only swished his tail at me several times and raced off into the night. The stanchion lamps had been lit. I blew out all but one, stripped off my clothes, and stretched out under the rugs, hearing Jemeret say "You're out of control" over and over again, like the echo of a distant song.

And something happened inside my mind as another door opened in the memory that was locked away.

The gala after graduation was winding down. Com Counselor Pel Nostro claimed the last dance for himself, and I bestowed it on him like a blessing. At the end of the dance I curtsied politely as he bowed to me. He said, "I hope to see you again before too many years go by."

I realized that tonight we would part company with Mortel John, though Kray and Coney and I had two more days of vacation together before we would be separated. After that I might not ever see them again, and if I did, we would all be far older. There were assignments aplenty for us to undertake—the business of the Com depended on us. It was what we had been trained for, what we had taken oaths to perform. I would not allow myself to feel a pang, so rigid was my unbending control.

My suite was in a building across from Government House, but part of the entire government complex. I put my wrap around me and went back to it to clean off my glittery face paint and brush out my hair.

Something had happened in those two rooms, I knew now, lying in the dimness of Jemeret's tent. Something I hadn't remembered yet. Something during which I was out of control. I concentrated on the minutiae of the memory: my reflection in the mirror with my face strangely little-girlish free of the cosmetics, the feeling of the brush in my hand, my hair loose around my face, crackling with electrostatic energy.

And then I started as Jemeret came in and tied the tent flap closed. Just the sight of his muscular shoulders as he stripped off his tunic made my body tremble again, and I closed my eyes to try to keep the excitement from building too swiftly.

I felt the closeness of his body as he slipped in beside me, and my breathing quickened. "Look at me, Ronica," he said, his voice thicker than I'd heard it before. When I still didn't respond, he repeated, "Look at me."

His face was very close when I finally opened my eyes, and the desire that I thought was already overwhelming suddenly doubled. I absolutely knew my body would not reject him this time, for it was already moistly preparing for him.

He bent and for the second time fastened his mouth on

mine, his lips and tongue skillful, drawing a response from me. I kept my hands tightly fastened in the rugs.

The fire, hotter than starfire, spread from his mouth through mine and into my body along the tracks the starfire had prepared for it. He handled me as if he knew exactly how I would respond to his touch, dropping his kiss to the point of my jaw, then to the hollow of my throat. Then, drawing the rugs aside, he continued downward.

I was lost in the heat, encased in it more completely than when I'd been engulfed by the roiling starfire. I may have murmured, "Please," or I may only have made incoherent sounds. I felt, rather than saw, him lean back from me, and as his fingertips stroked the curls below my belly, I knew that he was watching my face, measuring my reaction.

He could feel the moisture. For what seemed too long a time he waited, touching me only outwardly, building my sensation even further with small strokes that sent waves of desire through me, until I heard myself moan with longing. At that moment, he slipped two fingers into the moistness, and at exactly the same moment he moved the sting into my mind.

It is possible that I cried out. It is also possible that I broke apart into small flecks of light like the starfire that had danced on my hands and arms. Although my own control was gone, he was in control of me, showing me that there would be satisfaction, but not yet, because he'd placed the sting between the nerve receptors which needed to chemically connect to produce my orgasm. Thus, he could keep building my sensations without allowing me the physiological means to release them.

At some point he moved his hands to my breasts, then my hips, then beneath me, and entered my body truly, filling me with a burning sweetness that pulled me to it. A man with his power could maintain an erection for hours, but he did not try to, thank the stars. When he finally allowed me to experience the orgasm he had held at bay for so long, its power was beyond my comprehension, occurring in my body and my mind simultaneously, like being caught in an explosion.

My rhythm ultimately slowed, and he brought his own down to follow me to stability. I think I slept at once, at the edge of deeping even though I had never gathered and my reserves were full.

When I awoke, there was still enough time left in the night for him to make love to me again, this time more gently and without the sting. "What was I afraid of?" I asked him wonderingly.

"This isn't the end of the path," he said. "It is only the beginning, and we have a long way to go. I want you to think that there is a world of feeling still awaiting you."

"I don't think I have much more capacity for feeling," I said shakily.

Jemeret threw his head back and laughed, looking suddenly very young. "We will build your capacity," he said. "I know the potential is there, and I look forward to it."

I hid my face in his shoulder, all at once absurdly shy, and he laughed again. He pulled the rugs up over our sweat-glazed bodies. "Get some sleep," he said. "I have an idea for the morning, but it will take all of my strength and most of yours."

I settled against his body, tucked under his arm. Then something prompted me to say, "Jemeret, I've begun to remember things."

The slightest ripple of tension ran through him, but he mastered it instantly. "Don't think about it now," he said lightly. "Just get some sleep."

VIII. Stronghome

"We do know more today than we did last night, and it is remarkable knowledge," Sandalari said. Hundreds of pairs of eyes turned toward Jemeret and me. "We will hear Lord Jemeret's plans."

The wagons were packed and divided into tribal groups for the breaking of Convalee, but it was already near midday and no one had moved. Jemeret stepped up onto the box of the wagon on which I sat, and which Gundever was driving; Variel rode behind me. Tynnanna waited beside the right front wheel.

"I think we can avoid war," Jemeret began. "It won't be easy."

"Does this plan involve getting us home?" Krenigo of the Vylk called out in a drawl.

Jemeret masked a smile. "Of course, Lord Krenigo. I am anxious to return to my home, and I'm sure the Vylk want to be in Columbary before the storms begin." He reached down and laid his hand on my shoulder.

"I propose to use my power and the power of this woman, whom the stars have honored, to draw strength from all of the tribes in equal measure and to put the Honish guards to sleep. I propose to hold them in that state for the hours it will take the Resni, the Marl, and the Vylk to cross the Honish land. A Paja will go with each of them and return here when they are safe. Then we will release the Honish guards and continue on our own way home."

There were murmurings, and I felt a stirring from my other life. "The job of a Class A is often mundane, often unnoticed," said Mortel John to me in a class only composed of the two of us. "But the job of a Class A—overall—is to create scenarios that preserve or restore peace. Sometimes the scenarios for

219

ending war are a bit more dramatic than those for preventing it. For example, there was the Gandavian System dispute that threatened to split the Com with a violence even the Drenalion would have been unable to halt. Class A Bernetta Hansen, nearly four hundred years ago, went to the system and stung 108 of the key individuals fomenting the conflict. It nearly cost her her life, but the war was halted. This is the true fulfillment of the Class A promise."

And here was Jemeret, a truer, stronger Class A than any I had ever heard of, on a wilderworld, fulfilling the promise of the Class A. I wanted to cheer or to weep. I did neither.

Venacrona spoke for the plan, as did a number of other tribal leaders. Ustivet spoke against it, saying that he feared it would show the Samoth to the Honish as cowards and meggos. He glanced swiftly sideways at Jemeret as he said that, but it was possible not to take it as a personal insult, and Jemeret did not.

Sabaran laughed shortly. "Ustivet, they'll be asleep. They won't even know we've passed if we're careful. They'll just one day discover some of the tribes went home and they missed it."

"You're not going to have to cross their lands," Ashkalin said in reply. "You have nothing to worry about."

"Why, then, I'll come with you," Sabaran said easily. "That way the Paj only have to send out two messengers."

"As a matter of interest, that's not a bad idea," Jemeret said. "Since we don't want to slow down the trip across the Honish lands, I won't be able to draw power from the three tribes we'll be protecting. But I can link to you, Sabaran, and if you see anything untoward or alarming, you can signal immediately."

Sabaran nodded. "I have no objection to being a link."

Ashkalin accepted, and so did Zunigar, who had welcomed the plan from the beginning. Krenigo had little choice but to conform.

Venacrona announced the order in which the tribes would move toward the Honish border. The Paj would lead, because they knew the land best; then the Boru, the three tribes that would have to breach the Honish blockade, and the others thereafter.

The wagon roads through the forest were not plentiful, but they were wide and well-maintained. The stonehouses needed trade with the Samothen. We swung southward, then westward, and by dark had reached a place near the border. Jemeret, Venacrona, Sabaran, the two Paja messengers, the three leaders of the involved tribes, and I went forward to scout out the situation.

There was a partially sheltered thicket that gave a good view of the border, and we could see the line of Honish guards. They did not appear to be overly watchful, but they were well-armed.

Jemeret took my hand and concentrated for a moment, then turned to Venacrona. "About six hundred troops here and several thousand men at a garrison about two leagues north." He concentrated a moment longer, and this time I thought I felt a slight tug. "The far border is much less manned. They know we'll be coming from this side."

"How will you handle it?" Venacrona asked.

"I'm going to try to ignore the garrison as long as I can," Jemeret replied thoughtfully. "If we're lucky, we can avoid expending that energy altogether. Veen, I need everybody in a line, holding hands, the Boru first, then all the other tribes that aren't crossing. Intertribal linkages only between priests and priestesses. Hurry."

Venacrona hurried away, and in less than three handspans we'd made a human chain, with Variel linked to me and to Gundever and the rest—fifteen hundred strong—in a line that snaked among the wagons. Jemeret took a deep breath and let it out, gathering to touch his reserves against those of all of the rest of us. Then he looked at me. "Ready?"

"Anytime," I said.

He squeezed my hand, and I felt the beginnings of the surge that traveled all the way down through the gathered tribes of the Samoth, so that the amount drawn from any one person would be minuscule. Then he began to draw and to project at the Honish guards an overwhelming desire for sleep. Despite everything that I knew about power and control, I was amazed at how quickly the guards dropped.

"Start them across," Jemeret said tightly to Venacrona, who waved to Ashkalin. The Marl moved out beyond us, tivongs and wagons rattling toward the rise on which the guards had been keeping watch. As Sabaran went past, he glanced at Jemeret and nodded once.

Farther to the south, the Resni line began, and beyond it, the Vylk. Moving in parallel, they went slowly until they topped the rise, then sped up when the ground flattened out. Venacrona, the one remaining person who was not part of the line, went up to the hilltop, standing between the prone bodies of the guards, and kept watch.

Once, about four hours into the night, Venacrona made a series of gestures to Jemeret, which I took to mean activity at the garrison. Jemeret drew more power and expanded the scope of the projection to take in the garrison as well.

The day was entering its fifth hour—almost sun-high—when Venacrona signaled to us that the three riders were on their way back, and very soon Sabaran and the two Paj crested the rise and kept coming. Venacrona had tied Rocky and Jemeret's big tivong, Vrand, to a nearby tree. Now the priest went to Variel and said, "Be ready when my Lord Jemeret gives the order to break off. Let go of Ronica's hand, and you and Gundever run for the wagon. We'll take the Boru onto the North Road."

Variel nodded that she understood. I heard and saw it vaguely, but was concentrating on my role as a conduit.

Jemeret looked at me, his eyes focusing on my face from far away. "We have to hold it alone now," he said. "Can you do it?"

I said what I absolutely meant. "I think I can do anything." I felt he wanted to smile, but the enormity of the effort he was making precluded it.

He spoke past me, to Variel. "Break off *now*."

She let go of my hand.

I became aware in an instant that Jemeret had used the resources of the tribes and carefully husbanded mine and his own. Now there were only the two of us left, and we held the cap of sleep over the guards at this side of the Honish lands and over the garrison for almost another hour while the rest of the Samothen headed away for their various homes. Then it became too dangerous to continue, and he dropped the cap.

"Let's go," he said.

He was stronger than I was, not because he'd used more of my reserves, but because his were so much greater. Still holding my hand, he helped me to Rocky. Tynnanna, who'd been sleeping at Rocky's feet, rose and stretched as I swung up on the tivong's back. Jemeret untied the two tivongs and vaulted up on Vrand. A moment later we were pelting toward the North Road, Tynnanna racing lightly behind us.

We were both tired, but the exhilaration of the ride was still attractive. I was in awe of Jemeret's ability to accomplish so much without any waste of resources. I was certain that if I had been in charge, I would have thrown everything into the problem. His approach was infinitely wiser than mine would have been.

Of course, that has been proven to me many times over.

We caught up with the wagons half an hour later and discovered that the Genda were still with the Boru. Sabaran leaned across to Jemeret and embraced him. "No one else could have done it," I heard him say. "In the spring we will all start thinking about the unifying of the Samothen—especially if the winter goes as we hope it will."

"The Samothen were just unified for almost sixteen hours," Jemeret said with some satisfaction. "It's a start."

They embraced again. "Have a good winter," Sabaran said.

"And you," said Jemeret. "Weather the storms."

They clapped each other on the arms, and Sabaran reined his tivong around and rode back toward his tribe. I watched him go. Doing so, I became aware that Sandalari was sitting on the box of the second Gendal wagon. She waved at me, and I raised my hand in farewell, wondering if I would see her again in the spring, wondering what the Severance Storms were.

"Go get in the wagon," Jemeret said to me. "You need some sleep."

"So do you," I responded.

"I'll be there soon."

I turned Rocky toward the head of the Boru train. About twenty-five wagons forward, I passed the one Shenefta was riding on, and smiled at her as I went past. Then I realized that driving that wagon was Sejineth, and I nodded to him, too. He nodded back, and for the first time I sensed neither hostility nor reserve.

When I reached the wagon that Gundever was driving, I tied Rocky to the back, patted Tynnanna, and collapsed onto the pile of rugs by the tailgate. I wanted to think about what had happened, but I fell asleep almost instantly in the gentle swaying of the wagon.

I had been on the wilderworld for one month.

The trip toward Stronghome had been under way for a tenday when it really began to feel cold. The next day, the mountains came into view.

Jemeret had showed me a map of the route to Stronghome, which lay in a sheltered valley below the heights of the highest peaks on this world. Six major peaks more or less surrounded the valley—giant Marlith, the highest and steepest; massive Zuglith, which spread its immensity over the entire northern side of the valley; Harrilith, big anywhere except next to Zuglith, and whose southern face provided the only easy route up to the pass that gave access to Stronghome; and the three sisters, Kulith, Kunlith, and Kerlith.

Despite that, I was entirely unprepared for the aggressive reality of the range of mountains seen from a gentle slope as the foothills began. I had never seen mountains, except in vid studies, which, despite their simulations of reality, could not approach the originals. There was a grandeur, a magnificence, that nothing but the genuine article could convey.

"They're stupendous," I said breathlessly to Variel, who was riding beside me wrapped in her traveling cloak as I drove the team.

She looked at me curiously. "Yes, of course," she said. "Haven't you ever seen mountains before?"

I shook my head. "I've been on a number of other worlds, but there was never anything—anything like that."

"See the peak that looks split in the center?" Variel pointed. "It doesn't really look like a split, it looks like a shadow."

"Yes, I see it."

"Well, to the right of that peak is a low shoulder—you can't see it from here—and that's the pass we cross to get into Stronghome."

Her voice had a quality of longing. "You really want to get back, don't you?" I said.

She looked at me as if that were a remarkably silly question. "It's home," she said. "My family is there. Of course I want to be home again."

I realized as she spoke that I had never felt the call to a homeplace, because I had never really had a home. And if I had fulfilled my promise and gone to work for the Com, I would never have had one at all. It was a stunning realization. Almost as if she suspected what I was thinking, Variel spoke. "Tell me about the worlds you've seen. It's so strange to me to think there is anyplace else, anything up there"—she nodded skyward—"except the stars and the mysteries."

"Oh, there are hundreds of worlds," I said. "About 250 belong to the Com. Billions of people. And yet—" It was a strange thought. "There's a sameness among them. Werd and Koldor were in very different parts of the core, but the architecture was the same, the feeling was the same, and the overall civilization seemed the same. There was very little open space left, and what there was, was carefully designed to look like wilderness. We thought it was really wilderness—at least I did before I came here. The buildings were generally plasteel or alloy, and varied between six and about forty floors."

"Stop," Variel said with a helpless laugh. "I can't even begin to picture it. A stonehouse is big enough for me to think about."

She began singing lightly in a clear soprano, and as soon as I had heard enough of it to feel comfortable with the tune, I sang along.

Every evening when dinner was over, Jemeret and I left the wagon to Variel and Gundever, took our rugs and furs, found a place for a bed under the trees, and made love. He knew I was a beginner—except for Coney, there had never been a lover until him—and he reveled in teaching me about the physical joys of sex.

On the trip to Stronghome I was always passive, the student and the responder. The control was always his; the choice of acts was his; my response was invariably at his prompting, rather than my own, his power allowing him to govern every physiological aspect of the process—mine, as well as his. The depth of my passion, and the power of the orgasms, always astonished me, even if I was expecting them, for they were more than I remembered each and every time. In part it was because, as he learned my body the way he knew my mind, he could manipulate it more easily, and in part it was because of the sting.

I remember once reading that there really was no difference in the sex act from the dawn of history onward, but the person who wrote that didn't know about Class A talent. The sting directly affects the mind, the emotions, and the nerves, and the amount of effect is governed by the amount of power applied. Every night, Jemeret used a little more power. So that no matter where his hands or his mouth were, no matter how quick or how slow his penetration, his mind was the master of everything that went on, holding my own mind captive, giving me perfect pleasure.

By the twelfth night of the trip, when I felt as if I had dissolved into pure sensation, I heard him say, "Ronica, this is still only the beginning." I fell asleep bathed in the sweat of our coupling, but trembling in anticipation of a future whose limits I could not see, the thought of which both enchanted and frightened me.

On the twenty-first day after the end of Convalee, we reached the mountains.

There was a large open area where the track through the foothills became a true mountain road and began to climb steeply into the rocks. The wagons changed order then, the rear wagons going first and our wagon bringing up the rear. The warriors whose responsibility had been the guarding of the track while we were at Convalee fell into step along the wagons as we passed them. Some were the woman warriors, and everyone greeted each other with real happiness.

With us at the end of the train—the direction from which any attack might have come—we had the advantage of being able to preserve an unbroken view of the path behind us. As we climbed, except when it was obscured by the occasional boulder or stand of trees, the views of the plains and forest were more and more spectacular. Jemeret told me how hard the climb had been for him one spring when he and two of his companions were ambushed by Ilto raiders before the Peace of Jaglith was signed. There had been eight ambushers, and his friends were killed before they had come anywhere near evening the odds. Jemeret drained himself in dispatching the four who remained, leaving his reserves almost as empty as mine had been after the Drenalion. He said it took him three days to walk back to Stronghome, and if there had been one more Ilto, he would have died out there.

I could not picture him that weak. He seemed to me to be a focal point for incredible strength, incredible wisdom.

And, as we climbed, I began to see that, barring the development of manned flight on this world, Stronghome was probably impregnable.

"I don't understand why you won't teach us any military tactics," Kray said angrily to Mortel John. "It's something everybody needs to know."

"Not you three," Mortel John said stolidly. "The Com has generals and strategists and tacticians aplenty. You are to help maintain the peace, not participate in the conduct of war."

Coney seemed perfectly content with the reply, but Kray was even angrier. "All men know how to fight," he said, "and you're trying to keep Coney and me from that knowledge."

He sounded terribly pompous, and I couldn't resist laughing even though I tried to stifle it. He heard my sputter and threw me a nearly murderous look, which, unfortunately, made me sputter again.

"You have been taught eight separate methods of self-defense," Mortel John said. "The Com wishes to withhold no knowledge from you which may be necessary. Military studies is not considered necessary, because you will never direct an army, and because it can only consume limited study time better devoted to other subjects."

For the next six months Kray made our free time a hell, trying to convince us to study military tactics and history clandestinely with him. At first, united against the idea—Coney because it was a bad idea, and me because it was Kray's idea—Coney and I were adamant in our refusal. I suggested that Kray pursue the study alone if it was so important to him.

But the three of us had been studying together all our lives, and Kray's one effort to do it alone failed, so he returned to his campaign of nagging at us until, finally—for the sake of peace—we agreed to study with him.

It was a mistake, because Coney and I really had no interest in learning who had thought of taking the position on the hill first and why, or who first equated "the high ground" with "orbit," or who said that the seeds of an enemy's defeat lay in the enemy himself.

Once we had agreed to study with Kray, we did our best, but it was clear that we didn't enjoy it. Finally, unwilling to admit that he really did not like our forbearance, Kray broke off the studies and blamed it on us.

Coney and I talked about it in private. "He just can't admit he's wrong," I said, "and he just plain is."

"Well," Coney said, "let it go. He'll never admit being wrong in front of you, and you know it."

"I don't understand what makes him so damned stubborn," I said, and Coney grinned crookedly.

"Don't you? Strange. You're usually so perceptive."

I bristled. "What's that supposed to mean?" But even as I asked, I knew. I just refused to recognize it. Kray competed with me at every step, and he lost hard when he lost.

Coney just said mildly, and accurately, "You know."

Coney always knew me better than Kray did, and I was always less threatened by Coney. It's possible I cared more about him, or it's possible I was less like him. But it's also just possible that Coney simply accepted that he couldn't compete with me.

When Jemeret taught me there was another way of relating to people, a way that did not involve competition, I realized that I had never perceived it, even with Coney. I hadn't recognized that the game was any different—I just thought that Coney had refused to play.

At three places, as the track grew steeper, we crossed chasms on sturdy bridges that looked so solid I admired the workmanship. "In case of attack, we can take out one or all three bridges," Gundever told me with pride. "We become impenetrable under those circumstances."

"Have there been attacks?" I asked him. This seemed a better subject to discuss with him than with Variel.

"Not in my lifetime," he replied, "but after the original breaking of the Samothen alliance, when the High Lady was gone, there were a number of battles, and the Ilto and the Vylk mounted an attack on Stronghome."

"What happened?"

Gundever grinned. "They decided to go home while there were still enough of them to father the next generation. That's why those tribes still exist. Hold on, this is a very sharp turn."

It took two days to climb to the pass on the shoulder of Harrilith, and the tivongs had to sleep in the wagon harness because there was not any room to unhitch them. Sejineth fed them a concentrated grain mixture he'd brought along for just this purpose. The cold was severe here, but there still seemed no sign of the storms, for which I was grateful. A storm that caught us here on the narrow track would be devastating.

We all slept in our wagons, bundled against the cold, and Jemeret and I did not make love. Instead, we talked long into the night about nothing important, until, just before we finally fell asleep, Jemeret asked me, "What do you hope for?"

"I hope for a little quiet time," I said softly. "I don't think I've ever had quiet time."

He smiled against my forehead. "Some of us never get very much," he said, "but this winter, in this valley, we may be fortunate."

"What do *you* hope for?" I asked him in return.

"You knew from the very first day," he replied. "I want a child."

"I'm not sure I can," I said honestly.

He stroked my hair. "Give it time," he said. "We have plenty of time. We get to Stronghome tomorrow afternoon."

The valley in which Stronghome lay was immense, but it was dwarfed by the mountains that rose all around it. As we descended into the twilight, I could see a long, winding river that divided the valley nearly in half from north to south, its far side forest, cultivated fields, orchards, and pasturage. The near side was largely open fields, but to the west, nestled into a sheltered triangle made by Harrilith and Zuglith, was a village of many small buildings and a few larger ones. They were only pinpoints of light by the time we reached the valley floor.

Word of our arrival had naturally gone ahead, and many people lined the road with cheers and torches. Jemeret leaned from his tivong to touch hands as we passed.

We reached a fork in the road near the village, and Jemeret dismounted and gestured to me to join him. I swung off Rocky. Shenefta seemed to appear out of nowhere to take the reins of the two mounts. Jemeret took my arm, and we started to walk the remainder of the distance to the buildings in the torchlight. He was continually greeted by people who hadn't seen him in a while, and he spoke easily with them. There was a great deal of curiosity about me, and I was shy before them all. Luckily, I did not have to speak. Tynnanna created something of a sensation, and because he stuck close to me, I got a wide berth.

It seemed a very long time before we reached a house at the mountain end of the village. Behind it was an expanse of field, and then the soaring heights of Harrilith. Somehow Numima had gotten there first, probably because she did not have to stop and talk with everyone she passed. The house, behind the porch posts, was brightly lighted.

"This is home," Jemeret said quietly to me. "Get settled inside. I want to make certain everyone's in safely, and then I'll be back. If I'm very late, eat without me."

"Come in out of the cold," Numima called, and the klawit and I climbed the four steps to the porch and entered our new home.

It was definitely the house of a chief. The spacious front room ran the entire width of the house, divided roughly into a dining area on the left and a sitting area with two facing couches and a huge fireplace on the right. Numima took my cloak and disappeared into a doorway to the right of the fire-

place. Tynnanna went directly to the stone-flagged hearth,
turned around three times and lay down with a contented sigh.

I began to explore before Numima came back, finding a
nice-sized kitchen behind the long dining table, and a small
bedroom beyond that which I assumed to be Numima's. Back
in the sitting room, I opened a door to the left of the fireplace
and found a small bathroom. Numima passed me on her way
to the kitchen, and I went into the room she'd come out of. It
was a spacious bedroom, with a dressing area and a small fireplace with two chairs in front of it. A bathroom opened off the
room, and I glanced in, curious. It contained a deep tub, a sink,
and a wooden-seated disposer, all fed by a system of pipes that
vanished into the ceiling. I assumed there was a water tank in
the attic. When I turned a stop-cock on the sink, the water
came through warm. I smiled at it and went back into the bedroom. It was an altogether warm and cozy room, the wide bed
piled high with pillows and coverlets, including a deep, fluffy
one that was probably stuffed with feathers.

Once it started getting cold, talmas were inappropriate, and
all the women had taken to wearing tunics and leggings. Now
I saw a laba-fur-lined robe laid across a chest at the foot of the
bed, so I changed into it. The room felt surprisingly comfortable and welcoming. It was, too, strangely luxurious, the dressing area lined with trunks and a large wardrobe. A mirror of
polished metal, edged with filigree and probably of Genda
manufacture, hung over one of the trunks. I studied my face in
it for any signs of change and discovered that I looked older
than I remembered. I attributed it—a little stupidly, but perhaps
not without reason—to the maturity gained from weeks of the
most intense lovemaking imaginable. Despite the slight reddish
cast to the metal of the mirror, I saw an additional blush rise
to my face when I thought about the things Jemeret did to me
and the way those things made me feel.

Quickly stifling that, I turned away to investigate the view
from the back window. It overlooked the sweep of meadow
leading to the foothills of Harrilith.

Tynnanna lifted his head and looked at me as I came back
out of the bedroom past him, but then he put his head back
down and purred briefly before dropping off.

Numima was bustling around in the kitchen, and something
smelled delightfully mouth-watering. I went to the kitchen
door and watched her add a fingertipful of spices to the pot
hanging from an iron hook on the kitchen hearth.

"Numima, are you related to Jemeret?"

She looked at me, startled. "Stars, my lady, all of the Boru are my lord's family," she said, "but no, I've just cared for him since he was a young man."

"What about his parents?"

"His sire was gone before he was born," she said, not interrupting her work for a moment, "and his mother went back to the house of women to have him."

"So Jemeret was Lord of the Boru from birth," I said.

Numima looked even more startled. "Where did you hear that?" she asked. "Sejineth's sire, Brenadel, was the Lord Before, but my Lord Jemeret took the lordship from him when he came of age. It was after his many-year stay with the Genda. He challenged for the leadership and had to kill Brenadel."

I felt very stupid not to have ever asked these questions before, for it explained Sejineth's hostility. I was struck by a thought and pulled my robe closer in spite of the heat radiating from the kitchen. "Numima," I said carefully, "do you think I'm terrible because I never asked you anything about yourself before?"

If my previous two questions had startled her, this one was flabbergasting. Her mouth dropped open and she dusted her hands quickly on her oversmock, came to me and took my hands in hers, earnestly looking up at my face. "Terrible, my lady? By the stars, you have been unhappy for a long time. Of course it is not terrible to think of yourself when you are in such a state! Now it pleases me to see you becoming happy." She touched her forehead to the backs of my hands and bustled back to work, leaving me feeling very strange.

I turned to go see where my nomidar had ended up and found that Jemeret had come silently into the house and had obviously watched and heard what passed between Numima and me. The expression on his face was deeply thoughtful. Then he smiled and took off his cloak, scattering across the room a shower of melting snowflakes I hadn't even known were falling.

That first night in our house—I had not begun to think of it as "home" yet; I was too unused to the idea of having a home—Jemeret changed the nature of our lovemaking. I wasn't expecting it. I had grown accustomed to being entirely responsive, of allowing him complete access to my body and my mind and merely following his signals.

When we'd eaten and let the weariness of the journey sink in, I bid Numima good night and went into the bedroom, stripping out of my clothes in the chill of the room and slipping for the first time into Jemeret's bed.

He came in soon after, smiling to see me there, and I sensed some new purpose about him. He stripped quickly and said, "Slide over." As I did, he climbed into bed. It was the first time since Convalee that we had been naked together, as the trek had not allowed so much freedom. I wondered what he intended.

He lay back on the pillows, drawing me in against his side. "Tonight is up to you, Ronica. If you want me, I'm here."

I was stunned. It had been so long since I had controlled anything, and he was asking me to control something I had never done well before he took over. I couldn't move.

Jemeret's breathing was slow, deep, and even, and I was completely aware of the pressure of his body against mine. I would have known what to do if I had still had the sting; I didn't have the slightest notion of what to do without it. I couldn't think of what to do with my hands. I knew he was watching me in the fading light of the banked fire, and still I couldn't move. His steady gaze was disconcerting.

I swallowed to clear my throat and said in a whisper, "I don't think I can."

"Why not?" The deep voice was even, unchallenging.

"I can't—control you when you have the sting, and I don't." I hadn't known I was going to say it.

"Control me?" he repeated. "Is that what you think sex is about?"

"Isn't it?" I didn't voice the question as I asked it, but either he heard it anyway or read it on my lips.

He drew my head down onto the hard muscle of his shoulder. "No, it isn't," he said. "It's a sharing."

"You've been controlling me." That time, I did voice it.

"I've been leading you," he corrected. "It's like any other form of training. I knew more of the pathways than you did. You have to begin to develop your own style at some point, and I think this is the appropriate point."

I still couldn't move. It was as if his words had created a situation in which I had no way of succeeding, no way of attaining the level of ecstasy for him that he could achieve for me. But he had not ordered me to try to satisfy him, nor had he asked me to. He was only telling me that it was time for me to accept some responsibility to reach out for him. "I don't know how," I said.

He laughed once. "Now that, I don't believe. You're a good student, and you've learned well. If you have doubts, they aren't doubts relating to 'how.' " We were both silent for a time, and then he asked softly, "Do they relate to 'why'?"

I didn't understand, and I said so.

"Do you see no reason why I should want you to take the initiative in this?" He sounded casual, and his muscles under and around me were still relaxed, but I sensed an underlying tension. This meant something to him, and while I didn't know what, once again I did not want him to be disappointed.

I moved my hands down his sides. "I may not be very good at this."

He smiled. "Just use your imagination," he said. I did.

I awoke suddenly, looking around at the gray light filtering into the room, blinking to free my sight from a lingering veil of golden sparkles. It faded quickly. Either it was false dawn or it was snowing, for the sunlight was only a hint. Jemeret was already gone. I fished my laba-fur robe from under the clothes he'd abandoned the night before and slid it on, then opened the bedroom door.

"That gives me the right to ask," I heard a woman's voice say. "It used to be my place."

Jemeret's voice held a coolness I had never heard in it—not menacing, just detached. "There is a difference, Shantiah. She is my bracelet."

The woman gave a minute hiss. "You braceleted her?"

"I just said so," Jemeret said.

"I want to *see* her."

Before Jemeret could reply, I stepped out into the sitting room, holding the robe closed at my throat. The woman confronting Jemeret was taller than I, with dark hair bound up under a fur hat and dark eyes that flashed to my movement. She was very well built, lean and strong, but when she turned from Jemeret to me, she was moving a little too nervously.

Her eyes widened when she studied my face. "You do look like the High Lady," she said grudgingly. "I can see why he wanted you."

She was beautiful, and I had learned from things Variel said about her power that she was a talented Class C, but I had never feared either category of person. I could only think that

she had lost her chance with my Lord Jemeret, and I didn't
necessarily want to hurt her. I said, as kindly as I could, "No,
I don't think you can. I don't think the things that draw people
together or tear them apart are ordinarily visible."

Jemeret laid a hand gently on my arm. "Ronica, this is
Shantiah, once my claim. Shantiah, this is the Lady Ronica of
the Boru, my bracelet and my love." He chose the words deliberately. I could tell by the widening of Shantiah's eyes that
she didn't doubt their sincerity.

She let her breath out in a powerful sigh. "I will see you
again, lady," she said. She threw one more glance at Jemeret,
more resigned than angry or hurt, then spun on her heel and
marched out. As she opened the door, Tynnanna appeared out
of the swirling white beyond the porch and bounded past her
into the house. Shantiah jerked back, startled, her hand on her
dagger, but when she saw me stroke his damp head, she relaxed. "That, too," she said, went out and slammed the door
behind her. Through the porch windows I could see her pull
her hood up over the fur hat and stalk away into the snow.

I realized that Jemeret was watching me, and I turned and
went back into the unlit bedroom. I suspected that he would
follow, and he did. He leaned against the door frame. I went
into the dressing area, picked up my hairbrush, and concentrated on getting some of the tangles out of my hair. For a long
time neither of us said anything. I worked all the tangles out,
brushing my hair smooth, then stole a look at him.

His arms were casually crossed, and when he saw me glance
at him, he said, "Go on, ask."

"Did you love her?"

"In a way, yes, but not the way I love you. Enough?"

I almost said yes, and I almost said no, but I felt I had no
right to say anything, because I had never been able to say I
loved him. I knew—or thought I knew—what love was; it
was what I had felt in the hospital room on Werd when Lanya
and her parents had been totally engulfed by it. I didn't feel
that depth of devotion, of desperation, for him, and I couldn't
test if he really felt it for me, so I couldn't say I loved him.
Love was alien to my nature. Anger, petulance, selfishness,
arrogance—those I knew very well. But love had always been
what others felt *for* me, not what I felt. The night before had
been difficult for me, and I hadn't a notion of how well I had
succeeded. I wondered if Shantiah had been better at it than
I was.

And then I realized that it was possible for me to feel insecure, and I put the brush down with a snap that startled me. "*Is* it because I look like the High Lady?" I demanded.

"There may come a time when I agree to answer that question," Jemeret said carefully, "but I won't answer it now. Get dressed, and I'll show you around the valley."

He went out.

I thought about his hands on me in the dark, thought about the fact that I had nowhere else to go, no other life than this one, trembled, shook off all the feelings, and searched in the trunk for a heavy tunic and leggings.

A few months before graduation, I was introduced to a handsome young Com counselor-assistant named Lamar Acifica. He was breathtakingly good-looking, his features regular and even a little delicate, his body well made, if a little on the soft side. I thought he was gorgeous, and I made no secret of it to Coney or Kray.

"He's a puffball," Kray said dismissively, but he glowered at me when I laughed at that.

Coney looked more concerned, and I read him quickly, to learn that he was feeling apprehensive. At that time it seemed to me the height of bad taste on his part—I thought Coney was wondering if I would seduce Lamar the way I had seduced him two years earlier. It was clear to me, of course, that Lamar desired me, and the sting would not have been needed if I had chosen to take him to my bed. I didn't want to remember about Coney and me, and therefore I didn't want Coney to remind me of it.

"If I want to have sex with him, I will," I said to Coney. Out of the corner of my eye, without having to read him, I felt Kray's anger start rising up, and I instantly stung him for it.

"Ronica, we all know you'll sleep with anyone you damn well please," Coney said mildly, ignoring the fact that I had never slept with anyone but him.

"Anyone but me," Kray said hotly, and Coney, always uncomfortable in the presence of Kray's anger, turned away.

"You," I said to Kray, "have *never* deserved it." The provocation was very deliberate, very childish. I had never forgotten the fight Kray and I had had as youngsters, and I knew from the rage that flooded him that he hadn't either. "You broke my arm," I reminded him insufferably. "You don't love me or admire me, you don't want to be my friend anymore, you just want to tell me what to do! Well, soon—"

He came at me, with a suddenness I didn't expect, but I was nevertheless ready. In our first fight I had not been fully trained, and my physical capabilities were more highly developed than the mental ones. But now I was at the peak of my mental powers. Instead of even trying to defend myself physically, I lashed at him with the sting.

Coney had started forward to get between us, but as Kray staggered back, he halted in his place. I got hold of the pain and fear receptors in Kray's brain as he reeled from the first lash in confusion, and I made him go back across the room away from me until he was sitting on a couch, shaking his head.

I withdrew, soothing the neural pathways as I left, because I really didn't want to hurt him—just show him that I was the master. "I'm sorry, Kray," I said lightly, "but I can't let you hurt me anymore. I can't ever let anyone hurt me anymore."

Kray was looking at me without anger now, but with something I read quickly as discouragement. "I never meant to hurt you," he said. "You always push me until I just react."

"I should have thought you'd have learned better control by now," I said, not meaning to be cruel, but I saw Coney stifle a wince and look away.

I was somehow upset that Coney was disturbed by all this. From my point of view, it had been going on for a long time, and the latest incident was just one in a familiar sequence. I made a face at him, turned and started away, only to be stopped by his unexpectedly sharp words. "We grew up together, Ronica. Somehow I thought you'd have learned to *care* about us."

I spun back to the two men, but the expressions on their faces were such that I couldn't bear it. Kray could never admit hurt openly, but I felt it behind the discouragement he was radiating. Coney was always able to be openly hurt, and I refused to read him past the expression on his face.

I said, more to him than to Kray, "You don't understand that I always have to protect myself."

Coney nodded, sad now. "I do understand," he contradicted. "What I question is why protecting yourself always means attacking us."

"Leave it," Kray said to him, the edge of futility still on his voice. "It's too late, and we've come too far."

It was a very long time before I knew how right he was.

* * *

My tour of the valley took most of the morning and involved a stop at the house of women, where Shenefta greeted me with a hug and Jemeret introduced me to a beautiful older woman named Alissa. She was embroidering a set of talma borders. The work was exquisite, and I thought I recognized it.

"Did you make the borders for the talma I wore on the Day of the Fire?" I asked her curiously, admiring the red and gold patterns she formed with her nimble fingers.

She smiled at me, and there was something familiar about the smile. "Very likely," she said. "I'm responsible for a great deal of the embroidery here. They sell some of my work, even to the Elden, but they keep more. If you show me the talma, I could tell you if I did the borders."

Jemeret watched us speaking to one another with a curious expression on his face. She looked at him, raising an eyebrow. "So. I heard she brought a klawit with her. Do I get to meet it, as well?"

His eyes twinkled. "He's Ronica's klawit. Perhaps you'd like to come join us for dinner, and you can meet him then."

"And see my talma," I said, uncertain why I was feeling a little uneasy at the interaction.

"My time is largely uncommitted," Alissa said with a smile, her hands flying unerringly over colors, threads, and cloth.

"Tomorrow night, then?" Jemeret's voice was rich with warmth.

She agreed, and Jemeret led me back outside into the crisp, clear day. I looked at him curiously, and he said, "That was my mare." I stared at him, mouth open, until he said with a laugh, "Did you think I didn't have one?"

"You said your parents were lost to you," I reminded him.

"My sire and na-sire are gone," he said. "My mother moved back to the house of women, and after I took the office of chief, she refused to give me any more guidance or advice." He looked away from me. "I consider that lost, in a way." And before I could say anything else, he went on. "Come with me. We're going to the temple, and then I need to leave you with Venacrona while I make certain that we're ready to face our first Severance Storm."

We strode together through the snow toward the temple building. I slid my hands into the slits in my cloak, thinking that it had been years since I'd been in deep snow.

* * *

Coney and Kray and I had once been permitted to play in a field of snow. We couldn't have been older than nine or ten, and I remember snow fights, gales of laughter, the building and subsequent destruction of a snow fort, and a great deal more which fell into the category of utter nonsense. I thought of it now as a truly golden day, when we were permitted to be ordinary children. If only we could have held on to that feeling. If only—

The temple was the only elaborately decorated building in Stronghome, if smaller than the wagon sheds were. It had three levels, the lowest being an assembly hall that could hold about half the tribe. Jemeret left me at the doorway with a fast kiss on my nose, and I climbed the steps to the second level, where there were five separate worship chambers, one decorated in each of the four star colors and one in all four. I stepped into that one for a moment, seriously tempted to linger, before I continued up to the third level, which contained what was called the observatory and Venacrona's rooms. The assistant priest and priestess lived in the house of men and the house of women.

No one was in the temple as I went through, so I guessed they were all out helping with the work. I almost went back to the starfire chamber. I wanted to reach out to the starfire again, and I wanted it to answer me. I glanced down the third-floor corridor and saw that Venacrona's sitting-room door was open and he had seen me, so I put my head in.

He looked up from the scrolls spread across the desk in front of him. "Come in, Ronica." As I did, he fished among the scrolls, looking for one in particular. "Sit." He indicated the armless chair across from him, and I sat, watching him unroll and toss aside scrolls until he finally found the one he was looking for. "Here," he said with satisfaction, and showed it to me.

It was a star chart, drawn with this nameless world at the center, for I recognized the pattern on the paper. "We need to start gathering records on you, for you are our lady now. Can you show me which star you came from?" And he looked at me expectantly.

I was completely nonplussed, because of course a two-dimensional starmap looks totally different from widely separated vantage points, and I had never seen this angle before I crashed here. I took the most expeditious way out. I pointed at the table about a handsbreadth off the scroll and said, "Somewhere out here." It was easy to read his disbelief, but he was not about to call his lady a liar. He took a pen and made a note.

"What were the names of your sire and mare?" he asked next.

I decided to be honest about this. "I never knew their names," I said. "I was raised by strangers."

He thought about that for a second or two, then wrote, *Parented by the stars.*

I seized the opportunity. "The starfire—where is it when you're not doing services?"

"Offworld. It enters the receiving bowls when we call to it."

"It's alive, you know."

"Of course." But the casualness of his affirmation made me aware that he meant it in a different way. He looked up at me. "The next major ritual will be Midwinter Song," he said, "and as the lady, you will have certain duties. Mardalita has done them in the absence of a lady, but she will be glad to relinquish the responsibility to its rightful possessor."

"Will the starfire be present?" I asked.

He seemed surprised at the eagerness in my voice, and sat back in his chair to study me. "You did have an unusual experience with the starfire," he said thoughtfully. "If you had not been the bracelet of my Lord Jemeret, I would have chosen you to be a priestess."

On the trip to Stronghome he had told me their legend of the onset of the starfire worship. It had begun, it was said, very long ago, when there were no tribes and the land was still wild, when there was no such thing as a person of power. In that time, fire fell from the heavens, and many people were harmed. The stars fell in fireballs, always in the night, never in the daytime, and so the people began to try to placate them, that they might stop the fiery rain.

Eventually the correct way to please the stars was found. It involved worshiping them, and permitting them to select the couples who would be most likely to breed a strong future generation. After this approval process had been operating for some time, there began to be born people of power, and they became the Samothen. Those who never developed any power became the Honish, and they lived apart from one another. A caste of priests and priestesses—people with the ability to hear and speak to the starfire—arose to make certain the rain of flames never again devastated the world. The origins of some of the rituals had been lost, but the Samothen were cautious—

the rituals would not be varied unless the starfire let them know they could do it without risking the rain of fire again. Sometimes the starfire came when it was called, and sometimes it did not. "Even those of us who are worthy are not always judged so, I think," the priest had told me.

"Venacrona, the starfire is alive," I repeated now.

"Yes, I know," he said again, as if it were nothing.

"No," I said carefully. "I don't think you understand. The starfire is sentient. There were only five known sentient species in the Com, and two are human, us, or closely humanoid. The other three were created by human intervention—the protocanines, the protodolphins, and the protosimians, who have died out. The starfire is unknown sentience. That is information of vital interest to a great many people."

Venacrona looked at me indulgently during that speech. "Ronica, I don't know what you're talking about," he said. "As for creating other species—you could say the starfire created *us*. But we don't feel it necessary to tell anyone."

I couldn't convey to him that it was vitally important because, when I thought about it, what good would it do? Who could I ever tell? I was stuck here for the rest of my life. But perhaps I could learn more about the starfire anyway. That way, if the Com *did* come looking for me, I would have something of great value to give to them, even if my sting never came back. I made myself stop thinking about that.

"What am I expected to do in the Midwinter Song?" I asked him.

"You will need to sing these three prayers to the starfire on behalf of and with the Boru." He gave me three separate sheets of parchment, weathered enough to show me that they were very old. "You can return them to me when you've memorized them."

"Is that all?"

"It is more than you think. The starfire may respond."

"I look forward to that. Is there any way to speak with the starfire except during the rituals?" I barely looked at the prayers as I put them into the pocket of my cloak.

He nodded. "Anyone at any time may go to one of the temple star chambers and call to the starfire. It answers at its own whim."

"How do I call it?"

"When it's not a ritual celebration, each Boru finds his own way."

I rose, then realized he might have more questions or more to tell me. "I'm sorry. Are we done?"

Venacrona set all of the scrolls aside. "I will go with you," he said, and rose also.

Something occurred to me. "Does the starfire come when *you* call?"

He nodded. "Almost always. That's why I'm High Priest. But I never call irresponsibly."

I barely heard that. "If you are High Priest, why are you also priest of the Boru?" We moved through the building at a slow pace, and I quelled my eagerness to get the process under way. I wanted to feel again as I had on the bowl floor at Convalee.

"Because the Boru have the most power, and the starfire always goes where the power lies strongest," he answered.

I was certain that the starfire, having honored me so outstandingly on the Day of the Fire, would answer me now. We reached the lower floor and I went without hesitation into the central chamber for all four star colors.

Meeting another sentient species was vastly different from meeting the MIs. As a Class A, I was given the opportunity to encounter all the other thinking animals, but not the humanoids. The humanoid species was much like us, and its mutation had been caused by a periodic radiation that washed the world of Nailat. The planet had been surveyed during a time when the radiation wasn't present, and the settlers who had been dropped there to bring it to Com standards were unexpectedly exposed and mutated. The mutation affected the genes for maturation, lengthening its cycle until their childhoods lasted almost their entire lives, and they reached sexual maturity in time to mate, reproduce, and die. The world was proscribed immediately upon discovery of this.

At the outset of the experiments to create other intelligent species—years before I was born—arguments had raged over *how* intelligent a species needed to be, and if the protosimians were always going to be a good deal smarter than the protocanines, why develop a protocanine stock at all? But the upholders of diversity prevailed, and the species were created. The protosimians were very much like we were, and they might have done well as a species, but after two generations their colony was wiped out by a virus, and we were afraid enough of contracting it not to force their re-creation.

I met a protocanine female named Jessif when I was fifteen. It was one of the training assignments I went on without Kray and Coney. Mortel John did go along, and seemed slightly more uneasy than I was used to, for he was usually unshakable. And yet the protocanines were the friendlier of the created species.

I had seen pictures of the true canines—the eocanines, as they were called now—and when Jessif trotted into the room, her shiny black nose and lovely caramel-colored fur made her look very like the pictures I'd seen. Intelligence sparkled from her brown eyes, and as she tapped the voice simulator— artificial larynxes and palates could be implanted, but they did not breed true, despite numerous efforts—she winked at me.

"Welcome, Ronica McBride," the simulator said. "I have been nominated to greet you on behalf of my people."

"I'm pleased to meet you," I said formally. "I have always wanted to speak with one of you."

"It's not the speaking," the simulator said, and it was very strange to have a speaking machine tell me that speaking wasn't important.

I smiled. "All right," I said, and reached out to read her, projecting friendliness and curiosity simultaneously. I had only just been taught the techniques of the probe, and my use of it was still rather crude—one of my subjects had described it as "bashing my way in," which humiliated and angered me to the point where I almost showed him what a bash from me was truly like.

Jessif was surprised by feeling the probe. Not only could I read it, but her ears rose and she cocked her head. The speech simulator said, "That was interesting. Do it again."

No one I had ever read had asked me to do it again. I felt a thrill go through me and tried not to let it leak past the shields. I projected the warmth again and augmented it with some reserve power. Jessif wriggled with delight.

"We are a species that responds in really meaningful ways to friendliness and love," she said happily. "We think your Responsionists are right about that single tenet of their faith. Some of us are natural responders."

I think humans, too, respond in really meaningful ways to friendliness and love.

"We are fierce warriors," Jessif went on, pleased to be in a position to give me information in return for the projection which had so delighted her. "And fierce friends."

"Are you glad to have gained sentience?" I asked her.

She was amused by the question. "Are *you*?"

To my complete surprise, I burst out laughing, and Jessif nearly shook with pleasure at having made me laugh. There was a true innocence, an utter lack of sophistication about her, that I somehow associated only with children, yet this was a fully adult, highly intelligent creature. I wondered about that.

Some of my bewilderment must have leaked past the shields, for she looked closely at me. "You are confusing sentience with sameness," the voice simulator said in response to her input. "Not all sentient species will use sentience to be like human beings—so serious, so concerned with weighty matters and the futures of peoples."

"You're describing the MIs, not us," I said, and out of the corner of my eye I saw Mortel John twitch, but he did not intervene.

"We do not see much difference," Jessif said. "You believe you can mind-learn everything you need to know. We have always known that to be a false premise. But we would not expect you to learn from us."

I thought about that casual statement for a long time after my conversation with Jessif was over. *We would not expect you to learn from us.*

If the protocanines were happy, the protodolphins were uncompromisingly joyous. In fact, they came to represent for me the epitome of joy. They seemed to have been barely affected by sentience, but we knew they had it because every so often they contacted the Com to argue a particular government policy of which we'd had no idea they were even aware.

To me, it was incongruous that they should be a mixture of carefree joy and astute political reasoning, but I gathered they found no mismatch. When I met them through their representative, Glon, from the terraformed planet Sargasso, which was ninety-two percent ocean, Glon was very pleased to see me, but clearly more reserved than Jessif had been. The protodolphins had an intricate language all their own, so only a translator was necessary, and I wore mine against my ear when Glon rose from a massive tub of water and balanced upward at my feet, nodding at me.

"I am very pleased you consented to meet with me," I said.

Glon nodded again, emitting a series of high-pitched squeaks that my translator interpreted as, "It is an honor to speak with the new Class A, but it is also to our advantage.

When you come truly into your own, your understanding will be of vital importance to us."

"So you are meeting with me in hope of future gains," I said.

"It is why most people do any things relating to the government," Glon said with what I assumed was a trill of laughter. "Otherwise our natural tendency would be to avoid such institutions completely."

"Are you saying that you would rather not be involved in politics at all?" I asked him.

"I am saying that any species with any values centered in natural things would ordinarily not care to be involved in politics."

"Politics has been a moving force of civilization throughout all of history." It was strange to find myself defending a process I thought myself above.

"So has warfare," Glon countered, "and is not one of the primary uses of a Class A to eliminate war?"

I nodded, enjoying myself immensely. "Do you believe that another of my primary uses should be to eliminate politics?"

Glon trilled his laughter again, and my translator managed to convey something of a contradictory sadness in his voice as he answered. "Ah, Ronica McBride, if only you could. You have no idea how much happiness you could bring to the universe."

The central chamber was lit by a hanging lamp with four lighted nibs, each with a transparent wrap of colored mica around it. The flickering of the four colors made dancing shadows across the carvings in the walls and on the sides of the altar, which lined the back wall. Sunk into the top surface of the altar were four depressions lined with metal, much like the bowls carried in rituals.

"What do I do?" I asked Venacrona.

"I can't help you," he said. "You must find your own way to call."

I thought about that for a while. It seemed to me that the best way to let a totally alien species know I wished to speak with it was to recall, to the best of my ability, my only previous encounter. Filled with the confidence of previous interaction, I closed my eyes and reconstructed the scene on the ritual floor at Convalee, slowly building all the concrete details in my mind, including the exact way the starfire looked before it sent the tendril to take my wrist. Then, instead of waiting for it, I built in myself a thought that I wanted the tendril to come for me.

I heard Venacrona draw in a quick breath and opened my eyes.

The altar was alive with starfire, all four colors rising and dancing in the metallic depressions. I stepped closer to the altar and projected a desire to communicate, asking the starfire to speak to me. One long tendril reached out from the white, touching me in the center of the forehead as it had in the bowl of Convalee, and a tone seemed to form in the walls of the chamber, echoing like a bell. The tone had a strange sound to it, and for a few moments it was only a noise. Then I realized it had been a long, almost incomprehensible word, so drawn out as to be shapeless. The word was, "Tynnanna."

The tendril withdrew and the starfire whooshed away as it had on the Day of the Fire, leaving the chamber darker and emptier, but somehow still charged with an energy I'd been unable to grasp and hold on to. I tried not to feel rejected, but I did. I turned and looked at Venacrona, who was watching me closely. "Did you hear it speak?" I asked him.

"How could I?" he asked in return. "The starfire stalk was against your forehead, not mine."

I wanted to say that I had not heard the word in my mind, but in the chamber itself. I hesitated, however, because I felt lessened by my inability to make the encounter go as I'd wanted it to. It was, after all, an issue of control. I'd been reacting to things for so long now, going against everything I'd been taught, that I needed to know I could manipulate something again. I'd been sure this meeting with the starfire would be it, and I'd been absolutely wrong. I hated it, and I hated that someone else had seen me reach out and be rejected. I was swept by embarrassment, and then I was just plain angry. If I couldn't control the experience, I would have to downgrade it.

"What did it say to you?" Venacrona asked me, still watching me closely.

"Nothing I could understand," I said before I'd thought about it. "It seemed a waste of time."

His surprise was so obvious that I had to look away from him. "I have never known an encounter with the starfire to be a waste of time before," he said carefully.

And I snapped at him, as I hadn't snapped at anyone since my first day with Variel, as I used to snap at Kray when he challenged me. I had wanted to be right just this once, and I'd failed. Somehow, in my mind, I thought that made me as worthless as the Com must have found me, to throw me out. I reacted to Venacrona as if he were deliberately rubbing it in.

"How fortunate for you!" I threw at him, turned and spun out of the room, down the steps past the assembly room, and out into the snowy day. Even as I did it, I knew it was unbearably rude, which is, I suppose, growth of a sort, since I used to say and do rude things all the time without caring.

It was only my first day in Stronghome; I didn't really know my way around yet. As a result, I didn't know where Shenefta or Variel were likely to be, and I wasn't certain I could go to the tivong sheds without encountering Jemeret, for the storehouses and the animal sheds were all in the same area. So I turned and gathered and ran back along the track we'd entered Stronghome on, running full-speed for the entrance to the valley. I wasn't sure why I was doing it, but at least I'd made the choice to do it. Sometimes we can see ourselves getting deeper into angry choices, and yet we seem almost to take pride in it. I was caught in it now, unexpectedly, awash in disappointment and self-condemnation.

And yet there was this prediction that I was to become the High Lady. Just as, I supposed, there had been a prediction that I was to have been the Com's Class A, taking Jasin Lebec's place.

I ran until I reached the crest of the pass, where the two track guards waited. They were startled to see me, but said nothing. I glanced away from them, up the sides of the vee through which the track passed, and gauged its steepness, the amount of ice on the bare rock cuts, and the snow, which could provide easier footing or could be treacherous.

Barely aware I was doing it, I unhooked the clasp of my cloak and let it drop to the ground. I could run with it well enough, but it would hinder me during the climb. I chose the side that looked more challenging, because exhaustion was a weapon I could use to combat the sudden, irrational combination of depression, anger, and helplessness into which I'd plunged myself. Still gathering, I started to climb, damping out the cold, forcing myself to stay alert and concentrate on every hand- and foothold.

It took nearly two hours to reach a spot where there was a ledge wide enough for me to sit down for a few minutes, and I flopped onto it gratefully, letting the gathering slide away, checking to be sure that my reserves were sound. They were about two-thirds full.

The view from the ledge was breathtaking, nearly beautiful enough to shake me out of my mood. The shoulder of the mountain slanted away toward the plain and the forest that covered parts of it. There were clouds massing in the south, from which I'd heard the Severance Storms came, the dark and roiling cloud banks building almost visibly, but still more than a hundred kilometers away. Above me the sky was a bottomless azure—somewhere in which lived everyone and everything I'd known before this world.

I couldn't go back; I thought I had accepted it. But what had I here to compare with what I might have had? And why couldn't I remember anything else? My last return of memory had been on the Day of the Fire, and there'd been nothing since then. It was as if I were stalled in that room after the graduation gala, unable to recall what had happened to me—or what I had done—next. There were times when I could tell myself to be patient and wait for it, and there were times, such as sitting on that high ledge looking out over a beautiful world, when I wanted to try to batter down the wall that separated my consciousness from the missing memory.

Just at the moment when I'd decided I would try to force my way through the barrier, despite the damage I might cause, I realized I wasn't alone on the ledge. Tynnanna had dropped down beside me from higher up on the slope and now he butted his head against my arm, demanding attention and, incidentally, almost knocking me off my perch. I grabbed for him, twisting my hands in his coat, and he purred at once, as if I were petting him. As soon as I was stable on the narrow ledge again, I asked him, "What do you know about the starfire?"

The last thing I expected was an answer, but Jemeret's voice said coolly, "If you want to know anything about the starfire, either Venacrona or I would be happy to discuss it."

Even before I turned, I knew he was angry. It was a different anger from the cold inexorability with which he'd addressed Kowati at the Boru Court of Justice. It was hotter, more volatile, and while he was controlling it, he was letting it show, edged just slightly with the sting, so that I would feel it.

His face was unreadable when I looked around. "The starfire didn't tell me to ask you," I said, trying to match his tone with mine.

He seemed remarkably balanced and comfortable on the thin

shelf, and I wondered how he had gotten higher than me without my seeing or hearing him—though I didn't wonder how he knew where I was; he had doubtlessly sent out a sensory scout to find me. "From what I gather, the starfire didn't say very much to you at all. I gather you expected more. I'm not sure what else would have provoked such childish behavior."

I wanted to tell him that he had no right to speak to me that way, but he had every right, and we both knew it. If his power as a Class A hadn't given it to him, his power as lord of my tribe would have—and if that had not, his power as the man who had braceleted me would have. Triply caught, I looked back out toward the gathering storm clouds again, unwilling to watch him being right when I was so very wrong.

"Ronica."

I ignored him. He repeated it, his voice tighter. I ignored it again. He stung me, and my head whipped around toward him, the anger and indignation welling up in me to match the implacable purpose in him. The ledge was a dangerous place to explode, and there were three of us on it. That didn't deter me. All of the day's emotions, all the juvenile tyranny that had been so much a part of my life in the Com and had been so nearly successfully repressed—but not destroyed—here, rose up in me, and I sprang at him. He could have stung me to stop me, but instead he caught my wrists and turned me to press my back against the cliff, holding me there with his body, his heels at the very edge of the shelf on which we stood.

I hadn't gathered, nor would I. Only when he knew he held me securely did he sting me, and, angry as he had been, there was no sign of it in his sting. Instead he flooded me with arousal.

I gasped, going almost limp against him, for he'd thrown the full power of his reserves behind it, smashing my anger and blowing it away in the face of sudden, overwhelming need. He held me tightly for a moment, then turned his body so that we were both securely on the ledge, my left shoulder and his right one against the cliff face. Only then did he withdraw the sting and allow me to recapture some of my equilibrium as the hunger faded. He released my wrists and took my face in his hands, his long fingers buried in my hair. All the anger was gone from him now, and his gray eyes, so close to mine, were level and serious.

"I don't want to bully you," he said evenly, "but you have to grow up. It's imperative that you begin to deal in adult ways with frustration and anger. Hush." I'd started to speak. I shut my mouth. "Now tell me," he went on, "why it's so much easier for you to react in a mature way when I'm controlling our sexuality than when you are."

The quiet question jolted me. I'd made no connection between my uneasiness all day and the fact that he'd given the initiative to me in our lovemaking the night before, but the moment he said it, something rang true inside me. He watched—or felt—it register in me. And I said slowly, "Before you, I only ever slept with one man. I controlled it, and—" I forced the words out, ashamed, but determined that he should know. "—and I hurt him by it."

I tried to look away from him, but he held my head still. "What has that to do with us?" he asked deliberately. "You don't hurt me when you reach for me."

"The past governs the present," I said, slowing my heartbeat to try to keep my chemicals in balance.

"Only if we don't think about it enough to master it," he said. "You're letting something that happened to an entirely different man affect what's happening with me. That's inappropriate." He studied me for a moment more, seeing that I was listening, then glanced over my shoulder. "The storm's moving in. We've got to start back. We don't want to get caught out in it. After the first one, they'll be easier to predict." He held still for a moment, concentrating. Later, I realized he had been calling in the guards.

"How did you get up here without my seeing you?" I asked.

"There's a hidden trail." He nodded upward, and Tynnanna, who had sat quietly on the ledge all during our exchange, now turned and bounded up the cliff as if it were no work at all.

"Wait." I glanced down toward the wagon track, so far below us now, in some distress. "My cloak is down there, and the Midwinter Song prayers are in it."

"The guards will bring it," he said, as if it was already taken care of. "Come along." I followed him up a few more feet of cliff face and then between some large shoulders of rock onto a barely visible but not difficult trail that wound its way farther up the slope and then descended on the other side, opening out onto the track as it went down to the floor of the valley.

We waited a few minutes for the guards to come around the curve of the road at a trot, and, sure enough, one of them was carrying my cloak. I took it from him, and Tynnanna bolted down toward the level ground of Stronghome.

IX. Governing the Present

Shenefta had told me that Severance Storms, which had only come once before in her lifetime, lasted from three to six days each, and that the location for the village had been chosen to keep the worst of them from destroying the buildings. Variel had told me that the best preparation for the storms was to be in your home, with food and things to do, adding with a blush, "And with someone you love." Shenefta had teased her about that.

Tynnanna refused to come into the house with Jemeret and me. Instead he stood on the front porch, his tail whipping from one side to the other as we went in, and then I saw him dart away through the village as the first winds began to rise.

Jemeret sealed the door and went from window to window, making certain the latches would hold, while Numima slid the storm dampers into the chimneys in both the living room and bedroom fireplaces. I felt useless in the bustle of activity, so I pulled the Midwinter Song prayers out of my cloak and sat down on one of the couches to look them over. I'd barely gotten through the opening verse of the second song when the first blast of storm wind struck the house and seemed to shake it on its foundation.

I started for a moment, then got up and went to the window, standing and staring out at the storm, fascinated, as I had been by that first, gentler storm when I was in the tower of the Lewannee stonehouse. This storm was a very different one, creating kaleidoscopes of white and gray out of what might have been the sunset. Particles of white struck against the panes of glass, laying a base for the inevitable frost patterns which would follow in the sunlight after the storm cleared. The howl of the wind, and the violence of the ice beating on the window, in contrast with the calm and secure warmth of the house's interior, was somehow exciting. I wasn't sure why, but it transfixed me—so much wild power, so entirely uncontrolled.

Jemeret came up behind me and rested his hands lightly on my shoulders, his thumbs automatically massaging the muscles of my upper back. I realized that I was responding to the savagery of the storm in a nearly physical way, and suddenly, without his prompting it, I had turned under his hands, reached up for his face and pulled him down to me.

He circled me with his arms, as he had the first time we kissed, and the feelings built quite naturally, without augmentation, adding to the comfort and security of being inside and sheltered. We ended up on one of the couches, and I vaguely heard Numima give a squeak as she started to set the table, looked up and saw us. Jemeret laughed softly as his housekeeper scampered out of the room, moving much faster than she usually did.

That Severance Storm lasted only three days, which left us with two tendays until the start of Midwinter Song. I had successfully been the initiator all three nights. I suppose I should not have been astonished by the level of his response to me, but I was. One of the best things about Class C talent in a man is that he never has to worry about his sexual performance, and I sensed that Jemeret had not once in his life been uneasy about his ability. He was invariably wonderful, and sometime during the storm, I began to accept the fact that he found me wonderful, too, even when I reached for him first.

As soon as the storm blew itself out, Jemeret insisted on my going with him to confirm that everyone and everything had come through the weather. I was surprised to see that, instead of there being more snow on the ground, there was less. Jemeret explained that the violence of the winds scouring the inside of the bowl tended to move most of the snow against the slopes of the mountains and out of the village or the fields. The tivongs had already been let out of the sheds into the pens, and Sejineth and his workers were gathering the dung amassed during three days of forced enclosure. It would be carted to the potting sheds and made into fertilizer or soil. Shenefta waved a rake at me as we went past.

Jemeret's mother would be coming to dinner that night, her previously scheduled visit having been forestalled by the storm. Numima was bustling around to get everything ready, and I was nervous, but trying to ignore it. We went on to the storehouses to confirm their integrity, for they held the tribe's winter supply of food, except for the fresh meat the guards would gather on hunting expeditions. Once that was completed, we went through the village to ensure the safety of all the houses. One house had had some shingles blown off, but it was already being repaired before we reached it.

All in all, by early afternoon Jemeret was satisfied with the condition of his tribe, and he sent me back to our house while he went to talk with Gundever about arranging a hunting party.

I had been watching for Tynnanna everywhere we went, but had not seen him. On my way back to the house, however, I spotted a moving, furry body against the white of the slopes on the shoulder of Harrilith, and I watched it draw close, wondering where he'd been. As he approached, I realized he was carrying a fresh kill in his mouth. He danced alongside me, making certain that I noticed and was proud of him. He seemed taller to me than he had been, his ears now on more of a level with my shoulder, and I was glad I'd come to trust in his affection. Clearly, he had come through the storm well, though I couldn't have imagined any living creature, exposed, surviving the violence of that weather without augmented talent.

We went back to the house together, and Tynnanna stayed outside until he had finished devouring the kill, then came up on the porch and banged on the door until I let him in. Numima clucked and wiped the floor after him as he stalked with dignity to the hearthside, lay down, and began washing himself to remove all traces of his recent carnage. When Numima had made certain the floor was spotless again, she returned to her bustling, trying to make the house more minutely presentable than it already was. The cooking smells issuing from the kitchen were even more attractive than usual, so I guessed she had outdone herself there, too. Housework and cooking had never been occupations to me before I saw Numima taking such pride in her ability to do them. They had been background tasks, unworthy of attention—other than, perhaps, contempt—until now.

"Are you nervous, my lady?" Numima asked me.

The question was a surprise. "Why would I be nervous?"

"My lord's mare is a formidable woman," Numima said with conviction. "She made certain he challenged Brenadel and became chief, so we say she carried the legacy of the

Lords Before until my Lord Jemeret was willing to take it up."
She seemed to see an infinitesimal speck of ash on the hearth-
stones beside the klawit, and, glaring at him, she hurried to
wipe it up, as if she was afraid it would multiply if she did not.
"She was not entirely approving when he returned with you,
though of course she would never gainsay the stars' choice for
him. Who knows what would have happened if the braceleting
had failed?"

And I said nothing, thinking, *Who knows what might have
happened if I hadn't been sent here?* I excused myself, leaving
her cleaning an already immaculate room with such nervous
energy that she almost infected me. I bathed, glad that
Numima had thought to keep the fire built up under the water
tank that provided our bathwater. Then I dressed in front of the
bedroom fireplace, for the cold after a Severance Storm was
intense. By the time I went back into the living area, Jemeret
and Alissa were seated on the couch, drinking a golden liquid
from goblets. Jemeret rose and went to the table to pour me a
gobletful.

Alissa watched him with an amused expression, then looked
at me, hesitating in the doorway. "Sit with me," she said.

I went obediently forward and sank onto the couch, then
looked at her. "What happens if you don't approve of me?"

Her eyes—so like his in some ways—widened in surprise,
and she said calmly, "My son is an adult and Lord of the Boru.
It's not for me to approve or disapprove of what he chooses to
do." She paused infinitesimally as Jemeret returned to the
couch, holding out a goblet to me. "Or whom he chooses to do
it to."

Jemeret bent and kissed her cheek, then looked at me. "It's
me in general that my mare is warily approving, not you and
me. It's a characteristic of mares. You'll see that when it's your
turn."

The words were casual, but went through me like a bolt of
electricity. I'd forgotten.

Alissa turned toward me as Jemeret settled on my other side,
leaning inward as if to provide shelter for me with his chest
and shoulders. "Am I to be a na-mare?" she asked.

I analyzed my body for a moment and relaxed with relief.
"Not yet." I had realized that, should I have become pregnant,
I would have been sorely torn. I didn't feel I was in any way
ready to cope with having a baby, but I also knew that I had

reached a point where I could not simply expel a fertilized egg—it would be half his, and I completely recognized that.

"I have no intention of impregnating Ronica until she wants me to," Jemeret said quietly.

Alissa nodded, accepting the statement. I gathered, reflexively and hard, to stop the trembling that had sprung over me. He looked at me as I clamped down on my reactions, then sipped some of his wine.

"I've waited this long," Alissa said. "A good fifteen years of patience. I suppose I can wait longer."

Numima started putting dishes on the table. I heard myself ask Jemeret, "Why did you never have a child with Shantiah or—if there were others—with the others?"

Alissa got up and took her goblet with her to the table, complimenting Numima on the meal and asking her how this dish or that had been made. It didn't put much distance between us, but it gave the illusion that she was leaving her son and me alone. It was an extremely gracious gesture, and I appreciated it, even as I waited for him to reply.

Jemeret seemed to weigh his answer, his eyes never leaving my face. "Yes, there were others, but they don't matter now, and I trust you're not fool enough to think that they do. None of them had enough power, for one thing, and for another, I didn't love them. I might have had a child with Shantiah, but the Ilto ruined her for that." He paused. "And then I would not have a child by a woman I had not braceleted, and the stars refused her when I asked." His eyes glittered, almost warningly.

I knew that he was saying he would not have had a child without the blessing of the starfire on it. He had waited—fifteen years longer than he might have, according to Alissa—because he wanted to play for the highest possible stakes, because he wanted to unite the Samothen, and because he needed a woman of power to do it. If he had only known me when I had my full power—but I shut off that thought as ruthlessly as I had shut off the trembling.

"Not yet," I said, almost a whisper.

"I know." He took my arm and we joined his mother at the table.

After supper Alissa left, without kissing either of us. I could tell quickly that she was a woman unaccustomed to yielding to emotion, that, like so many people I had known in the Com and so few I had met here, she had fastened a veneer over her feelings and always kept it there. Before she left, she confirmed that she had indeed embroidered the bands that edged my talma for the Day of the Fire, and she fingered the exquisite material, glancing at Jemeret as if it had some meaning to them both.

Jemeret went with his mother when she bundled herself into her cloak and walked back to the house of women. I knew he'd also see to the guards before he returned. I put the talma away, then undressed, lay another log on the bedroom fire, put out the stanchion lights, and climbed naked into the huge, soft bed. The wind had come up outside, so I listened to its high-pitched moan until I drifted to sleep.

I awoke at the sound of movement in the room. The fire had burned down to mere embers, and Jemeret was undressing. He looked across at me, obviously aware that I was awake, and tossed his clothes onto one of the chairs by the fireplace. I watched the play of dim light on his muscles and thought his body beautiful in a way I'd never tire of. Wordlessly, he got into bed beside me, his hands already caressing me even before his mouth took mine. It was clear that tonight he was choosing to take control again, and I was both relieved and grateful. The depth and range of my response to him still surprised me; the speed with which my body signaled my readiness to receive him seemed altogether unreal.

He lay on his side beside me and lifted his mouth away, watching me closely. I felt him slide his hand between my thighs, and I closed my eyes, enjoying the caress. When he inserted fingers in both the openings at my body's core, I gasped and twisted toward him, shaken by the crashing of sensation. In a strangely controlled voice he said, "Ronica, I want you to open your eyes."

He had to repeat it, a little more harshly, before I could respond, but I finally managed to gather and force my eyes open. The second I had obeyed him, he moved his hand in a way that made me wrench and try to roll my face away, but he held me firmly in place. "Open your eyes," he said again, "and this time raise your shields."

The command was so unexpected that my eyes snapped open on their own. It had not occurred to me to shield my mind against him since the night he took it. With an effort, I dragged the shields up. The sensation in my body decreased

instantly by what seemed a factor of ten, even though I knew
he had not withdrawn his fingers.

"Let the shields down," he said. They dropped instantly, and
the rush of heightened arousal overwhelmed me again. Jemeret
used his other hand and began both internal and external per-
suasions. I might have cried out; I know I moved uncontrolla-
bly against his hands.

"Raise your shields," he said, his voice still steady.

It was much more of an effort this time, as if the sparks
thrown off by his touches took up all the neural pathways I
would have used myself, but I did it. Despite the fact that he
continued caressing me, the feelings of excitement diminished
at once, and dramatically. I still felt him, still felt the desire,
but I could control my reactions and focus my eyes on his
face.

"Good," he said, nodding. "Now try to let down just enough
of the shields to feel what you want to feel, but not to lose
yourself in it."

It was not a skill I had ever had to master. All my life it had
been vitally important that I stay in control, and for me the al-
ternative to being *in* control was being *out of* control. I tried to
release only a little of the shields, but they slipped downward
and I was overcome with feeling so intense that I clutched at
his arms and bit his shoulder.

"All right," he said thickly, his own control slipping away,
"We'll work on it later."

After a time, as we lay side by side with my cheek on his
chest, he stroked my tangled hair and asked, "Do you want to
try the shields again?"

At that moment, I admit, I wanted nothing less. And to delay the acquiescence on my part, which had always been so
much a part of our physical relationship, I asked, "Why is
there such a dramatic relationship between the shields and the
sensation?"

"You know," he said, but continued anyway. "You know
how the body works. No matter where the sensation originates,
it ends up in the brain, but I'm already there, so I can create
your pleasure both ways, where I touch, and—"

Without moving or touching anything but my hair, and despite the satiation I had just experienced, he flooded me with
desire, using only the sting. It felt much like being shielded
and physically manipulated. I liked it. It felt, I imagine, the

way sexual desire feels to people who make love without the Class A reflex. Jemeret withdrew the sting.

"I want you to learn to retain part of the control when I'm inside you," he said seriously. "It's important that you begin to share the responsibility for every one of our sexual acts. I want you to learn to use your shields gradually. Right now, it's all or nothing—either they're fully deployed or fully absent. There are gradations of shield use, and you have to find them and become comfortable with them."

From his tone, I knew it was almost vital, though I didn't know why. It was not a concept with which I was familiar—I'd always used my shields for defense, and a defense only half activated was no defense at all. "I've never needed to do that," I said softly.

"You've never controlled the shields at all," he told me. "They are triggered reflexively when they snap up, and you push them down again to clear them. But you can practice choosing to slide them up, pausing anywhere along the spectrum." He held me close as he spoke, his voice rumbling right over my ear. "Part of defending yourself is choosing the proper level of response, not just going all out. I want you to practice it while I'm gone."

I tried to lift my head, surprised, but he held me tightly against him. "Gone?"

"I have to go out of the valley for three or four days," he said, "and while I'd like to take you with me, I can't. You'll be fine here, and I'll want to see some progress with the shields when I get back."

I sensed that he would not answer questions, so even though I wanted to know where he was going and why, I didn't ask. I had not been separated from him since my first days on this world, when I was in the hands of the Honish. Even when the Ilto abducted Shenefta and me, we were in their hands only a few hours. I was uncertain about the prospect of spending time away from him, of sleeping apart from him.

As if he read my mind, heard my doubts, even though I didn't think he had, he repeated, "You'll be fine here."

I said nothing.

I felt his absence as keenly as I had felt his presence. The weather held, and I found things to do during the days. I wrote a lot in my journal; I played the nomidar; I visited with Variel and Gundever, and Shenefta, who took me once to her parents' home for dinner. I went tramping in the hills at the shoulders of Marlith and Zuglith, with Tynnanna dancing around me and kicking up great quantities of snow. I worked out with the other warriors, for men and women practiced together here, on a field almost sheltered by the tivong sheds on one side and one of the large storehouses on the other. Shantiah was there, but we avoided each other, not even exchanging polite nods. Most of the men—Gundever, Wendagash, and Tuvellen most prominently—knew enough to keep us apart, usually at opposite ends of the field. And while Shantiah practiced largely with the other woman warriors, of whom there were seven, I was kept preoccupied by the men.

On the morning of what would have been the fourth day of Jemeret's absence, I decided to take Rocky out for a ride. I hadn't been on his back since we arrived at Stronghome, and I found I missed riding. It was one of the few things I had done all through my childhood and adolescence that I could also do here—that and the nomidar.

Sejineth and Shenefta were working in the sheds, feeding and watering the stock. Pepali and Lutamo were filling barrels with manure to be stored outside and freeze-dried. We talked for a few moments about the storm, and Lutamo, who had ambitions to be an artist as well as a tivong trainer, showed me some of the sketches he had made of the tivongs reacting to the violence outside the sheds, for during the storm he and Pepali had slept with the animals to keep them fed and watered. I praised his work honestly, and then we conjectured on how much time we would have before the next storm, an imprecise but grossly accurate calculation made from the length and severity of the one preceding.

"The last time there were Severance Storms, I was only five or six," Shenefta said, "and I can't remember getting out of the house at all that winter."

"You can't remember what you did yesterday," Pepali teased. Sejineth ordered everyone back to work.

"I'll saddle Rocky," I told him, and he nodded and returned to his own chores, taciturn now. Shenefta watched him walk away, pressing her lips together. "His claim went back to the house of women before the storm. He's not happy about that."

I refrained from saying that I didn't think I'd ever seen Sejineth happy. Instead I went to the nearest tackroom, hauled out saddle and bridle, and took them to the shed gate, where Rocky was already waiting, as if he had known I was coming for him. Beyond the fence, I saw Tynnanna pacing back and forth, which explained why all the other tivongs were at the far end of the pen. I glanced over at them as I flung the saddle on the top rail, out of the way until I had bridled Rocky.

Tynnanna had finally been accepted by the Boru who had not seen him join me on the Plain of Convalee, but it hadn't happened quickly. He had to hunt by night for more than a tenday, without ever touching a tivong, a dralg, or any of the fowls, before the most outspoken of his critics admitted that he did not appear to be doing any harm.

I finished securing the bridle and was reaching for the saddle when something I'd seen in the herd registered, and I looked back again. Vrand was there, tall against the others, watching Tynnanna calmly but warily. Jemeret was back, and I hadn't seen him. He hadn't come to find me, or reached out to touch me with the sting to let me know he had returned. And Vrand wasn't in the pen for new returnees, but in with the herd itself, which meant he'd been here for several hours, long enough to be cleaned and pronounced unsullied by parasites.

For a moment I was tempted to skip the ride and go looking for Jemeret, but Tynnanna roared impatiently, and Rocky was tossing his head and turning himself to remind me I was supposed to be putting the saddle on him. I didn't want to leave him standing there, looking after me with hurt and bewilderment in those gorgeous eyes. So I went on with my plans as if I did not know that my lord was once again in the village. And while I was riding, I thought about my progress with the shields.

Until Jemeret had made me aware of it, I'd never realized that my reflexive snapping up of the shields had not been by my conscious choice. The shields never went up unless I needed them, and when I was safe from whatever psychological danger had caused me to raise them, I could lower them easily because they slid all the way back down.

In the first few hours of practice, the shields' strength made them too slippery for me to hold in the center of their range, but by the second day, I was finding fingerholds. By the third practice session, I'd discovered that the shields yielded to my deliberate choices for them, and while my control was no more subtle than my initial experience with any of my talent had been, I could feel the growing potential for some finesse.

Tynnanna must have sensed the presence of some game in the canyons at the foot of Marlith, for with a sharp, barklike noise he split off from us and vanished into one of the arroyos which led to the forested outskirts of the mountain. I knew he'd be back later.

I kept Rocky on the flats at the edge of the valley floor and gave him his head, enjoying his energy as he ran. He slowed himself when he was ready, and I turned him back toward the village, feeling contented with the day, which was now drawing toward the early winter dusk. I was also excited at the idea that Jemeret was back.

By the time I'd rubbed Rocky down and returned his saddle and bridle to the tackroom, it was nearly dark. I turned him out of the returnee paddock into the herd paddock, then put on my cloak against the increasing cold and ran back across the village toward the chief's house, toward what I had begun to think of as home.

He must have felt me approaching.

I looked up, slowing, as the house came into sight. Jemeret was waiting for me on the porch, and there was a peculiar tension in his stance, on his face, that I didn't think I had ever seen before. I had been improving steadily in my ability to read people in normal ways, but with Jemeret, my abilities seemed much greater. I was never certain if that was because he signaled to me or because I had simply spent more time with him than with anyone else. The tension made me wary, and the wariness was not dispelled by his smile. If he was reading me, he knew of it, but he seemed not to be reacting to it. He held out his hand to me. Walking slowly, I climbed the steps to the porch. Before he could speak, I asked, "What is it?"

"I was beginning to think you weren't going to come back," he said, his eyes fastened on me.

"I live here," I said lamely.

He pulled me against him, kissing me with a peculiar intensity that seemed not to be sexual. Then he took me by the shoulders, spun me around so that he was behind me, and walked me into the house.

There was a man sitting on one of the couches with a goblet in his hand. He was wearing one of Jemeret's tunics, and it was too big for him. When he looked up as he heard us come in, I had to suppress a scream. Jemeret's hands clamped down on my shoulders.

The man on the couch rose, smiling a little crookedly, and said, "Hi, Ronnie."

It was Coney.

I thought I would fly into a million pieces, and Jemeret, sensing it, stung me gently, calming me. He let go of my shoulders when he felt I was back in control of my nerves, but he didn't stop stinging me.

"What the hell did you do to get sent here?" The question was out of me in a flash, sounding more belligerent than I might have intended.

Coney shrugged and flushed, the smile fading. "I don't think I want to talk about it," he said softly, looking away from me. I glanced at Jemeret, whose face had hardened perceptibly. I couldn't imagine what Coney could possibly have done wrong, but then, I didn't know what I had done either.

"When did you get here?" I asked him.

And, looking back at me, Coney said, "It's good to see you, Ronnie."

I realized with a blush I didn't even try to hide how unwelcoming and rude I'd just been. "It's good to see you, too," I said to him, "though I'd rather it wasn't here." And that, too, sounded awful.

Coney glanced quickly at Jemeret's stony face, then looked back at me.

He cleared his throat. "So—you don't like it much here?" He tried to make it a statement, but the rising note at the end gave it away.

I realized what my words had implied. "That's not it, Coney," I said quickly. "I love it here. I guess you will, too. It's just that—" The words died in my mouth.

"Just that what?" That was Jemeret, his voice held expressionless.

For all its feeling, it came out of me as a whisper: "I'm nothing here, not compared to what I was supposed to be there."

Before Jemeret could respond, Coney spoke. "I don't intend to be nothing here, even if I wasn't what you were, Ronnie."

"*I* wasn't what I was." The words emerged quickly, almost without my willing them to. "Nobody could be, except for Jasin Lebec, and I don't know how he does it. Do you remember being sent here?"

Coney glanced again at Jemeret, and something in the look disturbed me, but I couldn't place it. Then the pale brown eyes turned back on me. "I said I didn't want to talk about it," he said firmly. After a moment he smiled. "Tell me what it's like here."

Words failed me. How could I describe the overwhelming sexuality, or Jemeret's love and support, without reminding him of the wrong I'd done him? How could I do for him what I had so wanted someone to do for me when I first arrived, bewildered and angry—neither of which emotions he seemed to be feeling at all? It was the recognition at last that he seemed so at ease here that made me uncomfortable. I wished fervently that I could probe him, to try to see what wasn't right. Granted, I had not fully expected him to react as I had, but he wasn't reacting at all as I might have expected *him* to act. Coney was an acceptor, but not necessarily of the catastrophic.

Then I felt a suspicion rise, and I frowned at him and said slowly, "They oriented you, didn't they?" He seemed surprised by the question, and once again his gaze slid for a split second to my lord, still standing behind me. I wondered if Jemeret was stinging him to provoke a specific reaction. "The Com told you what to expect before they sent you here!" I went on.

It was accusatory, but I was angry now, and I was unwilling to try to control it. Before Coney could speak, however, it flowed through me and left me wondering. "Did they orient me, too? Is it part of what I've forgotten?"

"I'm not going to talk about the past," Coney said carefully. "I gave my word not to. Don't ask me to break it, Ronnie."

I stared at him, torn. They had not tampered with his memory, only with his sense of honor, which was extreme, and he was asking me for the single thing that would be hardest for me to give. And yet, I owed it to him. After the slightest of hesitations, I bowed my head, acquiescing.

Jemeret had said nothing at all during the exchange, and I'd been barely aware of his hands still resting on my shoulders. Now he pressed tighter for a second, bent and kissed the top of my head. "I'm going to take our new arrival over to the house of men," he said and let go of me. "You can see him in the morning." He stepped around me as Coney rose. "We'll need to choose a tribal name for you," he said.

They walked toward the door. Something occurred to me, and as Coney drew on a cloak I heard myself say, a little awkwardly, "Just tell me—how is Kray?"

His hands faltered as they fumbled with the clasp. "I don't know. I hadn't seen him for more than two years."

Then, while I was still reeling from that statement, the two of them were gone, and I fled to the bedroom, to the dressing area, to the mirror, staring at my reflection as I had in the tower room when I first arrived on this planet. Two years. *Two years.* Where had they gone? Where had I been? What had I done? And why couldn't I remember?

The anger and frustration rose again, even more potent than they had been when I first confronted the existence of the wall in my mind.

And yet . . .

Slowly, watching my eyes in the polished metal, I went back over the memories that had been returning, carrying me through the graduation ceremony and the gala and back to my own rooms where, I felt certain, whatever it was that had happened—whatever it was that had caused them to send me here—had occurred. And it had occurred that very night, in those very rooms. I felt it with an absolute conviction unanchored in memory, almost cellular.

And then two years had gone by?

I felt something slipping, as if the ground under my feet had shifted, as if a ship entering roll had shuddered and failed to make the roll gradient, spinning out of control through normal space away from the roll point. Nausea almost overwhelmed me to a degree I hadn't experienced in years, and I already knew trying to overcome it would only make me sicker. I ran to the bathroom and threw up until my exhaustion, ungathered, was too great to support even the dry heaves.

All my control was gone. Two years of my life had vanished—perhaps more, because Coney had only said he hadn't seen Kray for two years, not how much after graduation that had been—and I couldn't seem to get my mind to deal with that. In some ways it was worse than when I had first awakened here, because then there had been hope of rescue. Now there was none, and there was finality in that, but just as I'd begun to accept that I didn't need rescue, that I could build a worthwhile life here, Coney had appeared and everything had come rushing back—except for those absent memories, so much greater and more perplexing than I had thought them to be.

I realized I was lying on the bathroom floor, sobbing, and I straightened up, mopping at my eyes with my hands. I made a barely thought-out decision that enough was enough. I would have to try to batter down the wall that stood between my consciousness and my absent memory, as I'd decided to do on the mountainside before the first storm. I figuratively picked up a rock and drew it back—

And Jemeret figuratively caught it, interposing his self between the wall and my blow, catching and absorbing its power so that the recoil did not hurt me, though I knew it must have staggered him. He was in the bathroom doorway, and now he bent and lifted me to my feet, holding me tightly against him. Even through my despair and anger, I could feel him trembling very slightly from the force that he'd absorbed. "I've been waiting for you to do that ever since you got here," he said softly to me. "I can't let you do it, love. You could do yourself irreparable damage."

"—didn't mean to hurt you," I gasped out, clinging to him.

"I know." He gently pushed my matted hair off my forehead and, wetting a towel, wiped my face with it, then tossed it aside and carried me to the bed. "I'm going to put you to sleep for a while," he said. "We'll talk when you wake up." And before I could say anything else, I was sinking away into darkness.

I had always known—until I came onto this planet—that I had more power than anyone else alive. It was an immensely comforting thought, even though I knew that it separated me from all other human beings. From the day Jasin Lebec had to ask my permission to probe me until at least graduation, I had been, simply, the strongest person in the Com. I had not given much thought to the morality of using that power; it was simply something I was supposed to do, and nothing could stop me from doing it. Or so I thought.

Awakening slowly, calmly, late into the night in our home, with Jemeret sitting in one of the chairs by the fireplace watching me, I realized consciously something that I might have suspected in other ways. It was not the Class A power or my training that gave me strength; my strength was not the ability to make things happen, but rather the ability to endure the things that happened to me. And I wasn't doing as well at it as I might have liked.

I sat up in bed. "Are you all right?" I asked him. "You took a hell of a slam from me."

He smiled at me, that open, completely loving smile that made me warm all over. "I'm fine," he said. "Tell me about him."

I knew at once that he meant Coney. I drew up my knees

and circled them with my arms, wondering how I could say what Coney meant to me. He waited, the smile gone, but his eyes still glowing. At last I looked at him directly. "We grew up together," I said. "He is a part of every one of my memories. He loved me, and—" I gasped. "—I hurt him." I looked away then, tears starting. "I hurt everyone who ever cared about me, just like I hurt you earlier today."

His voice surprised me with its power. "You didn't hurt me, Ronica." He rose and came to sit on the bed beside me, his arms around me. "You were trying to hurt yourself, and I stopped you. Look at me."

I raised my eyes. He took my face in his hands, stroking my cheekbones with his thumbs. "Believe me, you would have hurt me far more if you'd succeeded in mangling your brain than you did when I caught the blow."

"Two years," I said, my voice shaking in spite of myself. "I've lost two years. I need to know what happened."

He went on stroking my face. "You told me you were starting to remember."

"Not quickly enough."

"As quickly as possible. In the meantime, you will have to learn to live with the ambiguity. Come eat something. Numima put it on the table hours ago, and she'll be deeply offended if we don't eat any of it."

He got to his feet and pulled me up. I realized I was still dressed, and though I wasn't hungry, I went with him to the dining area and nibbled whatever it was. There was clogny, and I drank deeply, grateful for the warmth as it went down. After a few minutes I asked him, "Do you mind that he loved me?"

Jemeret set down his knife and leaned back in his chair. "He still loves you," he said evenly. "You must know that I probed him before I brought him to the Boru. He fell in the plains between us and the Genda, and he might have gone there as well as here. But when I probed him, I found him to be a fine, strong young man, and I wanted him for us. We were almost back here to Stronghome when he asked about you."

"He knew I was here." It was not a question. Jemeret neither confirmed nor denied it. I thought they had told him when they oriented him, or—the notion struck me suddenly— perhaps, somehow, he was here *because* I was here. There had to be dozens of wilderworlds. Why would the Com have sent both of us—and Sarai—to this world, unless they wanted us to be together?

I looked at my lord. "Do you mind that he still loves me?"

He shook his head. "As I said, he's a fine young man."

"Then why did they send him here? If he's not maimed, like me, they would have needed him. Kray couldn't possibly be handling everything himself. He's not temperamentally suited for it, and he was never—" I broke off suddenly.

"Go on," Jemeret ordered.

I'd been very careful, since my arrival here, not to use Com jargon for talent, but Coney's presence had disoriented me. When Jemeret told me to continue, I abandoned my caution and did so. "—he was never able to accept a Class A assignment. He hated that he couldn't."

Jemeret sighed and pushed his plate away. "Sandalari spoke to me once about the outside, so the words you're using are not completely alien to me. But they're inappropriate here. We don't divide people by their differing levels of power. We divide only those with power—the Samothen—from those without. Your friend has power, and he belongs with us." He had not meant Kray.

"What did you decide Coney's name would be?"

"He chose Mekonet." He waited to see if I'd come far enough in my understanding of the language of names to interpret it, but I shook my head. "The center of the circle."

Considering Coney's Epicyclism, the name actually made a great deal of sense. "I can still call him Coney," I said, pleased.

"Privately," he cautioned. "I'd rather the tribe didn't know you knew each other before if we can avoid it."

My question was out before I realized I was going to ask it. "Jemeret, does the starfire know?"

He seemed as surprised by the question as I was. "I think the starfire knows everything," he said at last.

I digested that for a very long time. "When the starfire touches you, what do you feel?"

He reached out and took my hand, rubbing his thumb across its back as he had rubbed my cheekbone. "Almost the same kind of joy I feel when I make love with you. What did you feel when it engulfed you?"

"As if nothing could ever hurt me." I lowered my head, watching the steady, even movement on my hand. "But things do." It came out as a hiss.

"Yes, they do," he agreed. "That's part of living, getting hurt and going on."

"And paying for it." It was as if someone else was speaking with my hushed voice, but I knew it wasn't him. I knew it was a part of me somehow coming to the surface of speech without reaching the surface of consciousness.

He squeezed my hand hard, making me suddenly look up at him. His gray eyes seemed to bore into me. "You have it mixed up," he said firmly. "You don't pay for getting hurt, Ronica. You only need to pay for hurting."

I stared at him, somehow bewildered by the concept. To me, being hurt meant that I had been too weak to *keep* from being hurt, and the Com had spent my entire life training me not to be weak. "But I feel as if I'm responsible," I said, trying to explain, perhaps choosing the wrong words.

His eyes glittered suddenly, and he took my hand in both of his. I realized—once again surprised by it—that something very important was going on. "Listen to me," he said, the tension in him so monumental that I felt it clearly even though I didn't think he was deliberately projecting it at me. "Responsibility is not fault. Do you understand the difference?"

I said I did. I think I do now. I didn't that night, and he must have known that I didn't, but he let it go.

After we finished the little we ate of Numima's meal, we went back to the bedroom and Jemeret tested my ability to control the shields. When he saw that I did not have much trouble holding them partially extended, even while he was stimulating me, he began to vary and increase the physical sources of stimulation, and to add more of his formidable power to the sting. Slowly, that night, I learned I could increase the extension of the shields, using just as much shield power as I needed to match him and no more, and then yielding to him when we were both ready.

From the first Jemeret had been, I think, secretly amused by my eagerness to experience the overwhelming pleasure of our sexuality. But that night he showed me that the sex and the shields could work together, and he told me he would become my teacher in ways I had never dreamed. I knew he was right. While I was studying with Mortel John, my training had been almost entirely mental—only the Class C work required physical exercise, and that was about eleven percent of the total. This training would begin physically, with the genitals, and grow to the mind along paths I had only previously guessed at.

My new schoolroom would be the wide, berugged bed in the dim bedroom in our home. My new teacher would help me not to be uncomfortable at whatever role I took sexually, passive or aggressive. He would, he said, teach me how to give him pleasure, putting more and more of the initiative, the direction of our lovemaking, in my hands or my mouth. I was looking forward to the lessons.

Coney's Class C talent and training in self-defense—the same as my training had been—qualified him for a fax as a warrior, and the day after his arrival, he joined us on the practice field. Unexpectedly, Jemeret came, too. He almost never practiced with his warriors, and I had never seen him fight with weapons—only with the sting—so I was fascinated at being shown his power with the physical implements of combat, as well as with the unarmed techniques.

Coney and I were still awkward with one another in the morning. I watched as he met Gundever and Wendagash and began to familiarize himself with the weaponry. I got to listen as a newcomer was weighed and discussed by the members of the tribe, who accepted me now as if I had not been the last person so weighed and discussed. I was fascinated by the depth and perception of the judgments made. Because I had known Coney for all but the few past, missing years, I knew that the observations of his personality the tribe made were much more accurate than not, even on only a momentary acquaintance.

That accuracy caused a bewildering suspicion in me that everyone in the Boru had some low level of Class A talent. It created a situation that I had not previously thought possible—indeed, that Mortel John had said was not possible: that there might be people with neither full Class A talent nor fluctuant Class A talent, but rather with *minor* Class A talent. In small amounts, Class A talent was supposed to be wild, renegade, undependable, even warping to its holder. And yet I thought I was watching it now, and it was both useful and controlled.

I felt stupid that such a possibility had never occurred to me, for just as everyone was thought to have some extent of Class C ability, and Class B's were graded because their talent levels differed from one another, it was utterly logical to think that Class A talent might exist in differing amounts, and that some of it might be stable. It was just that Mortel John had always said such a thing was impossible, and I had believed him.

I wasn't concentrating at all on my halfhearted sparring with Gundever, and he noticed it. He evaded a defensive move of mine, dropped his sword, and smacked me, open-handed, on the hip. We grinned at one another. "My mind is not on this," I said unnecessarily, and he nodded.

"You might want to sit down for a while," he suggested. "Or pick out a wrestling partner, so you won't get hurt."

I withdrew to the edge of the practice area, folding my cloak and sitting on it, automatically seeking out first Coney—working slowly, weaponlessly, with Wendagash—then Jemeret, holding his longsword two-handedly and moving more and more rapidly through the series of exercises called the Ladder of the Warrior. The exercises could be done unarmed—Climb 1—or armed—Climb 2. They grew increasingly complex and more demanding of concentration as the practitioner moved up the Ladder.

Even as I watched him, admiring his prowess, his strength, Gundever's casual caution kept resonating through me. His last words—"so you won't get hurt"—seemed to echo and reecho through my consciousness, consuming more and more of it. I frowned, trying to smother it, and instead I started hearing Jemeret's voice from the night before, saying, "You only need to pay for hurting."

Suddenly I could barely breathe, and tears were refusing to heed my command not to flow.

Jemeret must have been reading me, for he spun instantly out of Climb 2, tossing his sword aside and accelerating to me almost before I had realized I was going to start crying. I felt his arms around me and his sting touching my mind at the same moment, neither delving nor influencing. "Tell me," he said.

"I—never paid—for hurting him," I said, the spaces between the words consumed with the effort to swallow irresistible sobs. "I hurt Coney, and I never paid for it!"

"How would you want to pay for it?" His voice was right at my ear. I was too distressed then to realize what I did later—that he was pleased by what was happening.

"I'm not—" I had begun to say I wasn't sure, but then I remembered that when I first felt the truth of how much I had hurt Coney, I had been devastated to think that I would never have the chance to apologize for it. Now, of course, I did. It was such an elementary thought that I felt, again, abominably stupid. But its very rightness calmed me at once. By the time

I'd blinked back the tears and looked up, Coney was standing in front of us. I guessed that Jemeret had stung him to call him over.

The expression on his face was one of infinite concern for me, and I knew it as well as I knew Kray's mocking, challenging smile. I rose up out of Jemeret's embrace and threw my arms around one of the two men who was much more than a brother to me. Jemeret, behind us, must have warned the others back, for all at once it was as if the three of us were alone.

I barely gave a thought to Jemeret's expressed wish that the Boru not learn that Coney and I had known each other before our separate arrivals here. And Jemeret could have stopped what was happening, but chose not to.

Coney held me tightly, and I gripped him as if he were somehow the key to my future—which, it has turned out, he was, though not in any way I could have anticipated.

"What is it?" Coney whispered to me. "What can I do?"

He was so damned unselfish that I wanted to shake him. Instead I said, "You can forgive me."

He was honestly flabbergasted. "Forgive you?"

I nodded. It had become vitally important to me to do this. "I am so sorry I made you sleep with me. I know you didn't want to. I know I caused you pain. I need you to forgive me for that." I'd tried to keep my voice low, but it had scaled up.

Coney held me even more tightly against his chest. "Ronnie, I forgave you years ago. Don't do this to yourself."

"I'm sorry," I said again, almost helplessly, looking up at him. He turned his head, and I assumed he was looking once more at Jemeret. Then he bent slightly, only a little taller than me, and pressed his lips against my forehead.

"I forgave you," he repeated. "Now you have to forgive yourself." He set me away from him and turned me, in effect handing me back to my lord.

"He's right, Ronica," Jemeret said. "You are very hard on yourself, and you're judging yourself much more harshly than you ever needed to. Forgive yourself."

I began weeping in earnest now, and the men used their bodies to block me from everyone else. Somehow the thought of forgiving myself was almost paralyzing, as if it was a step I couldn't possibly take. After a few moments I felt Jemeret slide into my mind and make adjustments, and I began to calm. Coney had forgiven me, and that was, after all, what I wanted more than anything else. The tears dried.

"Coney, I never meant to hurt you," I said honestly.

"I know that. I always knew that." He smiled at me. "I was even flattered that you chose me instead of Kray."

"Were you?" I asked dubiously.

The smile went a little crooked at the edges, reminding me of the charming, sheepish Coney I knew so well. "Not at first," he admitted. "But later, after it was all right again, then I told myself you'd chosen me when I was—" He stopped abruptly, suddenly looking at Jemeret.

"You were what?" It was Jemeret's voice, coming from over my shoulder, and it was amazingly gentle. I would have asked it myself if he had not.

"—not as good as Kray." He tore it out of himself.

It made me angry. "Coney, stop it!" He stared at me, startled. "You were the best of us—better than Kray, better than me!"

Jemeret's hands closed on my shoulders, but he didn't try to keep me quiet.

Coney shook his head. "Ronnie, you were always, always the best of us. We knew that. We never forgot it."

And then there was something I heard myself say, feeling the hard, bare truth of it, letting it carve a piece out of me. "Oh, no," I said. "I was only the strongest. Strongest—isn't always—best."

Just as he had before, Jemeret blazed outward, surrounding me, holding me with him away from the world, far more tightly than his grip on my shoulders and far longer than I would have thought he could sustain it. Then the fire of his soul dropped away from us and he turned me against his chest.

I was no longer aware of anyone or anything else, only his arms around me, his heart beating steadily beneath my ear, and that I was clinging to him, panting as if I'd just run a hard race without the help of my reserves.

That night, the world changed again.

When we were preparing for bed, after my apology to Coney on the practice field, I thought about what Jemeret had told me, and remembered how much I was looking forward to beginning the lessons he had promised me.

I had no notion of what was to follow.

The evening had begun normally enough. Coney shared dinner with us, and I noticed, almost shyly, that we had nearly regained the easy familiarity of our time before. After he left,

Jemeret and I played a duet on our nomidars by the dying sitting-room fire. We had been playing for quite some time now, and our music blended and supported itself in ways that made me very happy. The nomidar had always been a private obsession, and to share it with someone of his skill and depth was, I believed, making me a better player, as Lyrafi had predicted it would.

When we went to bed and I reached for him, he caught my wrist and held it lightly away from his body. "We're not going to make love," he said seriously. "Not tonight."

"Why not?"

"It's necessary." His face was very sober in the firelight. "Lie back. And, Ronica, you have to trust me."

I lay back against the pillows, curious but not in any way alarmed.

Then, still holding me by the wrist, he said, "You're going to feel a need to snap your shields up, and I want you to control the reflex. Keep the shields down no matter what." My control over the shields had developed enough now so that I thought I could do it, but there was nothing he could have asked that was more calculated to test the trust he'd built up in me. The shields had always been my saviors. He watched me, waiting for acquiescence.

I nodded, not sure I could speak.

"I'm going to enter your mind and find a certain place, a certain set of nerves—not pleasure, not pain. You'll feel where I am. I want you to concentrate on touching me there."

Before I could say that was impossible, he used the sting, stilettolike, and slipped along a particular neuron chain I would have needed a month's study of brain physiology just to locate. I had no time to wonder how a primitive on a wilderworld would have the sophistication to identify this individual chain, small and subtle as it was, because he was right—I *could* feel where he was, and I *could* touch him there. And I felt the reflex threatening to slam in and try to thrust him out. I fought it, helped by fascination at what he was doing inside my mind.

As I grew more and more absorbed in the exercise, controlling the shields consumed less of my conscious energy and I paid more attention to what Jemeret was doing. He was moving the sting lightly back across the neuron chain, a millimeter at a time, drawing my awareness with him, deeper into the complexity of brain function.

The neuron chain seemed to terminate in a blank wall of

grayness, and I would have stopped, but Jemeret drew the sting past the wall and I followed, almost pulled along by the force of his own will. The moment I was past the wall myself, Jemeret withdrew his sting and took me back along with him. The outer world returned. I realized that we were still in the bedroom together, but that it was day, and I was physically exhausted. What had seemed only a few moments of contact within my brain had been eight or more hours of hard work.

I could see that Jemeret was very tired, too, but he was watching me so seriously that I guessed we weren't finished yet. He took my hand and stroked its back with his thumb. "Now, Ronica," he said in a very matter-of-fact voice, "I want you to tell me what I'm feeling at this moment."

Without thinking about it, I gathered and touched him to read him—and then I realized what I had done. My entire body spasmed at once; tears sprang to my eyes and I stifled a scream, pressing my free hand against my mouth.

Jemeret nodded, unsurprised. "It's all right," he said. "I wasn't certain I could do it, but it worked."

"You—I have my sting back!" I was afraid to believe it had happened, but I knew it had. He had given me back the sting.

I began to weep, and Jemeret embraced me, holding me against his chest and rocking me as if I were a child. I had thought that part of my life was over, but it had been restored to me.

"Try to sleep," Jemeret said, his lips against my hair. "You don't have much left in your reserves. I'm sorry I had to use so much, but I can't drain myself all the way down."

The gale of weeping blew over me and left me so drained that all I could do was fall asleep, and then deep. He may have slept awhile, too, but I had no way of knowing. He may also have gotten up and done whatever he needed to do all day, but when I awoke it was dark again, and he was beside me, watching me. I struggled out of an unaccustomed web of sleepiness.

"Are you all right?" he asked.

I was calmer now. "I'm fine," I said. "I'm whole again."

"Not quite yet. You still haven't remembered anything about what caused the sting to go away."

I stared at him, openly bewildered. "Jemeret, how do you *know* all of this?" I demanded.

"You keep forgetting how long and how often I've been in your mind. But you're getting better. Let's get something to eat."

We got up and raided the kitchen, for Numima was not in the house. I wondered if he'd sent her away.

As we sat at the table eating by the light of a flickering lamp, I reached out with my newly recovered perception, feeling his satisfaction with what he'd done and with me, but also a subtle undercurrent of anticipation, which he was not—intentionally or unintentionally—fully masking.

"Could you have restored my sting at any time?" I asked him.

He shook his head. "You weren't ready until yesterday night," he said. "You would have slammed the shields up on me if I had tried. And, by the way, I didn't restore it. All I did was remind you of where it was and how to reach it. You restored it yourself. Before yesterday, you might not have been willing to." He took a large swallow of clogny and watched me closely, reading me with a strength I could now feel and did not in any way resent.

I pondered what he'd just told me. I knew there was some connection for me to make, something he could see and I could not, something that might lead me to a portion of the memory still locked away from me. As I chewed on the bread and cold dennipin, I chewed, too, on what I knew.

First, that my Class A talent had been gone. But did "gone" mean it had been truly missing, or fluctuant, or did it mean that I simply could not access it? If it was fluctuant or gone, how had Jemeret known so positively that we had reached the point where *he* could access it for me? If it was merely inaccessible, how had it been made so?

Because I knew, second, that a fully developed Class A talent, one that was not fluctuant, could not be shut down without its physical destruction. Its reserves could be exhausted, its wielder could be killed, but it could not just be frozen in the presence of reserves. And yet, my sting had been gone.

I frowned, looking at Jemeret in confusion. "But no outside force—" I began, and then it hit me. I started to automatically reject the insight, in horror, pain, and instantaneous denial, but Jemeret overrode it.

"Don't shut it out! Say it!"

At the same time, he was stinging me with feelings of security and love, laying a ground on which I could finish my broken thought. I squeezed the chair arms so tightly that one of them split under my hand with a crack that echoed around the room. I held on just as tightly to the feelings he was sending me, forcing myself to slow my breathing and open my throat, which had closed so tightly as to make speaking impossible.

"No outside force can destroy an individual's power," I stammered.

"Which means . . ." he prompted.

I was sweating at the effort, but I found I *could* say it after all. "Which means I did it to myself."

His face didn't change into the smile I felt him projecting. "If I draw back the sting, can you bear it alone?"

I tested myself gingerly, the new knowledge entirely unsettling, and I found that now that I had faced it, had said it, it was bearable—if still infinitely painful. I nodded quickly, not trusting myself to speak again.

Gradually Jemeret stopped projecting, and I realized that, even without his using the sting, even without me making a deliberate effort to read him, he still gave me love and support. I drew in a deep, shuddering breath and explored the pain at its edges. He had said, when he caught the blow I'd tried to direct at the wall between me and my memories, that he didn't want me to hurt myself, but I already had. I had turned against myself, and he had known it. For reasons I still could not fathom, I had hurt myself worse than anyone outside could have hurt me. I had removed from myself the thing that made me special, that made me different from anyone in the universe except—I thought then—Jasin Lebec. I let myself cry for a while. This time Jemeret did not take me in his arms or comfort me, but only watched me, reading the surface of my reaction, not its depth.

At last I blotted the tears with the sleeve of my robe. "How did you know?"

His answer was absolutely the last thing I expected, at a moment when I believed nothing could surprise me any longer. "I did it to myself once," he said calmly. "If I had any more evidence, I would think it was just a brutal part of growing up with this kind of power."

"There really aren't very many of us, are there?" I asked.

"Not that I've ever heard."

"Why did you cut off your power?"

He rolled the stem of his goblet between his fingers. "Probably for the same reason you did," he said maddeningly.

"But I don't remember why I did it!"

He said nothing.

I frowned at him. "How did you know I would let you show

me where it was and bring it back? If I'm the one who took it away, how did you know I'd let it come back?"

He studied me. "You were ready," he said at last. "When you apologized to Mekonet—Coney—I knew you were ready. You only needed guidance, and I thought I could provide it."

We ate for a time in silence, and I reached tentatively, almost fearfully, for the sting a hundred times. It was there every single time, just as it had been every time I'd reached for it before I crashed here. I wore out my reserves casting sensory scouts into the village, finding and identifying some of the Boru I knew, touching Coney without letting him know, lingering a moment, voyeuristically, as Variel responded to Gundever's lovemaking, and then sliding away, embarrassed.

Jemeret didn't interfere with any of the explorations until it became obvious that I was straining. Then he said, "Don't weaken yourself too much. It'll still be there if you leave it alone for a while."

I started to ask him a question, but I was overcome by a yawn.

He smiled. "Go back and get some more sleep," he said. "We need to transfer a great deal of the winter fodder from one of the storage sheds tomorrow. We're expecting another Severance Storm, probably by tomorrow night."

I got up and started to leave, obedient to the direction, then remembered that Numima wasn't in the house and took the dishes to the kitchen. He watched me do it, neither stopping me nor helping me. When I was done, I was very weary, and tapping the edges of my reserves showed me that the emotional drain on them was as debilitating as the physical drain had been.

As tired as I was, lying in bed, I could not turn my brain off to sleep. Why, I wondered, would I have built a wall between my sting and myself? Cowardice, faced with graduation and the true beginning of my career? Unlikely. I had looked forward to being a graduate Class A and a free citizen for too long, and it had filled me with too much pride. Overload of some sort? Even less likely. The Com would always monitor and prioritize the incidents demanding my services. Had I tried something and failed? That was more worth considering, because I would abominate failure—I, who had always been taught the critical value of succeeding at all costs. Two months before, I would not have even been able to consider this reason. Failure would have seemed more than an abomination, it would have seemed an impossibility. Now I could speculate about it. But something in me did not accept it as an answer.

What choices were left? Why should I withhold my finest power?

The word formed in my mind before I was aware it was there, and with my sting active again, I *knew* Jemeret had not projected it at me.

Punishment.

There was a bone-deep, bone-hard truth to the word that struck an immediate chord in me. I sat up slowly in the darkness and tested some still unknown reality. I had punished myself for something. Something I had done? Something I had *not* done? I was too tired to wrench at the blocked memory, but I wanted to. What had merited such drastic punishment? And if I had done it to myself, what had forced them to expel me—a trained, graduated Class A—out of the Com entirely?

Still puzzling on it, I slept at last, and for the first time since we had come to Stronghome, I wasn't aware if or when Jemeret came to bed.

I was able to push the speculation to the back of my mind when I awoke the next morning. The level of activity in Stronghome had accelerated to a just-below fever pitch. Every able-bodied person—Sammod, Sammat, or child—deserted any normal tasks that did not involve food for either the Boru or their stock of animals. All morning, we worked transferring supplies—six days' worth of food to each private cottage, the houses of men and women, the temple, the dralg sheds, the fowl pens. By noontime we'd shifted just more than half of what we needed to, since the snow made the use of wagons impractical and we had to make a chain of people, winding from the storehouses across the pasture to the houses. At the very end of the morning we began the job of transferring bales of fodder to the tivong stables, where the line passed into the buildings and up into the lofts that had been emptied in the first storm.

I'd noticed that Shenefta, who was working in the loft just above my place on one of the ladders, had cast several long, appraising looks at Coney, who was one of the men lifting bales into the stable itself. I was not, therefore, surprised when she sat down beside me on a bale to eat her bread and cheese and asked, "Will you introduce me to your friend?"

I grinned. "Does everyone in the tribe know that we knew one another before?"

"After what happened on the practice field?" She sounded as if I were an idiot even to have asked the question. "All day yesterday, people were saying Lord Jemeret didn't let you out of the house because you and Mekonet had been best friends."

"But you didn't think so."

"I didn't care much," she corrected. "I just think he looks awfully nice, and I want a chance at him before any of the others move in. Do you think he'd like me?" It all ran together into sudden self-doubt that made me remember she was only fifteen.

"I think he'll like you very much," I said honestly, glancing around to see where Coney had sat, and finding him so deep in conversation with Jemeret that I didn't want to interrupt them. I did want to listen, to find out what they were talking about, but the stable was full of people, all of them talking at once, and expanding my hearing only made the cacophony more intense.

Instead I reached out with the sting, touching at the edges of their feelings. They liked and respected each other, and while that didn't surprise me, the depth of the emotions was entirely unexpected. These were two men who had only known one another for three days—or, if Jemeret's four-day absence had been to follow a fireball down and retrieve its occupant, at most for seven days—and yet they appeared to have bonded very quickly.

I wondered why.

Shenefta drew my attention back again, chattering about Sejineth and the women he was tentatively and sequentially sharing meals with, perhaps thinking of sleeping with. Suddenly curious, I asked, "Have you thought of sleeping with anyone?"

"Me?" She seemed stunned.

"Of course, you. You're an adult now."

"But I'm only fifteen. I haven't even—rounded out yet." She actually blushed. "No man would claim me yet."

"Do women ever claim men?" I wondered that I had never asked that question before.

She ate some of her meal before she answered. "I've heard that they do among the Dibel and the Paj, but not here. I don't know if those tribes have the custom because their chiefs are women, or because they're pacifistic, or just because that's how it is." She thought about it for a moment, finishing her meal along with the contents of a water bottle we were sharing. Then, with a grin, she said, "Of course, you can order everyone to take up the custom when you become High Lady."

I was astounded by the realization that I had forgotten I was supposed to become the High Lady of the Samothen. The reminder almost disoriented me, and then I accepted it without acknowledging anything to Shenefta. Now that I had the sting back, I felt more equipped to cope with the notion than I had before. As a Class A, I could do far more than anyone else, except, of course, my lord—and he could not become High Lady.

My glance strayed again to the two men, and I was struck by a strange sense of the inevitable. All my life, until I was sent here, there had been three of us—Coney and Kray and me. Now there were three of us again, but this time I wasn't the strongest, nor did I care to be. This time I would not be sleeping with Coney. And yet we were three; I could see that just in the way the men sat together, could feel it in their strangely rapid rapport.

Sejineth, in charge of the activities in the stables in his capacity as tivong trainer, gave the signal that the break was over. We all stuffed the remains of our food away and rose. "Come to dinner," I said quickly to Shenefta. "I'll invite Con—Mekonet, too." She flashed me a fast grin as we went back to work.

Because the storm was predicted to strike early in the evening, making passage between the houses impossible, we had to delay the dinner for Shenefta and Coney. It would have been awkward for all of us to be trapped together by the storm. But I did introduce them, Shenefta grinning with pleasure and Coney solemnly polite and secretly amused.

Jemeret sent me back to the house about a quarter of an hour before the storm was expected, to make certain the shutters were closed, the fire built up, and the dampers adjusted. I paused on the porch in the rising wind to look around for Tynnanna, whom I had not seen in several days. There was no sign of him, and I didn't call.

The house was empty. Numima had expressed a desire to spend the storm with her daughter, who was expecting a child at any moment, and Jemeret had gladly given his permission. That meant he and I would have the time of the storm to ourselves. I trembled a little to think about it, but put it out of my mind, tossed my cloak onto a couch and went from window to window, securing the latches. Then I moved to the three fireplaces—living area, bedroom, and kitchen—setting the dampers, and at the same time carefully feeding the fires. By the time I'd lighted the lamps, Jemeret had come in, laying his cloak on mine and sealing the door.

He barely beat the first blast of wind, which made the house jump and filled the air outside with howling and moaning. He smiled at me, and I smiled back and went to pour us some clogny. We were both tired after the full day, as were, I supposed, the rest of the Boru, for everyone believed in exhausting themselves when an approaching storm would mean enforced idleness.

Jemeret had washed his face and hands and sat back on one of the couches. I brought the goblets and gave him one before I sat down across from him, rather than beside him. He raised an eyebrow, curiously watching me, as he sipped some of the liquor.

"I haven't seen Tynnanna for a while," I said.

"I'm sure he's all right. He'll probably be back when the storm clears."

I took a long swallow of clogny. He rubbed his eyes wearily, then fastened them on me again. "What is it?"

"Can you help me remember—what I can't remember?" It was a far harder question to ask than I'd thought it would be. "Before Coney came, I thought it was just—a night, a single night, the night of graduation. But—*two years*. So much time gone, so much time—" I had begun to tremble, and I gathered and controlled it.

He watched me, his eyes strangely reflexive. He seemed to analyze my question—which I thought could not have been completely unexpected—for a very long while, but I knew he was not reading me, because I would have felt him now that my sting was back. At last he said, "You're not ready to remember yet."

The words were quiet and even, but charged with meaning.

"How do you know?" I tried not to be angry or demanding, tried to hold on to my impatience.

"I know."

For a moment we regarded each other across the space between the couches. Then I said, "I want to probe you."

He lowered the goblet and crossed his arms. "Come in, love."

But before I could enter his mind, I was frozen into the past by my first new memory in weeks, completely unexpected—another door opening, the missing time getting infinitesimally shorter.

Nothing had happened in my suite in the few hours of night remaining after the graduation gala. But Jasin Lebec had come to my rooms just before dawn. I hadn't slept, still riding on the adrenaline rush of the night before, and I felt no need of sleep. I had bathed and, still naked, was packing for my trip with Coney and Kray to Nanseda. I sensed his commanding presence before he actually tapped on my door, and pulled on a wrapper. As soon as he knocked, I opened the door, smiling at him, for now—I believed—we were truly equals at last.

"I didn't see you at the party," I said by way of greeting.

"I wasn't there," he said mildly. "Would you sit with me for a few minutes?"

"Of course," I said, and joined him on my couch, a little miffed that he had not congratulated me. "What are you still doing here? I should have thought the Com would not want us both to be in the same place at the same time now."

He studied me for a moment or two, his dark eyes sparkling. "It is necessary for me to probe you again," he said unexpectedly.

I was immediately wary, guarded. "I thought all that was over last night. I'm a graduate Class A and a free citizen."

He started to say something, then changed his mind. "You may probe me first, if you would prefer."

A thrill of apprehension ran through me. I had stung many people in my training, but I had never done a full probe on anyone with anything like the shielding ability of Jasin Lebec. The idea of probing him was as terrifying as it was exciting. The lure was also, as he knew it would be, irresistible. I nodded, and he made one quick, palms-up gesture that said, "Well?"

I began a normal read, enhanced it, and directed it into a probe. Most normal brains can be pictured as a sea of restless waves, moving, passing into and through one another, sometimes breaking on the shores of consciousness. Inner energy created the power of the tidal motion; in some people the water was shallow and serene, or barely disturbed, while in others it was almost wild.

In Jasin Lebec, the sea was unfathomably deep, and currents ran strongly on many levels. Yet, despite its complexity, there was a purity, a wholeness to the sea which was almost overwhelming. I could find no backwashes, no crosscurrents, no treacherous undertows, no shoals or reefs. The strength and power of the waves were undeniable and, in their own way, exquisite. I could feel the neural bases propelling them, but I did not linger to explore, because I was certain I would find no tangles there either. Tangles left shadows upon the currents, and there were no shadows in the sea of this man's mind.

With a sigh, I withdrew.

Jasin Lebec nodded. "Very well done for a first attempt at this level," he said. "It could have been a little less protracted, but on the whole it was quite skillful."

"Yes, I could have done it faster," I admitted readily enough, "but I didn't want to."

He understood at once; I felt it. And I wondered for the first time what kind of sea he would find when he probed me, which he did at once, swiftly and without any sense of intrusion. When he was finished, he stood, leaned down to me, and kissed me once on the forehead and once on the lips. "Serve well, and with all your heart," he said.

The memory died, leaving me still on the couch in the house at Stronghome. I had no idea if any time had passed, or if the memory had come in a timeless flash of insight. Jemeret's expression did not appear to have altered. "Have you forgotten how?" he asked.

I didn't tell him I'd just remembered something, and I didn't waste any time reading him. I simply created a probe and slid it up behind his eyes into the deeps of his mind. This sea, while bottomless, was far from sharing the tranquility of Jasin Lebec's placid ocean. Shadowless, unfragmented by crosscurrents, Jemeret's was a powerful surge of swells and boundless, heaving motion, sublimely untamed yet tirelessly controlled. Waves moved restlessly over the surface, carrying their roots throughout the mass of deep water, seeming to constantly change while remaining eternally the same. It was a majestic evocation of his greatness, and it was without deception, limitlessly rich and sensual, filled with power.

I had to force myself to withdraw; the sea I'd encountered was as fascinating, as hypnotic, as the man himself. And, like a shaft of sunlight striking through clouds to gild the surface of the waves and plunge a shaft of fire into the liquid depths, I read the absolute truth of his love for me. He gave it like a gift, knowing that I would recognize it, raising it above the solid glow of his responsibility for the Boru and high above the deep-buried swirl of a pent-up anger.

He was magnificent.

The room around me returned, and I gulped the rest of the clogny in my goblet as Jemeret rose, came across the space between us, setting his own goblet down on the floor, and gathered me into his arms, his mouth on mine. This time Numima was not there to interrupt us.

It hadn't occurred to me—stupidly—that my repossession of the sting would materially change the nature of our lovemaking, but of course it did. For the first time we were truly equals, and I could feed him pleasure by my presence in his mind, just as he could feed it to me in mine. I could circle and control his nerves, block and build his receptors, just as he did to me. We moved within one another, and he showed me how we could magnify the excitement through each other until it doubled, then quadrupled, and then I lost count.

We slept entwined in one another on the floor between the couches until it grew too cold, and then we gathered up our scattered clothes and went to bed.

He built up the fires again in the morning while I tried not to burn the porridge. I would never be even an adequate cook, and by dinner that night he'd ejected me from the kitchen and taken over the responsibility for the food himself. We spent a good deal of the day pathfinding and repairing the circulation of the hot water system that operated to fill the basins and the tub. The pressure had been dropping off enough to signal some narrowing of the conduit due to scale or debris smaller than the filter would remove. The pathfinding, though it was slow because the piping was very primitive, allowed us to identify the most deeply affected segments of the system so we could replace them.

There were several small lulls in the driving force of the storm, but they seemed to be only for emphasis, as the weather closed in violently thereafter. In one of the lulls, we climbed into the attic of the house to replace the section of pipe directly under the spigot that brought water from the large holding tank, kept from freezing by the low level of warmth rising from the rooms below.

We worked well together, often without even needing to speak to one another, anticipating each other's needs. By late afternoon I was as comfortable with him as I'd ever been with anyone in my life.

While he cooked a stew of refreshed dralg meat and cold-stored vegetables, I studied the prayers I would need to know for Midwinter Song. What with one thing and another, I'd only managed to memorize one of them so far. They were deceptively simple, and the rhythms of the words in the longest provided a real challenge, because the beat appeared almost at variance to the words, which spoke of relatively plain things in relatively complex ways. As quick and as—ordinarily—controllable as my memory was, something in the lattice of words and rhythm was strangely elusive. I enjoyed the challenge.

At dinner I asked a hesitant question. "Do you mind that now everybody knows that Coney and I knew each other—outside?"

"A little." His response was slow and cautious enough so that I knew he'd thought about it a great deal before I'd asked. "We don't like to raise any questions about the people who are sent here—over the years. Most of the Boru and the Genda know that the people the stars send had some kind of lives outside."

"I knew Sandalari, too." Somehow there was a great deal of relief in being able to tell him.

"She told me," he said, and while I wondered when, I didn't ask. "She said she'd no longer have known you, because you'd softened so."

"Softened?" My voice scaled upward. "I was always very hard-edged."

He smiled, his eyes lazily caressing my face, but he said nothing. I flushed a little and then concentrated on my food.

After dinner was over, I sat down on a cushion by the fire and picked up my nomidar. The concentration on the complex prayer had reminded me that I hadn't practiced for a little while, and I felt the lack. This was the first time I had tried to play since I had recovered my sting, and I wanted to replay something from the Dibeli song contest to see if it felt any different now that I could project.

Swiftly I ran through the choices. The nursery rhyme was in itself not truly a sympathetic piece, so it would not do. The song of the warrior I had not agreed with and had not enjoyed playing, so I rejected it. The third song had described the space between the stars as empty, and I got no joy out of interpreting that. The fourth song had been the one about secrets, and while I had played it, I remembered nothing of the song I'd played, so I couldn't repeat it. The Song of the Outcast Tribe I hadn't played at all; Jemeret had played it twice, once himself and once through me.

Then I remembered the words of the next-to-last selection: "The fires of the stars burn through time and are not consumed; there is no body great enough to contain the heart of a victorious warrior, or a mother with a newborn, or a lover who dances with Fire." I almost gasped at the memory, because now I *had* danced with fire, and now I *was* a lover.

I closed my eyes and stroked the nomidar, letting the sympathetic strings ring in a strong undertone to the melodic line. I felt the music move through me and the resonances emerge from the nomidar, the amplification comforting again.

When I was through playing, I realized something, and opened my eyes, frowning. "It didn't feel any different."

"What didn't feel any different?"

I'd been so absorbed in playing that I hadn't been aware of Jemeret's coming up to sit behind me on the floor. Now I glanced back at him. "Playing the nomidar. It didn't feel any better or any stronger than when I was playing without projecting."

He looked me straight in the eye. "You may not believe me, but you never played without projecting."

I went ice cold and didn't move.

"I said that one day I would tell you what happened when you played to interpret the 'secrets' selection in the game of the Dibel," he went on, almost inexorable, knowing the effect he was having on me. "I think this is the time."

I had played that song with such power, invested it with such strong emotional reality, that he had been afraid there was no way to keep the real strength of my abilities hidden any longer. So he had used all of his own projective strength to absorb the projection and dissipate it. The spectators had received no more than the barest hint of the ocean of feeling I had played into that piece. I realized why he had appeared so strained after I finished playing, and I remembered Shenefta saying it had been wonderful and horrible.

"I couldn't let the Samothen see how much power you really had," he said, "because I couldn't let you see it. You weren't ready." He reached out and gently stroked my cheek with the side of his forefinger. "And the only lie I've ever told you was to say I once stole the sting from myself when you asked how I knew yours wasn't really gone. Truthfully, I knew you had the sting because you used it when you played the nomidar. And you used it to call me when the Ilto took you. How else do you think I found you so quickly?" He kept stroking my cheek, dropping revelations in my lap. "You called Rocky with it that first day at the tivong pens, too."

Tears stung at my eyes. "Do you mean that I *never* lost the use of the sting? That's impossible. Because when I reached for it, it wasn't there!"

"Yes, it's impossible," he agreed. "You couldn't control it, so you didn't have it. But you couldn't play the nomidar without using it, so you kept it and used it without controlling it or being aware of it."

It seemed too fantastic, and I shook my head.

"The mind is a very complex thing," Jemeret said unnecessarily. "Your mind has been extensively trained to be far more complex than most. Look at it as a kind of hysterical blindness. You were blind, not to vision, but to your sting."

"Who taught you these things? These are things I was never trained in."

He smiled, brushing my hair off my forehead. "Living teaches us many things," he said. "You have done a great deal of learning and only a little living."

"You aren't that much older than I am."

"I've lived almost twice as long."

I was still trembling at the unbelievable truth. "But—I *know* when I affect other people with the sting. When I was angry at Dogul in the stonehouse, I'd have slashed at her with it if I could have used it. When you probed me against my will, I would have—" My breath caught in my throat with a ragged sob I was helpless to stop and unable to understand.

Jemeret took my hands in his and held me tightly. "You never used it to hurt anyone," he said deliberately. "Ronica, you have not misused the sting since you were here, if that's what you're afraid of."

He was right, I realized. I *was* afraid. It was the same kind of paralyzing fear that had come over me on the stage at Convalee when I couldn't play the Song of the Outcast Tribe. The same kind that came at the idea of forgiving myself. This time Jemeret did not slip into my mind to help drain the panic.

"It's just the two of us," he said, holding my hands with

enough pressure to hurt them. "There's no one else here. Fight it, love. Don't let it win."

He went on murmuring, even as I ached to pull him into my head so he could help me. Slowly, under the soothing encouragement of his voice, the dread began to weaken its hold on me, and I gasped as if my lungs had been paralyzed, too. I panted for a moment, then fought for the gather and forced the rest of the fear away, the adrenaline draining out with it.

"That's it." He pulled me against his chest, his mouth on my forehead, then on my eyes. "Every day you get a little more ready to put yourself together."

"This is *painful*," I said almost explosively.

"Of course. But not too painful to be borne."

Something in his voice made me draw back away from him, looking at him closely. "Can you see into the closed place in my mind?" I asked him, suddenly suspicious. "Do you know what I can't remember?"

He didn't answer.

I tried to probe him, only to discover that he was shielded against me. His face remained compassionate, but he gave me nothing. "You do know." I felt the truth of it sink down inside me. He had been inside the place in my head where I couldn't go. Just as he had been able to move past the gray wall that had kept me from controlling my sting, he had been able to move to the dark spot that held two years of my life. "Tell me."

He shook his head. "You'll get there," he said. "I know you can get there. It'll just take time."

My eyes stung with tears. I'd been crying so much lately. It seemed as if I had lost a lot of my life, really, and I didn't want to lose any more getting to the truth. Yet even as I thought that, despairingly, another thought was creeping in to tell me that time spent here, with Jemeret, would not be time spent badly. It was a kind of acceptance.

He seemed to feel it. He rose and picked up his nomidar. "I want to show you something," he said, nodding toward the wine-wood nomidar I'd put down.

I recradled my own instrument, feeling the familiar security of it and me as a team. He sat down opposite me and touched me lightly with his sting.

"Touch me back," he ordered. I did, and he immediately began to play. After a few notes I joined him. Though I didn't know the song, I knew what he would play, which made the duet remarkably easy for me, its harmonies even richer because we could both anticipate and follow each other. When the song was over, I was smiling as openly as I thought I'd ever smiled in my life. He beamed his love back at me, and we put the nomidars aside and went to bed.

X. The Voice of the Starfire

There was one more Severance Storm between my recovery
of the sting and Midwinter Song, and we prepared for it as
carefully as we had for both the others. The events of daily life
leading up to the ceremony of star worship and tribal unity that
would bisect the hard, cold season were fairly unremarkable.
Mostly, we just lived, as people do everywhere in the galaxy
except the School for Talent, on Werd. Jemeret and I entertained several times a tenday, for it was one of his obligations
as chief to meet with his people. My small dinner for Shenefta
and Coney expanded effortlessly to include Variel and Gundever, Morien, and Tuvellen, who had—inexplicably—shaved off
his beard and wasn't letting it grow back.

"I think he looks like a little boy," Morien said disparag-
ingly, trying to enlist me to her cause by adding, "Don't you,
Ronica?"

"I don't want to take sides," I said with a laugh. "I like men
with beards, and I also like men without beards."

Coney grinned. "That's about the limit of your diplomacy,
isn't it, Ron—Lady Ronica?" He was trying to remember, in
company, to use my title, and I admired the fact that he could
do it without sounding in the least forced, while I was having
trouble making "Mekonet" come out at all.

Variel smiled a little shyly. "We're none of us as tactful as
we probably should be."

"Power does that to people," Morien drawled. "It removes
the 'polite' gland."

"I'll beat her when I get her home," Tuvellen said lightly.

Variel and Shenefta giggled, and we all knew the threat was
an idle one. Variel had told me that beating his claim or bracelet was one of the offenses for which a man could be ejected

from the tribe. The practice was considered Iltolike or even Honish, and therefore degrading. But Morien was well known to have interesting sexual tastes, and there was every possibility that Tuvellen might indulge her, not with a beating, but with something or other mutually exciting.

Morien made a face at him and winked at me.

Jemeret changed the subject easily to a discussion of the hunting expedition that would preoccupy most of the warriors the next day. "It's not that we're running low on meat," he said to Coney. "It's that I'm endlessly cautious. I want to have half again as much of anything as I think I'll need." He smiled. "I may not get it, but I want it."

"I can't imagine you not getting anything you want." Coney's voice was rich with the kind of admiration he used to reserve only for me. I felt a small pang of jealousy, then laughed at myself for it.

Jemeret had gone very serious and shook his head at Coney. "I don't always win," he said softly.

Coney flushed, as if he somehow should have known better than to say it, and I looked at my lord with a curiosity I knew better than to express.

It was Gundever's turn to change the subject. He brought up the need to replenish the hard charcoal used in the single, small forge they employed to keep the weapons in good repair, rework the wagon wheel rims, and fix any pipes or farm implements that needed it. Somehow Gannelel had let one of his apprentices keep the fire going through the five days of the past storm, and that had depleted the supply far beyond safe levels. It meant cutting more trees, then reinsuring the caulking seals on the stone oven in whose interior the wood could be sealed and turned into charcoal.

Gundever watched Jemeret carefully as he told him, and I briefly wondered why. Then, as Jemeret folded his hands on the table and stared at nothing beyond Gundever's shoulder, I realized this was a more serious question than merely the charcoal supply.

Coney looked curious, the rest of the diners solemn.

"Do you believe," Jemeret asked at last, "that I should ask Gannelel to allow me to assess the neuron state of his brain?"

Gundever looked away from his chief and friend. "I hate to think it may be time," he said quietly. "His whole life has been the wagons since my na-mare died."

"I know." Jemeret's voice was even, emotionless. "But last

time I tested him, there was barely enough to knit together and shore up. I said then I didn't think I could do it again."

Variel surreptitiously ran her knuckle under her eye.

"How old is he?" I asked.

"Almost a hundred," Gundever answered.

And yet it seemed young to me. I thought about Jasin Lebec, still going strong at nearly 110 now, with many more years of service before him. Coney and I exchanged a glance. Life was harder here than it had been in the Com—in some ways—for technology extended some benefits in physical ease that a wilderworld did not.

And yet, over the span of time leading up to Midwinter Song, I made some discoveries about life—truths I had not previously perceived, truths that may have held as much in the worlds of the Com as they did here. I discovered that everyone lives a life of value, that importance is not, as I had always been taught, a quality created by the interface of talent and sociopolitical influence. The small things, the human things, were important because they made up most of what happened in most lives.

In Stronghome, I moved into the lives of the Boru, and the routine of them made the blank time in my memory seem less urgent. I began to learn the patience of passing time in everyday ways, not trying to hang on to every moment so that it would be imbued with the deeper quality of "meaning." I learned the happiness of being part of a community, a people. Having Coney there made it easier for me to see the joy of quietness as well as of influence.

And slowly, still nervous about it for reasons I could not then entirely understand, I began to use my sting, not as a device for control, but as I had in the hospital room long ago, when Lanya Ver Lenghy had therios fever. I began to help.

Numima's daughter had a prolonged labor, which she could not herself speed for fear of harming the baby, and I was able to ride out the final two hours with her, helping her to conserve her strength and not exhaust herself holding the pain at bay. Pepali slipped on some hidden ice coating a rail of the tivong pen and shattered his arm. I heard his cry for help almost by accident and ran to the pens, helping him control the pain long enough to begin diagnosing and assessing his injury. I discovered, to my astonishment, that he had never been formally taught how to splice bone and knit muscle cells. We worked together all the rest of the afternoon, beginning the slow process of healing he would need to continue on his own over the period of days that followed. It seemed that the Boru had always regarded self-healing as an idiosyncratic thing, rather than something scientifically structured in physiology.

I had been tempted to ask Jemeret to take me with him when he went to test Gannelel, but something made me cautious, and instead I went out running with Tynnanna, who had indeed returned after the Severance Storm. Once again he seemed to have gotten bigger, but he was more affectionate to me than he had ever been before.

After our run, we climbed a little in the steep slopes at the western side of Zuglith, and while we were sitting on an outcrop of rock with a view of the entire valley—I was catching my breath, and Tynnanna was stalking a sket that was trying to scratch out a winter living—I cast a scout back down into the village to see if I could find out how Jemeret was faring.

Instead I encountered a stab of sadness which was almost staggering. I must have reacted to it in an overt way, for Tynnanna's head jerked up, his fiery eyes burning at me. I scrambled to my feet, gathered, and started back down the slope as quickly as I could. Tynnanna abandoned the sket and followed me.

Gannelel had left the wagon sheds and walked across the frozen surface of the river to the circle canyon in Kerlith's flanks that sheltered the Boru graveyard. I wondered that Jemeret had just let him go, but he had. The old man was alone, kneeling in the snow brushing flakes and dead leaves from the small cairn that marked one of the graves. Unlike the Com, where death was postponed indefinitely and the remains of a body disposed of hygienically, almost like an embarrassment to science, the tribes of the Samothen believed in remembering that the dead were a part of them. The Boru customs honored the nomadic origins of the tribes, separating from the settled Honish as their power became apparent. Now that they had a home, they still marked their graves as they would have had they buried a lost member by the roadside, with cairns of stones. These cairns were, however, of Boru manufacture, not haphazard, and each contained a compartment in which something beloved by the lost person could be placed. Those who knew they were to die would choose the things they wanted in their cairns, but if someone died unexpectedly, without making such a stipulation, all those who loved him or her made the choices in a mourning group.

Gannelel heard me approaching, looked up, saw Tynnanna at my side, and started to shuffle to his feet. I went forward quickly and caught his shoulders to keep him in place as I sank down beside him.

"My lady," he protested, and I overrode him.

"I felt your sadness, Gannelel, and I wanted to see if I could help to ease it."

He laid his hand on the cairn beside him. "This wash my Lishanie."

"I can feel your love for her," I said, grateful beyond measure that the sting was back in such strength that I could use it subtly. "Finding that love in life is an incredible blessing."

He bobbed his head and said shrewdly, "You have found it."

I didn't deny it. "Why are you so sad now?"

He sighed once, caressing the cairn absently. "I've grown old," he said. "I knew I would, but I never pictured myshelf not going to the wagon sheds. Ever shinsh Lishanie died, it wash my life."

I found myself hoping I'd say the right things, and touched him lightly with the sting to assess the effect of what I was saying. "You built a second life once, which is a hard thing, and most people can't do it at all. Now you have a chance to build a third life. You'll have two more than other people do."

"What kind of life can I have now? I cannot do my work any longer." He looked at me, blinking. I felt a stirring of interest in him, not resignation or despair. He had not given up; he was willing to listen.

"You can have a good and full life, I think." I let myself sound a little tentative, though not as tentative as I felt. "What did my lord say to you when he tested you?"

He sighed again, not as deeply. "He shaid I had reashed that point when we need to let the tribe give me back shome of what I've given. But I don't want to take." He spat out the last word with a vehemence I hadn't thought him capable of. Then he seemed to talk to himself. "I wash never meant to be ushless. Harentig ish a good man, but there'sh shtill a great deal he needsh to learn about wagoncraft."

"Could you still teach him?"

He shook his head. "He'sh wagonmáshter now. It would be very rude of me to interfere."

I understood the etiquette, and then inspiration struck. "Gannelel, I think you should write a book."

He stared at me.

"You have a wealth of knowledge to share about the wagons, and Sejineth's apprentice Lutamo is an excellent sketch artist. He could provide illustrations." I gauged his hesitation and added quickly that Lutamo could probably do the writing down of the information as well, and that "then Harentig could choose to benefit from your knowledge and experience without feeling unworthy of his fax."

He was considering it, I knew. The idea was an alien one, but it drew him, flattering and challenging at the same time. Some of his sadness was beginning to dissolve. He talked to me for a while, a little ramblingly, about Lishanie. He missed her, but in the years since her death, he'd never stopped carrying her with him. He had been thinking that he could not carry the wagons with him in the same way, but now he saw a way in which it might be possible. I sat and listened, damping out the cold he seemed not to feel, until the sun was almost gone. Then we got to our feet and walked back to the village, Tynnanna pacing us to the house of men, then roaring once at me and darting off to hunt.

I remember thinking, as I went home, that I was building a second life, too, and wondering if it was something many more people did than I expected.

There were a few more incidents before Midwinter Song which seem meaningful to me now.

Coney was fitting in well with the tribe—better than I had at first—and he seemed to enjoy what he was learning about us. He saw Shenefta occasionally, but he did not appear to feel more for her than the kind of affection she inspired in everyone. Coney was preoccupied. I sensed it in him, and it bewildered me. He had always been so open, so uncomplicated before.

One afternoon, while Jemeret was occupied elsewhere, Coney and I left the practice field together and took tivongs from the pens. Rocky was recovering from a split pad and wasn't available for me to ride, so I was mounted on a spirited little female who seemed to delight in trying to make me think she was in charge.

We went up the road to the pass into the valley. Coney had expressed a desire to see the view of the outside world. When I asked him if he didn't remember it from his initial arrival at Stronghome, he hesitated a moment and then said, "I didn't notice much of anything when I first got here, Ronnie. It was all a kind of a muddle."

I accepted that, even though I sensed something not quite right about it. Coney was entitled, after all, to his privacy. It didn't occur to me then that that was not an attitude I would have recognized as valid in the Com, where I was the one entitled to everything, where the universe was mine to plunder—all for the greater good, of course.

The day was breathtakingly clear, and after we passed the guards, we tethered the tivongs to one of the bare, windblasted trees that twisted its way upward from scattered patches of dirt on the slopes along the road. We sat at the roadside, looking out over the long stretches of forest and plain to the south.

"It's beautiful here," Coney said softly.

"Did they tell you it wouldn't be?" I tried to keep the question casual, as if it had no real meaning for me at all.

"They don't define beauty in this way." He answered almost without thinking about it. "I mean, Epicyclism does, but the government doesn't."

We had brought water bottles and squares of the heavy winter grainbread with us. I broke a slab of mine into tiny pieces in its wrapper and popped one into my mouth. "They were wrong, then, the government." It was, for a probing statement, unobtrusive.

Coney kept studying the vista, drinking it in. "About some things," he admitted. "You don't see it when you're in training. You don't think to question the values or the methods." Something in his voice on the last word made me look at him. There was a judgment there, a maturity, a hardness I had not seen in him before. Even if he had not told me time had passed, vanished from my recollection, even then I would have known. Coney had changed.

I looked out over the land and swallowed hard. "I know you won't tell me what you did to get sent here, Coney. But will you tell me why you did it?"

And then we sat in silence for a long time, not looking at each other. I might have reached out and stung him to persuade him to tell me. Had I been the Com's Class A, I would have done it. But I knew now that persuading him to do something against his will before had caused both of us grief—and me rather more than him. I knew that he needed to be able to make his own choices without my influencing him; I would not deliberately hurt him again.

Before he spoke, the sun had changed position enough so

that there were long shadows accompanying us, and we'd eaten all our grainbread. Still, I was content to wait, not knowing why he felt the need to hesitate for such a long time, but crediting him with good reasons.

At long last he stirred and turned toward me. I met his gaze neutrally. "I don't want to lie to you, Ronnie. I don't think I've ever lied to you, and not because you could read me and tell."

"I'm not reading you now," I said.

"I know that. It's one of the reasons I want to be especially honest." He might have smiled, but he did not. "Everything I did, I did because I thought it was right. Now there's one thing I'm not so certain about. You're happy here, aren't you?"

The question seemed like a complete non sequitur to me, but I knew that, to Coney, it followed directly. "I haven't thought about happiness, really. We were brought up to duty, you and I, not to happiness." I folded up my bread wrapper and stuffed it into the pouch of my cloak. "But yes, I'm happy. Except now that I've got my sting back, I sometimes feel very guilty."

"About being happy?"

I half smiled at him, then looked overhead at the sweeping circle of a pair of hunting lattels. "You see, the Com needs Class A talent, and Jemeret and I are both here, hidden away. It's like I owe them something, and I never got to provide it."

He studied me, a closer, tighter scrutiny than I was used to from anyone but Jemeret. "Do you think you're being wasted here? Not doing things important enough for you?"

It was a very pointed question, and I smiled at it, unoffended. "When I first got here, yes, I did feel that way. But I haven't since Convalee."

"Why not?"

Even without using the sting, I sensed more tension in him. "Because Jemeret's convinced me that people are as important as tribes, and tribes are as important as nations, and nations are as important as worlds." I looked back up at the lattels. "A person *is* a world, Coney. I don't know why they never told us that in the School for Talent."

He said slowly, "I don't think they know—or if they knew, they've forgotten. Hey!"

I followed his gaze and realized Tynnanna was sitting on the road near the tivongs. I hadn't realized he'd come with us, and clearly, neither had Coney. "It's just Tynnanna." And the moment I said it, I realized it wasn't just Tynnanna. Behind him stood another klawit, bigger, darker, its expression predatory, its tautly muscled body motionless in the stalk.

With the sting, I was fearless. It also didn't hurt that Tynnanna was between us and the strange cat, even though both of them were facing us. Behind us the tivongs shifted nervously and pulled at their reins. But instead of lashing out at the klawit, which might have been my instinct had Tynnanna not been in the way, I just waited, laying a hand on Coney's arm as if to reassure him.

Tynnanna gave a small growl, directed over his shoulder. The strange cat jerked its head toward him, the stalk broken. Tynnanna growled again, more menacingly this time, but still did not turn in the direction of the other cat. The unknown klawit took one step backward, turned its back on us, and darted away down the steep slope below the road. Tynnanna waited until it was out of sight, and then purred at us.

Coney was a little paler than usual. "What the hell was that all about?" he asked, his voice unsteadier than I'd heard it before.

"I don't know, unless the bigger klawit was a female, and Tynnanna was introducing us to his prospective bride. Come on, it's getting late. We should start back." I rose, and Tynnanna butted me once with his head so that I had to pet him above the ears and at the base of his horns. Then he turned and raced off back toward the village.

"That is the weirdest thing!" Coney said in a rush of outgoing breath.

"Not in context," I said, not caring if he understood. We remounted our tivongs and went home.

Less than a tenday later, another incident stands out. A number of the men—Jemeret and Coney among them—had left the valley to hunt a large but relatively elusive creature of the high ice plateau in latitudes behind and above the peaks around Stronghome. The meat was needed to supplement the dralg meat stored in the sheds, not only because no one would hunt around the time of Midwinter Song, but because it contained certain mineral-rich oils that dralg meat did not supply.

The practice field was, therefore, peopled largely by women and some of the oldest warriors. Urichen waved as I crossed the edge of the flat area, which had been cleared again that morning to give us secure footing. Before I had much of a chance to look around, Shantiah saw me, excused herself from a woman I knew only casually, and came across the field toward me. I read a low level of hostility and some apprehension as she approached, but they were overlain with a strong sense of bravado.

"Have you an opposite?" she asked truculently.

"No," I answered, not about to lie to her.

"I offer myself," she said, the formula sounding like a direct order.

In a split second I remade the decision about fourteen times. Part of me wanted to beat her face in, and part of me wanted to show her how much better at this I could be than her, and both feelings made me certain I should decline. I didn't want her to think that I was afraid of her, and I didn't want her walking around saying I wouldn't practice with her, and that made me certain that I should accept. She had been Jemeret's lover and I didn't want to be around her, and that meant refusing. But I would welcome a good match, and if she had been Jemeret's lover she would be no slouch, and that meant accepting. In the end, I accepted because I just didn't see how I could refuse.

"It would be an honor," I said in the formula of acceptance, carefully keeping my voice neutral.

Shantiah immediately swirled her cloak away and dropped into a crouch. I hadn't expected the abruptness, but I was prepared. I ignored my own cloak long enough to deflect one fast chop, then tossed it aside before she could try to tangle me in it.

I carefully kept my Class C skills at exactly the level of hers, which were not at all bad, and I made certain I kept the sting out of it. As a result, I took as good as I gave. When the match had gone on long enough so that she would have absolutely nothing to be ashamed of, I added a little power, took one quick sidestep, and gave her two rapid-fire body chops to overcome her talent long enough to pin her decisively. She gave the gesture, and I held out my hand to pull her up to her feet. I thought she might reject it, but she grasped it firmly and accepted my help.

"It was a good match," I said.

She leaned in closer to me. "All right," she said, "so your power is adequate. Well and good." She looked at me narrowly. "But if you don't love him, I swear I'll do everything I can to get him back. He deserves the best." She turned away from me, gathering up her cloak before I could reply, but there was no hostility left in her.

I almost smiled. It was as if her anger had burned itself out in the match, and she was more willing to accept my relationship with Jemeret. I found myself thinking that if I had beaten her badly, as I could have, the anger might have fed and concentrated.

As I picked up my cloak to go on to the part of the field where I could practice the Ladder, I was struck by a thought. The Com largely operated by overwhelming intimidation on the world level—the Drenalion saw to that, crushing small stirrings of rebellion with sufficient force to hold fast to the planet. Now I was wondering if the government had lost far more than it retained. If I thought crushing Shantiah would have stoked her anger, how could I think—truly believing people were worlds—that a planet could be won by war, rather than completely repelled by it? The Com wanted member worlds who were docile and obedient; it put no value in their being happy to be part of the relationship.

I was still thinking about that when I began the Ladder, so I was already somewhat removed from the extreme level of concentration a climb usually required. Thus I saw Tynnanna sitting on a crate against the wall of one of the storage sheds, watching me. I almost stumbled, paused, took a step backward in space and on the Ladder to begin Climb 1 over, and then realized that Shantiah and the other woman warriors were standing at the edge of my working area on the field side. I let my concentration fail completely and straightened, waiting.

"You climb the Ladder as well and as far as Lord Jemeret," Shantiah said at once, not in the least apologetic for having interrupted me, but not at all hostile, either. "We've watched you. The lord never had the time to help us perfect our work on the Ladder. Will you?" She seemed to hold her breath after the question.

"Of course I will," I said instantly, and one of the other women quickly stifled the cheer she was about to give. "In fact, if you'd let me, I believe we can even speed the process along."

The woman to Shantiah's right, a rangy blonde with an almost masculine athleticism, asked, "What do you mean, if we'll let you?"

She was by far the tallest of us, so I had to look up at her to meet her gaze. "If I sting you as I do an exercise or take a position, you'll be able to feel instantly if you're in the right stance, with your energy directed correctly. You won't have to watch me or guess."

Eyes brightened all around as they understood. "How many of us can you sting at the same time?" Shantiah asked eagerly.

That brought me up short. I'd never stung more than one person at a time, though I projected widely, and thus weakly, when I used the sympathetic strings, playing the nomidar. But it seemed to me that Jemeret could sting a great many minds at once, for short periods of time, and something in me said that if he could do it, I could do it.

"I don't know," I said slowly. "Let's start with one and add another until I'm pulling too much energy from my reserves."

Shantiah stepped up beside me. I fell into the first form of Climb 1 and touched her with the sting. "I see," she said with real wonder in her voice, her body automatically duplicating mine. The blonde took her place beside Shantiah, and I found I could bifurcate the sting and extend it onward. Simultaneous, rather than sequential stinging, as pinpoint sharp as an electron beam, rather than the dissipation of a blanket. I was delighted.

The splitting only worked one more time before I could feel I would need to gather too strongly. I signaled the others to wait and led my three students up the Ladder. It took the rest of the afternoon to accomplish Climb 1, and we made arrangements to repeat the work the next day, with another three women linked to me and the first three working alongside us to cement the learning into their beings. They were all very excited; I was nearly triumphant.

As I walked home, Tynnanna bounding along beside me, I realized that for the very first time in my life—barring, of course, the time I still could not remember—I was a teacher, rather than a student. I was giving back, not taking. I glanced around to see if anyone was watching, saw no one, and skipped a little, next to my klawit.

The Day of the Song

Except for the days of my camenia and the times when he was gone from Stronghome, Jemeret and I made love every night, and every time we did, the experience was as engulfing as being swallowed by the starfire. I wish I could say now that I was able to make any connections between my life by day and by night, but I didn't then. I only knew that Jemeret had been correct in saying that living taught one things that aca-

demic study could not. I let him teach me the variations on our
theme, and I taught the warrior women—especially Shantiah,
who worked with me longest and most often, striving for
perfection—what I knew about Class C combat. In short, I
lived, and I enjoyed it.

And then it was time for Midwinter Song.

The last Severance Storm of the uphill winter had blown
through in only three days, leaving the air scoured clean and
deep breaths tingling the lungs. The weather held. Venacrona
told me it always dawned clear at least on the Day of the Song
itself, but this year the peculiar clarity of ice and sunlight
stretched on until it magnified the approaching ritual into a
natural as well as spiritual grandeur.

All but entirely necessary jobs were suspended for the day
before, the day after, and the Day of the Song itself. And since
Venacrona and Mardalita were in charge of the ritual, Jemeret
had a rare lightening of his responsibilities.

The day before Midwinter Song, he didn't rise before dawn
to get dressed when almost everyone else was still asleep.
We'd awakened together during the storms, but this was the
first morning I opened my eyes and saw him watching me,
smiling, his face illuminated by the sunshine that poured in the
window of our bedroom.

When we awakened together, we generally touched each
other with our stings at once. Not only was it a way of greeting each other that we knew to be unique to us, but if he
wanted to make love again, I would know it instantly and respond to it instantly. The morning before Midwinter Song,
there was no passion in his touch, only a wealth of love, and
something I barely fathomed until the next day—gratitude, not
to me, but strongly present all the same.

He gathered me into his arms and held me for a few moments, his mind stroking mine with the familiarity of months
of constant contact. "We're going across the valley today," he
said. "There's something I want to show you before tomorrow."

I looked at him curiously. His smile widened. I didn't ask
him what was going on, for it was clear from his manner that
I was going to find out soon enough.

He swung out of bed, dressed quickly, and by the time I was
ready for morning shilfnin and porridge, he had already eaten.
"I have to go see Veen this morning at the temple. I'll meet

you at the tivong pens," he said, and was gone before I could ask any questions.

By the time I got to the tivong pens, something had changed in him, though he was making every effort to disguise it. I wondered about it, but I didn't ask, and I wouldn't just probe. We mounted Vrand and Rocky and rode over a shoulder of Kulith, at the farthest northwest corner of the valley. Then we entered a small canyon between Zuglith and Kerlith that narrowed so quickly that we tied the tivongs and continued on foot, climbing from shelf to shelf as we worked our way toward the head of the eroded cut. Behind a wall of boulders jammed into the passageway by a giant force—probably spring runoff from snows at a higher level on the titanic peak—we came to what appeared to be a shadow, but was actually the slit entrance to a cave.

Jemeret nodded to me to slip into the opening, then turned sideways and slid his broad frame through the narrow space. "Iris your eyes out," he said, as if I hadn't already begun to do that.

After the tightness of the entrance, the passageway in which I stood, though small, seemed almost luxurious. It curved gently to the right and slightly downward. With what I knew about caves, I figured the irising would do no good at all within fifty feet of the entrance.

"Let me past," Jemeret said. "Part of this is in total darkness, but you won't hit your head or crash into anything."

"Maybe I should hit my head," I said half seriously as I gave him my hand. "Nothing else has worked to bring my memory back."

He sounded annoyed. "Everything else is working," he said firmly. "You just want it all now."

"What's the matter with now?"

He'd been leading me down the tunnel, but he stopped and turned toward me as if we could see each other. "Those of us with power can control many things, but we cannot control time. You will remember when it's time for you to remember. Now come."

We moved on down the tunnel, and he seemed so certain that I *would* remember that I was willing to let the questions go. Even then I did not see the patterns, the careful intentions, his guidance in everything I was becoming. I would feel entirely foolish now if it were not that a little knowledge wasn't enough to see the entire mountain, just as we could not see Zuglith from this hole in its side.

In another few steps I began to notice shapes. The roughness of the tunnel wall grew increasingly visible, if indistinct, and Jemeret's shoulders bulked dark ahead of me in his fur-lined cloak.

"What's causing the light?" I asked.

"You'll see."

And, shortly, I did.

The tunnel opened into a chamber, roughly oval and about the size of the practice field in the village. The floor was uneven, but relatively flat, and the ceiling was an upside-down forest of stone projections—thin fingers of rock that reminded me of the starfire's tendrils in the bowl of Convalee on the Day of the Fire. They sparkled, glistening with a faint light that illuminated the cave the way the starlight illuminated a moonless night.

"This is where the metal comes from." Jemeret's voice spoke very close to my ear. "With the refined mineral from this ore, we make the bowls the starfire appears in."

I reached up wonderingly and, standing on tiptoe, touched the very end of the longest stalactite near me. "You mean the starfire is in here?"

"I suspect the starfire is everywhere," he said so softly that I had to augment to hear him. The cave seemed to drink some of the resonances of the sound, while at the same time, unnervingly, magnifying others. "But it only comes to us through the medium of something else. This."

He let me look my fill, catching the elusive, dancing light at the edges of awareness. Then I looked at him, seeing the planes of his face as I had so often in the nights at Convalee and after. "Why did you bring me here, Jemeret?"

He took a long, slow breath. "There are certain things to be said before tomorrow, and they have to be said here."

I waited, tensing slightly. He had not wanted to say this in the temple. I wondered why. I touched his mind as gently as I could, but he was shielded against me. He was silent for a long time, and finally I asked, "I'm not the one who's supposed to do the talking, am I?"

"A little of it." His next words cleaved into me. "There never was a High Lady of the Boru—until now."

"What?" My voice sounded three octaves higher than normal to me, and the stalactites made it echo, which nothing else spoken in the cave had done so far.

He knew he didn't have to repeat the revelation. "My na-sire's sire, and Venacrona, who was then a very young man, created the legend of the High Lady to try and stop the wars among our people by making everyone believe we had once lived in harmony—and thus could certainly do it again if the circumstances repeated themselves. Venacrona is the only Sammod still alive who remembers the time before the legend. It was just before the legend was created that the people of the tribes began to recognize that we had powers different from the others. They wanted us not to fight among ourselves when we were so few, compared to the numbers of those who be-came Honish. So you are not a candidate for the Fulfillment, Ronica, so much as you could be the first of the rulers of a united Samothen."

I was trying to deal with it in a logical manner. "How could they get away with it? Creating a legend like that?"

"It was built upon a story that was deep in the conscious-ness of the culture—all of it, the powerless as well as those with power. That was the story of a long meteor shower that damaged the surface of the world and had to be appeased. It was easy to say that was when power had begun to develop in the people. It was easy to say that was when the starfire came." His voice was steady, emotionless. "Veen and Jandelin—that was his name, my double na-sire—put the ele-ments together and decided that the men of the family groups, which became the basis for our tribes, would never be able to accede to the rule of only one of them. Our men were too used to competing with one another. There were too many fights.

"So the two chose the idea of a woman who would rule, and to make it more palatable, they added the belief that it had happened already, that the woman had brought the power down to the world from the stars. I've known all this since I became Chief of the Boru. I always thought they were very clever about it, until this morning."

"What happened this morning?"

He looked away from me, up into the forest of stone ten-drils. "Venacrona told me that it wasn't entirely their idea. The starfire told them to say it."

I had to remember to breathe. "The starfire spoke to them? Both of them? In comprehensible words?"

He nodded, the motion barely discernible, looking back at

me again. "According to Veen—and I have no reason to doubt him, he was there—the starfire told him and Jandelin to find a woman who would fit the role it wanted them to create. It told them the predictions to make that she would fulfill to prove herself, and what she was to look like. All of it. And then it told them that it, the starfire itself, would be a judge of whether or not the woman they chose was worthy of the task. They obeyed it."

I was gathering to remain logical, but underneath I was churning in fresh revelation. "*How* did the starfire speak to the two of them?"

Jemeret gave a small laugh, as if he really didn't believe what Venacrona had told him a few hours ago. When he answered, I wasn't sure I believed it, either. "Through a klawit."

My breath sighed out of me. "Tynnanna." Then I was swept with the absurdity. "But he hasn't said a word to me so far!"

Jemeret crossed his arms. I saw the motion and realized that tension from him was blossoming beyond his shields—and then I knew that he had lowered them. "Ronica, what do you believe I feel for you?"

The question seemed to spring at me unexpectedly, but I knew I had to answer quickly. I remembered as clearly as seeing it again the shaft of brilliant sunlight cutting through the ocean of his mind. "I believe you love me."

His tension did not lessen. "What do you believe you feel for me?"

I searched inside myself, all except the part I still could not reach, and then it was surprisingly easy to answer. "I believe I do love you, Jemeret. Did you doubt it?"

"No, I didn't," he said, "but I needed to know that you didn't doubt it either." He seemed to be studying me, hard, but he was not using the sting. "It is not impossible that you could believe I was manipulating you and using you. You know I want the unification of the tribes as much as I want to live, and you know I want children. You also know I see you as a key to both those ambitions. Because of that—" He overrode me quickly as I started to speak. "—because of that, I want to give you a choice."

"Between what?" I was now openly astonished.

"As part of the ritual, we are going to ask the starfire to confirm you as High Lady. If it chooses to do so, it will give you, yourself, no choice in the matter. It will lay on you all the responsibilities that title holds in our minds, and in whatever it uses for a mind as well. But we don't have to ask it to confirm you."

I knew what it cost him to tell me that. He was letting me feel it from him, and its depth was monumental. I thought about our time together, and I understood that much of what I was learning to love about being in Stronghome could end. I laid a hand on his face. "Ask," I said. "I know what it means to you. And I was raised for responsibility. Perhaps I was supposed to be a ruler, one way or another. Just promise me you'll be with me, whatever comes."

Somehow he was ever so slightly shaken by that, and it was a reaction I had not in any way expected. "Whatever comes," he said. For a moment the tension swelled beyond its already high level, and then I felt it wash out of him as if he had rejected it at last. He opened his arms to me.

I moved in against him. "How do you know the starfire will confirm me tomorrow?"

"Veen wouldn't have told me about the starfire's part in creating the High Lady legend if he had any doubts left, and he knows the starfire better than anyone else."

My entire body trembled once, and he held me tightly. "I promise you," he said clearly against my hair. "I will be with you."

Previous Midwinter Songs had been held in the temple assembly room, but this year Venacrona had wanted it outside, under the sky. Everyone in the tribe was aware that this year it would include the request for the starfire to let us know if I was truly the High Lady, and excitement was running strongly through Stronghome.

The priest had had a stage built just at the edge of the village, beyond which the ground sloped upward to the foothills of Harrilith in a much smaller imitation of the bowl at Convalee.

Tynnanna had not returned the afternoon before. Of course, I was more than eager to see him and try to speak with him— even though I kept recognizing the inherent silliness of sitting down with the cat and seeing if he could hold a conversation. Jemeret had not seemed either surprised or disappointed by the klawit's absence, but was only waiting now, passing the last hours until the culmination of something he had dreamed of all his life.

I dozed a little that night as he lay awake, cradling me in his arms, stroking my hair. Every time I awoke, uncertain of how long I'd slept, he murmured to me and held me a little closer, but his gaze was distant, fixed on something beyond our bedroom. I wondered if he was envisioning a future for which he'd hoped and worked, and I smiled against the hard muscles of his chest. Seeing into the future was not part of Class A talent, and at the moment I was still having trouble seeing into the past. Once, when I was nearly asleep for the twentieth time, I heard him whisper, "I don't want to lose you," and I murmured nearly incoherently, confidently, "You can't lose me." He held me momentarily much more tightly, and I drifted back into my half sleep, forcing my adrenal glands to slow their function. As soon as I lost the volitional control over them, they would begin to revive, and I would swim back up to awareness again, several minutes later.

When the Day of the Song dawned just as spectacularly clear as the days before it, I felt calm. I had decided that, whatever happened, few real surprises could possibly await me now. Whatever had caused the Com to expel me, I had not been permanently damaged by it, for now I was a Class A again. I had Coney here with me, and there was a joy in that, even though it was tempered by what I perceived as a troubling reticence in him. I attributed it to his reluctance to talk about what he'd done to be sent here, and I thought it was likely to pass after he'd been here long enough. Ironically, I thought he would be more comfortable if he forgot what was troubling him, at exactly the same time as I thought I would be more comfortable if I remembered.

Seeing Coney made me think more often of Kray, whose memory I had been able to put aside when Ashkalin went back to Salthome. Kray had been a part of us, all our lives. I missed him, but I was completely aware of the fact that Kray and my Lord Jemeret would have been matter and anti-matter, and the explosion would have been horrible for Kray. He always wanted to be so much stronger than he was, always thought his strength should have made all things possible. I admitted to myself, a little shamefacedly, that I had once thought my strength should have made all things possible, as well. I had learned that it did not; I wondered if he had by this time, too.

I wanted to confront the starfire again. Now that I had my sting back, encountering a living being was an attractive challenge. Jemeret and I dressed for the ceremony, which put me back in a talma for the first time since we'd left the Plain of

Convalee. "Does every woman have to wear a talma to this?" I asked him as he pulled his tunic on. "If it's all of us, the Boru are about to freeze most of their Sammats."

"It's just you today," he answered, "and you can keep the cold out better than a less powerful woman could."

He set his silver brow-crown on his head, then handed me a smaller circlet and nodded as, for the first time, I raised it and set it on my own head, its surface icy against my forehead for a moment before my body warmed it. It felt strange. Except for the crown on my head, we were dressed exactly as we had been on the Day of the Fire.

Numima had left bread and shilfnin on the table before she went to join the other Boru gathering on the gentle slope, now covered with blankets, table coverings, and wagon canvases. Jemeret and I ate a bite or two, drank a little, and then studied each other silently for a moment, our stings quiescent, before he held out his hand to lead me from the house.

Sometimes you know when your life is about to change, though you have only a vague idea of its exact dimensions. Before graduation, donning the golden helmet in my suite, I knew that it was the equivalent of a roll—emergence from the moment would be qualitatively different from entrance. Midwinter Song was the same. I had known things would never be, after graduation, what they had been before, but I had in no way been able to anticipate the nature and scope of the challenge.

I was suddenly struck with the fear that this, too, would be a change of unexpected dimension, and my hand tightened on his. "Jemeret."

He looked at me, his even gray eyes curious.

"I don't want to lose you, either." I honestly hadn't known I was going to say it. I was rewarded by the most completely happy smile I had ever seen on his face, and he drew me toward him and kissed my brow beneath the line of my crown.

We went out of our house into the day.

Tynnanna sat at the bottom of the steps, waiting for us. As soon as we emerged, he turned and began to trot off in the direction of what I secretly called the staging area. I tried to touch him with the sting; I felt nothing I could identify as more than "cat," but then I had never tried to sting him before.

Venacrona, Mardalita, and the young male assistant priest, barely out of his adolescence, stood by the stage, beyond which sat the Boru, the children wrapped in fur or woolen robes, cloaks, and shawls. I looked along the rows of faces, finding most of them familiar and smiling at us. Shenefta waved surreptitiously and jerked her head to the left to make certain I saw that she was sitting next to Coney. I masked a smile and looked beyond her to where Sejineth sat, his face as serious as usual. Shantiah sat beside him, looking excited.

I thought to myself that that pairing made a lot of sense and could also solve a problem, and then Jemeret stung me lightly to tell me to pay attention.

Venacrona, once again in his starfire robes, came behind the stage to greet us. "My lord, my lady, I trust you're ready." He glanced at Tynnanna, now standing behind us.

"You may begin at any time," Jemeret said quietly, letting go of my hand.

"When I signal, you should join us on the stage," the priest said. "If the klawit chooses to accompany you, do not discourage him."

Jemeret nodded.

Venacrona and his two assistants mounted the stage, each bearing a metal bowl. The crowd quieted. I glanced backward as I felt a warmth on my shoulder, and saw that Tynnanna had moved very close to me. He dropped his head, moved his nose forward, and nudged my hand with it, and I absently scratched between his eyes. Even as I was petting him, I looked back at the stage again.

Venacrona set his bowl down in the middle of the expanse and stepped around it, carefully drawing his robe out of the way so that it did not rock the bowl. Then he raised his arms. "People of the Boru, we gather again to sing the praises of the stars, whose children we are, and to thank them for the blessings they have bestowed upon us since the Day of the Fire. We come together because we recognize the debt the Samothen owe to the life from the stars. Everyone join hands."

It took a moment, because people were not necessarily sitting in orderly rows, and Jemeret and I moved in front of the stage to make a pair of links between the Boru and the priests. We were not, therefore, holding each other's hands. "My lord, my lady, the Boru are joined," Venacrona said, and Jemeret swept through the priests and picked me up so that the two of us blazed through the tribe, linking everyone into one coherent being. I saw Coney's eyes widen with wonder. Using my strength as well as his own, Jemeret held the tribe together for slightly longer than usual, then let the link fall away, and we dropped the hands we were holding and returned to the foot of the steps, where Tynnanna still waited.

"We stand together as a tribe," Venacrona said. "As a tribe, we will sing together." He and his assistants, still holding their bowls, began the first line of an obviously familiar song, which the Boru joined in. The hymn was the same one that had been sung at the Sacred Spring on the Plain of Convalee. The richness of the combined voices rose into the daylight.

I was used to starfire ceremonies taking place just at last light, but I realized that night fell quickly here in the winter mountains, and my three prayers alone could consume the better part of an hour. At least they were scattered throughout the ritual, so there would be plenty of time between them. It was going to be a very long ceremony. Distractedly, I wondered what would happen if some of the younger children had to relieve themselves, and then realized that they would probably have been taught that control before almost anything else. Being Class C had ceremonial advantages.

Jemeret must have sensed my thoughts wandering again because he stung me lightly.

The hymn was sung with words the first time through, and then a second time without words, its light, repetitive syllables contributing to a humming that I realized was in part an imitation of the unearthly hum of the starfire itself. Then the voices slid into a nearly flawless harmony, six hundred strong, some of the singers more enthusiastic than talented, but all fitting into the almost seamless whole.

Neither Jemeret nor I sang yet. We were leaders, and as such, we were to receive and absorb the opening hymn as if we stood for the connection between the world and the stars. Because I wasn't singing, I was watching the ranks of the Boru, and I saw Coney begin to weep. He did it quietly, unobtrusively, as he'd done most things, his emotions always a gentle rippling under the surface of his equanimity, but he made no attempt to hide the tears. I reached out with the sting and touched him gently; the familiarity of his being was sweet to me. What he was feeling was so entirely a mixture of awe, regret, gratitude, and happiness that for a few moments I couldn't understand what was happening to him.

And then I thought I knew. Most of his life, Coney had been a religious person, but he had been isolated in his faith. Those of us closest to him, while not deriding his choice, had never shared it. He had held to his convictions steadily in the high levels of the Com, where faith was scorned and devalued. Here, among the Boru, he was surrounded by, bathed in, a shining faith that, while not his own Epicyclism, was as genuine as anything he'd ever imagined and stronger than he could have guessed. He was not lonely; instead, he was feeling, perhaps for the first time in his life, completely at home. I understood, and I rejoiced for him, even as he wept.

The song ended, trailing down until only the two priests and Mardalita finished it out. Then silence lay across the open area, and Venacrona turned and nodded to my lord and me.

As we took our first step up onto the stage, Tynnanna rose and, with a stately dignity quite unlike his usual bounding and darting, walked deliberately after us. Jemeret didn't look at the klawit; he was, once again, stronger than I. I stared so hard I nearly tripped on the makeshift steps, and my lord caught my arm and stung me a little.

We walked forward to the metal bowl that Venacrona had set down, and as we reached it, Mardalita handed me her bowl. Simultaneously, the young priest gave his to Jemeret. Tynnanna remained at the rear of the stage, his tail switching in time to the soft murmur of Mardalita's voice as she formally gave me the physical link with the stars.

Then Venacrona's voice reached out over the assembly. "Once again, we have reached Midwinter, and stand on the peak of the year, poised to start downhill toward the summer. We are still a tribe. We stand before the stars, our parents, and tell them of the changes that have taken place in our lives since last we stood before them as a complete tribe." He stepped to Mardalita's side of the stage.

"Some have left us," Jemeret said clearly. His level gray eyes moved up the tiers of his people—our people, I corrected. "Let their names be spoken again, in the presence of the stars and the community that gave them life." He waited.

One of the young women, a weaver who was studying with Alissa, rose; the man beside her, who doubled as builder and farmer, released her hand as she stood. "Our son, Tal." She sat down again, wiping tears off her face. Variel had told me that very few babies died, but that one had been lost in the mountains several months before the tribe had begun preparing to leave for Convalee.

I started to sting the young woman to help alleviate her sadness, but Jemeret caught my sting and contained it, saying out of the corner of his mouth, "No, let them mourn. It's appropriate."

One of the warriors had risen. "My mother, Halana."

Slowly, two more people rose and spoke names, each allowing enough time for the name to echo off the faces of the mountain, for the person to be remembered.

Then Sejineth rose, his thin face hard, but emotion trembling beneath the facade. "My brother, Kowati," he said firmly, his pale eyes locked challengingly on Jemeret.

Almost imperceptibly, my lord nodded. Sejineth stood a moment longer than the others had, then sat down again, the tautness sliding out of his shoulders. Shantiah slipped her arm through his and said something softly to him. I wanted to augment my hearing quickly to catch it, but I was too late.

Jemeret stung me lightly, and I sensed he was a little annoyed that I kept losing my concentration on the ritual, but I couldn't help it. More than the ritual itself, the people of the tribe had become important to me.

Venacrona nodded at me, and I hesitated only briefly. I had never sung publicly without my nomidar, but I could gather to control the spate of nerves, and the first prayer, in the context of the spoken names of the dead, was the simplest of the three. It was also excruciatingly beautiful. As a representative of the Boru, I sang a plea for us all to be worthy of becoming spirit-bearers, vessels to contain the goodness of those who had gone, guardians of their memories. I interwove the names of the people who had been mentioned, even Kowati, though I had to swallow hard and gather harder to do it with equanimity after what he had done. The last part of the prayer spoke of the unity of souls and the continuity of the stars, an ongoing chain of unbroken life force, from which all of us emerged and to which all of us returned.

I thought as I finished, as objectively as I could, that I had at least hit all the notes. I hadn't tried to project, so I wasn't certain about the feeling content of the prayer, though the two women who'd spoken names were weeping.

Jemeret allowed the silence after the prayer to stretch on a little longer before he spoke. "Some have joined us, to become part of the river of our lives, enriching us with the gift of their selves. We will speak their names once here, and they will be part of us forever." He paused briefly. When he resumed, his voice was strong. "My bracelet, Ronica."

Mothers spoke for their newborn daughters; fathers, for their sons. One of the new Boru was a young cousin of one of the farmers, whose mother had been claimed into the Paj and who had asked to rejoin the Boru after his manhood ceremonial at Convalee. He had returned with us to Stronghome. In all, the births and the two of us who had joined as adults had increased the tribe's membership to 619.

The second prayer was sung by Mardalita and the young male priest as Jemeret and I set our metal bowls beside the one Venacrona had put down, their rims touching with small, chiming rings. The prayer was one of welcome, of tribesfolk standing together as one people, casting one shadow in the light of the sun, in the light of the stars.

It trailed off into silence, and Venacrona raised his arms. "We all have secret wishes. We bear them in our hearts, and they are known only to us. Here, at Midwinter, when the cold lies deep and the spring is still only a promise, we nurture the stirrings of our wishes as we nurture the hope of the coming springtime, out of sight, but not out of possibility." He held his hands outward, toward the tribe. "The stars welcome those wishes, and this is the time to speak them to the stars."

With the now familiar whoosh, the three bowls filled with starfire, each bowl bearing all four of the colors in writhing, humming streams which climbed skyward. Their brightness seemed in no way diminished by the daylight, and the snow reflected back all of their colors, glittering red, blue, gold, and a silvery, ephemeral brilliance whiter than the surface that reflected it.

I stole a glance at Coney, seeing that he was as agog as I had been at the first sight of the power of the starfire.

Into the humming, the indistinct murmur of voices intruded, as those Boru who could verbalized their wishes. For a split second an old sense of scorn arose in me, superior, steeped in the science of the Com. Speaking a wish aloud was superstitious nonsense, a relic of the belief that it was easier to attain that which could be expressed in words. And then I looked at the unknown, unfathomable presence of the living starfire, and the scorn faded. I said softly, "I want to remember—whatever there is to remember."

Jemeret, beside me, went very still. I knew he'd heard me. I knew it had affected him, but I had no time to try and figure out how. For whatever reason, I was transfixed by the force of the emotion pouring out of Shantiah.

Ever since we had worked the Ladder together, I'd begun to

be more sensitive to the feelings of the woman warriors. I'd discovered that time spent linked to someone created a genuine bond. Now Shantiah was in pain, longing for something, and the bond drew me. I concentrated hard on the emotions, and it felt almost like mind-reading. I wondered if that was how Jemeret had always seemed to read my mind. But in the beginning, we hadn't been linked nearly as long as I had been linked to the women I worked with. It impressed me even more with his power, that he had developed so solid, so accurate a link so quickly.

I kept trying to understand what Shantiah was experiencing, and it came upon me slowly that her passion was a hunger, edged in hopelessness, wrapped around a stubborn refusal to give in. But to what? The priests resumed singing, expressing a hope that the starfire would hear the whispered words, and I probed Shantiah patiently, hoping that *I* would. All at once, I thought I knew.

She wanted a baby. Morien had told me that the Ilto had hurt her very badly, and that she was not a skilled enough healer to repair the damage. I turned the sting and began to analyze what actually needed to be healed, and it was extensive, requiring rebuilding of cells from the formative stage onward. But her systems were there.

Jemeret might have done it, but I also thought, objectively, that Shantiah was unlikely ever to have told him. I knew, too, that I wasn't supposed to leave the platform, but I wasn't thinking of ritual; I was thinking of seeing if I had the power to grant one Boru woman a spoken wish that I hadn't really heard. I thought, last, that these were my people, and if they were outraged by my actions, so be it. I believed that it would be right to try.

Moving deliberately, I turned away from Jemeret and walked past Venacrona toward the steps. Tynnanna backed out of my way, watching me with those burning eyes. No one tried to stop me.

Shantiah looked startled as I walked up to her, the Boru making a path for me. Sejineth's face was wary, but I barely noticed him.

"Stand up," I said to the other woman.

She obeyed, curiosity and apprehension struggling inside her.

The Boru had fallen completely silent, and the starfire, while it continued to writhe, had ceased to hum as well. In the quiet of the day, a bird called somewhere above us.

I put my hands on Shantiah's waist and began to seriously diagnose her capacity and her incapacity. There had once been a massive infection, and I knew it had taken everything she was able to do to keep it from destroying parts of her reproductive system; in that she had succeeded. But she had destroyed cells when she destroyed the infection, leaving gaps in each fallopian tube and scars on the uterus and ovaries.

I assessed the right ovary to be healthier, as if I were assessing my own body, and then I slid into her consciousness as I had so often recently on the Ladder. Lending her the power of my own reserves to speed the process, I began to show her how to knit healthy cells together, how to change chemical keys so that they could build more of themselves, how to heal herself.

She gasped, her hands clutching my shoulders, and she concentrated hard, frowning, her gaze going distant as she tried to use the power well, but stumbling in her haste.

I murmured something soothing and meaningless to her, demonstrating the step-by-step process of rebuilding the tube cells, the painstaking linkage of each to the next, the dissolving of scar tissue and its replacement with new, healthy cells. When I knew at last that she understood what to do and how to do it, I mentally stepped back, letting her perform the process herself, measuring the energy she would need to apply. When I saw that she was increasingly confident, I gently stopped lending her my reserves, and her eyes refocused on me. It would take her months to build up and use reserve energy over and over again to complete the task, but we both knew she could and would do it. I withdrew the sting. I had no idea of how much time had passed, but more than half my reserves were gone.

Shantiah's eyes sparkled. She held on to me as I let go of her waist and asked, "Why did you do this for me?"

I decided to be entirely honest. "At the beginning, I disliked you, because you preceded me. But I don't dislike you any longer, and I felt I wanted to make up for what I had felt before."

She blinked. "But you helped me on the Ladder."

"That was for all the woman warriors," I corrected. "This was for you."

"Thank you," she whispered, seeming to fight the urge to hug me.

I stepped backward and glanced over at Sejineth once, then went back down to the stage and remounted the steps. Jemeret was expressionless, his shields up. Venacrona was regarding me with wonderment. The starfire began to hum again, and I took my place on the stage almost as if I'd never left it. I knew it had been at least an hour, and I suspected it had taken longer than that, but no one at all seemed to have moved during that time, and the starfire had waited as well.

Venacrona nodded at me, reminding me that I was supposed to do the next prayer. I gathered a little, though I was tired, and began the second prayer. It was singularly complex, speaking of a tribe's need for dreams, of the need of the tribe's members for their individual dreams, of the starfire's need for the tribe and its dreams, of the tribe's need for the starfire, and then of dreams themselves. When the song was done, I was really weary. I gathered more and drew in enough energy from my reduced reserves to hold me up.

As I had sung, the starfire columns had sunk slowly back into the bowls, which now seemed to vibrate slightly, not rocking on their bases, but rather appearing to tremble within themselves. The quiet ringing of their rims against one another was like a soft bell.

When I finished singing, Venacrona and his assistants began the song that recounted the legend of the High Lady and asked the starfire to judge the candidate the Boru had brought forward to approach it. As soon as they were done singing, the priest signaled to his assistants, who turned and jumped lightly down off the stage. The moment they were clear of the platform—as if it had been waiting for that very thing—the starfire flowed out of the bowls and around the four of us who remained, then whooshed up to an incredible height all along the edge of the stage, shutting us away from the outside world.

Venacrona lowered himself to his knees. I grabbed for Jemeret's arm, and he pulled me in against his side, nodding to draw my attention to the klawit.

Tynnanna's face had completely changed, a fierce intelligence shining out of the burning eyes. His larynx and tongue were—I knew from the experience with the protocanines—badly suited to speech, but talk he did, a deep, sibilant rumble, aimed at Venacrona. "You need not kneel to us. We told you so when last we talked."

Chills ran over me. I was listening to the starfire, even as the body of its flames rose and roiled about us.

Venacrona rose, looking a little sheepish. "That was almost a hundred and forty years ago," he said. "I may have forgotten a detail or two."

Tynnanna turned his massive head toward me. "You have done well and more," he said in a hissing growl. "A High Lady must most of all be the servant of her people. We have decided to rest our hopes for your people with you. We accord you the responsibilities and the title of High Lady."

There was a silence, except for the humming of the flames, and I was enchanted by the old seductiveness of interacting with another sentient species. I started to reach for my sting, but Jemeret shook me suddenly, hard. "No," he said harshly. "Just say that you are honored." For a split second the grip of his hand on my shoulder was almost unbearably painful. Then he relaxed it.

I said obediently, "I am honored."

Tynnanna turned that strange, brilliant face to Venacrona. "Our priests will know that we have done this. You must move quickly. You may not wait until spring. There are reasons for this beyond what you may know now. The Councillors of your Inner Council must declare her High Lady as soon as possible." The klawit looked at my Lord Jemeret, standing so rigidly beside me, and if a rumble could be said to contain affection, the cat's voice—the starfire's voice—did. "You have done exceptionally well. We know your heart's most secret wish, though you have not yet spoken it. We tell you now, it is possible that it can happen. It is possible that you can help it happen."

"Will I know what I need to know?" he asked, tense.

I looked sharply at him. He was, incredible as it seemed to me, uncertain. I believed I had never seen him uncertain before. He always seemed utterly confident, completely sure of his own rightness.

"You already do," said Tynnanna, a conduit. "And you are no longer the only one."

A tendril of the red flame split off from the curtain of fire that surrounded us and came, fingerlike, to touch his forehead and linger, like a caress. Then it withdrew.

"Move quickly," the cat repeated, and then, even as we watched, the presence left him, and he was merely a klawit again.

With a sigh the wall of starfire dropped down around us, except for four tendrils of the four colors from the middle bowl. These tendrils twined themselves into a cord and rose to me, circling above my head and creating a circlet—not a bracelet this time, but a brow-crown.

Jemeret let go of me and raised his hands to take the crown from the starfire. He held it out for the Boru to see and, one by one, they rose to their feet, even the children.

"The starfire has spoken!" Venacrona cried out, "We have a High Lady!" Tynnanna roared. Jemeret lowered the circle of fire onto my hair, over the silver brow-crown I was already wearing. I felt its peculiarly characteristic cold, and then had to iris my eyes down as it grew unbearably bright before it dissolved into my skin. The Boru began to cheer.

Jemeret smiled. "Take off your crown and look at it," he said.

I irised my eyes to normal. The other priests climbed back up on the stage as I lifted the metal circlet from my head and brought it down in front of me. The silver, while still flat and featureless against my fingertips, glowed and danced with the starfire colors, as if the starfire were alive beneath the thin surface of the crown. I was beyond wonder, deep into the realm of acceptance of the incomprehensible, but even so, I stared in fascination at the coiling colors, slightly muted within the metal. The starfire had left a piece of itself in the crown; it was not, after all, silver, but instead made of the same metal as the bowls.

The crown before my eyes was suddenly blurred with tears I was too tired to gather more to contain, for I felt the same kind of delight, the same level of overwhelming honor paid to me, that I'd felt when the starfire danced with me on the Day of the Fire.

There was a slight thickness in my lord's voice as he said, "You've grown up, my love. Do you realize that?"

I was about to deny it, to say that I really felt no different than I had when I first arrived here, but that was patently ridiculous. Even as stubborn as I was, I couldn't fail to recognize that I had changed.

He took the crown out of my suddenly still fingers and set it back on my brow. The three priests had brought the cheering to an end and now they began to sing the ritual phrases of the Song of Life's Gladness, which the Boru joined in. I took

Jemeret's hands as he lowered them down the sides of my face. "There's no going back now, is there?" I asked him.

"You knew there wouldn't be," he said. He used one of my hands to stop a tear that rolled down my cheek.

We kept looking into one another's eyes until the lengthy song was finished, and by then my tears had ceased without my gathering to stop them. With the finish of the song of thanksgiving, we were into the final part of the ceremonial portion of the day. There were only three prayers left—Jemeret's, mine, and the last of the priests'.

Jemeret walked to the center front of the stage to lead the men of the tribe in the hymn of praise to the masculine aspects of the Boru and, hence, of the men of the world. It was a powerful prayer, unequivocal and strong, praising the qualities that made men men and unapologetic for some things I might have thought of as flaws.

I'd never heard the hymn before, but I saw how it fitted with the last prayer I would sing, which praised the feminine in the Boru and in humanity. It occurred to me that it might be best for everyone, in the long run, if we all sang both songs. The women should be able to praise their men, flaws and all, just as the men should be able to praise us.

I almost laughed. I'd only been High Lady of the Boru for about a quarter of an hour and already I wanted to change things. I had come to believe we all had to learn to love each other, and our male and female aspects were a good place to start.

I led my last prayer, trying to concentrate on the words and melody I'd carefully memorized, but half my mind kept straying to the as-yet-unfathomed task of being High Lady of the Samothen. I had known very well what it was to be the Com's Class A—and I had failed it, or it had failed me somehow. I knew nothing at all about what would be required of me here. Maybe that gave me a better chance at success.

The women finished the song with me, and the three priests stepped forward as Jemeret drew me to the back of the stage. Tynnanna had vanished at some point while we were singing, but I hadn't been aware of his departure. As the priests began the closing prayer, with faith that the springtime would come, as the next day would come, as our tribe would go on, I asked Jemeret, "What kind of hopes can the starfire have for us?"

"I'm not the starfire," he said.

It wasn't an answer, but I sensed it was as much as he was

willing to give, and I didn't press the issue. "Why didn't you want me to sting the starfire?" I asked, instead.

He was very serious. "The starfire has great power—for our purposes, unlimited power. You might have died."

I remembered Shantiah stumbling over the power I had let her use, and I understood what he meant. I closed my eyes briefly, the weariness pulling at me, and then jerked them back open. I had seemed to see, on the insides of my eyelids, the wash of sparkling golden light, with indistinct shapes somehow in it or behind it, that I had hitherto only dreamed. Now, seeing it while awake made it seem somehow frightening.

The song came to an end.

Jemeret put his arm around me again. The glittering curtain faded, and we left the platform so that I could receive the greetings and good wishes of my tribe. I don't remember much of what anyone said, except for two people. Old Gannelel bent and kissed my hand. "Sho you have a third life, too, my lady."

And Coney, kissing my lips lightly, murmured congratulations and then said quietly, "I never knew, Ronnie. I never understood."

"What?" I held on to his arm to keep him from moving on in the line.

He struggled for a moment with the words. "I always thought *we* made life sacred—the Epicyclists, the Macerates, the Purists, and the rest. But life *is* sacred. We're just the ones who recognize that."

And Jemeret drew him away from me so that the line of Boru could continue passing by.

XI. Among the Samothen

The crown lay in the center of the dining table, the muted colors still moving beneath the surface. Everyone's eyes went back to it now and then, almost as if the motion called us.

Jemeret and I sat at opposite ends of the table, listening to the discussion that had been proceeding for quite some time now. Venacrona and Mardalita, seated with Tuvellen and Coney—whose presence frankly surprised me—on one side of the table, had been arguing good-naturedly about which of them should go with us. We'd agreed to the necessity for the trip about an hour earlier, while I was still stifling yawns because I had not been able to deep yet to try to replenish my low reserves.

Across from them, Variel was insisting that Gundever could not go without her, and Morien was telling Wendagash that a large contingent of warriors would make it more difficult to travel quickly. Wendagash, on the other hand, was maintaining that to travel in winter was dangerous enough with protection, and would be even more dangerous without it, for the tribes were no longer under truce, as they had been at Convalee.

Venacrona interrupted his own argument with Mardalita to break into theirs, saying, "No, no, no. We will not be in any danger, because the priests have told the tribes that there is now a High Lady of the Boru, and the only ones we really have to worry about won't try crossing the Honish lands in force. The Honish would fight them every centimeter of the way." Then with barely a pause for breath, he turned back to Mardalita and went on giving her all the reasons why she had to stay in Stronghome so he could go.

The decibel level in the room rose until I was almost laughing. Numima brought a dish in from the kitchen, banged it on the table to make sure everyone would know she had brought it, snorted into the sudden break in the talking, and retreated into the kitchen, shaking her head.

Jemeret took advantage of the silence. He cleared his throat and waited until everyone had looked at him. "I don't think there's a great deal to discuss," he said genially, "though you're welcome to continue, and I've certainly enjoyed it so far." He glanced at the priests. "Veen, you'll have to come with us, and I hope the speed we travel at won't be too much for you. You and Sandalari are the Inner Councillors, representing the stars, and you have to be there for the whole Council to make the declaration. If the Resni, the Vylk, and the Marl won't come out from behind Reglessa Fen—and we don't yet know that they won't, but it's a possibility—the rest of us will have to go to them. That means a great many warriors would be conspicuous and provocative, so the fewer the better."

"I'm as spry as I was when I was a hundred," Venacrona said a little indignantly.

Jemeret's voice gentled. "I know, but we can't take wagons, and it's a long way to go on tivongs."

"I don't believe I'll have any trouble," the priest said.

I was too tired to wonder how it was that he, at what had to be a hugely advanced age, was in far better shape than Gannelel, who was many years younger. I had thought that only in the Com did aging get so long delayed.

"Also," Jemeret said, taking advantage of the continuing silence, "we need to send Peraldi ahead, even though that will leave us without a Paja. I need Ginestra to send messengers out to all the tribes to assess whether they're willing to go along with the declaration, or whether we're going to have trouble. By the time we get to the Forge, the Paj ought to have some of the answers, at any rate."

"Do you think there'll be any trouble?" Gundever asked.

"Of course." Jemeret said it lightly, but I sensed it was serious. "We won't go to war over this, but I suspect some of the chiefs will be reluctant, and I'm a little concerned over the fact that we can't wait until spring." He smiled, a little grimly. "I do believe eventually they'll all come around."

"I still want to come, too," Variel said, glancing at Jemeret as if she was certain he would deny her permission.

"Is there any reason why Variel couldn't come?" I asked. "I've gotten used to having women friends. I wouldn't want to just—turn aside from that."

Gundever looked at me as if he wished I hadn't spoken, but he didn't say anything.

Jemeret was gentle again, half smiling at me. "I think it would be best if Variel remained at Stronghome." He watched me levelly. "If, however, you order her brought along . . ." He didn't finish.

I understood. He was telling me that my status had changed now, and he wanted to see if I had decided how I was going to behave toward him as a result of it. He was telling me that the trip could present dangers, and that Variel was less equipped to deal with them than some of the rest of us. He was asking me if I was going to contradict his choices. I shook my head. "If we have to move really quickly, perhaps it would be better for the warriors to know that those they care for are safe."

Variel bit her lip and looked down at her plate. Gundever hid a smile.

Jemeret went on as if the moment had not occurred. "So we'll leave at dawn. We've nearly a tenday until the next storm, which gives us enough time to reach the Forge. That assembles five sets of Councillors at one time, and we can shelter there for the duration of the storm."

I retreated to my own thoughts as the planning continued, letting the words wash over me without taking much note of them until I heard Coney say, "I still don't have much in the way of winter clothes."

Jemeret replied, "Once we're out of the mountains, the cold won't be as severe."

I realized then that Coney would be going with us. That surprised me even more than his presence here, for while he was a skilled fighting man, he was not a Boru. I wondered if I was being given Coney because I could not have Variel, but I did not raise the question.

Tuvellen stood as Jemeret said to him, "You'll be in charge while I'm gone. I'm not sure how long this will take, and you did an admirable job while I was away before Convalee."

Tuvellen nodded. "I'll arrange to get the saddle cases packed. We'd better alert Sejineth early." He held out his hand to Morien, and the group began to depart.

I said good night with only half my attention. The rest, feeble as it was at that point, was directed to something that had finally surfaced fully and demanded I heed it.

Something was going on between Jemeret and Coney—

something whose depths I had sensed, but couldn't fathom. It had to do with the ease with which Coney had accepted and adapted to this world, and the familiarity I sensed in the relationship between them. It made me wonder where it came from, and it shook the very foundations of the trust Jemeret had earned from me, because I sensed very strongly that neither of them wanted me to raise the question. I didn't want to doubt; it seemed I had little choice but to be what this life had led me to be. And I did love them both.

And yet there was something suspicious going on, and I wanted to know what it was.

I held the uneasiness to me like a subterfuge, and if Jemeret sensed it—which I think he must have—he neither mentioned it nor let it affect his smile as the last of them left and Numima hurried in to begin to clear up.

"Come to bed," my lord said to me.

I turned toward the bedroom, knowing I'd never last through a bath. I almost let myself doze as I was walking in, and he sat me on the bed, stripped me, and rolled me into the blankets.

"Do you want to see if the High Lady makes love like the simple bracelet did?" I murmured, partly asleep.

"You were never a simple bracelet," he said, laughing. "I'm going to see to the guards." I was asleep before he finished talking, and I deeped immediately.

I thought, in the morning, when he woke me early, that I felt so very safe in this room. Of course, I *would* recognize that just as we were leaving, for who knew how long.

Two things happened on our trip to the Forge which increased my unease, but I still fought to keep from yielding to doubts. Both were things I overheard by accident.

I had learned to isolate my thoughts from the outside world—from Jemeret—by building a figurative bubble around myself. It was something it had never occurred to me to do in the Com, when only Jasin Lebec could have read me and when I was convinced that there was no possible way my Class A reflex could be cut off from the rest of me. Now, of course, I knew that there was a myriad of things I never suspected, and I'd begun to experiment. I'd discovered that unlike shielding, in which I still had a presence that could be detected, I could surround myself with a bubble of nothing, just as Jemeret used his ability to catch my projections and trap them.

I don't think I did it deliberately, to be able to approach him without his knowing it, but self-deception has always been one of my preoccupations. I have to admit that the bubble did—does—allow me to make myself transparent to my lord. It also consumes an inordinate amount of energy. It helped me to begin imagining the power Jemeret had expended trapping my projection during the game of the Dibel.

At any rate, after we camped in the forest on the third night of our journey, I had been taking care of the tivongs, since I was the one of us with the most in-depth experience of the animals. I was grateful that no one seemed inclined to stop me from doing it simply because the starfire had anointed my brow-crown with some still unknown destiny.

I was coming out of the relatively sheltered glade in which I'd picketed the animals. They needed shelter more than we did, because it was impossible for us to carry enough fodder for them. That meant they would have to eat the low-hanging branches, especially those of the conifers, which kept their hard, needlelike leaves even in the worst of the cold. I'd scattered the small sacks of treated, dried grain we could carry, which would make certain the animals didn't suffer any nutrient losses, and they were busily eating that first. The grain had the additional benefit of making it easier for them to digest the normally harsh wild provender. While I was spreading the grain, Tynnanna, who had accompanied us on this journey without the slightest hesitation, had switched his tail at me several times and bolted off into the forest to hunt.

When I saw that the tivongs were all settled down securely, I walked quietly out of the trees toward the little group of lean-tos we'd set up around the roaring fire. Gundever and Wendagash were gathering snow in empty feed sacks so that it could be melted over the fire for the tivongs to drink. Venacrona was crouched by the blaze, turning a spit with skinned laba carcasses on it, and the three other warriors we'd brought with us were scouting the perimeter, a precaution Jemeret took even though he and I had both probed over the surrounding area for a distance of several miles and felt no other presences. Jemeret and Coney had been gathering firewood, but now they sat on a log near the lean-to Coney would occupy with another of the warriors, talking in low voices.

I couldn't resist. I swept the sting around me into a protective bubble and augmented my hearing in time to hear Coney say seriously, ". . . come with us when we go?"

"Absolutely." Jemeret's voice held no hesitation. "Even if I hadn't given her my word, I worked too damned hard to risk her."

Venacrona saw me and rose, which drew my lord's attention first to him, then to me.

As he glanced in my direction, I let the bubble drop away and went to join them. Neither Jemeret nor Coney referred to whatever they'd been discussing.

The second time, two days later, I'd taken advantage of one of the short stops along the trail to relieve myself, and I was hidden by a boulder, my hearing augmented so that I could tell if anyone was approaching, when I heard Venacrona ask Jemeret, "How much are you going to tell Sabaran?"

"As little as I can," Jemeret answered. "He'll need to know enough to ensure his full cooperation, but he and I have played that game for years, and there's never been any trouble. I don't anticipate any now."

"And Ashkalin?" Venacrona's voice was slightly more doubtful.

"Ashkalin will ultimately have to know everything. We need his cooperation too much."

"What if it falls apart?" Venacrona's words were so low, so tense, that I felt he must have wanted to ask the question for a long time.

"I'm not about to let it fall apart, Veen," Jemeret said instantly. "No matter what it costs me. She—" He stopped abruptly. "Ronica?"

I pulled up my leggings and stepped out from behind the boulder, thinking that this time I would have to confront the situation, and still somehow reluctant to do so. "I'm here," I said, as if he had summoned me. "Are you concerned that the tribes might not accept me as High Lady?"

He nearly smiled, which I felt was an inappropriate reaction. "To a minor extent—very minor—yes, I am," he said, "but I think there will be ways to deal with reluctance. In any case, we'll know more tomorrow. The Paj should all have let Sabaran know who intends what and who will be coming to meet us where. I'll be able to make some choices after that."

I was reading him, and it was true, but this was not what he was worried about. This was a small thing, despite all previous evidence to the contrary. He was seriously concerned about something else, and under the concern, as I'd seen it so clearly when I probed him, was the anger, the knot of dark rage whose object I had not come to know at all.

We studied one another for a few moments. He might have been waiting to see if I would ask more, but my sense of him was that he hoped I would not. I was curious, but I understood that some revelations were not pleasant ones, and I gave a small shrug and let him have his way.

That night, lying curled against his chest under our lean-to canvas, I had to will myself to sleep, and I dreamed again of the sparkly golden veil that hung between me and the indistinct figures that moved on the other side of it, closer now, but still unseeable.

Sabaran, Clematis, and Sheridar came to the mouth of the low valley to greet us. Behind them I could see the longhouses that sheltered the Genda in their home territory. The slopes of the hills on which the houses perched also showed the neatly shored and braced entrances to the caves that this tribe used as storehouses, stables, and wagon sheds. Jemeret had told me that the major forge buildings themselves would be out of sight behind the tumbled piles of boulders to the left side of the valley, while the longhouses I could see in the distance to the right were those of the Dibel. He had also told me that the Elden Homestead was several kilometers to the south, behind the hills and out of sight.

Clematis embraced me warmly, her eyes sliding over the dancing colors in the brow-crown without her seeming to be at all inhibited by it. To my amazement, I was deeply relieved. In the Com, I'd welcomed the distance between myself and the "ordinary" people. It had been an indication of my uniqueness, my singular worth. Now, I feared that distance. Jemeret had been very successful at teaching me that I was indeed a unique human being, but so was everyone else, in different ways. I had begun to learn that I could find my worth in the interaction between myself and others, and I already knew that I needed that interaction; I didn't want it to vanish because the starfire had chosen me for purposes whose scope I hadn't yet seen. Very little I had ever done in the Com had rewarded me personally as much as the things I'd been able to do here, where I had been welcomed even when I was maimed, and loved for reasons I couldn't understand but was learning to accept.

Jemeret and Sabaran had clasped arms, and the big blond man said immediately, "The Genda will be overjoyed to stand with the Boru in this." Then, the formality over, he gave a hearty laugh. "When the messenger arrived, my bracelet shouted so loudly the Dibel thought she was auditioning."

Clematis swatted his shoulder, blushing.

"Will Lyrafi and Orion be joining us here, or do they want us to come to them?" Jemeret asked.

"Sandalari says they'll be here immediately after the storm. Their priest signaled that they have a death in the tribe and they need to complete the ceremonies." Sabaran bowed his head to Venacrona as he spoke.

I looked at the distant longhouses and automatically reached out, seeing what I could feel. "Do you know who died?" I asked the Lord of the Genda.

Clematis's expression softened apologetically. "We didn't inquire," she said. "Generally, a death is a tribal thing, and we let the Dibel live separate from us, even though we can see one another's homes and we share the same farms."

I nodded, unrebuked, but still wanting to know if it had been Tendoro who died. He had seemed so old, and yet like most creative artists, his energy, the generative power of creativity, could have masked even greater age. And I felt I owed him something, for he had built the nomidar that gave me such joy.

Then I realized, with a start, that no one I had ever cared about had died. I'd killed people—Drenalion, Evesti of the Ilto—but I had not mourned for them. I had never had to mourn for someone who was gone. My body began to tremble.

Jemeret was at my side instantly, his conversation with Sheridar broken off in mid-word, his hands on my shoulders. "Tell me," he said.

It took me a moment to find the words. "Something happened. Something—struck the things I can't remember—and it hurt." I looked at him almost helplessly, letting the anger and frustration wash over me and depart. "*Why* can't I remember?"

"You will." He barely whispered it, his lips on my forehead below the brow-crown. "Let's get the tribes together and get you declared. That's what we have to worry about now."

He must have been calming me, because I calmed, and I didn't analyze where it came from. Everyone around us had gone quiet.

Jemeret looked up at the Gendal chief. I sensed the motion over my head. "I'm going to take Ronica to the Dibel for an hour or so," he said evenly. "We'll be back in advance of the storm. Veen, will you take care of getting us settled?"

"Of course."

"I'll stop them from unsaddling your mounts," said Sheridar.

I made myself look up at Clematis, amazed to note that she was slightly hazed with tears. "Your prospective High Lady is not perfect," I said a little shakily, trying to muster up a laugh.

Her face was warm, affectionate. "We never thought she would be perfect," she said, "because she would be human. We always knew she would have an uphill climb. I suppose the surprise is that we just didn't know we would witness any of it." She pulled me into her arms and held me tightly, even though Jemeret had not let go of my shoulders.

He allowed her to hold me briefly, then tightened his grip and drew me away. "We need to go if we're to outpace the storm getting back."

We galloped Vrand and Rocky from one set of longhouses to the other, Tynnanna racing along beside us. The longhouses were just that—houses that rambled over a hundred meters of ground each, but were only two or three rooms wide. Each housed twenty or more families who shared a central kitchen, hearth, and hall. Venacrona had told me that smaller sheds attached to the backs of each longhouse held some individual supplies. I didn't pick out the central temple, but he had said it would be small, for only the Boru temple was a multistory structure.

Jemeret watched me, letting Vrand choose his own path. Sometimes I wondered at the unusual degree of his preoccupation with me. At the beginning, I'd been resentful of the centrality I held for him, seeing it as an indication of his possessiveness. When he'd poured reserves into me, saving my life, and later, as I began to comprehend the true extent of his almost unbelievable power, I became flattered by the attention. I was almost surprised when, now, I became embarrassed by it. His love I treasured, but his constant attention made me wonder if he were somehow unsure of me—and yet, he had probed me, and he knew he had nothing to be unsure of. What was it I still didn't know?

Despite having probed him and seen everything there was to see, I still had the notion that he had some purpose I could not grasp—which, I guessed now, involved Coney. The question was whether it had anything to do with what I couldn't remember. And if so, how?

Two years was a long time.

I felt the surge of Jemeret's energy as he signaled the Dibel that we were approaching, and as we drew up to the first of the longhouses, a woman in a beautifully beaded coat came out to meet us, smiling a little seriously, as if glad to see us but aware of the solemnity of the occasion. It was, I noted with surprise, Ginestra of the Paj.

Jemeret was also surprised. He swung down off Vrand and put his arm around his fellow chief. "I didn't expect to find you here," he said.

She kissed his cheek and nodded respectfully in my direction as I dismounted. "I thought it would save time if I came myself, instead of sending one of the messengers. I brought Rudenil to serve as Councillor with me. You know, I'm sure, that our priest told us at Midwinter Song that the Fulfillment was at hand." She smiled at me, a little more completely. "We wanted this to come fully as long and as much as you do." Jemeret cocked his head at her. "Well," she added, "perhaps not as much."

"Who else agrees with you?" He spoke the question casually, but he was tense.

Ginestra stepped back from him. "Everyone here at the Forge, and the Hall, you know. Henion is on his way here as well. Ustivet isn't happy, and so far he hasn't shown any signs of leaving the Lodge." Her eyes darkened a little. "And we've had no word at all from the other side of Reglessa Fen."

"Where is the funeral?" I asked her, interrupting as politely as I could. I was unwilling to simply scan for it, since I saw no one in the complex except the three of us, and there was something about the occasion which demanded a respect for privacy.

Ginestra pointed up the hill behind the sprawling longhouses. "At the very top, to the east," she said.

Without waiting to see if Jemeret wanted to follow me, I ran in the direction she'd indicated, scanning ahead now that I knew where to look and could therefore keep the scan very subtle. Despite the lightness of my touch, the strength of the sadness, the mourning I encountered, nearly made me stumble. And then, beneath that surface, just as I'd felt it beneath the layers of fear in the hospital room on Werd, I encountered the incredible, pure love. I'd been looking for it for such a long time. And now, when I finally found it, I was aware instantly that it was so much less than Jemeret gave me that I was humiliated to have idealized it for so long. I'd have laughed if it hadn't been entirely inappropriate.

The Dibeli cemetery was a large clearing in the trees that crowned the hill, filled with elaborately carved monuments very different from the stone cairns of the Boru. The monuments were not representations of the people who'd been laid in the ground beneath them, but of the artistry of those people. The Dibel believed it was right to remember people for what they left behind, and in art was their immortality.

I slowed to a walk, and several of the people in the crowd around the grave looked up. There were probably fewer than 250 people in the cemetery, a low number for a tribe, but I remembered that dozens of the players and musicians would be at other tribes or among the Honish, entertaining them. Dirian must have been one of them, for I did not see him among the people present.

The crowd nearest me parted, and at the graveside itself I saw Lyrafi and her brother. Then, beyond them, much to my relief, I saw the bent, fragile figure of Tendoro. He had just looked around, sensing a disturbance that rippled through the crowd like the wind heralding the approach of the storm. Tynnanna stalked at my side, tall enough now so that his shoulder was nearly on a level with mine, and therefore even more formidable than he had been the last time any of them saw him.

Lyrafi stepped away from the mourners and came to me, clasping my hands and touching her cheek to mine. "You are always welcome among us," she said. "Karaghida told us you would be coming." I had never met the Dibeli priest. "Excuse me," the Chief of the Dibel went on. "We have to finish singing Parto away." The two-syllable name told me it was a child who had died.

I stood at the edge of the crowd with my klawit as Lyrafi went back to the graveside, where the older priest in the four-colored robe raised his arms. The tribe began to sing.

The song would have been marvelous for the nomidar, for it had three distinct melodic strains, each of which was countered by a harmony. The Dibel sang it flawlessly, its complexities eased by long usage and unfortunate familiarity. As its richness washed over me, I walked around the outside of the crowd until I was near Tendoro.

When the song was done and the members of the tribe were standing alone with their individual thoughts for a moment, Tendoro turned to me. "We are honored you chose to come to the Hall," he said.

"I feared this was for you," I said bluntly. "I wanted not to let you go without a farewell." I looked away from him, somehow embarrassed again.

When I looked up, he was smiling, which deepened all his wrinkles and almost made his eyes disappear. "In such a case, *I* am honored."

And then I couldn't think of anything else to say to him that would not seem forced. I didn't understand why it had been so necessary for me to rush here across the valley, only that it had, and that I no longer needed to understand every nuance of my own motivation.

Lyrafi came over to me. "Lady Ronica, Parto's mare and sire have asked if, as our prospective High Lady, you would be willing to honor us all with a prayer or song to smooth the child on her way. If you would rather not, of course we will understand."

I was tempted to refuse, for this was an intensely personal time, and I hadn't known the people who were mourning. But instinct told me it was something the High Lady would do, and I wanted the Dibel not to be sorry they would declare for me. So I nodded acquiescence to the request, and then started thinking quickly about what might be appropriate.

A waysong was sung while the grave was being filled, so I would need to begin quickly. The first tribe members had already begun to file past the opening to refill it, a task everyone present would perform. How would I choose to mark the death of a child I had never known? I wished I had a nomidar, but then I thought that if I could project sympathetically behind the notes, I might be able to do it just behind words as well. Without preamble, I chose, and began to sing.

The song wasn't one of mourning. It spoke of simple childhood joys like discovering the world, running and playing, and then, as evening fell and the sky began to darken, returning home to safety. It spoke of the welcoming beauty of home, the security, sustenance, and love it offered to the tired child, allowing by its very existence the daytime adventuring.

"Home is the redemption of the world of day," I sang. "We need not fear when a child finds the way / to the loving embrace / of his own homeplace."

There was a silence when I finished, broken only by a few muffled sobs. Lyrafi touched my arm lightly, murmuring, "A beautiful choice."

Tendoro nodded in agreement. "You have triply earned your nomidar," he said, "and we are in your debt now."

"I remit it," I said instantly, touched.

Jemeret's voice spoke right beside my ear, startling me, because I'd been involved in the ritual and unaware of his approach. "You see, you've learned to love far more people than only me, Ronica."

I was about to turn and declare that I had always loved Coney, when I was stabbed with the recollection of using my power to make Coney take my virginity, and I bit my lip. When I looked up at my lord, his expression made me tremble. "That's one of the definitions of love," he said softly. "Using the power you have to help someone with less."

"I never—put that together." I stumbled on it lamely, and his smile barely moved the corners of his mouth. Even after all this time, after all the control, all the naturalness of our being together, I had to fight to keep from succumbing to the desire.

"It's not a thing people generally figure out for themselves." His deep voice smoothed the words past my ears and into my consciousness. "Someone has to teach it to them."

He let me absorb that for a few moments in silence broken only by the murmur of the Dibel passing, putting dirt in the grave, and saying farewell. I knew it to be a great truth; I knew he had taught it to me; I knew there was no way I could ever thank him for it.

"We need to get back to the Forge," he said. "The storm's nearly here." He was, of course, right. I just didn't know then how many ways he meant it.

Three days after the storm departed, six tribes and the stars had declared me High Lady of the Samothen, and we were on our way to the Lodge to see if the Ilto would join us without our invoking the blood debt. But even if we did have to call the debt, we were perfectly prepared to do so.

Something very wonderful had happened during the storm, and I happened to be in the right place to see it begin. Coney met, and was stunned by, Sandalari. I had thought it would be interesting to see them together, and had expected him to be as surprised by her as I had been. He was not so much surprised as he was enchanted, and Sandalari responded to him. From the first moment he took her hand in greeting, it was as if they had somehow been waiting for one another. Through the four days of the storm, they were together almost all the time. I didn't exactly deliberately watch them, but several times I came upon them talking, her bright head close to his sandy one. Sometimes she seemed to be nearly glowing, and sometimes she seemed to be deeply concerned. I couldn't help but wonder what they were finding to talk about, but I forbore from spying on them. Coney was delighted when she left the Forge with us and the other members of the Inner Council who had joined us.

The Ilto lived near the southern borders of the Honish lands, on the edge of a marsh leading eventually to the great sea. From the first moment I saw the Lodge, I thought that the Pit would have been a more apt description for it. One of the natural conditions of the tribe appeared to be a casual squalor that appalled me. I had to keep reminding myself that these, too, would be my people. That was a very humbling thought, even as I was outraged by it. As the Com's Class A, I would essentially have been responsible for everyone, but I would probably never have met personally anyone whose life choices might have disgusted me. In the Com, I could have safely ignored the existence of a group with needs, habits, or values vastly different from my own. I would always have known, academically, that they existed, and that part of my role as Class A would be to help them choose to be "normal" Com citizens; that process of assimilation generally took less than a decade.

The Ilto, on the other hand, were right before my eyes—and my nose—unavoidably real, stealing and breeding slaves for some of the others of us and the Honish. As I had known since they kidnapped me, they showed no visible evidence of any qualities I valued, and yet I couldn't turn my back on them. For their edge of Class C power, they were part of the Samothen. I could probably lean on them to clean up a bit, but some of their laws and customs had to be completely left alone. I swallowed my distaste and did my best to view everyone and everything with equanimity, but I could not keep myself from judging them.

Jemeret and Venacrona had both told me that the Ilto clung to their customs in defiance of every effort to change them, partly because the Vylk and Honish depended on the slaves they could buy and were opposed to any efforts to stamp out the practice. Jemeret's own influence was at a minimum with them, because of their hatred for the strongest tribes.

We met with Ustivet, who asked only if we were prepared to invoke the blood debt. When Jemeret said coolly that we were prepared to do more than that, if required, he glared at us, but agreed to give us no trouble over the declaration. "It means the debt is cancelled," he snarled at me.

"I hope you won't force me to create another one, on your successor," I said to him, trying to duplicate Jemeret's coolness. "I would like to think you and I can learn to work together."

He was taken aback by that, but he sneered and turned away to get the supplies packed and mounts saddled for him, his co-Councillor, and the guards they would bring. Each tribe that kept warriors duplicated our numbers, and we had brought six, counting Coney; by the time we were ready to cross onto the Honish lands, our party numbered more than thirty people, along with the tivongs and Tynnanna. Still, we had no fear of being detected by the Honish—whom, I had learned, outnumbered the Samothen by a factor of almost eight to one. Jemeret could shield us. As long as we didn't blunder into any stonehouses directly, we could slip across in a full day and night of riding. But even knowing that, I was surprised when we got through without any trouble at all.

I was expecting trouble. Somehow every nerve in my body was primed for trouble, so much so that when none came, and we cleared the Honish territory onto the massive peninsula that belonged to the Samothen, I was at a high level of tension.

A Paja messenger met us several hours after we entered the Samish lands to tell us that the Resni were more than willing to declare, and that Zunigar awaited us at the Hive. The Vylk, on the other hand, had thrown in their lot with the Marl, and Krenigo had left Columbary to go to Salthome. Ashkalin was, in his words, "unconvinced that this is the right time or the right step."

Jemeret looked grim, but not discouraged. "We'll camp here," he said. "A detour to the Hive would delay us because we can't run the tivongs on the moors. Ginestra?"

"This man's too tired," she said, "and I think Zunigar would be more flattered if I came myself. I'll be back with their party by tomorrow." She smiled at him, at me, and at the messenger, took a water bottle from Rudenil, and vanished on the narrow track leading over the moors toward the Resni home.

"Is she faster on foot than on tivong?" Coney asked from behind us.

"The moor track is too narrow for a tivong to do more than walk," Jemeret answered almost absently. "On both sides of the track, the moors will suck you down in a flash. Wagons can't go across there at all. The path is one of the few in the world where a runner can move faster than any other form of transport."

Sandalari was, as usual, nearby. "They'll return mounted. That's why it'll take Ginestra so long to get back. It's only about twelve kilometers across the moor." She touched Coney's arm lightly, but looked at Jemeret. "My Lord Jemeret, may I speak with you for a moment?"

Coney and I watched them walk off together—the golden flame of a woman and the dark, confident man who had come to mean so much of the universe to me.

I looked at Coney. "It's a slow way of accomplishing things, isn't it? No eftel conferencing. No propulsion systems. Mortel John would say it's terribly inefficient."

"Mortel John knew a great deal," he said, "but he didn't know everything."

"You've fit in here quite well." I don't think I meant anything underhanded by the comment. I had not asked him again about his adjustment to the wilderworld since he'd indicated to me that he couldn't talk about it.

He smiled at me, but I knew him well enough to know that he was troubled. "And you've risen to the top here, just as you did out there," he said. "You're utterly remarkable."

I didn't want him to say that. "Did we go to Nanseda after graduation, you and Kray and me?" He said nothing, but he didn't look away from me. "We didn't, did we?"

"Ronnie, I can't—" he began, then stopped. "I've loved you all my life. I can't imagine not loving you."

I knew more about love now than I had used to. We put our arms around each other and held tightly. "I love you, too," I said against his neck. "I wish I'd known all along how to do it better." I let go of him. "So, Coney, tell me. What harm can it do for you to answer my questions if we're going to be here for the rest of our lives?"

And the moment I asked it, I *knew*. Once again, something impossible was going to happen. I stared at him as the color rose in his face too rapidly for him to keep it down. My breath caught in my throat, and Jemeret was beside us almost instantly—as if I'd called him, which I didn't think I had. I was struggling with the thought, fighting it even as I reached for it, unable to make my leaping conjectures hold still.

Jemeret slid into my mind, comforting me. "What happened?" he asked Coney, who shrugged.

"I knew sooner or later my presence would cause problems," my lifelong friend said to my lover.

I felt Jemeret's anger, that nexus within him, grow and swell. He looked at me and damped down the fury so that I wouldn't think he was directing it at me. "Tell me about it, love," he said firmly.

I had to grasp at the strength of his calm to get my thoughts in order. Only then could I look at him directly. "There's a way off this world," I said as flatly as I could manage, "and Coney knows what it is."

Jemeret was not surprised, and I realized that I had not expected him to be. Neither of them denied it.

Then my lord said softly, "Hang on for another two days, Ronica. We must have you declared High Lady by all the tribes, and then we can tell you what you want to know." He waited, watching me, not trying in any way to compel me to agree.

From the very beginning, from the first night in his tent, it had been a question of my trusting him. He hadn't lied to me about that; I did not think he was lying to me now. I bowed my head and acquiesced. I think it was the hardest thing I'd ever done. I pulled out of his hands and let him slip from my mind, and I went to take care of the tivongs while the guards set up the camp, which was a fairly sprawling settlement now. Working with the tivongs gave me something to do with my hands. And all the while, as I moved almost automatically at my tasks, Tynnanna watched me, his flaming eyes unreadable and filled with no more than cat thoughts.

When I could stand it no longer, I looked at him and said sharply, "Go hunt."

His tail whipped around a few times and he darted off.

After Zunigar, his co-Councillor and brother Mitharin, and their guards joined us, we moved quickly up onto the high plateau in the center of the peninsula. I tried to appreciate the dramatic beauty of the landscape—the sweep of treeless heath, with its stark grandeur, and the almost overwhelming breadth of the sky, after so long being hemmed in by mountains or trees. Even on the Plain of Convalee, I'd not been able to see a complete bowl because of the Palier Cliffs.

In one way, I couldn't wait for the night; in another way, I dreaded it. For the first time, the sky would not be an insurmountable barrier, and now that I knew it would not, I didn't know if I wanted to surmount it.

The ground began to slope downward in the afternoon, toward the canyons above Salthome, and the expanse of the sea became visible. We would reach the home of the Marl the next morning. Almost at dusk, Venacrona and Sandalari chose a campsite at the head of the largest canyon.

The sea breeze rose up the face of the land and flavored the air around us with tangy freshness. Lyrafi sang as we all unpacked our saddle pouches, and when the guards started setting up the lean-tos, I realized that the lean-to Jemeret and I shared was being set fairly far from the others, on the plateau side of the tivong area. I knew immediately what that meant, and I marveled that the thought of our lovemaking still excited me so.

Lyrafi sang again around the fire that night, and I looked with equal frequency up into the sky and across the darkness to the place where the lean-to stood. The dinner meal was very bad and nearly fun, with Henion, Tatatin, and Zunigar trying to harmonize on a bawdy drinking song that somehow embarrassed Sheridar and made Sabaran roar. I found myself enjoying the horseplay, liking these people very much, and fiercely glad that I had been brought here, no matter what the reason.

Eventually Jemeret rose and took my hand, leading me away from the fire and across the heath past the tivongs to our campsite. Since neither of us would have to feel the cold, he stripped me efficiently, wordlessly, then himself. Once we were naked, he pulled me down onto the feather-filled softness of our bedroll. "No shields tonight, love. Not yours or mine. Tonight, I want you to feel—everything."

He gave me no chance to reply before he used his mouth to remove my facility for speech and his sting to remove my wish to speak. Soon we were so entwined in one another, psychologically and physically, that I couldn't tell where I left off and he began. And this night, for the first time, he used his power to maintain his erection far beyond what might have been wise, or even sensible, despite the pleasure I was flooding into him, again and again and again. When I finally succeeded in making his control unbearable, I drowned in the joy of his release as much as I ever had in my own. At last I dozed, the golden curtain of sparkles dancing at the edges of my awareness. I don't think he slept at all.

Neither of us wanted morning to come, though our reasons differed. I didn't want dawn because I didn't know what the day would bring. He didn't want it because he knew.

Coney stared at Danaller with the same kind of stunned disbelief the youth had evoked in me at the Council meeting on the Day of the Fire. We stood in the central square of the village of Salthome, the soft murmur of the sea a constant background to the human interaction in front of it.

Krenigo and those of the Vylk who had accompanied him stood on one side of the square, their backs to a row of crowded but cozy-looking houses that faced the waterfront, where a dozen or so multimasted wooden ships were moored alongside narrow piers.

Ashkalin, his son, and several other guards of the Marl came out to meet us as we all dismounted. What must have been a good number of the tribe stood in the doorways of houses overlooking the square, in the narrow alleys between those houses, on the wharves, and along the rails of the ships themselves, silent and watchful. The lean Chief of the Marl radiated caution, but I didn't feel a great deal of hostility from him.

He looked, as always, remarkably like an older Kray, but with a greater depth of patience in his eyes, which whipped over me, lingering on the brow-crown, before he confronted Jemeret directly. "Welcome to Salthome," he said formally, nodding to the other members of the Inner Council to include them in the greeting as well. "I see we're to be honored with the first Inner Council ever to meet outside a Convalee."

"The fact that it's unprecedented is part of the Fulfillment," Venacrona said in a strong voice. He had borne the journey well, thanks in part to our stay at the Forge during the storm, and now he seemed to be growing younger and more energetic.

Jemeret made a silencing move with his hand, which surprised everyone. I read him instantly, and the sense of purpose he projected was rock-hard, unstoppable. He looked directly at Ashkalin. "You and I must talk," he said. "The need is great."

With those four words, something changed in the Lord of the Marl. Jemeret had not stung him; I knew that, for I would have felt it. But despite the lack of influence, Ashkalin's wariness was overridden by something else, almost indefinable to me. "Come with me," he said, turning to issue some orders about refreshments, and then leading Jemeret into the largest of the clustered buildings fronting directly on the square.

I looked at the people around me in surprise, narrowing my gaze on Venacrona. "I absolutely know that something important is happening," I said quietly, "and this time I do not want to miss what is going on here."

"I think you can be certain it will involve you," Venacrona said.

"Everything appears to involve me," I said to him, a little exasperated, "but I never understand any of it. This time, I want to understand."

Some women appeared from the houses with trays containing cups of grog and some dried-fruit sweets. Venacrona helped himself to a particularly sticky variety of the latter, pointing to his chewing mouth when I became impatient for an answer. He never got around to swallowing while I was there.

Jemeret swung open one of the windows of the building he and Ashkalin had entered, a wood-frame square inset with rows of glass circles, and called, "Mekonet."

Without looking at me, Coney went to his tivong, took a package from his saddle pouch, and ran lightly across the cobbles of the square. He handed it to Jemeret, who shut the window again.

I forgot about Venacrona, instead using the sting to assess the feelings of the Council members. Most were as openly bewildered as I was. Sabaran was cautious. Sandalari was openly, deeply hopeful. I was trying to decide whether there was something else that I could do when I felt a light touch on my arm and looked up, startled, to find Coney beside me.

"I'm going in," he said, taking his hand off my arm. "Take five or six deep breaths, and then follow me." He vanished into the house.

For a moment I couldn't breathe at all. I tried to scan, then read, within the house into which they had all gone, but my attempts were repulsed at once, so I knew that Jemeret was masking it all now, with a bubble the likes of which I had just recently learned to create. I made myself walk forward.

The entrance gave onto a little area that I guessed was a storm guard, with a wall directly inside the door, blocking the view of the room behind. I hesitated an additional moment in the entry, slowing my heartbeat, banishing my sense of apprehension to be better able to cope with whatever lay behind the storm wall's innocuous wood paneling. I wanted to be prepared. At last I took one of the deep breaths Coney had advised and walked the three steps that moved me past the barrier and into the small room that was obviously central to the house.

I was not prepared.

Coney and Kray stood together in the center of the room, watching me, Coney still in the tunic and traveling cloak he had gotten from the Boru, Kray in the silver jumpsuit he'd be wearing in government service for the rest of his life. As I froze, feeling the beginnings of a panic I didn't understand and was helpless to control, I felt Jemeret touch my mind lightly with his, making an adjustment. The panic faded, and the last door opened in my memory.

I was in my rooms at Government House, the morning after the graduation gala. Jasin Lebec had just left my suite, and I had not yet had a chance to change out of my wrapper, when the knock came firmly on the door. I'd started for it, sensing Kray's presence, but he pathfound the lock and let himself in before I was halfway across the room. I stopped walking as he turned from the door to confront me, almost brooding. "I think we need to talk," he said.

"Is something wrong?" I was paying him the respect of not probing him, of letting him say his piece unhindered.

"When we leave today, we'll be with Coney," he said. "This may be the last time we're ever really together."

I recognized how painful that was for him and gestured for him to sit on the couch, sitting beside him, concerned about the nature of our parting. I wanted it to be all right between us. I felt as if I should be proud of finding ways to bring our relationship to a worthwhile end.

"We always knew this day would come," I said to him. "All the time we were growing up, we knew we would go separate ways."

He acknowledged that. "But I didn't think we would part with so much unfinished business," he said. "Not you and me, Ronica, not as alike as we are."

I was a fool not to have suspected it. I felt the lust coursing through him and started to rise, but his hand snaked out and I felt something bite my leg, through the thin wrapper. Automatically gathering to pull away, I tried to analyze the compound he'd injected into me, but it was gone almost instantaneously. In one corner of my mind I thought quite logically that it had to be some kind of experimental drug, and that if it was, he'd paid an absolute fortune for it. It seemed to interfere with my ability to use the gather for my Class C talent, for the strength to pull away from him was suddenly simply absent.

"Kray, stop this!" I said, growing alarmed and angry at the same time, wondering how he would dare, then realizing I should have guessed all along that he'd try something like this. "Stop!"

"I can't," he said, rising and drawing me down onto the couch. "I can't just let you go out of my life. I can't." And then his mouth was on my throat, my shoulders, my breasts, as he stripped the wrapper from me.

Stupidly, I kept trying to use the gather and failing, which cut me off from my most usual line of defense, and I was also helpless to locate and neutralize the drug. I tried for far longer than I should have, feeling inept, but determined to reexert control over the talent I'd lost. By the time I realized that I was not going to be able to recapture it and would have to do something else, he had thrown me down across the couch, my wrists pinned in one of his hands, the other between my legs.

I was overcome with a horror unlike any I had ever known, even in the attack by the Drenalion. This was Kray. This was not some brutal stranger. This was one of my lifelong companions. *This was a man who was supposed to love me!*

I struggled for a moment or two longer, wordless, gasping, bathed in a fury and fear I was unable to control, and then he took his hand away from my body to open his jumpsuit.

"You won't be sorry," he said to me.

He had left me no weapon but the sting, and I was past the point where I could have used it wisely. He had bargained, I think, on the speed with which he could seat himself inside me. He thought, as some men sometimes do, that his penetration of me would unite more than my body with him, when of course the exact opposite was true. He was so completely wrong, and my loss of control so completely enraged me, that I stopped trying to think and simply reacted. I raced past the gather reflex, not needing it now, took firm hold of the sting, and struck him with it just as he sank into me. At that range, and with all my power behind it, I must have blown his mind apart.

He slumped down onto me, his mouth half open, his eyes suddenly vacant. His grip on my wrists relaxed. For a moment I couldn't move at all, caught in the relief of being safe, wanting only to eject him from my body. Then I realized there was no life in the man who lay on me, and I began to scream. I screamed until I lost consciousness.

Now, in the house at Salthome, I began to scream again, but this time Jemeret was there instantly, his arms around me, his mind locked in mine, putting himself immovably between me and the madness as he had put himself immovably between me and death. He was solid and strong, unyielding and loving, making it possible for me to look at the true magnitude of what had happened those years ago without fleeing from it.

I had killed Kray. It was my first real test as a Class A, and I had used my power to destroy someone I cared about. And then I had tried to destroy myself as punishment for it. The self-hatred started to rise in me again, and Jemeret relentlessly beat it back down. Slowly I realized he was speaking to me, saying over and over again, "You can bear it, Ronica, you can bear it. Hang on to me. It's all right."

"I killed Kray," I said unnecessarily. "With my mind. I killed him."

"He didn't leave you any other choice," Jemeret said. "Look at me and hang on. You can bear this."

I looked at him, his face blurred through my tears, but infinitely precious to me. "I don't think—"

And more of the memory came flooding in, choking off the words. I actually remembered methodically taking my brain apart, to the point where awareness could no longer record the memories. Then there was the ghost of memory from what must have been a long time in which things imprinted themselves on a brain over which insanity and destruction reigned unchallenged. The sparkling gold curtain that had been haunting me resolved itself into the Com's radiant sustenance fluid, a substance that kept people alive when their autonomic nervous systems had been injured or paralyzed, rendering them incapable of such basic bodily functions as breathing.

Weeping, clinging to Jemeret's support as if to a lifeline, I realized where my missing years had gone—lost to a mindless madness self-inflicted for a misjudgment I couldn't forgive. The memory carried me forward through the endless time of golden-sparkled near-death, until I remembered that my brain had been rebuilt, but not by me. I'd thrown away all my tools when I threw away Kray's life and my own sanity.

I saw in memory, as vividly as if it were really happening now, the imprints left on my returning consciousness, the picture of the man who stood outside the radiant tank in which I floated, and who worked tirelessly, month after month, putting me back together from the cellular level upward, attaching neurons, rebalancing chemicals, reconstructing personality, compartmentalizing memories. I saw him clearly, his smooth-shaven face always solemn and determined above the plain, dark blue jumpsuit he wore.

And, of course, it was my Lord Jemeret.

Blinded by tears, choking on the sobs of memory, I held him so tightly I tore his tunic. He went on murmuring to me, but I no longer knew what he was saying. He had been in the Com. He had healed me.

Some of the images involved him and Coney together, and I remembered that they'd been together the day I was finally removed from the tank, which meant I could breathe on my own and govern my own organic balances. I understood why they had seemed to know one another. I understood why, from the very beginning, Jemeret had seemed somehow familiar to me. I understood at last why it was so easy for him to slip into my mind, how he could speak through me and play the nomidar through me, and where the bond had come from that let him read me with such ease.

Under Jemeret's steady, soothing comfort, I had begun to calm almost without noticing it, but the tears still made it impossible for me to see.

I heard Ashkalin's voice. "Was there no way to save him? You saved her."

"I couldn't, not him," Jemeret said above my head. "By the time they sent for me, he'd been dead for more than two years. And besides, when she ruined his mind, she took him out at the cellular level. There was nothing left to rebuild with. When she demolished her own brain, she pulled out every connection—like tearing down a house by taking away all the strapping, nails, bolts, and dowels, but leaving all the blocks in the rubble."

"I see." Ashkalin's voice was toneless.

"Is she all right?" It was Coney, anxious.

"I think so." Jemeret's mouth moved very close to my ear. "Come sit down, Ronica," he said. I couldn't move. "Come on, love." I felt his hands on my shoulders, gentle, steering me.

I realized that if Kray were truly dead, it must have been Ashkalin in the silver jumpsuit, and I unfastened my fingers from Jemeret's clothes to scrub at my eyes and get my sight back.

Jemeret sat me down on a cushion on a window seat and let me lean back against the window. I saw him first, the same face, bearded now, the same solemnity and determination in it, the eyes darker than his normal shade, grave, but still warm. "I love you very much," he said, "and I'm going to let you be on your own now. All right?"

I knew he meant he would withdraw the sting, and for a moment I was flooded with fear. Jemeret said strongly, "He should have known better than to strip your control away from you like that. He should have understood something of who you were, who the Com had raised you to be. He never learned to think with his brain, instead of with his balls. *He left you no choice.*"

He needed me to believe him, and that, more than actual belief, made me nod at him. He slid out of my mind with the same exquisite tenderness he'd always used sliding in. And I rocked for a moment, as the self-hatred started rising in me again. With every ounce of strength, I beat it back. I was no longer the girl who had killed Kray, and I knew it at such a visceral level that the old pattern couldn't hurt me this time, not now that I recognized it for what it was.

Coney was still standing beside the man I'd taken for Kray. I looked more closely, recognizing that it was indeed Ashkalin, beardless now, peeling off what appeared to be a deceiver—the thin, smooth, clinging mask that older Com citizens wore to counterfeit youth once their own skin would no longer support shrinking without breaking down.

Jemeret crouched in front of me, his gaze locked on my face, his arms resting on my thighs. He said softly, "Talk to me."

I reached out and laid a hand on his cheek, not bothering to still the trembling in my fingers. The words came almost unbidden, surprising me. "I seem to have learned what you set out to teach me."

He turned his head and pressed his lips into my palm, then rose, holding on to my hand, looking at Ashkalin and Coney. Both of them, I saw now, seemed pale and shaken. "I'm sorry you had to take the full blast of that," he said to them. "I couldn't protect you and keep her from blowing her mind out again. I'm afraid she's my first priority."

Ashkalin pressed his lips together briefly, then nodded once. "In any case, I wouldn't have believed you if I hadn't felt it," he said. "I need a drink." He seemed to fling himself into motion and crossed three steps to a table with a decanter and some mugs on it. His hands shook as he poured several mugsful, and he made no effort to stop them.

By the time he handed one of the mugs to me, I had begun to be able to think again. So many questions were whirling inside me that I wasn't certain I could choose one to ask. Coney accepted a drink and leaned against the room's dead fireplace, silent. I took a gulp of the liquid, which was a rough, searing fire as it went down.

Finally a question crowned, and I got it out. "*Is* this a wilderworld?"

"Absolutely." Jemeret's voice was utterly sincere, almost steely in its strength. "This world is everything it appears to be."

"But K-Kray—" I stumbled over his name, made myself speak it. "He looked just like—"

Jemeret looked at Ashkalin, who took a swallow of his own drink before speaking. "He was my oldest son, birth name Mahd."

"He was born here?" I asked. "This is Abranel?"

It was Coney who said, "This world is called Caryldon."

I frowned. "But Kray was born on Abranel."

"He was born here," Ashkalin corrected, his voice steadier now. "I can show you the house, if you like. You can meet his mare. You've already met his brother." Danaller.

Jemeret's words were measured and quiet. "You were all born here, Ronica. Everyone with talent. Caryldon is the only planet in existence on which talent arises."

I was having trouble absorbing this. As much as I now wanted information, in the aftermath of the crisis, I kept getting information I couldn't process. "But I was born on Steressor."

Jemeret almost smiled. "They told you you were born on Steressor, love. You've been a Boru all your life."

That, I absorbed. "How?"

Ashkalin said flatly, "The Com fishes here, Lady Ronica. For babies with power."

I realized that I was gaping, closed my mouth and looked helplessly at Coney. "I'm an Elden," he said. "Jemeret told me my tribe while we were working on you."

I drank the rest of my liquor down in one burning gulp and looked into the mug as if I expected it to grow more. "But no one's mentioned the Com to me the whole time I was here except for Sandalari. They weren't interested."

"Besides Sandalari, only four of us know." That was Jemeret. It began to frustrate me that they were all so calm about this, when I was being hit with revelation after revelation. "Venacrona, Sabaran, Ashkalin, and me. We power-test the children, and a few of those with real potential are sent from Caryldon to the Com to be raised there."

"Why?" I hadn't meant it to sound so anguished.

Jemeret answered. "Because it's the only way the Com won't conquer us, absorb us, ruin us. It's what buys our freedom to stay the way we are."

I shook my head. "That doesn't sound at all like the Com I know. Why settle for an occasional person with talent when you can have the entire population?"

"We've convinced them that they would destroy talent completely if they took us over," he said, "and the Com needs talent too much to risk it." He let go of my hand, turned to the decanter and refilled my mug, then Ashkalin's. Coney had barely touched his own drink. "They keep their hands off the rest of us to avoid damming up the flow."

"But—" I was trying to find a logical way into the moving stack of questions. "This world could use an alliance with the Com to benefit from some of the scientific advances, some of the technology."

Jemeret shook his head. "Technology kills talent. Why do you think talent has never arisen in the worlds of the Com?"

It disoriented me to hear him call it "talent" with the same ease he had used calling it "power." "What does one thing have to do with the other? There must be dozens of wilderworlds—"

All three men shook their heads. "Not inhabited ones," said Ashkalin, and Jemeret went on, "We are the only inhabited human wilderworld. We are the only natural cradle of talent."

"Why?" I was glad he'd refilled my mug. I needed it. The revelations kept on arriving. I kept trying to rationalize them with what I knew—what I thought I knew, at any rate—and it kept turning out that they didn't fit; I didn't know what I thought I knew.

Jemeret answered softly, "The starfire, love. The starfire creates talent. It created the Samothen; it created the High Lady legend to try to unite us."

"*Why?* Why is it doing all this?" I kept wanting to get to the bottom, and there was no bottom.

Jemeret looked away from me, confronting Ashkalin squarely, as if he had been the one who asked the question. "It won't tell us why until we have a High Lady."

"Ah," Ashkalin said. He put his mug down. "Get Venacrona in here."

Jemeret made a signal to Coney, who set his own mug on the mantel and went out of the room.

I was still struggling. "If you were with me in the Com, how did I end up with the Honish?"

"I needed you to accept absolutely the reality of your being on this world," Jemeret answered, "and your mind has been trained extensively to distrust simplicity. I needed a complex scenario to distract you from too much distrust. It happened that I'd recently bought the Meltress Lewannee's gambling debt to try to start normalizing relations between us and the Honish. I built a scenario around it. If I hadn't had it, I'd've developed another scenario."

I felt like I might start crying again. He knew all the Com vocabulary; he had known it all along. I fought the tears. Even as I did, I recognized how far I'd come. There were anomalies all around me now, which meant I had no control of what was going on, and while it was uncomfortable, it was bearable. I had some absurd faith that I would come through it.

For the first time, I reached out with my sting and touched the Lord of the Marl. He was mourning. I knew the feeling, having felt it recently at the graveside on the hill above the Hall. He had just been told, as I had, that Kray was dead—for the grief was too fresh, too raw, to have been of long standing. I stirred myself on the window seat, got up and went to him, leaving my mug behind.

"My Lord Ashkalin, I'm very sorry I couldn't love your son the way he wanted me to," I said. I wanted to touch his arm, but I was uncertain if he'd want me to, and I held back.

He looked at me wearily. "My son was a fool," he said. "He could have had a life, but he chose dishonor."

"You don't hate me for killing him?" My voice wavered badly.

"I might have," he said, "if I hadn't felt what you felt while it was happening and seen what you did to yourself because of it. You don't need any more punishment from me."

"Then—" I didn't know if I dared to ask it, but I wanted to

very much. "—will you let me grieve with you? I haven't mourned him either, and I think I need to, very much."

He stared at me, his eyes glittering as they had when he told Jemeret he wanted to challenge for me after the game of the Dibel. Then the glitter softened. "Yes," he said. "I can't mourn with his mare. She thinks he's been dead for more than twenty years."

I put my arms around him, reaching in to help him accept the grief, but also to mourn his son with him. From Jemeret, who had watched us from across the room, I felt an incredible surge of pride and love.

When we heard Coney returning with Venacrona, I let go of Ashkalin and stepped back, retrieving my mug and drinking some more of the liquor. It didn't burn so much now.

Venacrona's sharp black eyes flew from me to Ashkalin and back again several times before settling on the Lord of the Marl. "You asked to see me, my lord?" he said noncommittally.

"Set up the ceremony," Ashkalin said, more abruptly than the etiquette of the Council usually permitted. "I'll take care of Krenigo as soon as I've regrown my beard."

Even as we watched him, the hair began to sprout on his cheeks and jaw. Venacrona nodded to him, glanced once, triumphantly, at Jemeret, and then hurried back out.

Jemeret relaxed and upended his mug.

I let another question surface, strangely poignant. "Jemeret, do I have a family among the Boru?"

"Shenefta is your niece," he said. "Her mare was your older sister."

"How could you not tell me?" It was a whisper.

"I just did," he said. "At the first possible moment."

"What else haven't you told me?"

He put his mug next to the decanter, watching me out of the corner of his eye. "All right," he said. "I'm the one who broke your arm, cracked your ribs, slashed your ankle, and a few other things. We landed here together. And I'm the one who blew up the lander."

I was gaping again. Every answer I got sank into the turmoil of how everything was changing, and raised further questions. I began to think I'd never find my way through it all. I shook my head, momentarily overwhelmed.

Jemeret put his arm across my shoulders. "I know it's too much," he said, "but you're handling it. And I'm here."

"You were there, too!" Suddenly I was frowning at him. "When you were gone before Coney came, you were off-world, weren't you? How?"

"There's a fully equipped station in polar orbit above us," Jemeret said. "There has been since the Com first took a child from the Samothen."

The time scale was wrong. "Wait," I said slowly. "That's not possible. The starfire made its arrangement with Venacrona in your great-great-grandfather's time, which would be, what, a hundred and fifty years ago? The Com has records of Class A talent dating back more than five hundred years."

"The Com," Jemeret said quietly, "told you you were born on Steressor."

And I gasped, counting myself stupid beyond my capacity to imagine it. The Com had lied to me—to us—consistently. Our Com training was propaganda, not history. Our loyalty had been to false traditions and doubtful ideals, and I'd accepted it all. I covered my mouth with one hand. I couldn't ask "why" again. This was a precipice over which I was not ready to leap.

I looked at Coney, and he was watching me with such compassion that I wondered if he had known all along. I dropped my hand from my mouth and asked him.

He cleared his throat. "Jemeret and I spent a lot of time together while he was trying to heal you, up on the station," he said. "I thought I'd lost both of you, you see, you and Kray. He helped me through it. We talked for months, and I learned a great deal."

"Is that why they sent you here? Or did they?" I realized that there was no part of my knowledge of the Com that I could depend on any longer, that most of my assumptions were vapor.

"They did," Coney answered quickly, "but not because of that."

Sandalari put her head in past the storm wall. "We're largely ready out here," she said. "I'm afraid my Lord Krenigo doesn't quite believe it yet, and he said he was going to leave."

"Did he?" Ashkalin asked, fingering his new beard to make sure it was the right length.

Sandalari smiled a little embarrassedly, glancing at Coney. "He took one step toward his tivong, and Tynnanna pushed him over and sat on him."

Jemeret laughed. I said, "Oh," and jumped up to get

Tynnanna off the Lord of the Vylk. I thought I probably ought to apologize for my cat's behavior.

Jemeret caught my arm. "We'll all go," he said.

Outside, the Councillors and their entourages had been finishing the grog and fruit, along with some of the dried biscuits that formed a staple of the seagoing diet. When we reached the square, everyone was watching Tynnanna carefully hold Lord Krenigo down without crushing him. I was somehow surprised that the world looked the same as it had when we went in, because everything else had changed.

Tynnanna moved aside, and Ashkalin pushed past Jemeret and held out his hand to help Krenigo to his feet. They talked briefly in low voices. I was sure that Krenigo asked the same question at least three times before he was satisfied with Ashkalin's answer.

Venacrona had sent the priest of the Marl to the village temple to bring out the starfire bowl, and now he asked to borrow the younger man's robes. I realized I had begun clinging to Jemeret again, and I deliberately made myself let go of his tunic. By the time I had gotten myself more under control in the shifting truths of the world, Venacrona was raising the starfire bowl, and Sandalari and the Marl priest, both unrobed, went to stand at his shoulders. But only Venacrona chanted, because it was not a prayer that had ever been sung before, and the others didn't know it. At its end, he set the bowl down. "I am Venacrona and this is Sandalari. We speak for the stars, and we declare for the Lady Ronica as High Lady of the Samothen." The formality of the Inner Council introductions went on, pausing only when they reached Jemeret and me.

He hesitated, as if waiting to see if I would speak first, according me that right. I smiled at him a little, and barely shook my head. I didn't know how I could declare for myself and be believed. He spoke the introduction, once again placing myself equal to him, and declaring that I was already High Lady of the Boru.

The feeling around the Council circle was very different from my previous experience of Councils—subdued, the rivalries under the surface rather than flung at one another—and a current of excitement rippled through the assembly.

"We have gathered here, extraordinarily, for the purpose of the Fulfillment," Venacrona said, his voice rich with satisfaction. "In bringing forward this candidate as prospective High

Lady of the Samothen, we call upon the stars to bless our efforts and confirm or deny the rightness of our choice."

Almost before the last word was spoken the column of starfire shot upward from the bowl with a whoosh that seemed deafening, until its leading end vanished above us without ever giving us the feeling that it had stopped climbing. A sudden dazzle before my eyes made me realize my brow-crown was glowing in response to the column.

Venacrona cried, "The stars declare that the Lady Ronica is High Lady of the Samothen!"

Jemeret said instantly, "The Boru stand with the stars in this." And, one by one, the others confirmed what all had now agreed to, even Krenigo, who managed not to sound entirely reluctant. With a loud hum the starfire sank back into the bowl.

In the silence that followed, they all looked at me. I knew I had to say something, and with my mind still awash in the series of revelations and the heap of unanswered questions, I wasn't certain what I could say that would be meaningful or even coherent. But I would have to speak. I looked around the circle at all of them.

"It is a great moment when people join their lives to one another," I said at last. "It is a moment for rejoicing. But even in our joy, we have much work to do. We must formulate a common law which respects most of each tribe's individuality, even while setting a foundation of sameness for each and for all. We must learn to celebrate one another, and to respect the ways we differ without letting them tear us apart. We must treasure the ways in which we are alike without letting them blind us to our differences. None of us can build the edifice of our unity alone. Therefore, we will meet again in Convalee in the summer, as if four years had passed instead of one. And there, we will begin to learn who we will become." It echoed inside me. At Convalee, I had begun to learn who *I* would become.

I hoped I had done all right. I glanced at Jemeret, even as he touched me with his approval. Then Tynnanna, who had been lying quietly on his side outside the circle, got lazily to his feet and walked into the center, sitting down beside the bowl.

From the center of the bowl a single tendril rose, pure white, and swayed back and forth for a few seconds before it elongated and came to me, beckoning me to step into the center of the circle. I did, immediately. The tendril left me and beckoned to Venacrona, then to Sandalari, Jemeret, Sabaran, and Ashkalin—everyone who knew this world had a great many more secrets than was first apparent, except Coney.

By the time they were all assembled, I fully expected the starfire to rise around us, blocking out the rest of the world, so when it did, I was unsurprised. Then I watched the klawit as his fiery eyes once again took on the increased presence of an additional consciousness.

"You have done well," the rumble said to us.

Ashkalin swore under his breath; Sabaran gave a bark of astonished laughter, and Sandalari sank gracefully to her knees, watching with awe.

"Why don't you speak through one of us?" I asked it.

The burning eyes seemed amused. "Your minds are too complex to host us without comment, and comment means alteration. The klawit creates no such problems."

"We have a High Lady," Jemeret said.

"And not only you," said the starfire through the cat.

"The Honish, too?" Venacrona guessed. "We're to try to unite with the Honish?"

"And not only the Honish," the rumble said, and Tynnanna turned back to me. "You accepted the responsibilities of High Lady. Now we tell you that they are more than you know. You are High Lady of your entire species—and there is much we will ask you to do, because there is much that is needed."

"I don't know how much more I can deal with at this exact moment," I said shakily.

"There will be time."

I found myself overwhelmingly grateful for those four words.

"Why do you change us?" Jemeret asked.

"You were destined to change yourselves," the starfire said. "But it did not happen, and you were long overdue when we chose to try to help. If you do not grow, if you do not evolve, you will die."

Jemeret's voice was hard. "As a species?"

The starfire didn't answer that question directly. "We believe it can be avoided. We believe you will be the best possible instruments to accomplish that avoidance. We will contact you later, when we are nearer the nexus."

"Wait!" I couldn't let it just vanish, sigh away, when we knew so little more than we had. "What are we to do in the meantime?"

"Go on living," Tynnanna said. "You have obligations; meet them. It will not be long before we speak with you again. You have done well."

The wall dropped, the possession withdrew from the klawit like the withdrawing of the sting, and we were all of us back in view of the others.

For a time, none of us spoke. Sabaran reached down and helped raise Sandalari to her feet. Then Ashkalin shook himself as if awakening. "Stay the night. You've come a long way."

Jemeret nodded, saying softly, "And we have a long way still to go."

We sat up quite late that night, after the singing and dancing, after the feast of rather sparse winter fare. We camped in the square and on the docks, with small fires in fire pans donated by the Marl from their fleet. For the first time, Coney and Sandalari shared our fire, and we kept our voices very low, so no one would overhear. It was instinct; Jemeret had bubbled us all before we began speaking.

"Early in the winter," Coney said, clasping his raised knees with his arms, "Pel Nostro wanted to see if they could get you back. The government never wanted Jemeret to bring you down here in the first place, and Pel fought against it, but eventually he gave in."

"To whom?" I still didn't understand how Jemeret had gotten involved in all this. I found it nearly impossible to believe that he could use even such power as his to go against the full weight of the Com.

"Actually," Jemeret said, stroking my hair, "the MIs forced him to accede. I knew I had to have you here to heal you completely. You couldn't have been brought back safely in the environment that nearly destroyed you. Pel thought about the failed talent they'd dumped here and feared he'd never see you again."

"Will he?" I was amazed that the question didn't stick in my throat.

Jemeret was silent for a long moment. "Yes, he will. As soon as we get back to Stronghome, we're leaving Caryldon. We need to go back first because I have to prepare the tribe for a lengthy absence, but also because the spaceport is in the mountains above Stronghome."

I took a breath to protest, but Coney said quickly, "You're

still under Com oath, Ronnie. Jemeret had to swear he'd bring you back if you healed."

I took a minute to absorb that. "How does it happen," I asked my lord then, "that you and the Com are on such terms of intimacy?" I gathered and held myself hard, trying not to yield to trembling. Nothing was making any sense yet. The ground under my feet was still shifting treacherously.

"I was one of the children taken from Caryldon." He watched me, his hand still moving lightly on my hair. "I was trained on Werd for more than ten years. By Mortel John."

I had never lived with uncertainty until I awoke on this world. I had always known—in the most minute detail—who I was, what was expected of me, and who I would become. And I had been wrong. Now I was adrift in a sea of unknowns, larger than the sea on which Salthome sat, and with enough unanswered questions to fill the void between Caryldon and Werd. I had little control over events I had always thought I would be controlling completely. How was it that I was not running around shrieking from one place to another?

That brought me up short. I had done that. I was through with it. I leaned back against Jemeret's broad chest and tucked my head under his chin. He shifted his body a little to help me be more comfortable. Across the slowly dying fire, I saw Coney put his arm around Sandalari and draw her closer. She smiled at me. "You aren't going alone, you know."

"Jemeret has to come with me," I told her. "He promised he would be with me, and I intend to hold him to it."

"Coney and I are coming, too," she said, the smile widening. "He has to go back, and I want them to see what became of some of the failed talent they threw away. Jemeret agreed to let me come with you just a couple of days ago."

I was glad. "Why did they send you here?" I asked Coney.

"They wanted me to talk Jemeret into bringing you back," he said, sounding a little annoyed. "They thought he was unnecessarily delaying the process of healing you. I told them they were wrong, but I'm under oath to them, too."

Sandalari snuggled herself a little closer to him, then closed her eyes.

"In the morning, I'm going to have a hundred more questions," I told Jemeret.

His chest moved evenly beneath me. "You can ask me now, if you like."

I shook my head. "Now I just want to go on living. I have

the starfire's permission to." I felt his lips on my hair, and I thought about the two of us.

He was powerful, and he'd wanted me to be powerful, and I had been powerful.

He was caring, and he'd wanted me to be caring, and now I was learning what it was to be caring.

He was a whole person, and he'd wanted me to be whole, but I hadn't been, and so he had made me whole.

And now whatever trials and surprises lay ahead of me—ahead of us—I thought I would be able to face them with strength and perhaps the beginnings of something vaguely resembling wisdom. Even in the midst of all the uncertainty, I believed that.

I slept in his arms, and in the morning we turned our tivongs toward the first of the places we would need to go. Tynnanna raced out in front of us and vanished over a fold of the heath, hunting.

DEL REY ONLINE!

The Del Rey Internet Newsletter...

A monthly electronic publication, posted on the Internet, GEnie, CompuServe, BIX, various BBSs, and the Panix gopher (gopher.panix.com). It features hype-free descriptions of books that are new in the stores, a list of our upcoming books, special announcements, a signing/reading/convention-attendance schedule for Del Rey authors, "In Depth" essays in which professionals in the field (authors, artists, designers, sales people, etc.) talk about their jobs in science fiction, a question-and-answer section, behind-the-scenes looks at sf publishing, and more!

Online editorial presence: Many of the Del Rey editors are online, on the Internet, GEnie, CompuServe, America Online, and Delphi. There is a Del Rey topic on GEnie and a Del Rey folder on America Online.

Our official e-mail address for Del Rey Books is delrey@randomhouse.com

Internet information source!

A lot of Del Rey material is available to the Internet on a gopher server: all back issues and the current issue of the Del Rey Internet Newsletter, a description of the DRIN and summaries of all the issues' contents, sample chapters of upcoming or current books (readable or downloadable for free), submission requirements, mail-order information, and much more. We will be adding more items of all sorts (mostly new DRINs and sample chapters) regularly. The address of the gopher is gopher.panix.com

Why? We at Del Rey realize that the networks are the medium of the future. That's where you'll find us promoting our books, socializing with others in the sf field, and—most importantly—making contact and sharing information with sf readers.

For more information, e-mail ekh@panix.com